The disappearance of Edwin Drood

When Charles Dickens died in June 1870, he had completed only six of the twelve projected parts of his last book and only crime novel, *The mystery of Edwin Drood*.

It will come as a delight, however, to many readers to learn that from the legendary and seemingly bottomless battered tin dispatch-box containing the private papers of Dr John H Watson MD, late of the Indian Army, there has lately emerged a case-history which bears a remarkable resemblance to the extraordinary events related by the great Victorian novelist. In one essential respect, though, it differs: the mystery of Edwin Drood is satisfactorily solved.

In 1894 the celebrated sleuth of Baker Street was at the height of his powers, but the grave allegations made to him by a certain choir-master, John Jasper, about the 'murder' of his nephew, Edwin Drood, were to present Sherlock Holmes with a case whose tragic ramifications had no rival in Dr Watson's chronicle of the great detective's exploits.

The day after breaking off his engagement to Rosa Budd, and following an uneasy reconciliation with the strange young man from Ceylon, Neville Landless, after a long-smouldering row provoked by sexual jealousy, Edwin Drood disappeared off the face of the earth. Only his gold watch and chain, discovered on the river bed, remained as a tantalizing clue to his distraught uncle and guardian.

But if 'Ned' was drowned, where was the body?

A baffling time scale; the destructive effects of opium; the secrets of a family tomb; the pitiful inmate of a country asylum; the portrait of a lovely girl — these are some of the elements in a richly intriguing story of detection.

THE DISAPPEARANCE
OF EDWIN DROOD

Peter Rowland

Constable   London

First published in Great Britain 1991
by Constable & Company Ltd
3 The Lanchesters
162 Fulham Palace Road
London W6 9ER
Copyright © 1991 by Peter Rowland
ISBN 0 09 470350 7
Set in Palatino 11pt by
Servis Filmsetting Ltd, Manchester
Printed in Great Britain by
St Edmundsbury Press Ltd
Bury St Edmunds, Suffolk

A CIP catalogue record for this book
is available from the British Library

To the memories of
Willoughby Matchett
(*The Dickensian*, January 1914, p.14)
and S.C. Roberts
(Introduction to OUP edition of
The Mystery of Edwin Drood, p. x)

AUTHOR'S NOTE

'I am lost without my Boswell,' Sherlock Holmes once remarked.

The private papers of Dr John H. Watson, MD, late of the Indian army, are less voluminous than those bequeathed to a delighted posterity by the Laird of Auchinleck, but the question of their publication has posed problems of a more intractable nature. Their trustees, Messrs Cox & Co. of Charing Cross, have been advised that, the passage of many years notwithstanding, there are certain matters over which, even now, the veil of secrecy must remain firmly drawn. Such material as it has otherwise been possible to release has proved, in the main, disappointingly inconsequential.

Frustrating though this is for the dedicated researcher, anxious to sift the contents of that battered tin despatch box to his heart's content, there occasionally occur relaxations of the necessary constraints. Specified time limits expire and the records of a particular case can pass, at last, into the public domain. One such case-history is set out in the pages that follow. The present editor was intrigued to find, however, when perusing the manuscript, that parts of the story it had to tell, albeit incomplete and written from a totally different viewpoint, had already been chronicled elsewhere. Dr Watson's account, while a complete dossier in its own right, thus acquired something of a complementary character. This being so, I have taken the liberty of replacing its original title, 'The Adventure of the Missing Nephew', by one which (in the circumstances) appeared more appropriate. Other than this, editorial emendations have been kept to a minimum.

1

'Well, Watson, and what do you make of it?' enquired Holmes languidly, from the depths of his favourite armchair.

I pulled my own chair nearer the fire, digested the letter for a second time and passed it back with a shrug of the shoulders. 'Not a great deal,' I confessed. 'Your correspondent is obviously distraught and excited. Somebody — his son, presumably, or even a grandson — has left home and he is desperately anxious to find him. The notepaper is of good quality and the writer appears to be a man of substance, although the shakiness of the hand suggests someone of advancing years.'

The document in question, embossed with the address of 'The Gate House, Cloisterham' and dated 22 December 1894, was relatively brief. 'My Dear Sir,' it ran, 'I implore your assistance. You are the only person who can help me now. I must know, for my own peace of mind, whether my dear boy is alive or dead. This never-ending anxiety is driving me to the depths of insanity and despair. Only you, Mr Holmes, can solve this most baffling of problems.

Expense is no object. I will be with you tomorrow afternoon and beg that you will do me the honour of hearing my story and assisting me with every means at your disposal. I am, yours distractedly, John Jasper.'

'I fear', said Holmes, 'that since my much-publicized return to Baker Street those little articles by which you sought to bring my modest achievements in the sphere of elementary analysis and elucidation to the attention of a wider audience, although penned with the best of motives, are proving a mixed blessing. There appears to be an ominous disposition on the part of Mr Jasper to regard me, first and foremost, as a bureau for missing persons.'

'But he does refer', I remarked rather tartly, 'to an element of mystery in this affair, which is surely why he is coming to you, and he insists that you are the only person who can help him. I trust I am not to be blamed, Holmes, for attracting clients to your door at a time when you would otherwise be complaining of the dearth of business.'

Holmes smiled. 'The festive season', he said, 'does indeed have its *longueurs*. If Mr Jasper can relieve the ravages of boredom then he is most welcome, but my experience of reuniting fathers or grandfathers with long-lost heirs is limited and I rather fancy that I will be obliged, at the end of the day, to direct the gentleman elsewhere.' He glanced at his watch and then again at the letter, holding it up to the fading light. 'It may just be,' he mused, 'that this affair will not be totally devoid of points of interest. The note-paper, as you say, is of good quality, although sicklied o'er by a certain yellowish tinge which suggests a degree

10

of antiquity. You will observe that the date has been squeezed in as an afterthought and is penned in a different hand. A wife or secretary, perhaps? Cloisterham, as you are doubtless aware, is a cathedral city in Kent some forty miles hence. The dog-eared envelope which contained this letter, however, bears a Surrey postmark. Whether or not a curious address such as 'The Gate House' confirms that our client is a man of financial stature remains to be seen.'

We did not have to remain long in suspense, for the bell rang even as Holmes ruminated and a few minutes later Mrs Hudson ushered Mr John Jasper of Cloisterham into our room. He was a tall man, dressed in a long black coat which had evidently seen better days – and so, one was obliged to acknowledge, had Mr Jasper himself. His age was difficult to determine. His hair, once black, was heavily streaked with grey and there was an appalling haggardness about his features. The most striking aspect of the man was his dark eyes, which shone with an almost fanatical light. He collapsed with an air of exhaustion into the chair which I speedily made available and sat there without speaking for several minutes, breathing heavily. He eventually proffered a shaking hand and scrutinized each of us closely.

A look of mild surprise had passed across Holmes's face. 'I believe, sir,' he murmured, 'that you and I may have met some years ago, and in rather curious circumstances, but no matter – you will not recall the occasion. My name is Sherlock Holmes and this is my friend and colleague Dr Watson. You may speak freely in front of him and you have my assurance, if you so desire it, that what you say will not go beyond the four walls of this room. How may we be of service?'

Mr Jasper summoned up his strength, drew a deep breath, and launched into his tale.

'You must understand, Mr Holmes,' began our visitor, fixing my colleague with a gaze which, until the end of his narrative, never wavered in its steadiness and intensity, 'that I am a well-known and, I hope I might say, respected resident of Cloisterham. I am a music-master and also the choir-master at the Cathedral — although in recent months I have been unable, I must confess, to execute my duties with that degree of efficiency which would normally have been my wont.

'Many years ago my only sister, Elizabeth, married a Mr Martin Drood, an enterprising young business man who was building up an engineering partnership with far-reaching commitments in Egypt — developing, it seems, some ingenious contrivances of major significance for the sanitation of that country, but I confess I am unfamiliar with the precise details. The Levant was, at that time, not only an extremely unhealthy but also a singularly dangerous part of the world — little more than five years, indeed, had elapsed since the crisis engendered by Mehemet Ali had threatened to plunge the whole region into turmoil. Elizabeth, her parents' forebodings and distress notwithstanding, insisted on accompanying Martin back to Egypt and it was in Alexandria, a year or so later, that she gave birth to a son. The climate was, however, already far too severe for one totally unsuited to such latitudes. Fatally weakened by the additional demands now made upon a feeble body, she gave up the ghost while Edwin was less than a month old. Martin, heartbroken by this event, found himself unable to continue his business activities with anything like his previous zeal. He returned to England, a shadow of his former self, and became little more than a sleeping partner in the firm which he had done so much to create. The wheels which he had helped to set in motion were turning, however, with alacrity and he was now a comparatively wealthy man. He eventually settled in Cloisterham (with some idea, I suppose, of consoling Elizabeth's parents for the loss of their daughter by presenting them with a grandson) and it is, indeed, in Cloisterham that he is buried, for he followed his wife to the grave within the space of twelve years.

'This is a melancholy tale, Mr Holmes, and I will endeavour to be brief. My parents, although well advanced in years, lavished upon Edwin all the love and attention that they had formerly bestowed upon Elizabeth and myself. They set in hand the necessary arrangements for his education, first at the very best of our public schools and then, later, at an engineering college in the north (for it was Martin's dying wish that his son should inherit his partnership and make good the family contribution to the regeneration of Egypt), with the result that Edwin came to Cloisterham only at comparatively rare intervals. Both my parents died, however, before he could complete his studies and I myself then became his guardian. The intention was, indeed, that I should remain in that position until Edwin came of age, which would have been in the spring of this year. The engineering firm founded by his father continued to thrive and the annual income derived from that firm more than sufficed for his requirements. It was understood that, on the day that Edwin attained his majority, he would come into full and untrammelled possession of his inheritance. But that day, alas, is now seven months behind us, and whether or not that majority was actually attained is a question upon which, so far as I know, no one in this land is able to pronounce.

'But I anticipate. I must explain at this point that the dearest friend of Martin Drood, since their days at college together, was a Mr Ronald Bud who was also a widower and who also died young. He left behind him a seven-year-old daughter, four years Edwin's junior. The two young men, united in friendship and bereavement, made a compact before Ronald died to the effect that their entwined destinies should not terminate with the grave – for they recognized, already, that their own respective days were numbered – but should continue after death and bear fruit, as it were, in their children. It was agreed, in short, that the two potential orphans, Edwin and Rosa Bud, should (under the terms of their fathers' wills) be betrothed and that they should marry as soon as Edwin came of age. Such an arrangement might well seem strange in this day and age, but it was one born purely of a great friendship between two men whose emotions, agitated by great stress, were running at a fevered pitch – and it was accepted, indeed, that if the two young people, filial obligations notwithstanding, did not choose to unite in matrimony then there should be no compulsion upon them, financial or otherwise, to do so. The proposed arrangement was a sentimental one, expressive of their fathers' dearest hopes, but in no sense a legal commitment. Neither of them would be a penny the worse off if a union did not take place.

'So Mr Bud died and so Martin died and Rosa became the ward of a Mr Grewgious and I myself, in due course, became the guardian of Edwin. Miss Bud came to Cloisterham, where she was, until recently, a boarder at the Nuns' House, a seminary for young ladies run by a Miss Twinkleton. I myself kept a fatherly eye on her, in the capacity of music-master, and Mr Grewgious (a trustee of some description) came down from London from time to time to observe her progress. Edwin too came down to Cloisterham, when his obligations in town would permit, and invariably stayed with me at the Gate House – a bachelor apartment in close proximity to the Cathedral, where I have lived since my parents died. Relations between himself and Rosa appeared to be, so far as the outside world was concerned, all that their fathers could have wished and it was generally assumed that, when Edwin came of age, he and Rosa would marry and would then set sail for Egypt, where he would resume his father's commitments in the engineering profession.

'Ned – for so I almost invariably addressed the dear boy – had become, by this time, a living likeness of his father and had inherited, I must acknowledge, some of his father's slightly less attractive traits. In him they were, I fancy, little more than the impetuosities of youth and I am sure that he would soon have grown out of them, but a stranger meeting Ned for the first time would have found him – how shall we say? – somewhat bumptious, rather too self-assured for his years and perhaps inclined to speak casually or even carelessly of what others would have regarded as subjects more appropriate for graver discourse – subjects, certainly, that would have been accorded, in other quarters, a greater degree of respect or even reverence than Ned was apparently prepared to grant them.

'As ill luck would have it, there was indeed a stranger who encountered Ned for the first time in the autumn of last year – such a cursed stranger, I must confess, as I wish with all my heart had never left his native Ceylon – and that stranger was a young man called Neville Landless. From the moment that they first met there was bad blood between them. This dark young man appeared on the scene as the darkest of malign spirits and from the instant I clapped eyes on him I never knew a moment's peace of mind.

'Landless and his twin sister, Helena, were new arrivals in this country and had been sent to Cloisterham to complete their eduction – Helena at the Nuns' House and Neville under the guardianship of the Reverend Septimus Crisparkle, a Minor Canon who lives a short distance from myself. Ned and I were present at a dinner to welcome the young couple and after it had finished Ned and Landless escorted Miss Bud and Miss Landless back to the Nuns' House. The young ladies having left them, they instantly fell to quarrelling. Landless, it seems, took strong exception to some innocent enough expressions uttered by Ned and Ned responded angrily to what he regarded as his assailant's confounded impertinence. I chanced upon them at this stage and, in an effort to pour oil on troubled waters, insisted that they compose their difference and join me in a nightcap. A surly reconciliation (on Landless's part that is, not Ned's) was followed by a frightening scene within my very own sitting-room, when Landless physically attacked my dear boy, with the ferocity of a tiger, and had to be hauled away from him and evicted from the premises. Ned was shaken, although otherwise unhurt, but from that point onwards I went in fear of his life. It was a great relief to me, I do assure you, when Ned returned to London the following day.

'But Ned came back to Cloisterham two months later and I was prevailed upon, by Mr Crisparkle, to make one further attempt at composing relations between himself and Landless. On Christmas Eve, therefore, I played host to both of them at a convivial little dinner party and to all intents and purposes each of them was on his best behaviour and amicable relations were finally restored. But it was a night, Mr Holmes, of a terrible storm, which – although mercifully short-lived – wreaked havoc in the town while it lasted. (The Cathedral roof, to this day, bears some of the scars then inflicted on it.) At midnight my little party broke up, by which time the wind and rain had subsided to some extent. Ned announced that, before going to bed, he would stroll down to the river to observe the extent to which it had overflowed its banks. He invited Landless to accompany him and the latter agreed. The two of them left my gatehouse and that was the last occasion on which I ever saw my dear boy.

'Ned never returned home that night. I waited for many hours, endeavouring to convince myself that all was well and that, bearing in mind the impetuous nature of youth, he and Landless had perhaps returned to Minor Canon Corner (the home of Mr Crisparkle) to while away the early hours in conversation – perhaps, indeed, even to crack a further bottle or two, although intoxicating liquors at Minor Canon Corner are, I suspect, something of a rarity. When dawn finally broke, however, I felt that all was *not* well and that the time had finally come when I could no longer disguise from myself that something was dreadfully amiss. I eventually went to Minor Canon Corner, only to find that Landless had left there some hours before, while it was still dark, on what he was pleased to describe as a walking holiday. A party of volunteers immediately went in pursuit of him and he was apprehended at a spot some eight miles away. He resisted arrest, putting up a violent fight in the process, but was overpowered and brought back to myself and Mr Crisparkle. There was blood on his clothes, Mr Holmes, although he claimed that this was a result of the most recent fracas, and he denied that he had ever laid a finger on my dear Ned. They had, according to his account, surveyed the river and then strolled back to my gatehouse, Landless leaving him at the very entrance. To my own mind he was guilt personified, although the powers-that-be were less convinced and charges, I am sorry to say, have never been brought against him. He continues to protest his innocence.

'From that day to this, Mr Holmes, Ned has never been seen. Local volunteers scoured the area for him, and the river was dragged, but all to no avail. My boy had seemingly disappeared into thin air. He never returned to his London lodgings and his associates in town are as baffled as the residents of Cloisterham as to what could have become of him. Notices have been published, imploring him – if he was still in the land of the living – to make contact with me, but there has been no response – and I am certain, in my heart of hearts, that I will never see him again in this life. We were as close as two kinsmen could possibly be and I know that the thought always uppermost in my dear boy's mind was to spare me, if he possibly could, a moment's worry. Yet if he is dead, Mr Holmes, *where is the body?*'

3

There was a moment's silence after our client had finished.

'Curious indeed,' agreed Holmes. 'Are you able to explain to me, Mr Jasper, why it is that your nephew and Mr Landless should have fallen out in this unfortunate manner?'

Jasper stiffened. 'Is it really necessary for you to know that?' he asked.

'I think that the more I ascertain from the outset about this mysterious affair the greater chance there is of a solution emerging.'

'Very well then. The cause of the original altercation between them centred upon Miss Bud. Landless, although meeting her on only one occasion, appears to have formed an intense attachment to the young lady from the very first moment of that meeting – I suspect that the number of his female acquaintances is limited – and bitterly resented the fact that she was on the point of becoming engaged to Ned. Inflamed by passion and jealousy, he suggested that Ned was treating her in rather too casual a fashion and making light of something that ought to be held in much greater esteem.'

'And how has the young lady herself reacted to her fiancée's disappearance?'

Our client was silent for a moment and then spoke with the air of one choosing his words with great deliberation. 'She was, of course, greatly distressed and agitated. But I am unable to speak from first-hand knowledge about her present state of mind. She left Cloisterham several months ago and now resides somewhere in London.'

'You are aware of her precise location?'

'Unfortunately, no. On one point, however, I feel obliged to correct you. Miss Bud and my nephew, although seemingly predestined for one another from their earliest days, never reached the point of becoming formally betrothed. On the day before he disappeared Ned and she agreed, by mutual consent, that they were not really suited and that they should part as friends, to live henceforth in a relationship of brother and sister.'

'I see. Would Mr Landless have been aware of this?'

'I doubt it.'

'Were *you* aware of it?'

Again, a moment's silence before the answer came – and, when it did, it was as though it had been wrung out of Mr Jasper's innermost depths. 'No.' (Uttered hoarsely, with great emotion.)

Holmes deliberated for a while. 'Has any consideration been given', he asked, 'to the possibility that Mr Drood may have lost his memory?'

'It is, I suppose, possible,' said Mr Jasper, with the air of one who did not for one moment consider that this was remotely likely. He paused for a moment, engaged in some internal wrestle with himself, and then added, 'To tell the truth, Mr Holmes, I did at one time almost succeed in convincing myself that Ned had chosen to disappear of his own accord.'

'And why would he have done that?'

'Because the dear boy (so I ascertained afterwards) had feared for my peace of mind on learning that his unofficial engagement to Miss Bud would never be ratified. He had intended, in fact, that the news should be broken to me by Mr Grewgious – as, indeed, it was, but in circumstances very different from those which Ned had envisaged.'

'But you no longer believe that?'

Mr Jasper shook his head vigorously. 'Not since that moment . . .' he began, paused for an instant and then resumed in stronger voice. 'Not since that moment when Edwin's gold watch, with the chain still attached to it, together with his shirt-pin, were found in the river.'

Holmes sat bolt upright. 'Indeed! This is something that you have omitted to mention. Pray, where was this, Mr Jasper?'

'At Cloisterham Weir, some two miles upstream from that part of the river which Ned and Landless had intended to visit that night.'

'And who found them?'

'Mr Crisparkle, a week or two after Edwin's disappearance. There was no doubt as to their ownership – the watch bore the initials E. D. and was instantly identified as belonging to Ned. That he should have thrown them away himself is inconceivable.'

'Unless, indeed, he had determined to start a new life in

every respect, although without an intimate knowledge of the young gentleman's state of mind on the night it is difficult to judge why this might be.' Holmes pondered for a time. 'And is there anything else you wish to bring to my attention?'

'There is, and yet I scarcely know how to put it into words. Strange things have been happening in Cloisterham in recent weeks, Mr Holmes. I feel, somehow, as though a conspiracy were being waged against me, although it is difficult to pinpoint how it has developed or who the instigators are. I feel, almost, as though I were being put on trial. Attitudes have stiffened. People whom I have long been accustomed to look upon as friends treat me in a cold, antagonistic fashion – almost as though they suspected that *I* might have something to do with my dear boy's disappearance! Fingers are being pointed and remarks are being whispered. The most tangible development of all, perhaps, is that a stranger has appeared in the town – a genial old gentleman with a shock of white hair – who seems, all outward appearances to the contrary, to be keeping me under surveillance. He has moved into the house next door to mine and I see him wherever I go, try as I might to avoid him. You may feel, perhaps, that I am becoming deranged, and it may be that my nerves are now so finely stretched that it is difficult to distinguish between reality and imagination, but I do not feel' – and his voice broke at this point – 'that my equanimity can continue for very much longer. The uncertainty about Ned's fate needs to be resolved one way or the other. I am prepared for the worst, but it is the absence of knowledge about what happened on that terrible night that is gradually consuming me. How much longer can I go on like this? I appeal to you to abandon whatever other investigations you may have in hand and come to my rescue!'

'And the name of this amiable but watchful old gentleman?'

'Datchery, Mr Holmes. Dick Datchery. He is a total stranger – retired from the diplomatic service, so he claims – who has announced his intention of ending his days in Cloisterham.'

Holmes ruminated for a moment and our client grew still more agitated. 'The point that I must impress upon you above all things', he urged, 'is that Neville Landless (also now residing in London, in the vicinity of Staples Inn) is undoubtedly the perpetrator of this foul deed. Proof, sir, is needed, proof above all things, so that we might bring the villain to justice!'

'We must lose no time,' said Holmes, 'even at this late hour, in familiarizing ourselves with the scene of these events.' He turned to me questioningly. 'Do you have any objection, Watson, to our spending Christmas away from London? The arrangement would not, I fancy, be altogether unwelcome to Mrs Hudson, who has dropped a pointed hint or two about her desire to share the yule-tide festivities with a married sister in Croydon, and a brief change of scene might well be what you yourself, in your professional capacity, would prescribe for two middle-aged gentlemen who are otherwise only too susceptible to the attractions of a fusty atmosphere and a blazing fire.'

I willingly indicated my assent.

'Then that's settled. It is a thousand pities, though, that the trail, if one still exists, was laid so long ago, for it is a year, almost to the very day, since Mr Drood disappeared. Had the matter been brought to my attention at an earlier stage I would have been better equipped to deal with it.'

Mr Jasper looked surprised. 'You must remember, Mr Holmes,' he pointed out, 'that until very recently the nation at large was under the firm impression that your remains were somewhere in the vicinity of the Reichenbach Falls. Until you were brought back to life, as it were, the possibility of my being able to consult you simply did not arise.'

'Recalled to life,' said Holmes sorrowfully, shaking his head. 'You are, of course, quite right and I apologize for my oversight. The whirligig of time plays strange tricks with the mind. Or it may be, of course, that the whirligig of the mind plays strange tricks with time.'

Our visitor, tiring of what he evidently regarded as tedious sophistries, rose to his feet. 'If you are only able to recall Ned to life,' he exclaimed, 'or to ascertain, once and for all, what became of the dear boy, I shall be everlastingly in your debt.'

'We shall be with you by tomorrow afternoon,' said Holmes. 'There is, I believe, a relatively frequent train service to Cloisterham, even on Christmas Eve, is there not?'

'Trains?' repeated Jasper blankly, his eyes taking on a curiously glazed expression. 'I know nothing of such matters. You must make your own arrangements.'

'But perhaps there is a suitable hostelry you can recommend?'

'The Crozier,' said our visitor with a slight touch of impatience. 'Mr Bastewell maintains a good house, I believe. But these are mundane matters, Mr Holmes, which can surely be left to Dr Watson's consideration. I implore you to concentrate your own unique faculties on what has happened to Ned and to ascertain, for better or worse, what has become of him.'

'Indeed I will,' said Holmes smoothly, seeing our client to the door. 'You may rest assured, Mr Jasper, that this most intriguing affair will receive our full attention. All being well, we three will meet again within a very few hours. In the mean time, I wish you good-night.' He closed the door and lapsed into silence.

'A perplexing affair,' I remarked, crossing to the window and gazing down at the Christmas shoppers who were now intermingling with the homeward-bound office workers of Baker Street. Night had fallen, the lamps had been lit, the shop fronts were illuminated and odd flakes of snow swirled and twirled upon the garish scene. Our client, having emerged from the door of 221B, stood still for a moment as though getting his bearings and then strode off in a northerly direction.

'Perplexing indeed,' came the thoughtful rejoinder, 'although it may be that our attentions have been attracted by different aspects of the story. Mr Jasper's memory is oddly selective. My history is a trifle rusty, and my knowledge of the pressures brought to bear upon respectable choir-masters is scanty in the extreme, but I cannot help wondering —'

'Holmes,' said I, 'there is something strange here. It seems that our client is being accosted.'

Holmes joined me at the window. Two men in bulky coats and bowler hats, emerging from the shadows of a doorway, had overtaken and stopped John Jasper and engaged him in conversation. There was what appeared to be a short altercation. Jasper rounded angrily upon them for a moment, his head jerked back in fury, and then he appeared to resign himself to their company and all three walked on together – Jasper in the centre – to be caught up in the throng.

Holmes, without a word, seized his coat, hurried from the room and hastened down the road in pursuit, elbowing his way through the crowds. The three figures were, by this time, hopelessly out of sight and he returned some twenty minutes later, shaking his head with a rueful expression. 'Not a trace of them,' he remarked. 'Truly, a curious end to a curious visit. We must see what the morrow brings forth.'

No more did he say that night but retired to his room. And, a little while later, I heard the melancholy sounds of a violin.

4

Holmes was already out and about when I awoke the following morning but he returned soon after eleven. 'Great George Street,' was his curt response to my inevitable question – and, on interrogative eyebrows being raised, patiently explained, 'The headquarters of the Institution of Civil Engineers. I also endeavoured', he added cryptically, 'to renew a relationship with a certain royal personage of my acquaintance, but it transpired that Her Majesty was out of town.' This was the limit of what could be extracted from him. He remained in an uncommunicative mood for the next few hours and I knew better, by this time, than to interrupt such silences. My curiosity about his views on the subject of Neville Landless, let alone the purposes of the two men who had joined John Jasper the previous evening, would have to remain unsatisfied.

Our valises packed, we took a cab to Charing Cross station. Cloisterham having been, quite literally, off the beaten track for the best part of thirty years, as a consequence of never having been on it, and surviving its exclusion with equanimity, it was only as an afterthought that it had occurred to the managers of the London and South East Region Railway Company that this small, sleepy town might be usefully encompassed within a network which had extended its tentacles to almost every other community between the capital and the south coast. Having thus encompassed it, they appeared to have almost instantly repented of their decision. The great majority of trains shot through the town without stopping at all and those that did deign to draw reluctantly to a halt also insisted, for reasons of a savage perversity that defied all rational explanation, on stopping for several minutes at every other station *en route* regardless of whether anyone alighted or anyone boarded. The journey to our destination thus proved abominably slow and it was not until the early evening that we finally found ourselves strolling through the chilly main thoroughfare of the old Cathedral city. Dusk was falling, lights twinkled through the curtains now being pulled in the small and ancient houses and a great silence, in marked contrast to the turmoil of London, surrounded us wherever we went. The number of individuals out and about were so few that our footsteps positively echoed from one side of the street to the other.

'There is the Cathedral,' I remarked, as a great grey shape with a dominating tower, feebly illumined from within, loomed up.

'And there', added Holmes, 'is Mr Jasper's gatehouse. Shrouded in darkness, I observe. Obviously our client is not at home, but on this day, of all the days of the year, I would not have expected him to be. There is presumably a service either in progress or due to start in the near future.'

The medieval gatehouse, at the end of the High Street, surmounted a road which veered sharply to the left and ran towards the inky blackness surrounding the Cathedral and its environs. Still, grim and silent, somewhat in the posture of a squat, bow-legged sentinel, the gatehouse maintained motionless watch on a scene which grew increasingly indistinct. I shivered, involuntarily, and then brightened as I glimpsed our first port of call (its location ascertained from enquiries at the station) coming into view. 'The Crozier!' I exclaimed. 'And, all being well, a splendid repast with which to round off the day.'

The crowded interior of The Crozier was, indeed, all that one could have wished for in the way of a comfortable, old-fashioned, Kentish inn, and mine host, a plump, rubicund man, greeted us with a welcoming smile. 'Two pints of your best ale if you please, landlord,' said Holmes, loosening his overcoat and warming his hands by the fire. 'Have I the pleasure of addressing Mr Bastewell?'

Mine host, presenting us with two foaming tankards, looked puzzled. 'No, sir,' he said. 'There's no one of that name here, and *I've* been here the best part of fifteen years. Name of Appleby, sir. Never heard of no Bastewell.'

'No matter,' said Holmes. 'A small misunderstanding, obviously. More to the point, Mr Appleby, are you able to furnish us with a room for the next night or two? If your accommodation is as good as your ale, I fancy we'll have no complaints!'

The landlord's face dropped. 'Eeeh, sirs! I'm that sorry,' he exclaimed. 'Normally there'd have been no difficulty, but at this time of all times . . . If you'd only let us know you were

31

coming, a week or two back, I'm sure we could have fitted you in somewhere, but nowabouts it's a bit too late in the day, I'm thinking. It's the Convention, you see. You haven't come for the Convention yourselves, have you?' he asked with a sudden burst of hopefulness.

Holmes looked blank. 'What Convention's this?' I asked.

'Why of the Admirers, don't you see!'

Both of us now looked blank and Mr Appleby hastened to explain. A very great author, it seemed, had once lived in close proximity to Cloisterham and had died at this country home almost twenty-five years before — to be precise, twenty-four years and six months before. The Admirers of the great author had come together to pay homage, as it were, on the eve of this sad anniversary year, the Christmas period providing a suitable opportunity for the Admirers to converge from far and near.

'And what do they actually *do*?' I asked.

'Do, sir? Why, read chapters of his books out loud to one another and enjoy them and discuss them, like.'

'And that is the full extent of their activity?' asked Holmes, in some perplexity.

'Why bless me, no sir! That's the serious part of their proceedings, the sedentary aspect of their carryings-on if you take my meaning, sir.' And, on our still looking puzzled, the landlord explained that the Admirers also spent a considerable part of their time in dressing up as characters from the great novelist's books, in re-enacting scenes from those books, in processing through the streets in their period costumes and in feasting and revelry. And, to lend pictorial force to his explanations, there was at this point a sudden irruption of a group of the Admirers into that section of the inn. They were indeed in frolicsome mood, attired in costumes of a bygone age and bubbling over with seasonable goodwill. A seemingly elderly gentleman, a nightshirt pulled over his ordinary clothes and with an improbable shock of white hair, exclaimed, 'Bah, humbug!' two or three times, at which the other Admirers convulsed themselves with mirth, and they disappeared into a separate part of the inn which had been, so we gathered, especially set aside for their festivities.

'A singular but, I suppose, harmless pursuit,' said Holmes, shaking his head, as we took our seats in the dining-room — for the landlord had hastened to assure us that, while beds were in sadly short supply, he could offer us food in abundance. The meal that followed was all that we could have wished for and we devoured it in satisfaction. Holmes pushed back his plate, poured himself a fresh glass of brandy and groped for his brier pipe in absent-minded fashion. 'A curious state of affairs,' he murmured, almost to himself, as he filled it.

'You mean the disappearance of Mr Drood?'

'No, my dear chap; a strange business, certainly, but I refer to the activities of our friends in the adjoining apartments. That they should go to such lengths! Fact is fact and fiction is fiction and the dividing line between their respective territories should never be traversed. To mix one with the other is to meddle with the natural order of things,' He puffed contentedly and warmed to his theme, unconsciously making amends, perhaps, for his silence earlier in the day. 'Characters such as Don Quixote and Sancho Panza, say, loom larger than life in our imaginations, but if you and I were to encounter them walking towards us down Cloisterham High Street I fear we would almost certainly be sadly disillusioned. They would be mere mortals, the same as ourselves – for to make them, literally, larger than life (as our American cousins might be disposed to do, in their natural enthusiasm for such enterprises) would be to make them grotesques. Characters from Fact, similarly, should not be allowed to stray into the realm of Fiction, although historical romances – with the author of *Waverley* as an outstanding offender – have tended to obliterate the frontier to so great an extent that it is difficult to determine where the boundary now lies.'

'Perhaps', I suggested, 'we should draw a distinction between, say, the monarchs of Fact and the monarchs of Fiction? Between the Queen Elizabeth portrayed in our history books and the Queen Elizabeth portrayed in our novels?'

'That, certainly, is one solution, but scarcely a satisfactory one. The great majority of readers will surely be unable to distinguish between the genuine article and the counterfeit, with the fictional version aping the original model in every conceivable degree yet being, in the last analysis, nothing more than a two-dimensional pasteboard figure, incapable of doing anything that might be considered even remotely out of character. You and I, Watson, thanks to those little case-histories of yours which have attracted so much attention in recent times, are in some danger of being immortalized! Who will be able to tell, a hundred years from now, whether we were Fact or Fiction? Dare we contemplate what enormities, what fabulous exploits, might not be perpetrated in our names? Will there even be', he added with a shudder, 'duplicate versions of myself perambulating the environs of Baker Street at dead of night, equipped with deerstalker hats, bloodhounds and magnifying glasses and accompanied by their faithful Watsons?'

'Holmes,' said I, laughing, 'you are becoming altogether too fanciful in your old age (or in your cups), although – in general terms – I take your point. And as with persons,' I added, 'so, I suppose, with places.'

'Exactly. The London, say, of Fiction may closely resemble the London of Fact and may run on seemingly parallel lines, but it is a distinct entity and the two should never be confused. The Reverend Charles Dodgson came close to defining the situation with his creation of Looking-Glass Land, where – at first glance – the state of affairs on the other side of the mirror is basically the same as that of the real world, but should an Alice venture to intrude into that other world she will soon discover that things are strangely different. The same principle also applies, of course, to the weather. In this country a white Christmas is the rarest of events, for which we may be profoundly thankful, but when did you last peruse a Christmas tale set in England in which the snow was not falling fast or, at any rate, lying thick upon the ground? – and similar liberties may be taken, by our novelists, with the days of the week or even with the months of the year. But I have held forth for far too long and it is high time we were making a move. With no room at the inn on Christmas Eve, of all nights, we must exercise our ingenuity to its uttermost if we are to secure a roof for our heads.'

Mine host, with reiterated apologies, bowed us out (a lugubrious gentleman in the background, attired in the rustic garb of a bygone age, meanwhile making so bold as to inform us that he was willin' and being instantly hauled out of sight by unseen hands, amidst peals of recriminatory laughter from fellow Admirers) and we found ourselves walking, once again, through the deserted streets of Cloisterham as the Cathedral clock chimed the ninth hour of the night.

The night had become appreciably colder, and pulling our coats about us we retraced our steps to the gatehouse. It was still in darkness. We climbed the postern stairs, which carried with them an odour of peculiar staleness. 'There is a gritty state of things here,' said Holmes, shuffling his feet. 'These steps have not been swept for some considerable time.' He struck a match and rapped on the uninviting door revealed by its feeble light, but answer came there none from Mr Jasper.

'Perhaps he is still at the Cathedral,' I suggested, after Holmes had knocked again and we had waited several minutes. My companion grunted. 'If so,' he remarked, 'it is an unconscionably long service.' We waited a little while longer, after a third and final knock, and then groped our way back to the fresher air of the outside world.

A brief survey now led to the discovery that, squeezed between the lower portion of the far side of the gatehouse and the High Street proper, barely wide enough for the slimmest of travellers to pass through, was an exceedingly narrow alleyway. Holmes ventured down it, I following close at his heels, and we found that a tiny door was set into the wall of the gatehouse. The chances of anyone being in residence in this part of the building seemed equally unpromising, but after Holmes had thundered on the door several times it opened a few inches and the face of a very old gentleman could be dimly discerned peeping out at us. I was half prepared for a testy cry of 'Here's a knocking indeed! Who's there, i' th' name of Beelzebub?' but the old man held his peace.

'Good evening,' roared Holmes. The face was unresponsive. 'I'm exceedingly sorry to trouble you at this late hour but you may be able to help us.'

The old gentleman continued to peer out suspiciously.

'We are friends of Mr Jasper, your next-door neighbour.'

''E ain't 'ere!' came the suddenly spirited reply, and the door began to close at a great rate.

Holmes, however, had adroitly inserted his foot in the limited space available before the operation could be completed. 'I realize that,' he shouted, 'but my friend and I have come a very long way and there is no room at the inn. We are desperately anxious for accommodation. Are you able to take us under your roof for just one night? We will pay you well.'

At this final announcement the door wavered and then began to swing cautiously open again. Holmes, pressing home his advantage, produced a couple of sovereigns and they found a ready market.

'Wait 'ere,' came the command and the old gentleman disappeared for several minutes, returning with a candle. He led us into what were two remarkably tiny rooms – bearing, indeed, a closer resemblance to miniature dungeons than to ordinary living quarters. We were evidently in chambers which had been created some four or five hundred years before. They were sparsely furnished in the extreme, but there was a bed, a chair, a table and a corner-cupboard, the last of these features being virtually built into the wall. There was also another door to the outside world. "Tain't much,' grumbled the old man, with the merest hint of an apology.

'On the contrary, this will suit us splendidly,' bellowed Holmes. I vigorously nodded my agreement. The old gentleman, having lit a small lamp, saw no need to exert himself further and began to withdraw. 'One moment, sir,' exclaimed Holmes. 'Are you able to enlighten my friend and myself as to the times of the Cathedral services? Would we be correct in assuming that there will be one at midnight and one at the crack of dawn tomorrow?'

The old gentleman drew himself up proudly. 'Man an' boy,' he declared, 'I've been working at this Cathedral for seventy years, and there ain't much that I don't know about times of services!'

We signified, unfeignedly, our astonishment at this announcement and the old gentleman, encouraged by our interest, became still more expansive. 'I've been', he proclaimed, 'chorister, lay clerk, under-verger and now verger. I knows that Cathedral like the back of me 'and. The Bishop himself has been known to consult me on occasion. "Mr Tope," says he, 'would I be right in assuming that . . ." or "Mr Tope," he says, "please correct me if I'm wrong, but . . .". "Your Grace," I've said to him many a time, "you've come to the right man, Your Grace", and so 'e 'as, and I've put him right on one or two points before now and will probably do so again – *and* the next man arter 'im! Bishops come and bishops go, but Tope goes on for ever.'

Our wonder and admiration knew, by this time, no bounds and Holmes marked the occasion by the production of another sovereign, which speedily joined its pre-decessors. Thus encouraged, Mr Tope confirmed that there was indeed a midnight and an early morning service and, his duties done, abruptly disappeared. Holmes flung himself upon the bed, lost in thought, and I opened up the cupboard doors in order to stow away our modest travelling accoutrements. I was intrigued to see that, on the inside of one of the doors, a number of vertical lines, of varying lengths, had been chalked and that, on the other, there appeared (also in chalk) the word KIN-FREE-DER-EL, the second syllable being underlined, followed by first a question mark and then an exclamation mark. I called Holmes's attention to these mysterious jottings and he evinced a mild interest in them. 'The lines', he said, 'would seem to be an example of an old country method of keeping a tally, or score, while "Kin-free-der-el" is perhaps a jocular rendition of the word "cathedral", although the humour of the translation escapes me for the moment. Is it the kin or the letter L from which one is being set free? Of more immediate interest, I would suggest, is the fact that we have a door of our own to the outside world through which we can come and go, during the next few hours, without the necessity of having to disturb our worthy host on each occasion. Now, Watson, are you game for a tour of inspection?'

I willingly consented. With the lamp extinguished, and the door on the latch, we emerged into the precincts of the Cathedral, at a point exactly opposite the entrance to John Jasper's staircase, and walked towards the massive building. The moon was, by this time, high in the sky, casting a white light over the churchyard with its tombs, graves, miniature mausoleums, broken columns, sorrowing angels and lachrymose cherubs, their eyes rolled upwards, frozen in lamentation. We made our way through this shimmering city of the dead. Although the tombstones were railed off from the footpath, which made it difficult to decipher any of the words on them, even had we been so inclined, it was impossible to ignore the fact that some of them were in a sorry state of disrepair.

'I have devised', said Holmes softly, 'a little catechism for you, Watson. Let us suppose you had been so unscrupulous as to purloin a valuable book (as distinct from a letter) and that you wished, in the limited amount of time available before a search began, to hide it where it would be most likely to escape attention. Where would you go?'

I considered for a moment. 'To a library?' I suggested.

'Excellent! Now, in the words of a distant clerical acquaintance, where would you hide a leaf?'

'In a forest of leaves.'

'Excellent again! And finally, Watson, where would you hide a body?'

'In a forest of bodies,' I murmured, drawing in my breath and gazing at the wrecked tombs beyond the railings.

Holmes nodded. 'I commend the thought to your consideration,' he remarked quietly.

41

We strolled on, circumnavigating the Cathedral and its environs, and found ourselves at Minor Canon Corner, where Neville Landless had lodged with Mr Crisparkle before his banishment to London. We then turned into what was the definitely non-ecclesiastical and far from salubrious atmosphere of Gas Works Gardens. From the door of a seedy lodging establishment half-way along (the Travellers' Tuppenny, so a ramshackle sign proclaimed) streamed out a ray of light and the sound of ribald singing and raucous laughter from the inmates – the first human voices, other than our own, that we had heard for the best part of an hour.

'There is, it seems, an unruly element in Cloisterham,' said Holmes with a smile.

'On reflection,' I ventured tentatively, after a few minutes' silence, 'I cannot help wondering whether we are perhaps not making rather heavy weather of this business. Mr Jasper's account held us enthralled, and he virtually convinced us that Landless was the man responsible for his nephew's disappearance, but might it not be that Drood was simply attacked and mortally injured by some ruffian from that establishment which we have just passed? A shocking event, admittedly, but a relatively mundane affair scarcely necessitating your own involvement.'

'I would judge it exceedingly unlikely. The most significant aspect of this curious tale, although Mr Jasper almost forgot to mention it, is the fact that Drood's watch and chain and shirt-pin were thrown in the river. That would seem to rule out robbery as a motive.'

'Unless', I pursued, 'the assailant panicked when he found that he had killed the young man and threw away these

42

incriminating items lest they be found on him.'

'But in that case, where is the body? There are really only two possibilities. The first is that Drood divested himself of those items as a prelude to deliberately disappearing. That seems improbable, but cannot be ruled out completely. The second is that somebody else removed them so that a body, if discovered, would not be easily identified. That in itself, however, suggests one of two further possibilities: either that the body would not be found for a very long time indeed, in which case identification would be impossible, or that if it *were* to be found in a relatively short space of time it would somehow have been rendered unrecognizable by the process of decomposition being artificially accelerated. It may be that Mr Drood is, by this time, no more than the dust beneath our feet.'

We turned into the High Street for the second time that day, walking past the Nuns' House seminary which had been attended by Miss Bud, and – our immediate tour of inspection complete – fetched up at the gatehouse. There were now several groups of people converging on the Cathedral but Mr Jasper's quarters remained, as ever, in darkness.

'What now?' I asked.

'For you, Watson, the midnight service, for the witching hour is only twenty minutes away. It will doubtless be conducive to your spiritual well-being, but observe carefully and see if you can perceive our friend among the members of the choir. (But his absence from last year's service leads me to suspect that he will also be absent on this occasion.) Note, too, the time at which the proceedings conclude.'

'And you, Holmes?'

'I shall remain here until midnight and then stroll down to gaze at the river – at about the same time, so we are given to understand, as Messrs Drood and Landless strolled down to gaze at it exactly twelve months ago.'

'You are aware of its location?'

Holmes smiled faintly. 'There is an ancient map of the locality on display in the entrance hall of The Crozier: the jubilant distractions of the Admirers notwithstanding, I took the opportunity of familiarizing myself with the geography of Cloisterham before we took our leave.'

I left him standing in the shadow of the gatehouse and returned to the Cathedral, finding myself in the company of a fair-sized congregation. The service was indeed impressive. The choir was in splendid form and 'Once in Royal David's City' pealed out on the organ at the stroke of midnight. But of Mr Jasper there was no sign.

I made my way back to the gatehouse at the conclusion of the service and Holmes joined me about twenty minutes later. There being, he reported, a total absence of the foul weather which had so disfigured the previous Christmas Eve, the river was in an unspectacular condition. He had seen no one on his return journey, the Cathedral worshippers and clergy having dispersed to their homes, which suggested that no one would have been abroad to see Drood and Landless the previous year. He had knocked for one last time at Mr Jasper's door but, once again, there had been no reply. 'It seems', he concluded, 'that we must search for a missing uncle as well as a missing nephew. Truly, a perplexing state of affairs! But the twenty-fifth day of December is upon us and a few hours' sleep will not come amiss. You take the bed, my dear fellow. The chair will suffice for my requirements.'

And a few minutes later, as soon as we had settled ourselves and I had extinguished the lamp, there rang through the darkness a cheery cry of 'Merry Christmas, Watson!'

I was awoken, rather to my surprise, by an elderly lady shaking me gently by the shoulder. I sat up in some confusion, to find that there was no sign of Holmes and that the old lady had set down a cup of tea on the small table beside the bed. I accepted it with hearty thanks, coupled with the compliments of the season, and Mrs Tope (for she then begged leave to introduce herself) watched me drink it with much satisfaction.

Had I slept well? she wanted to know. On my assuring her that I had she lingered a while, with the air of one who did not often have the opportunity for speaking to fresh acquaintances, and became quite confidential. We had been, she explained, the first people to stay at the Tope residence for many years, although the rooms were always kept ready for unexpected guests and there had been a time, indeed, when she had hoped that they might make a regular "go" of the lodging-house business. For some inexplicable reason, however, the two tiny chambers had not aroused any great enthusiasm among potential clientele and had failed to prove the little goldmine confidently expected. One of the last of their lodgers, however, and one who had stayed there for several weeks, off and on, had been a dear old gentleman who (like myself) was very fond of his tea. 'Tea is capital, Mrs Tope,' he had proclaimed on several occasions; 'I am exceedingly partial to it, and *your* tea is the finest in all Cloisterham.'

I hastened to assure her that, on the basis of my own experience, the old gentleman could surely not have been mistaken in his opinion. It was, indeed, one which I most certainly endorsed. Thus encouraged, Mrs Tope excused herself for a few minutes and returned with a *second* cup for my benefit. I downed it with as great an enthusiasm as I could muster and Mrs Tope, while keeping an observant eye upon me, continued to ruminate on the character of her last lodger. He was, it seemed, a retired gentleman, very genial and easy-going in his ways although surprisingly active for a man of his years. But he must have been, all outward appearances to the contrary, an invalid. He had remarked several times towards the end, with a curious little smile, that he was living on borrowed time.

'Towards the end?' I queried.

'Towards the end of his stay here, sir.'

'Did he end his days in Cloisterham?' I enquired, more for some-thing to say than for reasons of any real curiosity on the subject.

'That was certainly his intention, sir, but it was all rather curious and, in a sense, I'm not able to say one way or the other. He came and went, not being a totally committed resident as it were, and there came a time when he went away and simply didn't come back, although paid up to the end of the following week. We didn't hear no more about him or from him, did Tope and me, and there was nothing of any consequence in these rooms to indicate whether he had relatives or forwarding addresses, but that was very many years ago now, sir, and I'm sure the old gentleman has passed on to wherever he was going by this time. It must have been in the autumn that he went,' she added rather inconsequentially, 'as he made some little joke about being in the autumn of our days when the leaves began to fall in the Close and that was one of the last times that I saw him.'

I could not help reflecting that the residents of Cloisterham were rather prone to disappear in unexpected fashion but I was tiring of the subject of Mrs Tope's last lodger and endeavoured to indicate, by a certain straightening of the back, that this was all very delightful but that it was high time that I was up and doing. The good lady instantly took the hint and, with a slight bob and an assurance that shaving water would be available whenever I required it, returned to her quarters.

Holmes reappeared a little while later, after I had finished dressing, and flung himself into the chair. The expression on his face was partly bemused and partly elated. He had, he announced, attended the early morning service. Again, the choir had been magnificent but there had been no sign of Mr Jasper. To my surprise, however, he dismissed this as a matter of no great significance. 'I have discovered', he announced, with undisguised relish, 'something that goes a long way towards explaining much that had been previously unclear – and, indeed, that confirms a suspicion that has been growing upon me from the moment that we arrived here.'

What this mysterious something was, however, he declined to reveal for the moment, but insisted that I immediately accompany him back to the Cathedral. Ablutions completed, we hastened out into the morning sunshine and returned to the churchyard, which looked far less eerie than on the previous evening. Holmes suddenly stopped, *en route* as it were to our final destination, and pointed at one particular monument. 'What do you think of that, Watson?' he asked with a smile.

The monument bore an inscription couched in terms of astonishing pomposity which proclaimed that it was dedicated to the memory of Ethelinda, departed this life in the month of December 1868, the Reverential Wife of Mr Thomas Sapsea, Auctioneer, Valuer, Estate Agent, &c., of the City of Cloisterham

Whose Knowledge of the World,
Though somewhat extensive,
Never brought him acquainted with
A SPIRIT
More capable of
LOOKING UP TO HIM.

The passing stranger was asked whether he could do likewise and sternly commanded, if the response were a negative one, to retire with a blush.

'I think', murmured Holmes abruptly, 'that we should act upon that final adjuration without delay.'

But it was too late. I suddenly became aware that, leaning

on a substantial stick a few yards away, a very elderly, somewhat portly gentleman had been observing our interest with evident satisfaction. He was dressed completely in black and equipped with so splendid a top hat and so imposingly gaitered that I felt, for a moment, that we could not possibly be in the presence of anyone less exalted than the Bishop himself.

'The greetings of the festive season,' roared this magnificent apparition. 'Chancing to pass this way on my way to morning worship, I could not help but observe that you felt compelled to linger at a memorial to a very simple but dear creature (gone these twenty-six years, gentlemen!) and to digest the sentiments so unworthily expressed thereon.'

'Indeed yes,' agreed Holmes with some enthusiasm. 'We were lost in admiration. But surely, my good sir, have I not the honour of addressing in person the author of those splendid sentiments? Is it really Mr Thomas Sapsea that I see before me?'

'*Sir* Thomas Sapsea,' came the reply, with a slight note of dignified reproach. 'The Crown, with that bounteous graciousness which is ever the hallmark and delight of our Constitution (and the envy of foreigners of every race and clime), saw fit to reward its most humble of servants, some years ago, for some modest functions performed in a civic, in a mayoral capacity, for this insignificant little community of ours. They also serve, gentlemen, however lowly their grade in life – they also serve,' and a hand was waved in deprecatory fashion, as a means of emphasizing that, whatever the insignificance of his achievements in the great

50

scheme of things, the Cloisterham that we saw about us was largely the creation of his labours.

'You are too good,' he said, smilingly, with a further deprecatory wave of the hand, after we had conveyed our congratulations, 'you are far too good. But may I take this opportunity, gentlemen, as a senior citizen of our small town (and some, indeed, have been so kind as to refer to me as the permanent *first* citizen, an unmerited accolade which I totally, nay absolutely, reject), may I take this opportunity of welcoming you to Cloisterham and trusting that your visit is proving to be all that you could wish it to be? Is everything, in short, to your satisfaction, gentlemen?' — with an air of one who would most definitely take it upon himself to personally seek out, reprimand, chastise and generally demolish any wretched denizen who had in any way, however unwittingly, crossed our path.

'A charming city,' said Holmes. 'One could wish, perhaps, that accommodation for passing visitors were in greater supply, for The Crozier is fully booked up, but we are lodging with Mr and Mrs Tope and they have made us more than welcome.'

'A worthy couple,' said Sir Thomas, magnanimously.

'My friend and I', added Holmes, 'are considering the possibility, indeed, of acquiring a small residence in this fair city, as a place of retreat at such times of the year as the present, and have been casting our eyes on one or two properties that appear to be in a vacant or semi-vacant condition. As the leading expert on valuation and property in this part of the world, Sir Thomas, what would you say about the possibility of such an apartment as *that*' — and he pointed to the gatehouse – 'becoming available at a modest price?'

'That particular property', said Sir Thomas, with a shake of the head,' is not on the market, gentlemen. It is the residence of Mr John Jasper.'

Holmes looked mildly surprised. 'I had the impression', he said, 'that it was unoccupied.'

'At the moment, sir, I fear that it is. My friend Mr John Jasper, sir, has been gone from Cloisterham for many a long day,' he intoned. 'For many a long day,' he repeated with emphasis. 'But I cherish the hope that he will one day return to us.'

'Ah!' said Holmes, as though an old recollection had struck him. 'Is this the gentleman whose nephew suddenly disappeared?' A portentous nod greeted this question. 'And there was some talk, was there not, of another young gentleman, a Mr Landless, being responsible?'

'A bad lot, sir, a thoroughly bad lot!' – and a contemptuous snap of the fingers as though to say 'There! I totally dismiss him.'

'And Mr Jasper, therefore . . .?'

'Went in pursuit of the Murderer, gentlemen, and pledged himself never to rest easy in his bed until he had brought him to justice.'

Holmes shook his head in mournful reflection on the evils of the world.

'I am impressed to learn, gentlemen,' continued Sir Thomas, 'that the events of our small community should have made themselves known to the outside world and been so long remembered in . . . in circles such as your own.'

This last in slightly questioning vein.

'We must look elsewhere for a residence,' said Holmes ruefully, ignoring the hint. 'But I must confess that the city of Cloisterham greatly appeals to us.'

'Its peace and stillness', I added in an unlucky moment, feeling that it was time I made a further contribution to the discussion, 'certainly provide a welcome contrast to the hustle and bustle of Baker Street.'

'Of Baker Street?' repeated the old gentleman with unexpected alacrity, his eyes opening wide and gazing at Holmes with newly awakened interest. 'And fully conversant with the disappearance of Mr John Jasper's nephew, Mr Edwin Drood! Have I the honour of speaking to one who is professionally involved in criminological matters? Is it a Celebrated Sleuth that I see before me?'

Holmes, who had darted a look of intense irritation at myself, spread wide his hands with the air of one who, hopelessly outmatched, judged it best to surrender without further ado. 'Sir Thomas,' he said, 'you are far too deep for us. It is useless to conceal my identity so far as you are concerned. But you will appreciate, Sir Thomas, that my colleague and I are visiting Cloisterham in a strictly private capacity, as a break from the turmoils of London, and it would be greatly appreciated if you would preserve our secret.'

Sir Thomas tapped his nose in knowing fashion. 'Gentlemen,' he declared, manfully suppressing his excitement, 'you may rely upon me. I am the soul of discretion. Upon my word, a Celebrated Sleuth in Cloisterham! I must now take leave of you but I hope that we shall have the opportunity for further converse and I trust, again, that your stay proves a pleasant one. Once more, the compliments of the festive season!'

'Sir Thomas,' said Holmes, 'we are forever in your debt – and not least, I must add, for the inspiring sentiments with which you have enlivened our morning,' with a gesture towards the churchyard.

The venerable first citizen of Cloisterham vigorously shook his head. 'A poor thing, gentlemen,' he declared, 'a poor thing, but mine own!' And he took his leave. I was not at all clear, in my own mind, whether he was referring to the inscription on the tomb or to the late lamented Mrs Sapsea.

'I fancy', said my companion drily, 'that our presence here will be known throughout the streets of Cloisterham by the time the Cathedral clock strikes twelve. Of Baker Street, indeed! But here, Watson, is what I noted earlier this morning.' Holmes pointed through the railing at one particular headstone. SACRED TO THE MEMORY, it ran, OF MARTIN DROOD, DEPARTED THIS LIFE 14 MARCH 1861.

'Well, that certainly confirms,' I remarked, albeit not greatly impressed, 'quite apart from the remarks of Sir Thomas, that there is some tangible basis for Mr Jasper's story.'

'Think, man, think!'

I looked again and enlightenment dawned. 'Good heavens, Holmes! Of course, that date is quite impossible!'

'Exactly. Martin Drood was a gentleman of some technical ingenuity, I gather, and the genetic sciences have made great strides in recent years, but I fail to understand how even he could have fathered, twelve years prior to the

54

year 1861, a son who would not come of age until the spring of 1894.'

'But this makes nonsense of virtually everything Mr Jasper told us! Are we the victims, Holmes, of some monstrous practical joke?'

'I doubt it. Mr Jasper, whatever else he may be, is no practical joker. The humour of our quandary escapes me and even the late Professor Moriarty, I fancy, would not have thought it worth his while to send us on a wild-goose chase to this inoffensive little town. No, there is nothing at all comic in the situation – just the reverse. The story that this Mr Jasper told us was narrated, I believe, in good faith and we have had the independent corroboration of Sir Thomas Sapsea on that score.' He paused for a moment, in some slight embarrassment. 'I fancy, Watson, that you will not believe me when I say that I half expected some development of this kind, or even if I add that it tends to clarify rather than obscure matters?'

'I know better than to doubt your word after all these years, Holmes, but I must certainly confess that I am totally bewildered.'

'Let us take a turn in the cloisters. This path is becoming rather too well frequented and I have no desire to draw undue attention to ourselves or to attract the conversation of another Sir Thomas Sapsea, if such there be! The morning service will be commencing shortly, and seclusion is required if we are to put our thoughts in order.'

The stream of pedestrians, of good-humoured families of all ages and sizes muffled up and chattering happily as they converged upon the Cathedral, was indeed growing formidable. We strolled into the precincts, gently illuminated by wintry sunshine and as deserted as one could wish, and perambulated them in silence for a time.

'You will recall', said Holmes at length, 'that I asked Mr Jasper several questions towards the end of our interview and that he was unable to enlighten me as to either the frequency of the rail service or, as it transpires, the identity of the present landlord of The Crozier. He acknowledged that Christmas Eve was upon us, but I did not think to ask him – indeed, I could scarcely have ventured to do so, even had the thought occurred to me! – what year of Our Lord he thought we were in. Had I done so, and had he retained sufficient control of his temper to answer a singular but simple question in a straightforward manner, I now suspect that he would have opted for 1870 rather than 1894. By this reckoning, Edwin Drood disappeared at midnight on the Christmas Eve of 1869 and we are investigating an event that occurred a quarter of a century ago. Our client's letter, of course, was correctly dated but you will recall that the date was inserted in another hand.'

I digested this information, shaking my head in wonderment.

'The trains, of course, did not run to Cloisterham until after 1870 and I feel certain that mine host at The Crozier in that year (and some elementary research will soon confirm this) would indeed have been Mr Bastewell.' He paused. 'What should instantly have alerted me to the strangeness of Mr Jasper's narrative – and, indeed, suspicions were slowly dawning that all was not right with it from the chronological viewpoint – was his reference to Mehemet

Ali. The Levantine crisis that he referred to occurred in 1840, or thereabouts, which means that Mr Martin Drood and his wife would have arrived in Egypt in, say, 1845. You will recall that visit I paid to Great George Street yesterday morning. I was hoping that the Institution of Civil Engineers would be able to enlighten me as to the professional qualifications and career of one or other of the Droods, but I drew a blank on both counts. It simply did not occur to me to go further back into the records.'

'So Mr Jasper is suffering from some kind of amnesia?'

'We are now venturing into what are more properly *your* realms rather than mine, Watson, but that would certainly appear to be the case. A most curious kind of affliction, however: while convinced, as I take it, that he was talking to us on the twenty-third day of December in the year 1870, he had nevertheless been able to keep abreast of certain current events — being particularly (and flatteringly!) familiar, it seems, with the events of my own recent career.'

'But where is Mr Jasper now, Holmes? And, even more to the point, what do we do next?'

I realized, at this point, that Holmes had steered us out of the cloisters and that we were now approaching, once again, our curious lodgings.

'Do, my boy?' he exclaimed, with a positive hint of glee. 'There is only one course open to us on this beautiful Christmas morning. While the good people of Cloisterham are at their devotions a little breaking and entry on the part of a pair of old reprobates such as ourselves will surely not come amiss. Cometh the hour, cometh the intruders!' And he raised his stick and pointed at Jasper's gatehouse.

So, once again (and, as it proved, for the last time) we climbed that dusty postern staircase. Such daylight as could penetrate to the steps made it clear, had we still been in any doubt, that no feet but ours had trod them in recent months.

It took Holmes little more than five minutes' careful probing at the lock, with a curious instrument which he invariably carried on his person (akin, perhaps, to a remarkable penknife but with attachments that would have been the envy of any schoolboy), to secure our admission to the music-master's chambers. We found ourselves in a large room with two latticed windows directly opposite one another, the first overlooking the High Street and the second gazing towards the Cathedral and its precincts. It was an impressive, respectably furnished room – the abode, obviously, of an erudite man – with a pair of comfortable easy chairs on each side of the fireplace, a wall lined with shelves of books, a grand piano in a recess (although how *it* could have gained access to the upper storey of the gatehouse defied all rational analysis!) and a music stand, with one or two folios still on it. But dust was everywhere and the atmosphere was stale and musty in the extreme. One's initial inclination, which had to be restrained for obvious reasons, was to fling open wide the windows.

'Undoubtedly,' said Holmes, 'this is the residence of Mr John Jasper, although I should not like to hazard a guess, for the moment, as to when he last resided here.' His attention was caught by what was, perhaps, the one human touch in the room – a painting, which hung over the fireplace, of a pretty young girl with long brown hair streaming down to her shoulders and an impertinent twinkle in her eyes. It was amateurishly executed and apparently unfinished but succeeded in conveying a captivating impression of the young lady's character. It roguishly enlivened what was otherwise a rather solemn bachelor apartment. 'A striking young lady,' said Holmes. 'And that brooch she wears is equally striking' – he pointed to an amethyst in a gold setting of peculiar intricacy, designed to resemble a budding rose. 'That may give us a clue', he added with a smile, 'as to the identity of the young person!'

A small dining-room lay beyond this austere chamber with a door at the far end (leading, we surmised, to the quarters of Mr and Mrs Tope). Holmes poked and probed around both rooms without finding anything of interest and then led the way up a short flight of steps to two modestly-sized bedrooms. The smaller of them appeared to be principally for guests, there being nothing of a personal nature in the wardrobe or chest of drawers, but the main bedroom, which was clearly Mr Jasper's own, was more rewarding. 'See here!' exclaimed Holmes, holding aloft (after blowing the dust away) a notebook which he had found on the bedside table. 'This appears to be some kind of diary kept by our client — and, yes, the entries relate to events in 1869 and 1870! Look at these, Watson — both written in September 1869.'

The first entry ran as follows:

Past midnight. — After what I have just now seen, I have a morbid dread upon me of some horrible consequences resulting to my dear boy, that I cannot reason with or in any way contend against. All my efforts are vain. The demoniacal passion of this Neville Landless, his strength in his fury, and his savage rage for the destruction of its object, appal me. So profound is the impression, that twice since I have gone into my dear boy's room, to assure myself of his sleeping safely, and not lying dead in his blood.

And the second, written the following morning:

Ned up and away. Light-hearted and unsuspicious as ever. He laughed when I cautioned him, and said he was as good a man as Neville Landless any day. I told him that he might be, but he was not so bad a man. He continued to make light of it, but I travelled with him as far as I could, and left him most unwillingly. I am unable to shake off these dark intangible presentiments of evil — if feelings founded upon staring facts are to be so called.

I shivered. 'Poor Mr Jasper', I said, 'had full justification for his terrible forebodings. He seems, indeed, to have been virtually clairvoyant! Neville Landless must surely have behaved like some kind of uncaged wild beast, on the occasion of his first visit to the gatehouse, to have aroused such apprehensions on the part of our client.'

'I certainly agree', replied Holmes, 'that he was finely attuned to the tension between these two young men. The quarrel between them, you will recall, concerned Miss Bud, and on such a subject as a member of the fairer sex passions can be aroused to an alarming degree. But what have we here? A letter from Mr Drood himself, it seems, written at the beginning of December 1869!'

The letter in question, which had been folded up and inserted in the diary, ran as follows:

My Dear Jack,

I am touched by your account of your interview with Mr Crisparkle, whom I much respect and esteem. At once I openly say that I forgot myself on that occasion quite as much as Mr Landless did, and that I wish that bygone to be a bygone, and all to be right again.

Look here, dear old boy. Ask Mr Landless to dinner on Christmas Eve (the better the day the better the deed), and let there be only we three, and let us shake hands all round there and then, and say no more about it.

My dear Jack, Ever your most affectionate,
Edwin Drood

P.S. Love to Miss Pussy at the next music-lesson.

'A frank, impetuous, good-hearted youth!' I exclaimed. 'His character emerges very clearly from this letter, and from the second of those two diary entries. One can fully see why Mr Jasper was so fond of him. And the young man appears to have been equally fond of his uncle.'

'Miss Pussy', said Holmes, somewhat drily, 'is presumably Miss Bud. That young lady evidently has a significant part to play in this tale. So, the stage is set for that fateful meeting on Christmas Eve 1869. What else does the diary have to tell us?'

There were a number of blank pages and then came a further entry, penned towards the end of January 1870:

My dear boy is murdered. The discovery of the watch and shirt-pin convinces me that he was murdered that night, and that his jewellery was taken from him to prevent identification by its means. All the delusive hopes I had founded on his separation from his betrothed wife, I give to the winds. They perish before this fatal discovery. I now swear, and record the oath on this page, that I nevermore will discuss this mystery with any human creature until I hold the clue to it in my hand. That I never will relax in my secrecy or in my search. That I will fasten the crime of the murder of my dear dead boy upon the murderer. And, that I devote myself to his destruction.

'It appears', I said, 'that Mr Jasper broke his oath when he came to see us.'

'Unless', said Holmes, musingly, 'the day *did* come when he held the clue to the mystery in his hand. But perhaps he regards me – not altogether flatteringly, it must be confessed! – as being in a category one stage removed from the ordinary human creature. He was also, of course, far less emphatic, both in his letter to me and in our conversation, as to the ultimate fate of Mr Drood. The man who wrote this diary entry had no doubts whatsoever on the subject; the man we saw two days ago desperately wanted to know, simply for his own peace of mind, whether Drood was alive or dead. That suggests that something happened, prior to his memory playing strange tricks with him, to shake Mr Jasper's certainty on the matter.'

'But these diary entries (and, of course, Mr Drood's letter)', I pointed out, 'amply confirm your conjecture that these are events which happened a quarter of a century ago. Is there really any point in our further involvement in what could almost be classed as ancient history?'

'These documents are certainly extremely convenient,' Holmes agreed. 'So convenient, indeed, as to suggest that we – or somebody else – had positively been *intended* to see them. But there is a mystery here, Watson, irrespective of whether it happened yesterday, twelve months ago or twenty-five years ago, and I think we need to penetrate a little deeper before washing our hands of the affair. Does this diary have anything more to tell us? Ah, see here!'

He had been turning the blank pages of the volume and came to a halt at two entries written on consecutive days at the beginning of July. The first ran as follows:

I have said what I had to say to Rosa. I could not help myself. I have laid my all before her and I have warned her of the consequences of rejection.

And the second:

> I am spurned. The bird has flown the nest. I warned her of
> the consequences! So be it.

'There is', observed Holmes, 'a positively threatening
note about these later entries — written, you will observe, in
a larger hand than before. I am not at all sure that we were
intended to see *them*! Is there anything further, I wonder?'

He continued to turn the pages, which had reverted to
the status of blank sheets, and it was not until he approached
the end of the year 1870 that two further entries appeared.
The first, written on 23 December, ran as follows:

> Rosa is to marry another! So much for her devotion to the
> memory of my dear boy. Mr Grewgious, whose attitude
> towards me during recent months has been abrupt to the
> point of rudeness, positively sought me out today, after
> calling on Miss Twinkleton, to tell me what he described
> as the glad tidings. And poor Ned, this time last year, was
> so close to winning her! — closer, now, than I had ever
> appreciated before.

And the second:

> A year ago today that Ned disappeared. But I have a
> curious feeling upon me that retribution is at hand and
> that the Murderer, at long last, is to be revealed. The
> Lord's will be done!

There were no further entries.

'So matters came to a head, it seems, on the Christmas

64

Eve of 1870,' said Holmes, closing the book. 'In what way, I wonder? And what could it have been that Mr Jasper learnt about his nephew from Mr Grewgious that he had not been aware of before?'

He stood there, absorbed in conjecture for some minutes, before shaking his head. 'It is futile', he said, 'to engage in speculation in the absence of sufficient data. But the other point of interest to emerge from these entries is that Mr Jasper, with his nephew out of the running, apparently offered himself to Miss Bud as an alternative suitor and was soundly rejected for his pains.'

'A grotesque idea!' I exclaimed.

'Not necessarily. We need, of course, to re-orientate our thoughts on this affair now that we know of the passage of twenty-five years. Mr Jasper, when we saw him two days ago, was a haggard gentleman with greyish hair. When due allowance has been made for the anxieties that he has undergone (and also, for that matter, a certain type of medication that I suspect him to have been indulging in), I would judge him to be in his early fifties. It appeared perfectly reasonable to us that a middle-aged gentleman should be concerned about the disappearance of a nephew aged no more than twenty. He referred to him then, and he refers to him in this diary, as his "dear boy", yet at the time Edwin Drood disappeared he himself could surely not have been more than twenty-seven or twenty-eight — perhaps even younger. If there were, say, an age difference of no more than six or seven years between them then a rather different picture begins to emerge. They would have been more like brothers than uncle and nephew.'

'Then the difference in age between Mr Jasper and his sister must have been substantial?'

Holmes nodded. 'It is time, I think, that we put some provisional dates to the sequence of events. Elizabeth Jasper married Martin Drood in, let us say, 1847 – almost six years after the Levantine crisis – and Edwin, destined to come of age in 1870, was born in 1849. John Jasper would have been born in 1843 or therabouts, being some fifteen years younger than his sister. Elizabeth dies soon after the birth of Edwin. Father and son then return to England, where they settle down in Cloisterham, in close proximity to the elder Jaspers. In the meantime, Miss Bud would have been born in 1853 – for she is four years Edwin's junior, you will recall – and her father, Martin's dearest friend, dies in 1860. Martin himself dies in 1861. Mr and Mrs Jasper die sometime in the mid-1860s and John becomes Edwin's guardian. We are now, I think, fully apprised of all we need to know of the immediate historical background.'

'So Miss Bud, by this reckoning, would be only ten years younger than John Jasper.'

'Quite. But the prospect of their being united in matrimony obviously did not appeal to her, despite a mysterious threat that he apparently coupled with his proposal, and she instantly fled to London – to take refuge, presumably, with Mr Grewgious. But what have we *here*?'

Holmes had been casting a speculative eye over the contents of the bedroom all the time that he had been speaking. Plunging a hand into the inner recesses of a bedside locker he now brought to light, with a cry of triumph, a small pipe of rather curious design. 'You will recall, Watson,' he remarked with a smile, 'that I thought that I had once encountered Mr Jasper on a previous occasion under rather strange circumstances – this little item may give you some inkling of what those circumstances were. But no more of that, for the present!'

He carefully replaced the pipe in the locker and led the way down the short flight of stairs. On the way, however, his attention was caught by a slight protuberance from the medieval wall, a foot or so above his head. He paused for a moment, felt over the area with singular intentness and then gave the protuberance a wrench. The brick in question, after a brief resistance, came away in his hand and he placed it carefully on one of the steps and then rummaged in the small cavity that it had left behind. Again, a cry of triumph as he brought to light a very large, very rusty, and very heavy metal key. 'Now what could *this* be?' he mused. 'I have the feeling, Watson, that if we could only find the door that this key unlocks we might be materially advanced in our quest.' He weighed it in his hand, frowning.

'Now *that* surely is pure fancy, Holmes!'

'You are quite right, of course, and yet it puzzles me. Far too big for a safe, but not the normal kind of key for the normal kind of door. And why, in any case, should it be hidden?' He replaced it in the cavity and restored the stone, shaking his head in perplexity.

'For safekeeping, obviously.'

'But Mr Jasper is the only person who lived in these chambers. From whom should he wish to hide it?'

We had returned, by this time, to the main apartment and I was about to answer Holmes (although, for the life of me, I cannot now recall what I was going to say) when we were disturbed by a slight sound. Turning, we found that Mrs Tope, framed in the distant doorway, was gazing at us with astonishment from the tiny dining-room.

'Do not be alarmed, Mrs Tope!' called out Holmes reassuringly, for the good lady was obviously much distressed. 'As I explained to your husband last night, we are friends of Mr Jasper and had arranged to call on him. Since he is not in residence, rather to our surprise and concern, we had hoped that we might discover some clue as to his whereabouts.'

'But he's not been here for years, gentlemen!' cried an amazed Mrs Tope. 'Not for years and years. And you're friends of his, you say?'

'Acquaintances, perhaps, would be a more accurate description. Yes, we met him two days ago and it was agreed that we should visit him without delay. It had not occurred to us, obviously, that we would not find him at home.'

Mrs Tope shook her head in wonderment. 'But how did you get in?' she asked. 'Did Mr Jasper give you a key? And how is he? How does the poor man look?'

We explained that, yes, we did have a key to the chambers, that Mr Jasper had seemed reasonably well, apart from shortness of breath and a shaking hand, but that he was much concerned about the fate of his nephew and had sought our advice on this matter.

'After all these years!' exclaimed Mrs Tope. 'The good man always was too much wrapped up in Master Edwin — he was that worried about him, you would scarcely credit.' She had recovered, by this time, most of her composure and suggested that we might like to accompany her back to the Tope quarters to partake of (yet another) nice cup of tea, an invitation which we thought it politic to accept.

'But I wonder, Mrs Tope,' said Holmes, just as we were on the point of leaving Mr Jasper's apartment, 'whether you could perhaps enlighten us as to the identity of the young lady in the picture over there? Would one be right in assuming that it was a portrait of Miss Rosa Bud?'

Mrs Tope confirmed that our supposition was correct and added that it had been painted by Master Edwin. She explained, as she led the way through to the Topes' own modest living-room on the far side of the gatehouse, that she had been accustomed to play the role of housekeeper to Mr Jasper, when he was in residence, and that since it was at a Christmas time that he had left Cloisterham very suddenly, many years before, there had never been a Christmas since when she had not half expected his reappearance — and hearing the sound of voices, on her return from morning service, she had excitedly jumped to the conclusion that the long-awaited event had finally come about.

'You miss him, then?' asked Holmes sympathetically.

'Ah, he was that good a gentleman, sirs, and so much

worry to bear — and the choir, it's said, has never sung nowhere near as good since he left!'

We were seated, at this time, round a small table while Mrs Tope did the honours with her teapot and here we were joined, a few minutes later, by her husband, his Christmas Day duties as verger now fully discharged. He joined in the ensuing conversation from time to time, although evidently hard of hearing (as we had suspected the previous evening), and we learnt virtually all that they had to tell us on the subject of Mr Jasper. That his music, and his concern for his nephew's welfare, were his two consuming passions — although there had been a time, thought Mr Tope, when he had contemplated writing a history of the Cathedral, being jovially accused by the Dean (no less) of intending to put them all in a book, and to this end had accompanied the then stonemason (a Mr Durdles, long since deceased) on a midnight tour of the crypt and the cloisters and goodness knows what else. That the disappearance of Master Edwin, in mighty suspicious circumstances, had come close to unhinging him. That he had regained control of himself and resumed his activities in the local community to some extent, although wounded, perhaps, by the manner in which one or two folk who ought to have known better had seemingly turned against him. That Miss Bud, whose talents as a singer he had spent many long hours assiduously cultivating, and who might have been expected to be especially sympathetic to him in view of the great loss they had both shared, had abruptly terminated her musical studies and flounced off to London. That Mr Jasper himself had gone away suddenly on a Christmas Eve, exactly a year after the day on which his nephew disappeared. That there was a strong school of thought (exemplified, as we were already aware, by Sir Thomas Sapsea) which understood him to be pursuing the Murderer and was thoroughly convinced that he would never return to Cloisterham until the villain had been brought to justice. That it was not clear how or where this theory had originated, except that it seemed to fit the known facts. That nothing more had been heard of him, from that day to this, except on two rather curious occasions — occasions, indeed, oddly akin to our own visitation, for both had involved a pair of gentlemen not altogether dissimilar from ourselves.

'Indeed!' said Holmes. 'Perhaps you can tell me more?'

'The first time', said Mrs Tope, 'was some three years after Mr Jasper went. These two gentlemen called, bearing a note signed by himself, which gave them authorization to fetch away some of his books and his writing paper.'

'And why could Mr Jasper not call in person for these items?'

'They said he was . . .' There was much intense concentration on Mrs Tope's part, as she struggled to recall the elusive word.

'"Indisposed,"' put in her consort, gruffly.

'That's it, gentlemen! "Indisposed",' said Mrs Tope in triumphant relief.

'And the second occasion?'

'This would be some ten or twelve years back. Two gentlemen arrived who said, like yourselves, that they were looking for him and wondered whether he had been home recently. They said that they were friends of his but had temporarily lost touch with him.'

'But you were unable to help them?'

Confirmation from Mrs Tope.

'And were they the same two gentlemen who had called previously?'

One of them, she thought, might be (although she was not prepared to swear to this) but the other had been unfamiliar. On the subject of Master Edwin's disappearance, neither she nor her husband was able to tell us anything that we had not learnt already from Mr Jasper. Questioned about Mr Neville Landless, she recalled him as a rather wild, headstrong person who, even before the disappearance of Mr Drood, had been regarded with a certain degree of aversion in the town. And as for *after* the disappearance, the good lady's indignation was scarcely strong enough to contain itself. That such a man should have been allowed to walk the streets was nothing short of a public disgrace! His guardian, Mr Crisparkle, had spirited him away to London as soon as he had been officially cleared, in the absence of any positive evidence, of having committed a crime, and just as well it was too!

'And Mr Landless never returned to Cloisterham?'

'No, *he* never came back, although of course —'

But at this point Mrs Tope was vigorously cautioned by her husband to say no more on the subject of Mr Landless or anything pertaining to him. 'There are certain matters, gentlemen,' he sternly advised us, 'that is best left undisturbed. London looks after its own, gentlemen, and Cloisterham does likewise.'

There being, by this time, a certain restlessness on Mr

Tope's part, which had evinced itself even before these final enigmatic utterances, we thought it best to bring the interview to a close, to thank them warmly for the tea and information, and return to our own quarters. 'So Mr Jasper', said Holmes thoughtfully, 'has had encounters with two gentlemen of a vaguely officious character on more than one occasion, which suggests that he was not altogether surprised by the events of the other evening – resentful, yes, but seemingly resigned (as I recall it) to his fate. Does that suggest anything to you, Watson? And what, I wonder, was the item of information relating to Mr Landless which Mrs Tope was about to impart? No matter – we are sure to learn it from some other source. Of more immediate concern, I would suggest, is the fact that it is now one o'clock. I propose that we call once more at The Crozier to see what further delights Mr Appleby can offer us in the way of festive fare.'

But, before we could set out, there came a tap at the door and our landlady ushered in a breathless small boy. He pipingly announced that he had come post-haste from the Deanery with a message to the effect that the Dean and his family would be greatly honoured if the two gentlemen visitors currently staying at the Tope residence would care to join the said Dean and said family for lunch in about one hour's time. 'The first citizen of Cloisterham', murmured Holmes to me, 'has, I fancy, been at work here' but to the youthful messenger he conveyed the tidings (simultaneously pressing a shilling into the small palm) that the two gentlemen would be delighted to avail themselves of the kind and unexpected invitation.

Our credentials of respectability fully restored, as it were, in the eyes of Mrs Tope (for I had been unable to rid myself of the uneasy feeling, cups of tea and sundry confidences notwithstanding, that we had rather fallen from grace after being discovered in the Jasper apartment) we sallied forth to our Christmas lunch at the Deanery.

Pangs of conscience, however, also smote me when we arrived at the Deanery, a substantial red-brick residence of the Queen Anne period, for I was struck by the sudden realization that, unlike Holmes, I had not set foot in the Cathedral that morning (except in the earliest of hours) and yet here I was, on this day of all days, accepting clerical hospitality at the highest level. Trusting, however, that my absence from the two morning services would not have been remarked upon, I accompanied Holmes into the spacious Deanery and found our new surroundings a welcome relief after the claustrophobic atmosphere of the gatehouse.

A maid, relieving us of our coats, showed us into the drawing-room and here we waited while our arrival was announced to the master of the house. The distant sounds of high-spirited laughter came to our ears, indicating that younger folk were in evidence, and Holmes, in relaxed mood, strolled round the room studying the furniture and a small gallery of portraits. What took his fancy, in the first instance, was a massive sideboard of curious design. 'I have not seen one of those', he remarked, 'since my childhood, but I remember it well. An ingenious idea, Watson: only one section can be opened at a time, the top half of the cabinet being completely unaware, as it were, of the bottom half's existence.'

We cast our eyes over the portraits. One of them, which dominated the room, was of a very striking, dark-haired young woman, slim and tall with stern, belligerent eyes, which virtually challenged the onlooker (or, for that matter, the world in general) to cross swords with her if he (or it) dared. There was a smouldering intensity about the figure which the artist had captured with remarkable adroitness. The characteristics of her face were reflected, to some extent, in a small head-and-shoulders sketch of a young man which hung a short distance away, except that *his* expression was of a more melancholy, brooding kind: one felt that *he* had wearied of fighting battles, and simply waited for the end. The third portrait was far different again, being that of a sweet, dimpled old lady, who gazed at us half in welcoming pleasure and half in warning admonition.

'My mother, gentlemen,' came a voice from our left, as the Dean entered the room. 'The dearest of souls, but the sternest of taskmasters! God rest her soul. Gentlemen, I am heartily glad that you are able to join us for Christmas lunch. Welcome to Cloisterham, Mr Sexton Blake!'

Holmes, unable to help himself, let out a loud whoop of delight which he endeavoured, totally without success, to convert into a cough. While he spluttered and, indeed, almost choked in his merriment, I endeavoured to explain to our puzzled and embarrassed host that there had been something of a misunderstanding and that Sexton Blake was a fictional creation who had recently begun to appear in the crudest of cheap magazine papers — a character based, admittedly, upon that of my friend, even to the extent of residing in Baker Street, but a shocking travesty of the original.

The poor Dean hastened to make amends for his mistake. 'A thousand pardons, gentlemen,' he exclaimed. 'You must appreciate that we in Cloisterham, though relatively close to London, are woefully behind the times in our awareness of current events and personalities in the great city. It was Sir Thomas Sapsea who informed me, in tremendous excitement, that a personage no less important than Sexton Blake himself had arrived in our little town and that Cloisterham was being shockingly remiss in offering him and his companion adequate hospitality. The name was slightly familiar to me but your own, I must confess, is even more portentous! You really must forgive us for our stupidity, Mr Holmes. We lead a sheltered existence, and that is all I can say.'

'There is nothing to forgive, I do assure you,' Holmes managed, at length, to reply. 'It is I who should be apologizing for my mirth, which is disgracefully remiss, but the sheer delight of your unexpected greeting caught me totally unprepared! This is a salutary reminder of the vulnerability of those with allegedly well-established reputations when they venture into foreign climes. It confirms a theme which I was developing last night in conversation with my friend Dr Watson here, that the dividing line between fact and fiction is one that is blurred with increasing frequency in this day and age, even in the best regulated circles. I only hope, Dean, that you will not consider me guilty of accepting your hospitality under false pretences.'

The Dean assured us, with a hearty laugh, that he would most certainly harbour no such suspicion and, to demonstrate that his word was his bond, promptly opened up the top half of the sideboard in search of aperitifs. He was a large, good-tempered gentleman whose receding grey hair led me to conclude that he must be in his early sixties. His open, ruddy complexion rendered him, however, the picture of health and he gave the general impression of being much younger than his years. Conviviality firmly established, he beamingly shepherded us into the dining-room and introduced us to his wife and family and fellow-guests (among whom, I was pleased to note, Sir Thomas did *not* feature). His wife, some fifteen years younger than himself, was instantly recognizable as the original of the young woman in the drawing-room portrait. Her dark hair had now become silver and her eyes had lost, perhaps, something of their fire, but her overall demeanour was that of someone who was relaxed and generally content. She welcomed us warmly and declared (when the misunderstanding had been explained) that *she* was perfectly capable of distinguishing between the genuine and counterfeit Sleuths of Baker Street and had been convinced from the outset that Sir Thomas had been gloriously confused. She then rushed away to supervise operations in the kitchen, from which promising aromas were emanating.

The absurd confusion over Holmes's own identity had

put a curb on the social niceties in the opposite direction, for the Dean had not had an opportunity to introduce himself formally and the longer we were there the more impossible it became to enquire his name. Holmes, however, was evidently unaware of any such problem, and simply addressed our host as 'Dean' and his wife as 'ma'am'. I followed suit, but when the time came for us to be introduced to the junior members of the household – a high-spirited lad in his early twenties and two young ladies who were, it transpired, still attending the Nuns' House seminary (the current principal of which, Mrs Tisher, was one of the guests) – my heart missed a beat, for the name of the young man was Neville and his sisters were called Helen and Rose. I began, at that point, to have a very strong inkling as to the name of our host (who was addressed, by his wife, as 'Septimus'), and the identity of the gloomy young man in the sketch, who bore an uncanny resemblance to the son of the house, was a mystery no longer.

The Christmas dinner was all that one could have desired and I flatter myself that we needed little encouragement to fall to and do it ample justice in the time-honoured tradition. A splendid goose, with all the trimmings, speedily came and went and an impressive plum pudding suffered a similar fate (although we were informed that its twin, equally impres-sive, was ready to take its place if the need should arise).

'So, Mr Holmes,' said the Dean at length, pushing back his plate, 'I gather that you contemplate taking up residence in Cloisterham at such time as you retire – or is it simply a holiday retreat that you have in mind?'

Holmes confessed, a trifle awkwardly, that the idea of

taking up residence in this pleasant little town had indeed crossed his mind. 'For the ambience', said he, 'is agreeable – as, too, are the residents – and the country air comes as a welcome relief after the fumes of London. But I believe that I am not the first fugitive from the great wen to have had this idea – there was a Mr Datchery here before me, was there not?'

'Old Dick Datchery!' said the Dean with a surprised smile. 'I haven't thought about him in years – fancy you knowing about old Dick! Yes, you're quite right, he too came to Cloisterham to retire – and he lived in the very same lodgings as those in which you and Dr Watson spent last night. Quite a character, in his way – a retired old buffer of independent means, or so he described himself, and that was all we ever learnt about him. Sir Thomas – or *Mr* Sapsea, as he then was – was convinced that he had been something to do with the diplomatic service, but I fancy old Dick was pulling his leg. Yes, he took to Cloisterham like a duck to water during the short time that he was here. You remember him too, don't you, my dear?'

Mrs Dean regretted that, for various reasons (and a shadow crossed her face as she spoke), she had been obliged to be elsewhere during the period in question.

'Of course, of course,' said the Dean hastily, resuming at top speed (as though to put as much distance as he could between himself and some disagreeable recollections) his reminiscences of Dick Datchery. 'A funny old boy,' he continued, affectionately, 'but a real Christian gentleman. One often saw him strolling about the town, buttoned up in that tight blue surtout of his, talking to whomever took his fancy, totally regardless of who they were or where they came from. Old Durdles, the stonemason, was one person who appealed to him: they got on famously together, and take my word for it, there weren't many people for whom Durdles could spare more than a passing grunt! On another occasion I saw him helping a poor wreck of an incredibly dirty old woman on to the London coach (for that was before the trains came direct to Cloisterham) with as much solicitude as if she had been the Queen herself. I said as much to him afterwards. 'Mr Crisparkle,' said he, with twinkling eye, 'that lady, sir, is a genuine princess, take my word for it!"'

Holmes appeared to take a keen interest in these stories. 'You say, Dean,' he responded, 'that Mr Datchery was only here for a short time. Did he end his days in Cloisterham or did he move on to some other resting place?'

'The strange thing is,' said the Dean, 'that I really don't know what became of Mr Datchery. I never saw the coming of him and I never saw the going of him — one simply became aware that he was no longer with us, although I don't recall any farewells. A curious old gentleman, but one to whom I (and, for that matter, my wife, although she never met him — and, indeed, she had not then done me the honour of actually becoming my wife!) am much indebted for invaluable advice and assistance. There was something of a crisis in our affairs at that time, the details of which I will not pursue, and he played a considerable part in seeking to remedy matters. I will not say that he was wholly successful, but he was a good friend to us at a time when good friends were in rather short supply.'

The Dean's wife had been observing my colleague intently for some little while and now steered the conversation back to its original starting point. 'In looking for your ideal retirement home, Mr Holmes,' she said, with a slightly ironic note in her voice, 'did you alight upon Cloisterham purely by chance or was it recommended to you?'

'The truth of the matter, ma'am,' replied Holmes, in the most casual, agreeable of tones, toying with his glass as he spoke, 'is that we were invited here by a gentleman with whom you are no doubt acquainted — Mr John Jasper.'

This announcement came as a bombshell so far as Mr and Mrs Crisparkle and Mrs Tisher were concerned. The Dean's wife instantly went deathly white, Mrs Tisher dropped her spoon with a cry of horror and the Dean started back as though Banquo's ghost were advancing upon him. He swallowed for an instant and found some difficulty in speaking. All this while the three younger members of the family, evidently unaware of any cause for consternation, stared in amazement at their elders. It seemed, for a time, that the silence would never be broken.

'The gentleman you refer to', said the Dean at last, almost croaking the words, 'has not resided in Cloisterham for a very long while. I do not think that he will be returning to this city.' He helped himself to a glass of water and drank it down with shaking hand.

'When did you see this man?' demanded Mrs Crisparkle coldly — and she was, once again, the combative spirit whom the artist had depicted some twenty years before.

'Two days ago,' replied Holmes, seemingly unaware of

the sensation he had created. 'He called upon myself and Dr Watson and solicited our help in ascertaining what had become of his nephew, Mr Edwin Drood. We agreed to come down to Cloisterham without delay — unaware, of course, that he was referring to events which had taken place many years ago and totally unprepared for the fact that he would not be here to receive us.'

Again, the same stunned silence.

'And have you discovered anything?' asked Mrs Crisparkle at length, making no attempt to conceal the note of contempt in her voice.

'Some interesting items of information, certainly,' replied Holmes with equanimity, 'but I fancy that it will be some little while before I can formulate definite conclusions.'

The Dean's wife, livid with rage, rose and swept out of the room, much to the astonishment of her three children: the two girls hurried after her and the son stood up awkwardly, not comprehending the cause of this domestic upheaval but aware, obviously, that these two strangers were to blame for it and gazing at us with smouldering indignation. 'You must excuse my wife, gentlemen,' said poor Mr Crisparkle, doing his best to make amends. 'Helena is subject, at times, to the most appalling headaches. They overwhelm her without warning and she is obliged to instantly lie down on such occasions.'

We assured him that we totally understood and rose to take our leave. The conviviality of the dinner-table had now, alas, been totally destroyed and I was horrified at the effect that Holmes's announcement had had upon these good people. Their Christmas Day had evidently been ruined by our arrival on the scene and by this introduction of a spectre at the very conclusion of our feast. It seemed a poor return for their warm hospitality and I was consumed by far greater feelings of guilt than any others I had experienced that day.

The Dean's appeal to us to prolong our visit being politely declined (much to his evident relief) on the grounds that we must catch the five o'clock train to London, he saw us to the door. 'I appreciate, gentlemen,' he said, 'that you are strangers to this whole wretched Drood affair, that you are innocent parties, as it were, and have presumably come here with the best of intentions, but I really cannot wish you well of your investigations. What may be largely of academic interest to you, Mr Holmes, as something that happened many years ago and was never brought to a satisfactory conclusion, is an issue that is as alive, to other people, as though it happened yesterday. For twenty-four years we have lived here in peace. I feel that your probings can do nothing but harm and I beseech you to return to Baker Street and concern yourself with matters of more relevance to the present day and age.'

Holmes listened gravely to this appeal. 'I am sorry', he said, 'for the distress that I have evidently caused your wife and yourself but I can make no promises, Mr Crisparkle, about my future course of conduct. I hear what you say and I will give your sentiments my full consideration, but you must know that there is an allegiance I owe that must take precedence over all else.'

'To Mr Jasper, I suppose?'

'No, Mr Crisparkle, to Truth. Pray thank your wife for her

hospitality and I trust that she will soon be recovered from her indisposition. Once more, my apologies.'

We returned to the gatehouse. I said nothing, for I felt an overwhelming urge to escape from this little town where we had caused so much ill-feeling in so short a space of time, and Holmes for his part was sunk in thought. 'You will note', said he at length, 'that the Dean referred to a period of twenty-four years rather than one of twenty-five: the question of what happened on the Christmas Eve of 1870 is, obviously, as relevant to our investigation as what happened on the Christmas Eve of 1869.'

I returned what was, I fear, a rather brusque reply to this remark – for it was now abundantly clear that Holmes did indeed intend to pursue his enquiries – and busied myself with packing our bags while Holmes settled up our account with Mr and Mrs Tope.

It was at this point that I made the first of two curious discoveries. It had been dark when I stuffed our modest travelling accoutrements into the corner-cupboard the previous night and I had not appreciated the full extent to which it receded into the ancient stone wall. Stretching my hand deep into the middle section, in which the back of the shelf rather fell away from the front, I was startled to encounter what I took to be, at first, the remains of a cat or dog – for it was undoubtedly hair or fur of some description that my hand had fallen upon. Unpleasant though it was to the touch, I grasped the grim relic and brought it forth. To my astonishment, I found myself holding a very bedraggled, very dirty, very cobwebby mane of what had once been an abundance of white hair – in short, a wig. In dragging it out, however, I was aware of having disturbed something else. Plunging my hand back into the cupboard for a second time, and groping once more in its innermost depths, I now came up with something slightly stiffer and bulkier. This second item proved to be a hat. Within it was written, in faded ink, the name 'Datchery'.

'Excellent, Watson!' exclaimed Holmes, who had re-entered the room by this time and quietly come up behind me. 'Not for the first time, I am greatly indebted to you.' He held the hat between finger and thumb and examined it with great care, with the aid of his magnifying glass, by the fading light at the window. 'Seemingly worn', he remarked, 'by somebody with a very large head (in the same league, indeed, as that of Mr Henry Baker!), although the wig, when properly spruced up, would have accounted for most of its capacity. *Not* the type of headgear sold by the normal London hatters, but the remains of the label (apparently emanating from Messrs Bergstone and Ritchie, who once upon a time catered for thespians of all shapes and sizes) suggest, rather, that it would have been purchased in a theatrical costumier's. Some thirty or forty years back there was a vogue for rustic comedies on our stage and I suspect that it would then have adorned some village sage or yokel who would have been the prize performer of the evening. So far as the inscription is concerned, you will observe that the upper stroke of the 't' is in a darker ink than the rest of the name — it was evidently added as an afterthought. We must conclude, I think, that the gentleman who wore this battered headpiece did indeed contrive to free himself of the letter L.'

'And very fond of his tea,' I added, '– or could it have been the letter T?' For it was clear to me, now, that the old gentleman who had been Mrs Tope's last lodger could have been none other than Dick Datchery. I passed on to Holmes the information that the good lady had imparted to me earlier in the day, such as it was. He listened in silence, with the air of one not greatly surprised, and then stuffed the hat and wig into his bag. 'These may', he said, 'come in useful sometime. I doubt whether the original owner has any further need of them.'

We walked briskly to the station through the silent and increasingly chilly streets of Cloisterham, passing not a soul on the way, only to find that the five o'clock train was running some fifteen minutes late. I stamped up and down the platform to keep warm while Holmes engaged the burly porter in conversation. 'You must have seen', I heard him say, 'some remarkable changes since the railway came to Cloisterham.' I made no attempt to catch any more, for my irritation at Holmes's continuing interest in this affair – momentarily swept aside by the discovery of the Datchery wig and hat – had now renewed itself. It was impossible to forget the look of fury on Helena Crisparkle's face and the anguished appeal of the Dean, which had fallen, all too evidently, on unsympathtic ears.

Our near-empty train eventually arrived and we scrambled aboard, it being a relief to sink back into the seats. 'No stone, however seemingly insignificant, should be left unturned in an investigation of this kind,' said Holmes, who was (for once) in a more talkative mood than myself. 'That worthy custodian of the platform, a gentleman by the name of Joe, worked here as an omnibus driver in the days before the railway and was responsible for transporting Neville and Helena Landless into Cloisterham. He remembers the young man well and was, in fact, one of those who made up the party which apprehended him for the alleged murder of Edwin Drood on that Christmas morning of 1869. Landless resisted like a tiger, so he tells me, although our friend soon got the better of him. He also remembers Miss Rosa Bud ('the sweetest little lass in the town') and was responsible for transporting her *out* of Cloisterham some six months later. She was, it seems, in a state of great perturbation, as though the seven furies were pursuing her.' I wished, however, to hear no more about this affair and indicated as much by the shortness of my responses. Holmes, not one whit abashed, continued to muse aloud on what Joe had told him. 'I appreciate', he said at length, 'that you now have strong reservations, Watson, about our involvement in this case, and the Dean's appeal did not leave me wholly unmoved, but I fancy that we are at the midway point of our investigation. Having come so far, one might as well go on as turn back. Much has become clear, and yet certain crucial aspects remain in tantalizing, impenetrable darkness! If I can only pierce that veil, and clarify one or two outstanding matters to my own satisfaction, I am convinced that nothing but good can come of this investigation. The Crisparkle family, indeed, may even be the ultimate beneficiaries of our labours!'

I was mollified to some extent, although still inclined to the view that we were venturing into regions better left unexplored. And so, for the moment − for twelve whole months, in fact — we bade adieu to Cloisterham and the lights of the little town slipped away from us as the train gathered speed. 'I wonder', said Holmes dreamily, leaning back and composing himself for a nap, 'what Sexton Blake would have made of it all.'

10

My narrative has thus far been relatively straightforward, being concerned solely with the Christmas of 1894 and the events of three somewhat curious days. From this point onwards it becomes, I fear, far more disjointed and I must ask the reader to make every allowance for the fragmented character that it now assumes.

The year 1895, as I have recorded elsewhere, was an exceptionally busy one for Mr Sherlock Holmes and was the herald, indeed, of that period of unceasing, intense activity that lasted until his retirement from professional consultancy work some eight years later. My small Kensington practice having been purchased by young Verner (with Holmes's assistance, as I subsequently discovered), I was free to accompany my friend on a good many of his expeditions and to assist him wherever I could, although I can scarcely flatter myself that my ruminations and suggestions contributed anything of great substance to the eventual outcome of his investigations. But my observations, such as they were, almost invariably received his full attention and were sometimes the unwitting means of setting him off in a totally opposite (and, it would transpire, far more rewarding) direction. He would also use me as a sounding board for various theories of his own when they were still at the semi-formulated stage, being convinced that a second opinion, on such occasions, was always of some value. At other times, however, when engaged on cases of either a particularly abtruse or a confidential nature, he would make no attempt to enlist my services and I knew better than to press them where they were not required.

His powers were now at their height. Throughout this hectic year, in which scarcely a week went by without some new and deeply mystifying problem being brought to his attention by a range of clients which varied from the highest to the lowest in the land, I was aware that he still pondered upon the Drood affair and that he made, from time to time, some further attempts to probe it. Correspondence with the local Kent constabulary and approaches to the Criminal Investigation Department of Scotland Yard resulted in confirmation that the official file on Edwin Drood, insofar as it had ever existed, had long ago been closed and enquiries in the vicinity of Staples Inn brought to light no news of Neville Landless. It was established that Hiram Grewgious, the one-time guardian of Miss Rosa Bud, had also resided at Staples Inn but had died some twelve years before. 'You will doubtless be familiar, Watson,' he said on one occasion, 'with a certain pursuit, popular on race tracks and at street corners alike, of "Find the Lady". Well, I am trying to find *two* ladies — one of them still moderately young and the other (if she is still with us) extremely old.' I was aware of the "Baker Street irregulars" being called in to assist with one or both of these searches, but I was not aware of any successful outcome.

'Holmes,' I once asked, 'why do you go on with these enquiries?'

'Curiosity, my dear chap; sheer, simple curiosity. Some strange things happened in Cloisterham twenty-five years ago and for my own peace of mind, if nothing else, I would dearly love to get to the bottom of them.'

Then towards the conclusion of breakfast, one morning late in February, he pushed back his coffee cup and remarked, with a twinkle in his eye, 'What say you, Watson, to a further meeting with Mr John Jasper?'

'You've tracked him down, then?' I exclaimed in astonishment.

'Tush, man, that was no great problem. Having established that he was suffering from amnesia, and that he was clearly not a free agent but under restraint of some kind, with two solicitous gentlemen ever concerned about his whereabouts on those occasions (at least two) when he managed to evade that restraint, all that remained to be done was to locate the institution in which he was housed. You will recall that his letter was posted in Surrey – from Guildford, to be precise – and a scrutiny of the excellent Ordance Survey map for that area showed that there were three such establishments in that part of the world. Telegrams to the two nearest at hand produced negative results, but I have struck gold with the third.' And he passed me a telegram which ran, 'Your surmise correct. John Jasper has been resident in this asylum since 1871. James

Wakefield, Warden, Stazeby Nanton.'

'And our seeing him again will serve some useful purpose?'

'Ah, that I can't say! But it is worth a visit, I think, and even if Mr Jasper himself is uncommunicative the warden may be able to shed some light upon his curious state of mind. Technically, of course, he remains my client, although the prospect of my ever receiving a fee for my services now seems decidedly remote.'

And so it was that three hours later a pony and trap from the nearest railway station, some four miles distant from the establishment itself, carried us through bleak, unappealing, midwinter countryside to the asylum of Stazeby Nanton. The building itself was an impressive mansion, set in extensive grounds which were surrounded by a high red-brick wall. A formidable porter, in the lodge at the main gates, scrutinized us closely before sanctioning our entrance and I noticed, as we came nearer the house, that some of the windows were barred.

Mr James Wakefield, a dark-haired, short, fussy and rather self-important little man, his stub of a nose surmounted by a large pair of horn-rimmed spectacles, greeted us in the entrance hall (in the presence of two or three members of staff as burly as the lodge-keeper, all of whom surveyed us just as keenly) and bustled us into his well-furnished study. 'Pray be seated, gentlemen,' he began. 'I am, of course, familiar with your reputation, Mr Holmes. What can I do for you?'

'I am interested', replied Holmes, 'in whatever you can tell me about the history and state of mind of Mr John

Jasper. Perhaps you have a file of papers on this gentleman? You stated in your telegram, I believe, that he had been an inmate of this establishment since 1871.'

'Not an inmate, gentlemen, but a *resident*,' returned Mr Wakefield primly. 'A file is not necessary for our present purposes, for I have been here almost as long as Mr Jasper himself. I arrived at Stazeby Nanton twenty-four years ago next August, by which time he had been in residence for six months, and am fully acquainted with every detail of his case – or, at least, with every detail that can be humanly ascertained. I have known this worthy gentleman so long and so intimately that I might almost claim, in the fullest possible sense, to be my brother's keeper.'

'And he is no doubt a peerless kinsman,' said Holmes drily. 'Yet I believe – forgive me, for no slight is intended – that there have been one or two occasions when Mr Jasper has not been kept as well as he might have been?'

'Mr Holmes!' exclaimed the warden in outrage. 'You must understand, once and for all, that Stazeby Nanton is *not* a prison. It is operated on the most enlightened and philanthropic of principles for the benefit of those members of the more genteel or select of our classes who, for one reason or another, find themselves either temporarily or permanently unable to cope with the stresses and strains of modern life or who are subject to unfortunate delusions or confusions. Stazeby Nanton was established some forty years ago and has acquired a status of some repute with the passing of those years. You may be interested to learn that its activities received the personal blessing of Mr Luke Honeythunder (whose statue you doubtless observed in the village on your arrival) and that it was, indeed, the Honeythunder Bequest which has enabled it to thrive, and build upon that reputation, during the past decade or so. The twenty residents are not always, perhaps, so free to come and go as you or I might be, and it might sometimes happen that a departure of an unauthorized nature is effected, but they are not criminals, Mr Holmes, and no attempt is made to treat them as such. They move freely within the limits of the house (unless confined to their quarters for medical reasons) and meet one another, if they so desire, at the dinner-table and in a residents' lounge. Or they can, of course, remain in their rooms if the fancy so takes them.'

'I stand corrected,' said my companion, deferentially. 'Nevertheless, you will be aware that Mr Jasper called upon me two months ago, to all intents and purposes master of his own destiny, and presented me with an intriguing problem to ponder upon. You will appreciate my surprise at discovering that he was apparently under some form of restraint – although my mind is greatly relieved at learning that he is in such good hands as your own – and Dr Watson and I, having made this gentleman's acquaintance, would be interested in learning more of his ailment. It may have some bearing upon whether or not we should continue with our investigations.'

Mr Wakefield, mollified to some extent, recollected his duties as host and poured a glass of port for each of us. 'Mr Jasper', he said, resuming his seat behind his splendid desk, 'suffers from two delusions of a singular nature. He is convinced that he is living in the year 1870 and he is also convinced, for much of the time, that he is living in his small apartment in the town of Cloisterham. All evidence and information to the contrary fails to impinge upon his consciousness and we have reached the point, I must confess, when we no longer endeavour to make him think otherwise. The only item of information that he has assimilated in recent years, Mr Holmes, has been the fact of your own existence, and he has followed the news of your exploits with remarkable intentness. You are now incorporated, as it were, in his 1870 scenario. The news of your apparent death plunged him into gloom, but the recent revelation that you were alive after all and had returned to Baker Street was greeted with intense excitement and apparently determined his resolve to write to you and seek your assistance.'

'I am most flattered! But can you explain how the letter came to bear the correct 1894 date and how, indeed, it came to be sent to me at all?'

'One of the other residents, with whom he has struck up an acquaintance,' said Mr Wakefield, rather grimly, 'thoughtfully inserted the date on his behalf and also arranged for the letter to be dispatched, on Mr Jasper's behalf, by a relation who visited him on that day. Needless to say, Mr Holmes, the staff of this establishment were totally unaware that such a communication had been dispatched (for all outgoing post is, as a rule, scrutinized most vigorously) and I have taken the necessary steps to ensure that such a breach of procedure does not occur again.'

'And Mr Jasper's visit to me was itself, of course, a breach of procedure – an "unauthorized departure", as you phrased it earlier?'

'Yes, most certainly! Fortunately, we were able to ascertain from the other person – from the other resident – his most likely destination, and my staff were able to apprehend him the moment he left your premises.'

'An operation most skilfully executed,' said Holmes, with a gentle touch of sarcasm. 'And can you furnish me, Mr Wakefield, with rather more precise details of the form that Mr Jasper's malady takes?'

'For the greater part of the time,' said the warden, absent-mindedly fondling his gold watch and chain, 'he seems as sane as you or I and it is possible to converse with him on a wide range of subjects. He is a cultivated man and not without a sense of humour. But there are occasions when he works himself up into the most ferocious rages, seemingly possessed by a demoniacal fury, and has to be physically restrained before he can do the other residents or, indeed, himself some dreadful injury. At other times again, he sinks into a mood of bewildered apathy in which he recognizes nobody and seems oblivious of his surroundings.'

'But these outbreaks,' I said, 'distressing though they must be, are presumably not uncommon among your residents and not confined to Mr Jasper alone?'

'No, Dr Watson, such moods are all too familiar to those of us who labour in the vineyard at Stazeby Nanton. What is quite unique, however, is Mr Jasper's fixation about the year 1870. His behaviour in this respect follows what is basically an unchanging pattern. He was originally much distressed, as you are no doubt aware, by the disappearance of his nephew on the Christmas Eve of 1869. At the beginning of the year he is in a state of great perturbation. By the end of February (the present time, in fact) he has become more resigned to his loss but is bent upon bringing the villain of the piece, a Mr Landless, to justice. In the months of June and July he grows greatly agitated and it is usually at that time that we experience the violence which I referred to just now. By the late autumn he becomes more relaxed, as though things are going well, and is almost invariably amiable. At the approach of Christmas, however, he becomes steadily more excited. By the time Christmas Day itself dawns he has taken utter leave of his senses, being appallingly confused and suffering, obviously, from the after-effects of some terrible shock of which he cannot bear to retain the remembrance. He remains in this state for several weeks. The cycle then resumes. Every year he grows older, and the century draws towards its end, but every year he is totally convinced that he is living again through that traumatic year of 1870. At times he is, admittedly, quite capable of realizing that he is *not* living in Cloisterham, but those times are few and far between – and I am not certain that such realizations, when they come, are necessarily all to the good.'

'Thank you, Mr Wakefield,' said Holmes. 'A most graphic account. And does he have many visitors?'

'No, none at all. Although it is not generally known, I believe, that he resides here, for the Cathedral authorities were very unwilling that the news of his breakdown should become public knowledge. He apparently had no surviving relations and no close friends.'

'And who pays for his board and lodging?'

'The Public Trustee, in co-operation with the Cathedral authorities. Mr Jasper is a relatively wealthy man and there is no danger of his not being well provided for. His apartment in Cloisterham, I understand, remains just as it was twenty-five years ago, in the theoretical expectation of his eventual return, but I fear that will never be.'

'And how does he occupy himself?'

'By writing, reading and singing. And also in prayer – for he is, of course, most religious – although he usually seems to have some strange difficulty in effectively terminating his devotions, and they appear to degenerate into incoherent mumblings. He is hardly ever a relaxed man, Mr Holmes, and I'm tempted to say that he has never enjoyed a proper night's sleep since he's been here. It is, at times, necessary to sedate him.'

'And would I be correct in surmising that it was also in the month of December that he made an earlier escape – I beg your pardon, an "unauthorized departure" – some twelve years ago?'

Mr Wakefield looked surprised but nodded. 'Yes, that's right, Mr Holmes.'

'And that he was apprehended in East London in rather curious circumstances?'

'Good heavens!' exclaimed Mr Wakefield, in genuine astonishment. 'However did you know that? Yes, as I have said, he always becomes especially restless as the festive season approaches. It is clear that we shall have to keep an even closer eye on him in the future.'

But your security measures are most impressive. I am

surprised that he has managed to elude the vigilance of your staff on two occasions.'

Mr Wakefield shrugged his shoulders. 'Where there's a will, Mr Holmes,' he remarked, 'the way will invariably present itself.'

'Very true. And as he has managed the seemingly impossible on two occasions, there seems every likelihood, however elaborate the precautions you adopt, that he will repeat his success. I wonder, Mr Wakefield, in the event of a *third* "unauthorized departure", whether you could notify me of the event without delay?'

Mr Wakefield, still impressed by my colleague's reference to the East London incident (which had equally impressed myself), willingly promised to do so.

'And now, if you have no objection, perhaps we could pay our respects to Mr Jasper? I assure you we shall not trouble him for long.'

Mr Wakefield had no objection of any kind and shepherded us up to a room on the first floor, pausing a while until he had selected the appropriate key from the bundle which had been hanging in his study. The large room into which he showed us did bear, curiously, a quite striking resemblance to the rooms over the gatehouse except that there was no piano. There were shelves with a number of books on them, two small barred windows not unlike their latticed counterparts and two comfortable chairs by a fireplace, in one of which sat the choir-master of Cloisterham.

I was shocked by the change in his appearance. He had looked haggard on the previous occasion: he looked doubly so now. His hair had then been heavily streaked with grey: it was now all but white. A pair of deeply sunken eyes gazed uncomprehendingly at us and he endeavoured, with a shaking hand, to rise from his seat. He failed and fell back again, collapsing into it like an elderly marionette.

'Please don't disturb yourself, Mr Jasper,' said Holmes softly. 'You may remember that I am Sherlock Holmes and that you came to see me a little while ago.'

'Sherlock Holmes,' the old man repeated to himself. 'Sherlock Holmes,' he said again, and this time there was the faint glimmer of a dawning recollection.

Holmes lowered himself into the other chair and Mr Wakefield and I remained standing at the door.

'Sherlock Holmes,' said Mr Jasper for a third time, and this time with an air of triumph. 'Why, I thought I'd dreamt you!' And he gazed at my colleague with a mixture of elation and wonderment.

'You came to see me,' said Holmes. 'About your nephew.'

'Yes, yes!' exclaimed the old man, in excited confirmation. 'And I thought, afterwards, that it must all have been a dream – though how I could dream about you since I never sleep (or do I?), is more than I can say!'

'I called in', continued Holmes gently, 'to reassure you, Mr Jasper, that enquiries are proceeding. I hope to have some news for you one of these days.'

Mr Jasper waited hungrily for more, his eyes narrowing as he scrutinized my friend's face. But Holmes remained silent. 'And have you', asked Mr Jasper at length, 'apprehended Neville Landless for that foul deed?'

'Not yet, Mr Jasper,' returned Holmes. 'But be patient.'

'I rely solely on you, Mr Holmes – and my dear boy relies upon you, for I know he is near me – to bring that villain to justice. Incapacitated as I am at present (for my good friend yonder tells me I must stay in the gatehouse until restored to health), I am dependent upon you, Mr Holmes, to act as my eyes and ears. Rot his hide!' And with this extraordinary cry he jerked himself to his feet, virtually clawing at the air, before toppling back again and glaring at us all with terrible eyes from the depth of his chair.

We left Stazeby Nanton soon afterwards. It had not been a pleasant visit and for some time neither Holmes nor I spoke. The pony and trap bore us back to the station and we caught the train to London a little while later. By degrees, normality returned.

'I seriously wonder, Holmes,' I said at length, 'whether there is anything to be gained from pursuing these enquiries. Is it not simply morbid curiosity that drives you on? Mr Jasper, semi-demented as we saw him just now, is scarcely your usual type of client and we really seem to have come to a full stop. The Crisparkles know something but will obviously not assist us and the other characters in this drama, if they are not actually deceased, have vanished into thin air. After 1870 we have no idea what happened to them.'

'Not quite,' came the response. 'I am able to inform you, for example, that Miss Bud married a Mr Jack Tartar, a retired officer of the Royal Navy, in April 1872 and that she gave birth to a daughter, Florence, in the spring of 1874. They were living, at that time, in a cottage in Hampstead, but subsequently moved on.'

'By all that's marvellous, Holmes!' I exclaimed. 'However did you find this out?'

My companion shrugged his shoulders. 'Elementary in the extreme,' he responded, with a slight touch of impatience. 'We were aware that Miss Rosa had become engaged towards the end of 1870 – or so, at least, Mr Jasper was given to understand – and an hour or two's research in the records of Somerset House sufficed to yield the relevant facts. A remarkable repository of information, Watson, and a source unaccountably neglected by the English detective force! The annals of that building, setting out births, marriages and deaths over the past sixty years, complete with details of addresses, occupations and ages, present us with an unparalleled number of peepholes into the past. The place is a veritable time machine. But it is the present we are concerned with, and I must confess that the current location of the Tartar family is totally unknown to me. The Admiralty records of officers on the retired list are, I regret to say, woefully incomplete. It may be that some enquiries initiated in the Portsmouth area will prove more felicitous, but I have my doubts.'

'And is there anything else that you discovered at Somerset House, Holmes?'

'There is one line of enquiry that I have, certainly, neglected to pursue and I must follow that one up as soon as opportunity permits. But time is in short supply, my dear fellow, and it is the harassment of Mr John Vincent Harden which requires my more immediate attention.'

Bringing the persecutors of the tobacco millionaire to book, however, was a task that overlapped with our involvement in the tale of Miss Violet Smith, chronicled elsewhere as 'The Solitary Cyclist', and no sooner had *that* been brought to a satisfactory conclusion than the strange business at the Priory school was upon us. Then came three weeks in one of our great University towns, where Holmes (in the midst of carrying out some crucial research into Early English charters) was caught up in the intriguing problem of the Fortescue Scholarship. This was succeeded by the singular episode of the six Napoleons. The next item on the agenda was the mysterious death of Cardinal Tosca, which Holmes investigated at the specific request of His Holiness the Pope. This was followed by a variety of other commissions. No sooner had Wilson, the infamous canary-breeder of East London, been placed under lock and key than we were involved in the Woodman Lea affair and the hideous murder of Captain Peter Carey. In the second week of July I accompanied Holmes to Norway, in an investigation into the circumstances surrounding the mysterious death of

Halvard Solness (the precise details of which, I regret to say, I am still not at liberty to divulge). At the end of that month Holmes was summoned to the Vatican, to clarify some outstanding matters relating to the Tosca affair, where he was granted a personal audience with His Holiness. On the return journey he stopped off in Paris, to be presented by the French President with the Order of the Legion of Honour for the instrumental role he had played in helping to track down Huret, the Boulevard assassin.

I was left to my own devices for some two weeks, therefore, and found the period of unaccustomed repose by no means unwelcome. I devoted some of the time to pure relaxation and the rest of it to putting my papers in order and writing up the case notes of some of Holmes's earlier investigations. It was while I was thus preoccupied, one sunny day in early August, that Thurston dropped in and insisted on bearing me away from what he regarded as my tedious labours. I accompanied him, albeit with somewhat muted enthusiasm, to the summer exhibition at the Royal Academy, which had attracted its usual clientele to gaze at what were, by and large, the usual somewhat insipid offerings. There was, however, one picture which was attracting a fair degree of attention from the passing throng.

'By Jove, old lad!' murmured Thurston, as we drew near. '*She's* a bit of a stunner, eh?'

The painting in question, entitled 'Morning Glory', depicted a young girl wearing a pale blue dress sitting in a garden under a parasol on what was obviously a glorious summer's day, an impish expression on her face and long brown hair cascading down her back. She was undoubtedly, as Thurston had put it, a 'bit of a stunner', and I grunted my assent.

'Ah,' said Thurston, consulting his catalogue. 'One of Dupont's latest productions — I might have guessed. Basically one of the Impressionist school, and owing a lot to that chap Renoir, but he seems to spend more time in this country than he does in France. One of our home-grown Impressionists, you might say.'

The name was familiar to me, since Edmund Dupont was as well known as an illustrator of books (especially children's fairy tales) as he was as a portrait painter. What was vaguely disturbing, however, was the fact that the portrait also seemed familiar. I could not call to mind having met the young lady in question but was convinced that I had nevertheless somehow encountered her, and in the not too distant past. It was not until later that night, as I tossed and turned in the early hours, trying in vain to lose myself in slumber, that the answer came. The portrait had something in common with the amateurish daub of Rosa Bud that Holmes and I had seen in Mr Jasper's gatehouse living-room.

The following day I returned to Burlington House and gazed for some time at the portrait. The features, so far as I could recall those of the earlier picture, were by no means precisely the same, but when every allowance had been made for the difference in styles and skills the two portraits did indeed have much in common — including the fact, I was now startled to find (although I may have marked it subconsciously the previous day), that the dresses of *both* sitters were adorned with a brooch composed of an amethyst in an extremely intricate gold setting that resembled a budding rose.

The coincidence, I concluded at last, was too great to be ignored. It might well be that there was more than one such brooch, but the similarity between the faces of the wearers was unmistakable. I had assumed, it being five months since our second meeting with Mr Jasper, and taking into account the number of cases with which Holmes had become involved since then, that he had abandoned his investigations into the Drood affair, and — for reasons indicated already — I had been rather relieved at this. But I was aware that he had been trying hard, at one time, to ascertain the whereabouts of Mrs Jack Tartar, the former Miss Rosa Bud, and I was excited by the possibility that I might succeed where Holmes had failed.

My mind made up, I had a word with the attendant in that particular room and was directed to the staff of the Academy offices for further information. I was immensely interested, I told them, in the painting entitled 'Morning Glory' and wondered if they could supply me with further details of both the artist and his address. This they obligingly did, indicating (in the process) that there was no great secret about any of the information. M. Dupont, it transpired, was indeed of French extraction, but had escaped from Paris at the time when it was under siege in the Franco-Prussian war, had made his way to London in company with many of his compatriots, and (unlike most of those compatriots) had remained in England when the war came to an end. He had established an impressive reputation, both as a portrait painter and as a book illustrator, and his services were much in demand by a number of publishers, both in England and on the Continent. He was now, it seemed, living in Peckham, and they supplied me with the address in case I wished to write to him.

Throwing caution to the winds, however, I resolved to get in touch with M. Dupont without delay. Hastening to Charing Cross I caught the first available train to the leafy suburbs of Peckham and, within two hours of leaving the Academy, turned in at the gate of a large house in Linden Grove. Before I could pull the bellrope at the front door, however, it burst open and a short, dapper gentleman with pince-nez and pointed beard burst out in some excitement, carrying a travelling bag and umbrella, evidently with an urgent appointment to keep. He was dressed in a smart brown suit of check design and wearing a bowler hat, quite unlike the garb which I associated with artists (although my first-hand experience of them was, admittedly, somewhat limited). He pulled up short at the sight of me and, despite his hurry, came to a halt, raised his hat and bowed stiffly from the waist. I returned his salutation and introduced myself, noting as I did so that M. Dupont had a slightly blotchy face and surmising that his poor skin complexion might account for the beard.

'*Bonjour, monsieur!*' he exclaimed. 'And to what do I owe ze pleasure of zees visit?'

'I have just come from the Royal Academy,' I explained, 'where you have a painting of a young girl, 'Morning Glory', on display.'

'*Mais, oui!* You like it, yes?'

'I like it enormously,' I confessed. 'But the fact is, M. Dupont —'

'Ah, no!' he exclaimed. 'Ze painting, she is not for sale. *Non, monsieur*, in zees I cannot oblige you.'

'No,' I said, 'that's not the point. The thing is —'

But again, he would not allow me to finish. '*Non, non!*' he exclaimed impatiently, with much waving of the arms. 'Ze picture is not on ze market, I cannot part wiz it, not for – 'ow you say? – not for ze King's ransom.'

'But I don't want to buy it!' I almost shrieked, aware of how absurd this scene was as we both stood there on the garden path.

M. Dupont stopped gesticulating and gazed at me in astonishment. 'You don't want to buy it?' he repeated, in evident disbelief. 'You don't want to buy my painting?' His face grew thunderous as the sheer enormity of what I had said evidently sank in.

'It is a marvellous painting,' I hastened to reassure him, 'but the fact is I believe I know — that is, I am distantly acquainted with — the young lady in question. I am very anxious to see her and wonder whether you could possibly let me know where she is living.'

'Zounds!' exclaimed the artist. 'Zis is a new ploy, You Zinc I introduce you to my sitter, yes? You zinc I bring togezzer ze elderly military gentleman and ze pretty young girl, yes? *Mon Dieu*, ze Eenglish have ze cheek of ze very Devil!'

'Sir,' I cried,' you are grossly insulting. My intentions are, I assure you, strictly honourable.'

He grew extremely red in the face and I fear that I did the

same. I somehow managed to convince him, in the end, that I had no underhand motives in making this request, that I believed the young lady in question was a Mrs Jack Tartar, formerly a Miss Rosa Bud, and that I was very anxious to establish contact with her with a view to exchanging some information to our mutual benefit. M. Dupont listened impassively to these remarks, neither denying nor confirming the identity of his sitter. 'Zees iz ze strange kettle of ze fish,' he concluded at length. '*Monsieur*, I have ze train to catch – I have ze urgent appointment in Hampshire. I must refer you to my clerk, yes? You give eem ze full particulars and we consider further on zees matter.'

He bowed stiffly, stepped back into the house for a moment and summoned his secretary to attend to me. 'And now,' he announced, 'I must run, as you English say, like ze clappers, no? *Monsieur*, good day!'

And with that he disappeared down the drive, his legs twinkling rapidly and his umbrella and travelling bag swinging wildly. I gazed after him, concluding that, for someone who had spent so many years in England, he had a remarkably poor command of the language.

I was relieved to find that his clerk, at any rate, was English. The gentleman noted down, albeit in a disbelieving fashion, the details of my request, snorting and puffing as he did so. 'We shall be . . .' he said, and paused.

'Yes?' I asked at length.

'In contact,' said he, and closed the door.

I was disconcerted by these exchanges and resolved to say nothing about them to Holmes, when he returned, until such time as they had achieved (if it were possible) some tangible result. I could not help reflecting, as I walked glumly away through the sun-dappled streets of Nunhead, that my colleague would have handled things somewhat differently.

'Come, Watson!' exclaimed Holmes's impatient voice, which was accompanied by a vigorous shaking of my shoulder. 'There is a cab waiting at the door and no time to lose. We must be up and away! And bring your bag,' he added. 'I have need of your professional services.'

I was thus rudely awoken, one dark, chilly morning in mid-October, by my friend in one of his most brusque, intolerant of moods, but I wasted no time in recriminations. I pulled on my clothes, noting that Holmes himself, as he paced up and down the room, was wearing a remarkably long overcoat and carrying a small carpet bag, and within five minutes we were clattering away through the slow-clearing mists of autumn, which had succeeded in penetrating even into Baker Street. We were heading, I noted after a time, in an easterly direction and the cab threaded its way through the heavy morning traffic of the City, past the Honeythunder Memorial, into the streets of Stepney and thence towards the docks.

Holmes, tensed up all this time, like a greyhound straining at the leash, barely uttered a sound until we were on the last lap of our journey, when it suddenly occurred to him that something in the way of an apology (and also an explanation) was due. 'I am sorry for the rush, my dear chap,' he began, 'but it was less than an hour ago that young Dawkins arrived hotfoot with the news and we cannot afford to waste a single moment. The irregulars have finally tracked down one of my missing ladies, but she is on her last legs and I fear that, if this confounded traffic jam does not clear in the near future, we may yet be too late.'

He gazed moodily out of the window, drumming his fingers against the clasp of the bag, then permitted himself a brief smile. 'I have, I fear, been withholding certain particulars from you for far too long, Watson,' he continued, 'and you have borne the suspense with commendable patience.' (Aware, as I was, that I for my part had not been altogether frank with Holmes, for I had received a curt note from M. Dupont a day or two before to the effect that the young lady depicted in his painting had no knowledge of a Dr Watson and that there must therefore be some mistake, I guiltily waved aside this remark with the most subdued of deprecatory rejoinders.)

'You will be aware', went on my friend, 'that from time to time, and particularly in the earlier part of my career, it has sometimes been necessary for me to frequent the opium dens of East London in search of information. Some twelve or thirteen years ago I chanced to be imbibing (in the guise of a Lascar seaman) the delights of a particularly insalubrious establishment presided over by an old woman known, to all her clients, as "the Princess Puffa". I say "old" because she undoubtedly seemed greatly advanced in years, although you will be familiar, of course, with the fact that opium has a peculiar ageing effect upon those of its addicts who sample it upon anything approaching a regular basis. It may be that she was no more than in her mid-sixties when I saw her last, but she had long borne the reputation of being a secret midnight hag *par excellence* – in certain underworld circles, indeed, something of a celebrity! At one time, I believe, small groups of distinguished visitors were escorted to her premises by senior members of the local constabulary, and she was in some danger of becoming what might almost be termed "a tourist attraction". Some eight years ago, however, Princess Puffa retired from her trade, and until young Dawkins (who is now guiding our driver) arrived this morning I had no means of knowing whether she was alive or dead.'

Holmes gazed, reminiscently, through the window. 'On the occasion of which I speak,' he continued, 'the only other patrons of the Puffa establishment were two Chinamen, both of them in a state of insensibility. I was making up my mind to leave, for my particular quest on that occasion was evidently proving fruitless, when a well-dressed gentleman, with a rather wild expression on his face, suddenly joined the clientele. That gentleman was John Jasper.'

I reacted with astonishment to this news and Holmes smiled. 'Your own surprise', said he, 'was fully equalled, if not surpassed, by that of the Princess Puffa, who appeared to be dumbfounded in amazement – and, what was still more interesting, gave every appearance of being terrified out of her wits. "So you've come again, deary," she croaked out at length. "It's been a long time. The mixture as before, was it? Sit yourself down, and I'll mix it for ye." This she proceeded to do, with trembling hand, and Mr Jasper gazed intently about him in the mean time. I feigned unconsciousness but contrived to observe, through half-closed eyes, what followed. He took the mixture, complaining that it was not so potent as it had been previously, but within half an hour he had fallen into a deep slumber in which he twitched and groaned to himself. The old woman, after reassuring herself that the rest of us were still asleep, plucked up her courage and approached the recumbent body of our friend. "Oh, you're a fine one, you are!" she cried, shaking her fist at him, and then – so incensed did she become – she actually kicked him, twice or thrice, so that he groaned and cried out, while not awakening. Her feelings thus relieved, she hastened away – to return, some little time later, with a police constable in tow! She pointed at our friend and there was a certain amount of whispering which I was unable to catch. "Not in here, you don't!" she hissed at one point. "Suppose he comes back here again? No, it's outside for you, my lad!" and she bundled the constable out of her den. Some forty minutes then elapsed, in which she resumed her place in her chair while watching Mr Jasper intently all the time.

'Our friend eventually regained his senses and staggered to his feet, declining her casual offer of another dose and complaining yet again, this time to the effect that the "vision" had been so poor as to scarcely justify his coming. Before leaving her den, however, he scrutinized both my two companions, listening intently to such mutterings as they gave rise to. When he came to myself I obligingly uttered some gibberish which he decided, at length, signified nothing. "Unintelligible!" he exclaimed, threw down some coins for the Princess (which she spat upon, the moment his back was turned, and swept contemptuously to the floor) and took his leave. I promptly regained my own consciousness, perhaps rather *too* promptly, for she gave me a mighty suspicious look, settled up my account and then hastened in his footsteps. I found that he had been detained, a short distance from the Puffa establishment, by the constable I had seen previously and by another one as well. But the affair was, of course, none of my business and my curiosity had to remain unassuaged. You can imagine my astonishment when, twelve years later, this particular client appeared in Baker Street! That was my first encounter with John Jasper and my last with Princess Puffa – but one of the tales of Mr Datchery told by our friend the Dean, which you will doubtless recall, strongly suggests that she had made her way to Cloisterham on at least one occasion and it is vital that we find out what she knows. The fact that she is alive at all is nothing short of a miracle, but her time has come and she is, so I gather, not long for this world.'

The cab eventually halted at one of the most dismal of the dockland hovels and Holmes, preceded by young Dawkins (playing Gooseberry, as it were), hastened inside. 'She's a-going fast, sir,' I heard a voice say, 'you're only just in time.' I paid the driver, instructing him to return in an hour, and followed Holmes into a darkened room from which the most revolting of stenches was emanating. On a tiny bed in the corner lay a very old woman. Another woman, who had been in attendance, bobbed as we came in and made herself scarce, hovering in the vicinity of the door and shaking her head sorrowfully. Dawkins retreated into the background and Holmes bent over the poor creature on the bed.

'So here we are again, Princess Puffa!' he said, quietly and almost jovially.

The old woman opened her eyes and slowly brought Holmes into focus. 'I dunno you,' she muttered.

'Ah, but you do, you know! But I looked rather different on the last occasion that we met.'

Princess Puffa continued to gaze at him uncomprehendingly. She was, all too clearly, on the last lap of her journey and in no mood to bandy words with strangers.

'Look to the lady, Watson,' murmured Holmes, straightening up, and he disappeared into the darkness of the room behind me. I did what I could for the poor woman, which was little enough in the circumstances, and she contrived to nod her head in gratitude and mutter, 'Thank ye! Thank ye!'

Some minutes went by, and then . . .

'Do you know me now?' asked Holmes gently, reappearing at the bedside. He had donned the Datchery wig (freshly laundered since its last appearance), together with the Datchery hat, and was clad in a blue surtout. I am not at all certain that I would have recognized him had we passed in the street.

The old woman's face positively lit up and she struggled to raise herself on her elbow. 'It's the dear old gentleman!' she exclaimed in joy. 'Yes, of course I know you now, dearie. Fancy it being you all the time!'

'You remember we met in Cloisterham?'

She nodded, with great vigour.

'And do you remember Mr John Jasper?'

'Remember him?' she screeched, with terrible vehemence. 'Oh, yes, I remember *him* all right, don't *you* worry! I'd remember him for a thousand years, and then some.'

'And you remember what you told me about him?'

Again, a vigorous nod, followed by much coughing.

'Could you tell me again, do you think?'

'But I told you it all once, dearie,' she pleaded, looking perplexed. 'You knows it all.'

'But my friend here', said Datchery-Holmes, indicating myself, 'was not present then and he would dearly love to hear it from your own lips. Come, one last favour.'

'John Jasper was the organist,' she said, 'in the Kin-free-der-ell.'

'That's it! And he came to see you in London, didn't he?'

'That he did!' was jerked out of the poor woman, with nods galore. 'Many and many a time. Oh yes, *didn't* he come and see me, though!'

'And what happened?'

'He sang so sweetly — or leastways, he did in the early days — and he had this dream, about someone called Ned, and about what he was going to do to him. Over and over again, he had it!'

'And then?'

'And then I tried to track him back to his lair, for the third time, and that was when you saw me and that was when I told you everything I knew.'

'But what about those other occasions? Your first and second visits to the town?'

'That first time, as I told you, he gave me the slip and I didn't even get as far as the town. That second time, on the Christmas Eve, I didn't do much better, neither, except at the very end of the day I met that nice young man called Edwin who gave me three-and-six for me lodgings and me fare back to London.'

'Did you, indeed?' exclaimed Holmes involuntarily, and slightly out of his assumed character. But Princess Puffa, engulfed in a fit of coughing, failed to notice. 'But what of Ned?'

'No,' she said sadly, after clearing her throat, 'I couldn't find no Ned.'

'And you had wanted to warn him?'

'Oh yes,' she exclaimed, emphatically nodding her head, 'I wanted to tell him, see. But the next time that Jasper came, just before I met you, I knew it was too late. He'd done for Ned, though he seemed none the happier for it — and the dream warn't the same, neither!'

'How so?'

"Cos he saw somethink that he hadn't seen before, dearie, and he didn't like it one little bit, not he!'

'And did you ever see Mr Jasper again?'

'Once more, dearie, and that was many years arter — but I settled his hash *then*, all right! I soon got him back where he belonged, didn't I just!'

'You knew where he belonged, then?'

'I'd kept tabs on him, all right. It was that —' and she used an expression which indicated that she was fully acquainted with Stazeby Nanton and the purpose it served. The vehemence with which she ejaculated that expression brought on another fit of coughing, and I knew that the end was near.

'There is just one thing more, Princess,' said Holmes, with a rather curious expression on his face. 'Did you have any ulterior purpose of your own in keeping tabs on Mr Jasper? Was it simply the desire to have justice meted out in respect of this unknown Ned, or did you have a private score to settle? Had Mr Jasper done you or your family wrong at some distant period in the past?'

The old woman, looking greatly excited, again tried to rouse herself but the effort was too much. She fell back but continued muttering. My friend bent low, listening intently, but the sound gradually faded away.

'Unintelligible,' said Holmes at last, straightening up. And he slowly removed his hat and wig.

13

It seemed, in a sense, that the mystery of Edwin Drood had finally been solved. All the information at our disposal pointed to the fact, horrible though it was, that John Jasper had been responsible for the murder of his own nephew and for the disappearance of the body. Yet this conclusion was curiously unsatisfactory and I knew that Holmes himself remained far from happy about the point at which our investigation had apparently terminated. 'There is', he said on one occasion, as the winter evenings drew on and we pulled our chairs closer to the fire, 'something not right here. If Mr Jasper was the murderer, why should he be so obsessed in bringing the alleged villain of the piece to justice? He himself was, after all, clearly above suspicion. Had it not been for the vehemence with which, in his semi-demented state, he has pursued Neville Landless, we ourselves would not have been drawn into the affair and the revelations of Princess Puffa would have remained a closed book for evermore. One can only surmise that Mr Jaspher wanted it to be clearly established that somebody else was definitely responsible for the crime. "To be thus is nothing, but to be *safely* thus" is a dictum which murderers have certainly been known to practise, yet in this instance I am not at all sure that it fits the bill. The story remains tantalizingly incomplete and we know, as yet, less than half the facts.'

So matters stood until, three days before Christmas, I chanced to linger at the breakfast table over the columns of *The Times* rather longer than my normal wont (a result of having been tempted into an additional cup of Mrs Hudson's coffee). Casting a brief eye over the announcements of births, deaths and marriages, while my companion skimmed rapidly through his post, I happened to glimpse a not unfamiliar name in the adjoining column and let out a cry which attracted his attention.

'Good gracious, Holmes!' I exclaimed. 'Listen to this, from the "In Memoriam" column — "Landless. In ever-loving memory of Neville Landless, a dear brother and friend. 'Love is Immortal and Life is Eternal.' Helena and Septimus."'

Holmes snatched the paper out of my hands and read the entry over to himself. His expression, much to my surprise, was one of intense annoyance — but of annoyance at himself, I soon realized, rather than anyone else. 'I have been slow, Watson,' he exclaimed, 'damnably slow! I half suspected this months ago but there was always some other matter of particular urgency on hand . . . Procrastination, my dear fellow, is ever the culprit! Pray Heavens that I am not too late to make amends.'

He left the house almost instantly and several hours elapsed before he returned, exhausted but seemingly triumphant. 'I have done all I can,' he said, 'and we must await the outcome.' He poked the fire vigorously and flung himself into his favourite armchair. I judged the moment propitious for making a small confession.

'Holmes,' said I, 'there is something which I ought to have mentioned to you before now, except that it is information of a purely negative kind. Whether it has any relevance at all to your investigations must be for you to decide.' I then told him about that visit to the Royal Academy with Thurston, the coincidence of the apparent similarity between the two portraits (seemingly supported by the rosebud brooch), of my subsequent farcical encounter with M. Dupont and, finally, of the curt note which I had received from that excitable gentleman, which I passed across to my friend.

Holmes listened to my narrative with a quite extraordinary expression on his face and shook his head in disbelief as he read the letter. He put it down at last and gazed at me for a moment without speaking. 'Good old Watson!' he finally exclaimed, in affectionate exasperation. 'As always, running true to form! You have truly excelled yourself in this little affair and I must confess that I scarcely know whether to laugh or cry. You diligently took note of every fact of consequence – every fact except the most vital one of all, which was confronting you from the outset.'

'Now see here, Holmes!' I began, jumping indignantly to my feet, but there came an unexpected interruption. The door burst open, a protesting Mrs Hudson being elbowed contemptuously aside, and in strode the formidable figure of Mrs Crisparkle. 'Mr Holmes,' she cried, 'if ever a fiend walked the face of the earth in human form, that creature was John Jasper!'

'Capital!' exclaimed Holmes in delight, rubbing his hands in eager anticipation. 'At last we are getting somewhere! Mrs Crisparkle, please be seated. Mrs Hudson, some tea for our visitor.'

Helena Crisparkle, her face burning with passion, loosened her coat and sat down. 'I apologize', said she, after a moment, 'for what may have been my rather unconventional entry, but my blood boils whenever I think of that reptile. I must control myself. Thank you for your telegram, Mr Holmes. My husband and I came to London as soon as we received it. We are staying at the Strand Hotel. I left Septimus in our rooms and came straight here, for I can sometimes speak more freely in his absence – I have done so already, in fact! He is a wonderful man and understands much, but I sometimes fear that my outspokenness shocks him a little. Mr Holmes, how can I help you? And, even more to the point, how can you help *me*?'

By way of explanation, my companion had silently passed across the table to me, while Mrs Crisparkle was speaking, a copy of the telegram which he had sent to Cloisterham earlier that day. 'Neville Landless,' it ran. 'Do you still wish to clear his name? If so, I am at your disposal. Sherlock Holmes.'

'Thank you for coming,' he said now. 'I trust that you will

be able to clarify matters, Mrs Crisparkle, to our mutual benefit. There is no rush. Tell me, in your own words, about yourself and Neville.'

'Neville and I were twins,' she began, 'and the bond between us was thus far stronger, I think, than that between most brothers and sisters. We looked alike to some extent and we thought alike to a large extent. There were times, indeed, when there was an almost telepathic communication between us. Our childhood in Ceylon was, I fear, an extremely unhappy one and our education was shamefully neglected. I will not trouble you with the details. Suffice it to say that we came to England hoping to make a fresh start in life. Through the agency of a philanthropic society, we were both sent to Cloisterham — Neville being domiciled with Septimus (then a Minor Canon) and his mother, the intention being that he should carry out his studies under Septimus's supervision, and a place for myself being found at the Nuns' House seminary.

'Septimus and his mother, with the best of motives, had arranged a small dinner party at Minor Canon Corner as a means of welcoming us both to Cloisterham — but it proved to be, alas, one of the most fateful and horrible evenings of our lives. The guests included John Jasper, Edwin Drood, Rosa Bud, who was another pupil at the seminary, and Miss Twinkleton, the principal of that establishment.'

'And what did you make of Edwin Drood?' enquired Holmes.

'This was the one and only occasion that I ever encountered him, so it is unfair to form a judgement on such a limited acquaintance. He was a cheerful enough young

127

man but perhaps inclined to be slightly too free with his opinions. Something of an extrovert, I would say.'

'And what do you think Mr Drood made of yourself?'

Our visitor seemed rather surprised at this unexpected question. 'Really, Mr Holmes,' she exclaimed, colouring afresh, 'I haven't the faintest idea. He addressed two or three remarks to me, and seemed gallant enough in his general attitude, but I was chiefly conscious of the fact that he was surprisingly patronizing towards Miss Bud, to whom he was supposed (albeit in an unofficial capacity) to be betrothed.'

'And what did you think of *her*?'

Helena Crisparkle smiled, for the first time. 'She was a perfect dear,' she said. 'The prettiest little child that I ever met — for she was no more than seventeen at that time. It was impossible to be in her company for long and not be attracted to her. Neville, I know, was most certainly smitten, and he was inclined to resent, in his rather hotheaded fashion, young Drood's cavalier attitude towards her.'

'And what, finally, did you make of Mr Jasper?'

The smile instantly disappeared. 'He was', she said, 'a handsome, courteous and extremely intelligent man but the most cold-blooded, calculating and repellent of creatures that I have ever encountered. It may well be, of course, that my opinion has been coloured by subsequent events, but even on that very first evening I soon realized (although, amazingly, nobody else did) that he was intensely interested in Rosa and that he wanted, above all things, to make her his own. He observed her from afar with a cool, calculating eye, with the air of one who bided his time. He was her music-master and when she was prevailed upon to sing he accompanied her at the piano in the most sinister, domineering of fashions, exercising so strange and tight a control over his pupil (especially when she seemed in danger of wandering from the tune) that she eventually broke down in tears. She confessed to me, later that night, that she was terrified of him. I find it incredible, even now, that no one else at that party — not Septimus, not Neville, and definitely not Mr Drood, who regarded his uncle with great affection — was aware of the extent to which he virtually mesmerized her and the horrible passion that he evidently felt.' And she shuddered at the recollection. 'Rosa herself', she added, 'did not fully realize, at that time, the extent of his obsession, although it would soon be made brutally clear to her.'

Mrs Hudson entered at this point, bearing cups of tea and a telegram for Holmes. He perused it, his face remaining impassive, then pushed it to one side.

'I imagine, Mr Holmes,' Mrs Crisparkle continued, sipping her tea, 'that you know something of what happened later on that first evening. Neville and Edwin Drood escorted Rosa, Miss Twinkleton and myself back to the seminary, but the moment we parted a row developed between them on the subject of Mr Drood's almost contemptuous treatment of Rosa. Jasper chanced upon them, just as they were coming to blows, and insisted that they both return with him to the gatehouse in an attempt to restore amicable relations. In the event, however, relations became far worse – deliberately enflamed, Neville later concluded, by something that Mr Jasper had added to both the young men's drinks – and passions reached such a sorry pitch that Neville actually flung himself upon Drood and had to be hauled off by Mr Jasper, being thrust into the street as a consequence. From that moment, I fear, our hopes of a happy life in Cloisterham were doomed. Mr Drood returned to London the following morning and Mr Jasper lost no opportunity for proclaiming, far and wide – chiefly, indeed, through the medium of unwitting mouthpieces – that Neville Landless had tried to murder his "dear boy", that he feared for Mr Drood's safety on future occasions and that, in short, a wild animal was lodged at Minor Canon Corner. He even had the temerity to suggest to my future husband, on one occasion, that Septimus's own life was in danger.

'It was Septimus who was instrumental in bringing about a reconciliation between Neville and Mr Drood on Christmas Eve, at a dinner party at the gatehouse presided over by Mr Jasper himself, and my brother returned to his lodgings convinced that all would be well between them in future. Deliberately absenting himself from the scene, for fear that his presence would otherwise cast a blight on sundry festive gatherings, he set out on a walking tour early the following morning. He had gone only a few miles, however, before he found himself pursued and taken prisoner by a gang of men who bore him back to Cloisterham, accused of the murder of Mr Drood. It was only the absence of a body that prevented him from being brought to trial.

'Thereafter, of course, it was impossible for Neville to remain in Cloisterham. Every man's hand was against him and Jasper was instrumental in ensuring that he was treated like a leper of old. Branded as a murderer, he eventually moved to London and took up lodgings in rooms found for him by Mr Grewgious, Rosa's guardian. Here he endeavoured to continue his studies, and Septimus looked in from time to time to see how he was faring. I joined him there myself a little while later and you may have observed, gentlemen, when you visited the Deanery, a little sketch that I made of him then. Even here, however, he was not safe from Mr Jasper, who pursued him with the implacable fury of an avenging angel and eventually caused it to be generally known that a Murderer was living in that particular tenement building.'

'You say "eventually",' interposed Holmes. 'There was, then, a short delay between Mr Jasper ascertaining your brother's whereabouts and his generally sounding an alarm in the neighbourhood. Would you be able to account for that delay?'

Helena's face looked troubled. 'It was, I fear, the execution of a threat,' she explained. 'Mr Jasper called upon Rosa one day that summer, when the pupils and most of the staff at the Nuns' House seminary were away, and threatened that he would, in effect, pursue Neville to the bitter end unless she agreed to surrender herself to him. He made this threat, you understand, not because there was a relationship of any kind between Neville and Rosa — for they had met only on that one occasion — but because he was the brother of someone of whom Rosa was very fond. It was blackmail of the vilest kind.'

'So the proposition was, as you understand it, that Neville would remain unmolested if Rosa undertook to sacrifice herself in marriage to Mr Jasper?'

Helena nodded. 'The poor lamb, scarcely able to comprehend what hideous passions she had awakened in this monster, fled to London without delay and flung herself, understandably, upon her guardian for protection. Mr Grewgious, who had already had strong cause to revise his earlier good opinion of John Jasper, took control of the situation. He initially found her rooms in a nearby hotel – Wood's Hotel, on the north side of Furnival's Inn – and she stayed there for a short time, but Jasper was observed lurking near its entrance on more than one occasion and Mr Grewgious subsequently arranged for her to go into lodgings in Clerkenwell, some little distance away, with Miss Twinkleton to act as her temporary companion.

'Neville, in the mean time, became steadily more depressed. He worked hard at his studies, never venturing out except at night, but eventually became increasingly subject to acute melancholia. A Mr Tartar, a gentleman whom he had encountered in these lodgings (by a strange chance, my husband's old fag), was originally well disposed towards him, and a friendly face at a time like this was a boon indeed, but Mr Tartar gradually became somewhat cold in his attitude – reserving judgement, as it were, but indicating that he had distinct doubts about my brother's innocence. There may have been a slight tinge of jealousy so far as Rosa was concerned – although my brother and

Rosa never came into contact, despite their relatively close proximity for a short while – but I cannot help suspecting that Mr Jasper found some insidious means of working his poison. The loss of Mr Tartar's comradeship was a determining factor in plunging Neville further into depression. He eventually moved to Lincoln, accompanied by myself, in the hope of lying low until the mystery concerning Edwin Drood was brought to a head, but even here John Jasper managed to pursue him. That man, Mr Holmes, was possessed of a demoniacal energy – it often seemed that he had perfected the art of being in two places at once! Once again, word got around that there was a murderer in the city and Neville found himself shunned by his new neighbours. Like Cain, he was treated as a fugitive and vagabond on the face of the earth.

'Our hope', she continued, 'that the mystery of Mr Drood's disappearance might be resolved at an early date was not entirely without foundation. A friend of Mr Grewgious, who had been keeping John Jasper under careful observation for several months past –'

'One moment. This friend of Mr Grewgious. It would be Mr Datchery, I assume?'

'That's right.'

'And Mr Grewgious had sent him to Cloisterham, I take it, for the express purpose of watching John Jasper?'

'Not exactly,' she said, frowning. 'I never met Mr Datchery myself, but I have the impression that he came out of the blue, as it were, and offered his services to Mr Grewgious of his own accord. I do not believe that they had been previously acquainted. It may be that he was a distant connection of Bazzard, Mr Grewgious's clerk – a most peculiar man, so I gather, but one who moved in theatrical circles – but this is mere surmise.'

'I see. Pray continue.'

'Mr Datchery, as I say, had been keeping Mr Jasper under careful observation and had also made diligent enquiry into his activities during the months immediately preceding Edwin Drood's disappearance. He formed the conclusion that Jasper had himself murdered his nephew and hidden his body somewhere in the churchyard – immured, in all probability, in quicklime, so that there would be virtually nothing left of him. The removal of the watch and shirt-pin, which would have been identifying features in view of their known resistance to the properties of quicklime, certainly suggested this. He also suspected that Mr Jasper had somehow gained access to the Sapsea tomb and had secreted the body in the spot reserved for our worthy mayor. You will think me, I fear, incredibly cold-blooded to be sitting here calmly narrating these conclusions without turning a hair, but you must remember that I have been familiar with this tale for more than a quarter of a century and it long ago lost its power to shock.'

'Not at all,' said Holmes. 'Please go on.'

'Mr Grewgious's friend, shortly before he left the area (for reasons I never could ascertain), had devised a plan whereby Jasper was to be startled into confessing his guilt. On the night that he disappeared Edwin was carrying, on his person, a ring which he had originally intended to present to Rosa as a means of marking their formal betrothal – it was of great sentimental value, having belonged originally to Rosa's mother, and it was only with great reluctance that Mr Grewgious (who had developed misgivings about the advisability of the match) parted with it to Edwin. In the event, however, Edwin and Rosa agreed of their own accord that they should not proceed with their engagement and Edwin had retained it, presumably intending to return it to Mr Grewgious's safe-keeping. The person responsible for murdering Edwin, however, while removing his gold watch, its chain and his shirt-pin, would not have been aware that a valuable ring, quite distinct in its appearance and instantly identifiable, was also secreted about the body.

'Mr Datchery's plan, therefore, was that Mr Grewgious should casually inform John Jasper, a day or so before Christmas 1870, that Rosa Bud had become engaged to another (a Mr Jack Tartar) and that it was a thousand pities that she could not wear her mother's engagement ring, which Edwin had had in his possession when he disappeared. It was surmised that this would be startling news to Mr Jasper, especially in view of the fact that Mr Sapsea was no longer a young man and might be joining his wife in the family tomb before very much longer, and that – in short, that John Jasper would hurry along to the churchyard and seek to retrieve the ring from what, if anything, remained of his nephew's body.' And at this point, despite her earlier brave words, Mrs Crisparkle's voice faltered and she was unable to repress a shudder.

'Take your time, Mrs Crisparkle, there is no hurry.'

She swallowed, and then continued. 'The plan was, briefly, that just as John Jasper reached the point where he had last seen the body, and was about to search for the ring, a young man who to all intents and purposes *was* Edwin Drood, clad in clothes identical to those which Drood had been wearing when last seen in the land of the living, would step out and silently confront him. Mr Jasper, so it was thought, would then break down and confess his guilt.'

'And where was this duplicate Edwin Drood to come from?' asked Holmes.

'The intention had been that Neville should play that role. He had been familiar with the clothes and hat that Edwin had been wearing on that fateful evening, was of approximately the same age and build and would have been quite capable, for a few moments, of convincing Jasper that he was gazing upon the spectre of the murdered man. Mr Grewgious, Mr Tartar, Lobley (Mr Tartar's man) and Septimus would then have emerged from their sundry places of concealment and apprehended him.' She paused, reflectively, for a few minutes and gazed unseeingly at the wall.

'But all did not go according to plan?' suggested Holmes.

Mrs Crisparkle shook her head. 'Neville', she said bitterly, 'was struck down by a brainstorm on 22 December – exactly twenty-five years ago today, in fact – and died within minutes. He was John Jasper's second victim, Mr Holmes, for that swine had hounded him – or been responsible for others hounding him – until he could endure no longer. He died like a beast at bay, totally innocent of any crime, but pursued from pillar to post until he could go on no longer.'

There was a moment's silence. 'I was aware of this,' said Holmes gently, at length. 'I ascertained from Somerset House, earlier today, the time, place and cause of his death. So the plan had to be abandoned, then?'

Helena Crisparkle shook her head. 'Oh no!' she cried vehemently. 'Not for the world! If there had been cause before why we should hunt John Jasper down and thrust him into the condemned cell, there was double the cause now. The plan went ahead.'

'And the young man?'

'Was myself. Don't look so surprised, Mr Holmes! It was not the first time that I had dressed up in boy's clothes, although it was certainly the last.'

'I have had some experience', said Holmes, smiling at the recollection, 'of another young lady who did precisely the same thing. But I am interrupting. Please continue.'

'It all went horribly wrong,' said Mrs Crisparkle bitterly. 'On the first night, nothing happened. On the second night, 24 December, Mr Jasper did indeed come stealing into the churchyard, holding a dark lantern, and he made straight for the Sapsea tomb. He paused a moment, apparently searching for something about his person, and I stepped out to confront him. But instead of breaking down and confessing all, as we had innocently expected, he broke out into an exultant cry of delight. "So, Landless," he snarled, "the old adage is correct – murderers *do* return to the scene of the crime! At last, I have you!" He flung himself upon me and the next moment his hands were around my throat. He was totally convinced in that instant, not only that I was my brother (of whose death he was evidently unaware) but that Neville was indeed the murderer of Edwin Drood. We fell to the ground, but now that we were at close quarters he realized his terrible mistake — that it was a woman he was trying to strangle, not a man — and the next instant Tartar and Lobley were upon us and pulling him free. His rage, mixed with his disappointment, was awesome to behold — he collapsed in a heap, foaming at the mouth, and we found ourselves calling for medical assistance instead of the local constabulary. It transpired (though I cannot express any regrets) that his mind was permanently unhinged and we heard, later, that he had been committed to an asylum. The rest you know.

'So the matter, Mr Holmes, never was resolved. John Jasper, far from confessing his guilt, had evidently believed, during those frightful few minutes, that he was grappling with the murderer of his beloved nephew. But I am equally convinced, whatever the world might say, that my poor, dear brother could not have been responsible for the death of Mr Drood. If you can indeed clear his name, then I will be everlastingly in your debt.'

There was a moment's silence. 'I blame myself to some extent,' she continued, in a dull, colourless, ruminating voice. 'I had, unfortunately, only seen Edwin Drood on that one occasion and I obviously bore a far greater resemblance to Neville than I did to Mr Drood. Yet I cannot help thinking, strange though it is, that if only Mr Datchery had not gone away things might have worked out differently. Although I never met that gentleman, he appears to have possessed an unerring touch for overcoming difficulties. Without him, the rest of us – myself, Mr Grewgious, Mr Tartar, Mr Lobley, Septimus and even Rosa – were bereft of a guiding force that might have made all the difference. It could be said, perhaps, that we were six characters in need of a stage-manager! Mr Grewgious was a good, kind man, extremely resourceful and capable, yet he somehow lacked the force, the guiding purpose required, to seize control of the situation and see it through to the bitter end. But these', she said, wrenching herself out of her mood of abstraction, 'are foolish fancies, Mr Holmes, and I am wasting your time.'

'Not at all, not at all. And what happened to you all after this unfortunate outcome to your little scheme?'

She laughed rather bitterly. 'In essence,' she said, 'we went our separate ways, for there was nothing to hold us together any more. Rosa married Mr Tartar some months later and I returned to Cloisterham, teaching at Miss Twinkleton's seminary for a time until Septimus did me the honour of making me his wife.'

'And you lost contact with Rosa and her husband?'

'Yes, for all practical purposes. My relations with Mr Tartar had become, as you will have gathered, somewhat strained, for Neville's innocence remained unproven and Mr Tartar had seen no reason – especially in the light of what took place in the churchyard that night – to banish his doubts on that matter.'

'So you haven't seen or heard from Rosa for twenty-five years?'

'No, I haven't seen her but we communicate occasionally

– and I wrote to her, of course, when her husband died.'

'Indeed!' said Holmes, sitting up. 'And when was this?'

'Oh, seven or eight months ago now – there was a small item in the *Telegraph* to the effect that Mr Jack Tartar had been killed in a climbing accident in the Swiss Alps, and I immediately sent Rosa my commiserations. I had a brief line in response.'

'I would be grateful,' said Holmes, 'if you could supply me with Mrs Tartar's current address. It is imperative that I see her without delay.'

Mrs Crisparkle promised to send a messenger to Baker Street with this information the following morning, adding that Rosa was living somewhere in Bournemouth.

'One final question,' said Holmes. 'You mentioned, a little while ago, that sketch (and a very evocative one it is too!) which you made of your brother. We could not help observing, when we had the pleasure of lunching at the Deanery last Christmas, that there was a remarkably fine portrait of yourself hanging alongside it. I wonder if you could tell me who the artist was?'

Mrs Crisparkle looked at my friend in some surprise. 'I cannot recall his name,' she said. 'It was done many years ago, soon after the events which we have just been discussing and at a time, indeed, when I would much have preferred a period of seclusion. The young man in question was a penniless French refugee (for this was at the time of the Franco-Prussian war) and Mr Grewgious had taken upon himself the role of patron. Mr Grewgious was anxious to obtain some commissions for the young gentleman and the painting served, indeed, as a wedding present from him

140

to Septimus and myself.'

'Thank you,' said Holmes. 'You have been immensely helpful. There are no further questions but I would be grateful if you and the Dean could delay your return to Cloisterham for a day or so. Ideally, I know, the Dean would wish to be there on Christmas Eve, but I have the feeling that events of great moment are upon us and I would wish you to remain close at hand for a little while longer. There are at least two visits that Watson and I need to make, with Bournemouth being our first port of call, and our investigation will then, I trust, be complete.'

Mrs Crisparkle willingly consented to my friend's request. 'One final word,' she said, as she rose to take her leave. 'It was never officially established that John Jasper was responsible for the death of Edwin Drood, and I must confess that, after the lapse of so many years, I no longer greatly care whether it is or not. What I do know, however, is that he was responsible for besmirching the memory of my dear brother, as well as for his death, and that is something about which I still care very much indeed.'

'If the record can be put straight,' said Holmes, 'then rest assured that it most certainly will be – and the pen of my colleague, here, will be primarily responsible for ensuring that, sooner or later, the public are made fully aware of what befell Mr Drood and at whose door the blame for his disappearance should be laid.'

Warmly acknowledging this potential commission, and pledging myself to discharge it to the best of my ability, I escorted Mrs Crisparkle downstairs to the waiting cab.

When I returned to our quarters Holmes held out to me, without a word, the telegram delivered earlier. It was from James Wakefield and stated that Mr John Jasper had made an 'unauthorized departure' from Stazeby Nanton.

That night, the heavens opened. The sound of intense rain drumming on the roof rendered sleep almost impossible and I managed, in the event, no more than a troubled doze, wondering, from time to time, whether Mr Jasper was likely to pay another visit to Baker Street and, if so, whether there would be a sudden thunderous hammering at the door of No. 221b.

There was indeed an early-morning visitor and at the sound of the rat-a-tat-tat I leaped out of bed and was half-way down the stairs only to find that Holmes was there before me, that Mrs Hudson was there before us both and that the caller in question, water streaming from his cape, was simply a lad from the Strand Hotel who had brought round the details of Rosa Tartar's address from Mrs Crisparkle. He was amply rewarded for his pains and splashed his way back to the hotel. The rain continued to stream down incessantly.

'Scarcely the weather', said Holmes, 'for a trip to the south coast, and I must confess – when all is said and done – that the points that Mrs Tartar will be able to clarify, in the light of what we learnt last night, are now unlikely to be of more than marginal importance. But she is the last of our witnesses — or, at all events, *almost* the last — and it is imperative that we see her without delay. Are you game for an out-of-season trip to Bournemouth, Watson? I fancy that oilskins and galoshes will be required!'

I confirmed that I was, as ever, fully prepared to accompany my friend wherever he wished. As soon as breakfast was concluded, and appropriately armed against the foulest of foul weathers, we were in a cab heading for Waterloo Station. Arriving there in an acutely wet condition, we caught the first available train and slowly steamed our way towards the south-west. The rain continued to pelt down in a monotonous torrent and we made but sluggish progress. I had bought a copy of the *Daily Graphic* at the station bookstall, with a view to familiarizing myself with the latest dispatches from its special military correspondent in Cuba, while Holmes, as was his wont, had purchased a large collection of newspapers of every description, which he skimmed through with no great patience. 'Ha!' he exclaimed at one point, after perusing the drama critic of the *Saturday Review*. 'If we wish to familiarize ourselves with the spectacle of a young soprano under the spell of a mesmerist, a visit to the Haymarket in the not too distant future may prove instructive — for Tree, I note, is essaying the role of Svengali.'

'Also instructive in this context,' he added thoughtfully, a little while later, after tossing the last of his papers to one side, 'is the strange story of what befell that Scottish member of your profession some ten years back. There are, it seems, precedents for virtually everything, although problems of identification are such that it is sometimes difficult to say which of them actually came first.' He was lost in thought for some little time, gazing from the window at the rain-swept landscape. 'It is certainly not inconceivable,' he added whimsically, 'that Gaelic mists might drift as far as the south of England, though whether they could be wafted across the Channel to Gaul, despite the obvious affinity, is another matter.' And then, after an even longer silence: 'One might conclude, I suppose, that the Scottish Queen has much to answer for!'

I had found it difficult to follow Holmes's train of thought and could not see, for the life of me, what Mary Queen of Scots had to do with our investigations. But he had murmured these final inconsequential words so drowsily that it was clear that he too had passed a troubled night, with only fitful slumbers, and that loss of sleep was finally making itself felt. This seemed to be confirmed, a little while later, when he slipped into a doze.

I stared, through the streaming windows, at the leaden, sullen landscape through which we were slowly making our way, much enveloped in mist, and reflected on the whole strange story of the Edwin Drood saga, which had now had us embroiled for almost exactly a year. I must have nodded off in my own turn, for the next thing I knew was that a tremendous screeching of brakes, and expulsion of steam, were proclaiming the fact that we had finally reached the end of our journey and had arrived at Bournemouth. Scrambling down, to be greeted by the incessant drumming of rain on the roof of the station, we eventually hired a cab and clattered off, through monumental puddles, to Voredale Towers, a residence located in Wenskerry Gardens.

The cab dropped us at the gates and we squelched our way up the drive, our umbrellas proving a sadly inadequate protection against what had developed into a howling tornado of a storm. I was much impressed by the size of the house, for it was nothing less than a small mansion. 'Mrs Tartar', murmured Holmes as he pulled the bellrope, and noting my surprise, 'is now a very wealthy lady. Quite apart from whatever funds the late Mr Tartar may have left her, she inherited a substantial sum from her parents and also, for that matter, from Mr Grewgious, a bachelor gentleman who seems to have regarded her as his own daughter.'

The door was opened by a maid, who noted our bedraggled condition with a certain degree of sympathy but was obviously loath to invite us inside. 'Is your mistress at home?' enquired Holmes. 'We have travelled a considerable distance, on a matter of some urgency, and would be grateful if Mrs Tartar could spare us a little of her time.'

'Oh no, sir!' exclaimed the girl. 'The mistress is away for a few days – I can't rightly say when she'll be back, I'm afraid.'

But at this point there was a call of 'Who is it, Edith?' and a very good-looking young lady appeared in the hall. I was almost certain (but hesitated to mention the fact, for fear of proving mistaken) that she was the girl whose 'Morning Glory' portrait I had admired at the Royal Academy some five months before.

'Miss Florence Tartar, I believe?' exclaimed Holmes. 'My name is Sherlock Holmes and this is my colleague, Dr

146

Watson. We are very anxious for a brief interview with your mother in connection with some happenings many years ago which have never been satisfactorily resolved.'

'Do come in, gentlemen,' said the self-possessed young woman, her eyes sparkling with interest. She led us through to the drawing-room. 'You're too late for lunch, I am afraid, but perhaps I can interest you in some sherry?' (She could indeed.) 'I'm very familiar with your name and reputation, Mr Holmes – fancy Mamma being involved in one of your cases! This is certainly going to liven up a soggy old day. And how wet you are!' A few minutes later, however, she was pouting with vexation as Holmes explained, regretfully, that it was a confidential matter on which he wanted to see Mrs Tartar, that he was not at liberty to reveal any of the details and that he would be greatly obliged if he could be informed of Mrs Tartar's whereabouts.

'Oh, that's not fair!' exclaimed our young hostess. 'You want me to tell *you* something but you won't tell *me* anything in return. I'll throw you out into the rain without further ado unless you give me at least a hint of what it's all about.'

Holmes, unaccustomed to playful exchanges of this fashion, breathed rather heavily. 'Miss Tartar,' he said at length, 'have you ever heard your mother refer to a Mr Edwin Drood?'

She shook her head.

'Or to a Mr John Jasper?'

Again, a shake of the pretty head.

'Then I fear I am unable to elucidate further. As I say, our visit concerns matters which happened many years ago and

147

if your mother has not seen fit to enlighten you concerning these gentlemen then it seems best that I emulate her example. Miss Tartar, I wish you a very good afternoon.'

He bowed and then made for the door, with myself following suit, but there came a petulant cry of 'Stop!' from the young lady. 'You really are', she said, 'the most provoking of men that I have ever encountered. You arrive here out of the blue (in a figurative sense), mention the names of some strange people that I have never heard of, arouse my interest in my mother's early life, about which I know virtually nothing, and then take your leave without a single word of proper explanation. What have I to do with your Edwin Droods or John Jaspers?' And she stamped her foot in annoyance.

Holmes waited patiently until she had finished. 'I am sorry,' he said at length, 'but the secrets are not mine to divulge. If you are unable to inform us of your mother's whereabouts, then our visit is at an end.'

'Oh, very well,' she said crossly. 'Mother has gone to London for two or three days. There! Now you know.'

'She is staying with friends, presumably?'

'No, she's gone to a hotel, but you'd never guess which one. It's nowhere near the West End or the bright lights, where all the exciting things happen and the best people are, but it's stuck in that frowsty, dry-as-dust, legal part of the City, where they have all those Inns and gentlemen rushing about in long gowns and short wigs and silly things like that.'

Holmes stiffened. 'That would be Wood's Hotel, I believe?'

'That's right! How clever of you. A funny little place, and very off the beaten track, but Mamma always stops there on her visits to London – not that she makes many, you understand. I think it has a sentimental attachment for her – she was staying there when she first met my father.'

'Miss Tartar, I am much indebted to you,' said Holmes, and this time we really did take our leave. The young lady, her curiosity unsatisfied as her day's excitement came to an end, saw us reluctantly to the door. We emerged into the same torrential downpour and, there being no cab at hand, were obliged to walk to the station. A local train took us to Mugsby Junction. Here we found that there would be a wait of forty minutes for the next train to London but this break in our journey did enable us, at any rate, to fortify ourselves at the refreshments room.

Holmes ate the unappetizing sandwiches with no great enthusiasm and looked frequently at his watch. 'You will appreciate, of course,' he said, 'the reason for my unease. Mr Jasper, so we learnt last night, was detected "lurking" in the vicinity of Wood's Hotel on two or three occasions when Rosa Bud was staying there. It does not follow, of course, that he will go there on this occasion, assuming that he somehow contrives to make his way to London, and nor does it follow that he would necessarily recognize the lady in question after a lapse of twenty-five years. But stranger things have happened already in this curious tale!'

Little more did he say for the moment. Our journey was unduly protracted and I was aware, every time that the train halted or slowed down, of his mounting impatience. By early evening we were back in London – finding, to our great relief, that the rain had finally eased – and in a cab heading for Wood's Hotel in Furnival's Inn. It was indeed, as Miss Florence had described it, off the beaten track and by the time we had alighted from our conveyance the darkened streets were almost deserted.

Wood's Hotel, used chiefly for the accommodation of court case witnesses obliged to stay in town overnight, was unassuming to the point of being positively unprepossessing. The receptionist, from his poorly lit cubicle, peered out at us in some surprise.

'Have you a Mrs Tartar among your guests?' Holmes enquired.

The receptionist shook his head emphatically but slowly moved his ink-stained finger down the hotel register. 'No sir,' he firmly announced at length, with an air of triumph. 'We have no Mrs Tartar.' And he slammed the book shut.

'Could she be using her maiden name, I wonder? Have you a Miss Rosa Bud staying here?'

The receptionist raised his eyebrows. 'Ah, that's a different matter,' he responded, without pausing to consult his register. 'Room 18 on the first floor. You're her second visitor this evening, sir,' he added. 'A gentleman went up to see her not five minutes since.'

Holmes, without another word, and much to the clerk's astonishment, bounded up the stairs two at a time, with myself in hot pursuit. He raced along the shabby, ill-lit corridor, peering at the numbers on each of the doors, and eventually flung open that of Room 18. There were two people in the room, a man and a woman sitting close together by the fireside, who started up in bewilderment and alarm as Holmes burst in. 'A thousand apologies for this interruption,' he exclaimed, but with a note of intense relief in his voice.

'Monsieur Dupont!' exclaimed I, close upon his heels, in astonishment.

Holmes shook his head. 'Not quite,' said he, with a smile. 'Allow me to introduce you, Watson, to Mr Edwin Drood.'

A few minutes later, with the briefest of introductions and explanations having been effected and with the hotel management having been prevailed upon to provide some liquid refreshments, Holmes and I drew up two chairs of our own to that fireside. Mrs Tartar, now, alas, a rather full-blown rose but a cheerful little woman with a twinkle in her eye, made us both very welcome, bustled about whenever the need to refill our glasses arose, and beamed upon all three of us in the happiest of manners. M. Dupont, as I still found myself thinking of him, had dispensed with the pince-nez and seemed altogether less foreign (and even slightly taller) as he sprawled at his ease in a comfortable armchair. He seemed, rather to my surprise, totally unconcerned by the fact that his true identity had now been revealed.

'My apologies, Dr Watson,' he began, with an affable smile,' for that altercation in Peckham a few months ago. I hammed it up unmercifully, I'm afraid, but it's a trick that I've often had to resort to as a means of getting rid of unwelcome or awkward visitors. When you started mentioning Miss Rosa Bud I began to realize that my past was catching up with me, and no mistake! Having not the faintest idea who you were, a quick exit seemed prudent.'

'My friend noticed', said Holmes, 'that your English was very poor, but had he been much longer in your company I suspect that he would scarcely have failed to perceive that your French was even worse.'

The artist cheerfully confessed that this would indeed have been the case. 'The months I spent in Paris', he said, 'certainly helped me to pick up some of the lingo, and I can manage the odd phrase or two without too much difficulty, but the smattering which I acquired during that period has now almost left me. A genuine Frog would spot that I was an impostor in an instant.'

'In recent months,' said Holmes genially, his glass having been refilled by the busy little woman, 'I must confess that I have been taking a keen interest in the works of M. Dupont.'

This was news to me, for I had had no reason to suppose that my friend had even heard of the artist prior to our conversation of the previous morning. 'I was not aware, Holmes,' I interposed, somewhat stiffly, 'that you were an expert on the French Impressionist school of painting.'

My companion chuckled. 'Now that,' he said, 'I cannot lay claim to. But did it not occur to you, my dear chap, that it was remarkable that Mr Edwin Drood and M. Edmund Dupont should bear the same initials? By what was, I must acknowledge, pure chance, I happened to see in Cloisterham on the Christmas Day of last year, within the space of a very few hours, two portraits. One of them was a poorly executed daub of a pretty young girl; another was a brilliant depiction of a striking young woman. Both very different in style, yet they had one feature in common. In the bottom right-hand corner of the more accomplished production there appeared, in very tiny print, the initials E.D. The other was unsigned but had been executed, so I discovered, by Mr Jasper's nephew. The portrait of Miss Landless was clearly not the work of an untrained amateur. I ascertained that the only portrait painter of any repute in this country bearing the initials E.D. and (for my purposes) of approximately the right age, was a certain Edmund Dupont. On a recent visit to Paris I made some discreet enquiries about the origins of this M. Dupont and discovered that he was completely unknown in what purported to be his native land.

'But it was not until yesterday morning,' he continued, addressing himself directly to the artist, 'when my good friend Watson showed me a note you had sent him, that my suspicions were finally confirmed. A comparison between the writing of M. Dupont, in October 1895, with what I recalled of the writing of Mr Drood in December 1869, proved extremely instructive! There was also', he added reflectively, 'another Frenchman bearing the initials E.D. who came to mind – and, indeed, another Edmund – who masqueraded as a Count, if I mistake not, as a means of revisiting the scenes of his youth undetected. But *that* Edmund played, I believe, a rather more active role than *this* one!'

'You're quite right, Mr Holmes,' the portrait painter acknowledged. 'Edwin Drood, for all practical purposes, came to an end twenty-six years ago and Edmund Dupont has been content, by and large, to lead a totally separate existence. Apart from anything else, nature intended me to

154

be an artist rather than an engineer, but having assumed an identity more congenial to me than my previous one, and taking all the factors into account, it seemed the most prudent course of all to keep things as they were.'

'You must remember', said Holmes, 'that I am not yet acquainted with all the factors in this case. You are certainly under no compulsion to tell me anything at all, M. Dupont (since this is the persona you prefer), but I feel that, even at this late hour, it could still do some positive good if the true story were revealed once and for all. While uncertainty remains, I fear that there are several quarters in which unhappiness still prevails.'

'Go on, Eddy,' urged the little lady. 'It can certainly do no harm, after all these years, and – as Mr Holmes says – some good may still come of it.'

'And confession', acknowledged M. Dupont, 'is good for the soul. Not that I have much to confess, mind you! I may have assumed an identity that was not my own, but it wasn't anybody else's either. Anyway, now that you have tracked me down, gentlemen (and I seem to have given you a pretty good run for your money), you must hear my tale and judge for yourselves.'

I did not find his flippant manner altogether agreeable, and I wondered whether he fully appreciated just how much trouble had been created by his failure to proclaim that he was alive and well. As his story unfolded, however, I gradually inclined to the opinion that his careless approach was, to some extent, yet another mask, and one that had been adopted as a means of hiding a fundamental insecurity. The little woman, at any rate, saw nothing to complain of in his attitude, and hung upon his every word with rapt attention.

'I am not sure, Mr Holmes,' he began, 'how much you already know about that terrible Christmas Eve twenty-six years ago. You will presumably be aware that there had been bad relations between myself and Neville Landless for several weeks and that Mr Crisparkle was primarily responsible for seeking to bring about a reconciliation between us. My uncle, John Jasper, played host to us at the gatehouse that night and things went, in the circumstances, far better than could have been expected. Both Landless and I were on our best behaviour towards each other and a genuine amicability appeared to be established between us. A fantastic storm raged throughout the evening, although dying out towards midnight, and when the time came for Landless to return to Minor Canon Corner it was suggested, although I'm not too clear whose idea it was, that before he and I went to our respective slumbers we should stroll down to the river to observe the extent to which it had overflowed its banks. Truth to tell, I had evidently drunk rather more than I ought to have done. The alcohol was having such a strange effect upon me that I thought it would be all to the good if I broke away from the rather too convivial atmosphere of the gatehouse and managed to shake off some of the fuzziness that was beginning to affect my wits.

'I walked down to the river with Landless and we gazed at the strangely unreal sight of the turbulent waters churning and slurping against the banks. The effects of the drink remained very strong, however, and everything

156

began to take on a strange, dreamlike quality – I heard my own voice, and that of my companion, coming from a long way off. There was a strange buzzing sensation in my ears and I appeared to be cushioned all around, like a man walking in a dream. I am under the impression that I returned, at length, to the gatehouse and said what was, to my own ears, a muffled goodbye to Landless. I leant against the door to regain my senses, with the world reeling about me, and a moment later was gripped by the arm. A distant voice said, 'Come, you do not seem well; we'll walk in the churchyard for a while. The night air will help to revive you.' My arm was taken and on we walked – or rather stumbled, in my case. I was steered towards the churchyard and was aware of the gravestones looming up. It was impossible to identify my companion. My senses were deadened and the buzzing in my ears became louder.

'The voice eventually commanded me to pause a moment and my arm was released. I suddenly found it exceedingly difficult to breathe and became aware that something was tightening around my throat. I struggled, feebly, to dislodge the mysterious something, but all in vain – I had no strength at all and felt myself falling into a pit. My senses virtually took leave of me, although I was dimly aware of a hand fumbling with my waistcoat. I realised, later, that my watch and shirt-pin were being removed at this point. Then I had the sensation that all was over and that I had been left alone. The fresh air was cut off, to be replaced by indescribable putrescent odours. A door closed and I heard, from afar, the sound of a key being turned. There was a roof over my head and dust in my mouth and I

157

was cold, but all I wanted to do was to curl up and go to sleep in this claustrophobic, uncomfortable yet strangely soft, squelchy resting place. But a little while later – it might have been minutes, or it might have been hours – there came, once again, the sound of a key being turned and the next thing I knew was that I had been seized by the legs and dragged out, coughing and choking.'

'Like Belzoni from the ruins,' interposed the little lady.

'Like Belzoni from the ruins. It transpired, when I had returned (after a fashion) to my senses that my rescuer was the stonemason – Durdles, the queerest of old chaps but the most wonderful of life-savers – who had seen me being attacked from afar, had hidden until my assailant left the tomb into which I had been stuffed and then came to my rescue. He was joined, a few minutes later, by an appalling urchin of a boy and together they helped me to a strange little hovel of a dosshouse – the Travellers' Tuppenny, I believe they called it – where I did my best to wash away the hideous material in which my clothes and face were plastered (although I retain some scars to this very day, hence the beard) and rested a while to take stock of the situation.

'The situation was so incredible that I had difficulty in taking it in! It was unbelievable that somebody had made an attack upon me and actually tried to kill me, but I somehow forced myself, during the hours of that terrible night, to accept the inconceivable. My reason told me that it must be Landless, who had indeed made a physical attack upon me on one occasion – although I now have reason to believe that the quarrel between us had been largely fomented by my uncle – but I could not, even so, believe that it was truly he. We had spent the evening as friends and past enmities between us had appeared to be genuinely at an end. Yet if it was not Landless, it could only be Jack – and that, to me, was equally unbelievable. In short, Mr Holmes, I did not know which of them had done this thing! Durdles, alas, had been too far away to be able to identify my attacker. Not knowing what to think, and with my head reeling from the enormity of what had happened, I decided that the best thing I could do was to leave Cloisterham instantly and to seek counsel with wiser heads than mine. Attired as a tramp – for, in the only spare set of clothes that the demon-child of the Travellers' Tuppenny was able to provide, I could not masquerade as anything else! – I returned to London and flung myself upon the protection of Mr Grewgious, Rosa's guardian.'

'And your rescuers?'

'Durdles and the boy were both sworn to silence. I made it my business to ensure, later, that Durdles was richly rewarded for his labours but I doubt, on the whole, whether the boy had much conception of what had actually happened. He appeared late on the scene, armed (incredibly!) with a handful of stones to hurl at Durdles as a way of encouraging him to go home, and was under the impression, I believe, that I was simply one of the stonemason's drinking companions who had met with some kind of an accident.'

'And why *was* the stonemason abroad at so late an hour of the day?'

'A curious tale, Mr Holmes, and one that I have never

been able to fathom. It seems that, on the *previous* Christmas Eve, the Christmas Eve of 1868 that is, Durdles was asleep in the churchyard in a drunken stupor at about that time and was awoken by what he described to me as the "ghost of a cry — the ghost of one terrific shriek". And that was followed, he claimed, by "the ghost of a howl of a dog — a long dismal woeful howl, such as a dog gives when a person's dead". But nobody else, according to Durdles, had heard these strange sounds, although he had enquired far and wide, and he had returned to the churchyard on *this* Christmas Eve to see whether they would be repeated.'

'A night-shriek,' said Holmes with interest, 'and followed by a howl. Singular indeed! If wolves still roamed abroad in this part of the world, to serve as a murderer's sentinel, an explanation might, perhaps, come to mind. But this is Kent in the nineteenth century, not Inverness in the eleventh, and we must banish such thoughts from our conjectures. Pray continue.'

'I went, as I said, to Mr Grewgious, who was astonished by my story. He decided that, until such time as further investigations could be carried out, and it had been clearly established whether Mr Landless, or Jack or even somebody else, had been responsible for this attempt on my life, it would be best if I disappeared from the scene completely. He considered that, for my own security, I should leave the country altogether and stay away until it was safe for me to reappear. We agreed that I should go to Paris, which seemed a pleasant enough destination, and that Bazzard, Mr Grewgious's clerk, should accompany me and act as my companion and bodyguard. Before the year 1869 had come to its end, therefore, we had crossed the Channel and had taken up residence in the artists' quarter of the city. It was here that I had the golden opportunity to study the rudiments of painting and discover the true vocation of my life.'

'And Mr Bazzard was with you for the whole of this time?'

'He was indeed!' Dupont agreed enthusiastically. 'He proved a marvellous companion and we came through many an adventure together.'

'Just in passing,' said Holmes, 'and you must forgive me for this odd digression, do you have the slightest reason of any kind to suppose that Mr Bazzard — or even, indeed, yourself — was acquainted with an elderly gentleman called Dick Datchery, who took up residence in Cloisterham six or seven months after your disappearance?'

Dupont looked mystified. 'That's a new name to me,' he said. 'I certainly never knew anybody called Datchery and I doubt whether Bazzard did either — but I'll make a point of asking him.' (He did, and the answer proved to be a negative one.)

'So,' said Holmes, 'you had been saved from a dusty death, you took up residence in Paris and you became absorbed in painting. What followed?'

'What followed,' said Dupont with a grimace, 'was the Franco-Prussian war and the German siege of Paris — factors that had *not* been allowed for when I decided to take up residence there! Bazzard and I made our escape and eventually returned to England. By this time I had grown my beard and was virtually unrecognizable as the young

161

man who had left its shores some eighteen months before, but I thought I'd play safe by pretending to be a Frenchman until Bazzard had seen Mr Grewgious and ascertained how the land lay.'

'And how did it?'

'Not at all well, unfortunately. He discovered that Neville Landless was dead, that Uncle Jack was in an asylum and that the mystery of who had made that horrible attack upon me — and whether, in fact, he was still at large — was as much a mystery as ever. (It has remained a mystery ever since — to me, at any rate!) It seemed, one way and the other, decidedly inopportune for Edwin Drood to come back to life. No one would have been particularly glad to see me — and Rosa, I found, had married Jack Tartar, so that it might have been a mite embarrassing for her (formal disengagements notwithstanding!) if I had reappeared on the scene. This being so, I decided to retain the identity of Edmund Dupont, to pass myself off as a refugee and to try to earn my living as a portrait painter. Bazzard, having had some theatrical experience, was able to give me a few tips on how to build up my character as an eccentric Froggie and Mr Grewgious was instrumental, in the early days, in finding me one or two commissions.

'I was eventually able to establish myself and have made, though I say it myself, a fair success of my career. Whether I could have had the same success under an English name is another matter! Peckham seemed as good a place to settle down as anywhere if one wished to assume a new identity without attracting too much attention, and there I've been to this day. And Bazzard, when Mr Grewgious died, came to me as secretary. Until I heard, earlier this year, that Rosa had unfortunately become a widow, and rushed off to offer my condolences and resume our old friendship, the ghost of Edwin Drood had ne'er been seen in the land. I little thought, however, when I did that painting of her daughter (who looks now as her mother did twenty-five years ago) and had it accepted by the Royal Academy, that I would have Dr Watson knocking at my door!'

'I believe', Holmes suggested drily, 'that you are being slightly disingenuous in disclaiming any connection with your previous existence. Did you not return to Cloisterham on at least one occasion?'

Dupont, with a glance at Mrs Tartar, seemed vexed by this question. 'Yes, you know about that, of course,' he conceded ruefully. 'I must confess that Helena Landless had struck me, on the one occasion that I met her, as a fine figure of a woman and I had a strong desire to do her justice on canvas. I won't deny, in fact, that one or two other thoughts had also occurred to me, and I persuaded Mr Grewgious, against his better judgement, to introduce me to her in the character of an artist. I had had some idea of revealing my true identity, if things showed any signs of turning out as I vaguely surmised they might, but I soon realized that it would be best for Edwin Drood to keep out of sight. She was still deeply in mourning for her brother at that time and could well have held me in some way responsible for his death had I declared myself – and it soon became obvious, in any case, that the possibility of *any* nephew of John Jasper making headway with that particular lady stood very little chance of success! Apart from anything else, I soon realized

163

that Mr Crisparkle, a man whom I've always admired, was paying court to her and it seemed best, in the circumstances, that I should complete my commission as soon as I could and steal quietly away into the night. I gather, in fact, that Mr Grewgious presented the picture to them both as a wedding present.'

'And while on the subject of weddings,' said Holmes, 'are you able to enlighten us as to what became of a certain engagement ring?'

'I returned it to Mr Grewgious, when I stumbled into his office on the morrow of that attack. He kept it in his safe thereafter, for to have revealed its existence would have been tantamount to acknowledging, of course, that he knew what had become of me. In his last days, rather than raise any old skeletons so far as Rosa was concerned, he passed it to Bazzard to do with as he thought best.'

'And its present whereabouts?' enquired Holmes.

'I thought, Mr Holmes,' exclaimed a beaming, blushing, giggling Rosa Tartar, 'that nothing escaped your eagle eye. Why it's *here*, of course! – where it ought to have been years ago, if only Eddy and I had not been so silly!' And, delighted as a schoolgirl, she held out her left hand for our inspection.

Later that night, in a private sitting-room at the Strand
Hotel, Holmes introduced the Dean and his wife to the
plump little woman who had once been Rosa Bud and then,
much to their astonishment, to the bearded French artist
who had once been Edwin Drood. There was much
embracing and weeping between the two ex-pupils of the
Nuns' House seminary and an awkward shaking of hands on
the part of the two men, for Mr Crisparkle gazed at M.
Dupont in a wonderment not untinged with a certain
degree of anger. The artist was speedily prevailed upon to
tell his story once again, however, indicating why (in his
opinion, and also in that of Mr Grewgious) it was
considered impossible for Edwin Drood to proclaim himself alive on his return to England in 1871, and the Dean
and his wife listened to him with a steadily increasing
sympathy and understanding (although Helena pursed her
lips, and had a most curious expression on her face, when
he recalled the occasion on which he had painted her
portrait).

'So the long and the short of it', said the Dean at last, 'is that *nobody* killed Edwin Drood – except, in a sense, M. Dupont – and for establishing that basic fact, Mr Holmes, we shall be everlastingly grateful to you. But are you now in a position to tell us who was responsible for that murderous attack?'

'In one sense,' said Holmes, 'there is no great secret about the matter. It was indeed, as Mr Datchery had surmised, John Jasper who endeavoured to remove Edwin Drood from the face of this earth, in the most literal of fashions.' He paused for a moment and gazed unseeingly at the room's smouldering fire. 'But if we ask ourselves', he continued, '*why* he carried out that terrible assault we are confronted with a strangely complex situation. It is one which I am, indeed, scarcely competent to penetrate. The mind of that man could be likened, perhaps, to a dark cavern in which dreams jostle with reality for supremacy, but it might be more rewarding if we were to think of it, in the first instance, as two separate caverns which share a common entrance and, let us say, a short length of corridor but which thereafter completely diverge. Two totally distinct identities, as it were, inhabit the same body and bear the same name but are unaware of each other's existence.

'Problems of nomenclature, to digress for a moment, have been a curious feature of this investigation. Mr Drood was christened Edwin but was known to his uncle as Ned and to his fiancée as Eddy and he has now acquired – and proposes to retain for evermore, I assume – the name of Edmund. When a poor old woman visited Cloisterham twenty-six years ago she came with the express purpose of warning someone called Ned that his life was in danger, but being unable to track down such a person she passed the time of day with a young man called Edwin, who thoughtfully gave her three shillings and sixpence.'

'I remember her!' exclaimed Drood-Dupont, in great excitement. 'She did indeed manage to warn me, after a fashion, for she told me that Ned was a dangerous name to bear and that it was a threatened name. I remember her very well – she reminded me, in some peculiar fashion, of Jack, for she had a curious seizure while we spoke and it was similar to one which Jack himself had experienced in my presence.'

'The reason being,' said Holmes, 'that both of them were addicted to the drug of opium and it was, indeed, their common craving that brought them together. The Princess Puffa, as she was known in less salubrious circles, was able to keep your uncle – the darker side of him, that is – supplied with the stuff, and he frequently patronized the den over which she presided. You referred to him just now, M. Dupont, as Jack although the rest of us have tended to think of him as John – but Jack is a common enough alternative, as Watson here will readily testify! You yourself, M. Dupont, have lived a double life in the sense of two separate existences, but one of them followed close upon the heels of the other whereas your uncle lived two separate existences simultaneously.

'It may simplify matters,' he continued, 'if we refer to the two personalities as Good Mr Jasper and Bad Mr Jasper. Good Mr Jasper was the gentleman who served as music-master in the town of Cloisterham and choir-master in its Cathedral, who was intelligent and courteous, respected by his associates and revered by his housekeeper. He was renowned, moreover, first and foremost, for being extremely fond of his nephew. Bad Mr Jasper, on the other hand, was the violent character who visited opium dens and (I suspect) other places of ill repute and was the man who terrified Miss Rosa Bud and aroused the contempt of Miss Helena Landless. The passion that dominated Bad Mr Jasper, above all others, was a terrifying hatred and resentment of his nephew. The reasons for this can only be surmised. Edwin, let us say, had been unwittingly responsible for the death of Bad Mr Jasper's sister and had afterwards supplanted him in the affections of Bad Mr Jasper's parents. Finally, and most crucial factor of all, Edwin was betrothed to Miss Rosa Bud, a young lady for whom Bad Mr Jasper had developed an intense desire. These are, as I conceive it, the basic factors that motivated Bad Mr Jasper into carrying out the murder of his nephew. It was Bad Mr Jasper, too, who somehow contrived to make a copy of the key to the Sapsea tomb, concealing it in a place where the Good Mr Jasper would never find it. It was Good Mr Jasper, on the other hand, who devoted himself to the task of bringing the Murderer to justice.'

There was silence for some moments. 'I seem to recall', said M. Dupont at last, in shaken tones, 'Mr Grewgious depicting for me, on one occasion, what he took to be the character of a true lover. He described him, if I remember aright, as "living at once a doubled life and a half life" – a description that seems terribly apt so far as poor Jack is concerned!'

Holmes nodded. 'The transition from one personality to

the other', he said, 'appears to have been strangely abrupt, and where one ceased and the other commenced, and the frequency at which such transitions occurred, are matters which are, I fancy, almost impossible to determine.

'But it would seem that, within a year of the apparent murder of Edwin Drood, the wall that separated the two Mr Jaspers was wearing strangely thin and that possession of their common outer shell (almost equivalent, indeed, to a tomb in its own right!) was taken first by one and then the other in bewildering rotation. It was Bad Mr Jasper who set out for the churchyard, on the Christmas Eve of 1870, but Good Mr Jasper who was in charge at the point when he left the gatehouse – for he failed to bring with him the key that would open the sepulchre. It was Bad Mr Jasper who went unerringly to the Sapsea tomb, and groped for the missing key, but it was Good Mr Jasper who recognized, as he thought, the figure of his nephew's murderer standing there and hurled himself upon Helena Landless. An appalling cataclysm then occurred and it is probable that the two Mr Jaspers fused together in frightful unity for a time. Later, they once again separated, but the wrecked personality whom the outside world knew as Mr Jasper was left, I surmise, with a faint recollection that someone who (in Bad Mr Jasper's eyes) might have been Edwin, had confronted him in what must have seemed a ghastly dream – that the three of them, as it were, had met together once more, for the last time – and thereafter was seeking reassurance and definite confirmation, one way or the other, of what had become of Edwin.

'But these are', he concluded, 'the conjectures of one who

is an amateur in this particular field, which is more properly, indeed, the province of my friend and colleague here, and I put it to you as a working hypothesis and nothing more.'

Those present, myself included, shook their heads in wonder at this strange assessment and, little by little, some further recollections of episodes involving Mr Jasper, tending to confirm the validity of Holmes's diagnosis, were brought to light. A mystery that had endured for a quarter of a century (and had seemed, indeed, destined to endure indefinitely) had finally been cleared up. Wonderment was replaced, after a time, by heartfelt relief among our four companions and it was clear, as their conversation became more general and happier memories were recalled, that the long separation between the Crisparkles and Rosa was at an end and that there would be, henceforth, a close relationship between the two couples. (Just how close would be demonstrated some eighteen months later, when I drew Holmes's attention to an item in the *Telegraph* announcing the engagement of Miss Florence Tartar to Mr Neville Crisparkle.) Refreshments were supplied by the management of the Strand Hotel and it was, indeed, a singularly convivial gathering that finally came to an end as the witching hour approached. 'And pray give our esteemed regards', said Holmes, as we took our leave, 'to Sir Thomas Sapsea.' There was a roar of laughter at this and as the door closed behind us I could almost swear, save for the sheer impossibility of the thing, that I heard the words 'Old Tory Jackass!' escape the lips of the Dean.

When we returned to Baker Street, soon after midnight, we found a further telegram from Stazeby Nanton awaiting us. It bore the news that John Jasper had been found lying in a field within two miles of the asylum, that he was suffering from acute pneumonia and was not expected to survive for more than twenty-four hours.

'There is,' said Holmes, 'one last service you can perform for John Jasper.'

'For that man? Never!' exclaimed the Dean, his normally open countenance darkening.

'For those *two* men,' said Holmes, 'for John Jasper is, as you surely appreciate by this time, a divided personality. It is your duty, Mr Crisparkle, to relieve a soul in torment.'

It was the following morning and we had called once more at the Strand Hotel to inform Mr and Mrs Crisparkle of the life that Jasper had been leading at Stazeby Nanton, including his 'unauthorized departures', and to acquaint them with the latest developments. The Dean swallowed hard but nodded, his momentary intransigence at an end. 'You are quite right, of course,' he said. 'Please continue, Mr Holmes. What do you wish me to do?'

'You are to go without delay to Stazeby Nanton and greet John Jasper as an old friend, as though it were 1870 and you had seen him but recently. Appear unaware of his illness. Tell him afresh that Rosa Bud is about to be married and tell him again the tale of the ring which Edwin Drood had been carrying on his person on the Christmas Eve of 1869. So far as *I* am concerned, that is all you have to do — but it may well be that some additional duties will suggest themselves.'

'A singular request!' exclaimed Mr Crisparkle. 'If the man *is* mortally ill, what is the point of this elaborate pantomime? And if he is *not* ill, he must surely be too weak to escape for a fourth time! Are you expecting a death-bed confession of some kind? I'll go, by all means, but I am not at all clear what useful purpose these tales will serve.'

'Not *tales*, Dean, for Rosa is indeed about to be married, and you can say, if you wish, that she is to wed a middle-aged artist called Edmund Dupont, but humour me in my strange designs. I agree that a death-bed confession is unlikely, although it is something that we would be ill advised to rule out completely, but I wish to try an experiment which may result in an even greater degree of relief — not only for ourselves but also for John Jasper.'

'And you will accompany me?' asked the Dean, compliant but still puzzled.

'No, our business lies elsewhere today — but, most certainly, our thoughts will be with you!'

Like the Dean, I was unable to discern the purpose of this exercise, but I knew better than to seek, at this stage, further information from Holmes. That night we returned to Cloisterham, exactly a year since we had first visited the little town, and commenced our Christmas Eve vigil in the Cathedral churchyard, a short distance from the Sapsea tomb. An hour went by, and then another. The moon rose high, though encompassed with clouds, and the night grew colder. I was finally about to suggest to my companion that we must surely be on a fruitless errand, when the moon broke through and I was aware of his sharp intake of breath.

A figure had appeared. It was that of John Jasper, but of a John Jasper we had never seen before − a young man, smartly attired, adorned with lustrous black hair but with an expression of stern intensity on his countenance. He paused for a moment, produced a large key from beneath his cloak, and then approached the tomb.

'Holmes,' whispered I, 'this is something diabolical!'

But Holmes was not listening. He had stepped out, and now confronted the apparition face to face. 'Edwin Drood is not here,' said Holmes distinctly. 'He has escaped from the grave. He is free of you for ever.'

The apparition's face was convulsed with a terrible expression of rage and there burst from it a frightful cry − or, at least, there surely must have done, had we been granted the ears to hear it. And on that instant it ceased to exist.

And at that moment, so the Dean afterwards informed us, as he kept his parallel vigil at the bedside, there died in the Stazeby Nanton asylum an old man called John Jasper, a look of contentment on his face and at peace, at long last, with the world.

'A fetch,' remarked Holmes, as we took our seats in the train bound for London later that night. 'A ghostly double that appears at the moment of death − a quite well attested phenomenon, although I was doubtful of my ability to raise it.'

He puffed at his pipe, as the train gathered speed, although not so contentedly as I had expected. On my congratulating him on the success of his investigations he shook his head in a restless fashion. 'I do not flatter myself', he said, 'that I have got completely to the bottom of the mysterious double life of John Jasper. I suspect that things happened in Cloisterham, Watson, during the lifetime of that strange man, of which you and I can have no conception. Perhaps, so many years after the event, it is best to let sleeping dogs lie – although in this instance, if we bear in mind the curious tale of Durdles concerning the Christmas Eve of 1868, there *was* a dog that did something in the night-time.' He shook his head yet again. 'A strange business,' he murmured.

'And are you able to shed any light, Holmes, on the identity of Dick Datchery?'

'Oh, that! A commonplace little problem, although its wider implications (if any) are obscure. The stroke across the 't' of the name Datchery had been added, you will recall, as an afterthought – the name that originally appeared in that hat had been Dalchery, an anagram of 'Charley D'. It may be that the gentleman in question thought that he would be rumbled too quickly if he adopted the name Dalchery, but who this gentleman was – and why he should equip himself with the Christian name of Dick and disappear so abruptly (at the midway point of the proceedings, as it were) – is something that I am unable to fathom. But it is not worth, I suspect, any further cogitation on our part.'

175

I was obliged to confess myself similarly baffled. Holmes knocked out his pipe, dismissed the problem as a matter of no great consequence and, as the train rumbled on its way, composed himself for sleep.

Equivalent Measures

This table is designed to do the mathematics for you when you want to divide ingredients in a recipe.

Ingredient to Be Divided	¼ of	⅓ of	½ of	⅔ of
¼ teasp.	pinch*	pinch*	⅛ t	2 pinches*
½ teasp.	⅛ t	2 pinches*	¼ t	⅓ t
1 teasp.	¼ t	⅓ t	½ t	⅔ t
1 tablesp.	¾ t	1 t	1½ t	2 t
2 tablesp.	2¼ t	2 t	1 T + 1½ t	4 t
5 tablesp.	1 T + ¾ t	1 T + 2 t	2 T + 1½ t	3 T + 1 t
7 tablesp.	1 T + 2¼ t	2 T + 1 t	3 T + 1½ t	4 T + 2 t
¼ cup	1 T	1 T + 1 t	2 T	2 T + 2 t
⅓ cup	1 T + 1 t	1 T + 2⅓ t	2 T + 2 t	3 T + 1⅔ t
½ cup	2 T	2 T + 2 t	¼ c	5 T + 1 t
⅔ cup	2 T + 2 t	3 T + 1⅔ t	⅓ c	7 T + ⅓ t
¾ cup	3 T	¼ c	6 T	½ c

*Pinch is as much as can be taken between tip of forefinger and thumb. If ingredient is a liquid, use 4–5 drops per pinch.

Abbreviations:

t = teaspoon   T = tablespoon   c = cup

◆CUTCO◆ Cook Book

By Margaret Mitchell
Director, Home Economics

Published by CUTCO DIVISION
Copyright 1972

Wear-Ever Aluminum, Inc.
Chillicothe, Ohio

*C*ooking, today, is different than ever before. To begin with, social, civic and recreational activities leave less time for cooking. In addition, home entertaining is again becoming very popular. This is true whether it is for two or twenty people. And, due to increased travel and special magazine features, wants and desires for different foods have increased.

The one thing about cooking that I hope never changes, however, is the individual personality of you, the cook. No matter what your tastes and likes are, these can and will be reflected in the type of table you set. We have tried to keep you in mind when we prepared the Cutco Cookbook. Rather than devote the entire book to a variety of recipes, we have attempted to be as comprehensive as possible in helping you plan and prepare interesting menus. Charts and guides were developed to help you buy, prepare and store food products.

A special section on entertaining might give you different and interesting ideas on how to make your next event—large or small—even better. We have even included conveniently located charts on can sizes, equivalent measures and substitutes. The only advice I would like to give you is this: look through the entire cookbook before you use it. This will give you a real good idea what the contents are and how you can best use the cookbook to your personal advantage.

Margaret M. Mitchell
Director, Wear-Ever Kitchens

◆CU̅TCO◆ French Chef's Knife

Directions for Use:

1. Place food to be chopped on chopping board.

2. Grasp handle of FRENCH CHEF'S KNIFE between thumb and forefinger with fingers following curve of handle.

3. Place tip of blade on cutting board at a 45 degree angle with surface of board.

4. Place thumb and fingers of other hand on tip of blade, holding it firmly to the board.

5. Move knife down and up in a rocking motion keeping tip of blade on the board; at the same time move knife back and forth across board in a quarter circle.

Note:

1. When dicing celery, carrots, green beans, etc., place 8–10 pieces lengthwise on chopping board.

2. Hold pieces firmly with left hand.

3. Slowly push pieces under blade of FRENCH CHEF'S KNIFE, at same time move knife down and up in rocking motion.

Uses:

● Chopping greens (cabbage, celery, lettuce, endive, radishes, watercress, romaine) for salads.

● Dicing apples, pears, canned fruits.

● Preparing potatoes for French frying, hashed brown, scalloping.

● Dicing celery, carrots, onions, potatoes, all greens, peppers, green beans, turnips, parsnips, beets.

● Cubing bread for stuffing, puddings.

● Chopping nuts, raisins, candied fruits.

● Dicing cooked meats, fowl.

◆CUTCO◆ Butcher Knife

Directions for Use:

1. Place food to be cut on cutting board.

2. Grasp handle of BUTCHER KNIFE between thumb and forefinger with fingers following curve of handle.

3. Place portion of blade nearest to handle of BUTCHER KNIFE on food to be cut.

4. Pull back on knife at same time pressing downward, using a long firm stroke. Never cut through bone.

Uses:

● Disjointing chicken, turkey, duck.

● Preparing pork loin; preparing spare ribs.

● Cutting short ribs from rib roast.

● Cutting chuck roast, rump, brisket.

● Cutting squash, pumpkin, rutabaga, cabbage, watermelon, sweet potatoes.

● Cutting lobster, crawfish.

● Removing head of fish, scaling fish.

◆CU͞TCO◆ Trimmer

Directions for Use:
1. Grasp handle of the TRIMMER between thumb and forefinger with fingers following curve of handle.
2. The TRIMMER is held in the same position regardless of the task: slicing, cutting, trimming, coring, boning, scraping.

Uses:
● Slicing tomatoes, oranges, cucumbers, hard boiled eggs, green peppers, peaches, pears.

● Cutting and sectioning grapefruit, oranges.

● Making celery curls, carrot sticks, cutting corn from cob.

● Trimming cauliflower, broccoli.

● Peeling pineapple, grapefruit, oranges, melons, eggplant, squash.

● Coring lettuce, green peppers.

● Boning rib roasts, steak, fish, fowl.

● Removing tough outer rind, gristle and excess fat from steaks, chops, roasts; blood vessels from heart, membrane from sweetbreads, kidneys.

● Scraping steaks, roasts, skin of fish before cooking.

● Removing fins from fish; pinfeathers from chickens.

● Gashing edges of steaks, chops, ham slices before broiling.

◆CUTCO◆ Petite Carver

Directions for Use:

1. Place food to be cut or sliced on cutting board.

2. Grasp handle of PETITE CARVER between thumb and forefinger with fingers following curve of handle.

3. Place portion of blade of PETITE CARVER nearest to handle on food to be sliced.

4. Pull back on knife with a long sweeping stroke, at the same time exerting a gentle downward pressure. Never use a sawing motion.

Uses:
- Carving steaks, small roasts, hams.
- Carving chicken, duck, game, small turkeys.
- Halving grapefruit, slicing pineapple, small melons.
- Slicing eggplant, squash.
- Cutting layer cake.

6

◆CUTCO◆ Carving Knife

Directions for Use:

1. Place meat or fowl to be carved on platter.

2. Grasp handle of CARVING KNIFE between thumb and forefinger with fingers following curve of handle.

3. Grasp handle of CARVING FORK in the same manner in other hand; insert tines in meat or fowl.

4. Place portion of blade of CARVING KNIFE nearest to handle on meat or fowl to be carved.

5. Pull back on knife at same time pressing firmly downward to cut through the meat, using a long sweeping stroke rather than a sawing motion.

Uses:

● Carving large roasts with bone such as standing ribs of beef, leg of lamb, pork loin, baked ham.

● Carving turkey, chicken, duck, wild game.

◆CU[CO◆ The Slicer

Directions for Use:

1. Place boneless meat or other food to be sliced on cutting board.

2. Grasp handle of THE SLICER between thumb and forefinger with fingers following curve of the handle.

3. Place portion of blade of THE SLICER nearest to handle on food to be sliced.

4. Pull back on knife with a long sweeping stroke, at the same time exerting gentle downward pressure. Never use a sawing motion.

Uses:

● Slicing rolled roasts, white meat of fowl, ham loaf, ham and other boneless meats.

● Slicing all kinds of cheese, eggplant.

● Cutting bread, sandwiches, layer cake.

● Shredding cabbage, lettuce.

◆CUTCO◆ Carving Fork and Turning Fork

Directions for Use:

Grasp handle of the CARVING FORK or TURNING FORK between thumb and forefinger with fingers following curve of handle.

CARVING FORK:

● Turning large roasts or turkeys.
● Holding large roasts or turkeys in place during carving.

TURNING FORK:

● Turning bacon, liver, steaks, chops, fried chicken, ham, fish.
● Serving meats, fish or fowl.
● Removing beets, turnips, rutabaga, sauerkraut, corn on the cob, spinach from cooking utensil.
● Stirring foods in fry pan while sautéeing.
● Tossing ingredients together, such as, crumb mixtures, meat loaf mixtures.

**TURNING FORK
AND CARVING FORK
TOGETHER:**

● Lifting large roasts or turkey from the roasting pan to the serving platter.

◆CUTCO◆ Paring Knife

Directions for Use:
1. Hold food to be pared firmly in fingers and thumb of left hand.
2. Lay PARING KNIFE across fingers of right hand with cutting edge of knife pointed to the left. Allow fingers to follow the curve of the handle.
3. Place the thumb of the right hand gently against food to be pared.
4. Make a cut through the skin of the food to be pared; continue cutting a thin layer of the skin using the right thumb to rotate the food and guide the blade of the knife. (Reverse procedure if left-handed.)

Uses:
● Paring potatoes, apples, cucumbers, peaches, pears, parsnips, turnips, rutabaga.

● Removing roots and stems from carrots, beets, rhubarb, radishes, spinach, cauliflower, celery.

● Scaling asparagus, trimming Brussels sprouts, scraping carrots.

● Cutting eyes from potatoes and blemishes from fruits.

● Pitting plums, peaches, nectarines, pomegranates.

● Seeding and skinning grapes.

● Making radish roses, celery curls, pickle fans.

● Removing black line from shrimp.

● Removing stomach sac from lobster.

◆CUTCO◆ Spatula Spreader

Directions for Use:
Grasp handle of the SPATULA SPREADER between thumb and fore-finger with fingers following curve of handle.

Uses:
- Icing cakes, cookies.
- Spreading sandwiches with butter and sandwich fillings.
- Cutting sandwiches.
- Cutting and removing bar cookies from pan.
- Spreading tea sandwiches and canapes with filling.
- Perfect for lifting that first piece of pie from the plate.

Kitchen Tool Set

Directions for Use:

1. Grasp handle of each KITCHEN TOOL between thumb and forefinger with fingers following curve of handle.

2. When using MIX-STIR, slide coil back and forth across bottom of pan or bowl for fast, efficient, easy stirring, mixing, beating and blending.

Uses:

● **MIX-STIR**—mixing, beating, stirring, blending and whipping.

● **TURNER**—turning and lifting foods.

● **SOLID SPOON**—serving foods in liquids and sauces.

● **PERFORATED SPOON**—removing foods from liquids; skimming soups and stocks.

● **LADLE**—serving soups, gravies, beverages; pouring batters onto griddle.

● **Mixes and Beats**—gravies, sauces, batters, puddings, fillings, candies, frostings.

● **Stirs and Blends**—flour and sugar into egg whites, sugar into whipped cream, soups and chowders.

● **Whips and Aerates**—milk shakes, eggs, toppings, fruit juices, instant puddings, instant potatoes.

◆CUTCO◆ Kitchen Shears

The KITCHEN SHEARS is the perfect tool for many cutting jobs around the kitchen. They come apart for easy cleaning.

The KITCHEN SHEARS simplifies the job of chopping many foods, such as parsley—merely hold the leaves of a sprig of parsley together and snip. When cutting sticky type foods such as marshmallows, dried and candied fruits—merely dip blades into granulated sugar several times while cutting to prevent food from sticking to them.

Uses:
- Snipping parsley.
- Cutting marshmallows.
- Cutting dried dates, figs, apricots, etc.
- Cutting candied fruits.
- Snipping shell on lobster tails.
- Cutting skin from chicken.
- Snipping top edge of grapefruit and orange halves for decorative effect.

13

◆CU⍑CO◆ Meat Knives

Directions for Use:
Grasp handle of the MEAT KNIFE between thumb and forefinger with fingers following curve of handle.

Uses:
Styled to complement the finest china and silver in your dining room and to be equally at home in your kitchen or at the barbecue grille. For cutting all types of steaks, chops, roasts, fowl.

Wear-Ever Fondue Set

Discover Fondue—the simple, convenient and fashionable way of cooking at the table; an elegant way to entertain friends and family.

A fondue pot is one of the few communal eating containers still in use in the Western world. The Swiss originated the fondue in the early days. Since that time, the fondue has been expanded to include many things.

As the custom continues today, we find people in the United States and other parts of the world gathering around the communal fondue pot enjoying all types of fondues. For instructions on how to prepare fondues, see Fondue Recipes on pages 111–115.

Combo Servers

Cutco's unique COMBO-SERVERS are the perfect companion pieces for elegant dining or an informal buffet table. Their contemporary design and attractive combination of wood, anodized aluminum and ceramic material makes them ideal for the following multi uses . . .

● Individual Steak and Chop Platter

Prepare steaks or chops in the usual manner. Preheat ceramic platters in oven for 10 minutes at 400°–425° F. (or place in oven for 5 minutes while steaks or chops are broiling). Place preheated platters in aluminum cradles; place steaks or chops on platters; garnish and serve. The meat will sizzle when placed on a hot platter. (Note—Platters should be preheated in oven only—never use on range top.)

● Hot Food Server

Preheat ceramic platter in oven about 10 minutes at 350° F. (or 15–20 minutes at 200° F.) just before serving. Place preheated platters in cradles; use for meat and vegetable course. Ideal for serving TV dinners.

● Cold Food Server

For cold dishes and salads, place food on platter and store in refrigerator. When ready to serve, platters may be used alone or placed in aluminum cradle.

● Snack Tray

Fill the aluminum cradle with pretzels, crackers, cookies, nuts or assorted fresh whole fruits.

● Auxiliary Serving Tray

Use ceramic platter alone as a small meat or vegetable dish or for relishes, fruit, salads, etc.

● Buffet Serving

Place COMBO-SERVERS side by side on table. Fill ceramic platters with relishes, cold cuts, cheese, salad, etc. The aluminum cradle alone makes a handsome bread or snack tray.

Menu Suggestions

ENTRÉE	APPETIZER	STARCHY FOOD	OTHER VEGET
Roast Beef	Consommé	Golden Potato Wedges	Stuffed Articl
Delicious Meat Balls	Onion Soup	Cottage Potatoes	Chinese Green Bea
Swiss Steak	Tomato Juice	Au Gratin Potatoes	Browned Ca
Beef Burgundy	Fruit Cup	Parsley Rice	Spinach
Corned Beef	Clear Soup	Boiled Potatoes	Cabbage We
Roast Leg of Veal	Tomato Juice	Mashed Potatoes	Mushroor Baked in F
Wiener Schnitzel	Consommé	Buttered Noodles	Corn Cur
Exotic Greek Stew	Vegetable Juice	Steamed Rice	Buttered B
Sesame Veal	German Lentil Soup	Noodle Pudding	Brussels Spr
Veal Loaf	Creamed Vegetable Soup	Glazed Sweet Potatoes	Creamed O

BREAD	ACCOMPANIMENT	SALAD	DESSERT
Soft Rolls	Celery-Olives	Jellied Vegetable	Rhubarb Custard Pie
French Bread	Tomato Wedges	Lettuce with Roquefort	Coconut Cake
Hard Rolls	Spice Peach	Mixed Green	Canadian Apple Kuchen
Salt Rye Rolls	Celery Hearts	Lettuce and Tomato	Gingerbread with Nutmeg Sauce
Poppyseed Rolls	Mustard Sauce	Head Lettuce	Raspberry Cream Parfait
Muffins	Currant Jelly	Cucumbers in Cream	Deep Dish Apple-Cheese Pie
Hard Rolls	Toasted Almonds	Cole Slaw	Ice Cream
Rye Bread	Pickle Relish	Molded Vegetable	Chocolate Pudding
Biscuits	Celery-Olives	Tossed Green	Hot Fruit Medley
Blueberry Muffins	Tomato Sauce	Head Lettuce	Southern Pecan Pie

Menu Suggestions

ENTRÉE	APPETIZER	STARCHY FOOD	OTHER VEGETABL
Roast Leg of Lamb	Fruit Cup	Baked Potato	Stuffed Zucchini Boat
Maggie's Lamb Chops	Apricot Nectar	Hashed Browned Potatoes	Spanish Green Peas
Lamb Patties	Celery Soup	Home Fries	Eggplant-Tomat Casserole
Grecian Lamb Balls	Tomato Juice	Rice	Baked Asparagu
Fry Pan Kebabs	Vegetable Juice	Toast Points	Souffléed Cauliflower
Baked Ham	Gazpacho	Escalloped Potatoes	Green Beans, Almonds
Glazed Ham Balls	Consommé	Baked Sweet Potato	Buttered Peas
Roast Pork Tenderloin	Split Pea Soup	Wild Rice	Asparagus a la King
County Kerry Pork Chops	Tomato Juice	Lima Beans	Carrots in Sauc
Spareribs	Vegetable Soup	Boiled Potatoes	Sauerkraut

BREAD	ACCOMPANIMENT	SALAD	DESSERT
Bread Sticks	Mint Sauce	Jellied Vegetable	Nut Pie with Ice Cream
Hard Rolls	Currant Jelly	Lettuce and Tomato	Black Bottom Pie
White Bread	Brown Gravy	Cole Slaw	Spice Cake
Corn Sticks	Sweet Pickles	Grated Carrot	Blueberry Buckle
Soft Rolls	Steak Sauce	Head Lettuce	Fruit Curry
Biscuits	Raisin Sauce	Tossed Green	Blueberry Pie
Raisin Bread	Celery Hearts	Cottage Cheese	Danish Apple Cake
Cornbread	Broiled Half Peach	Sauerkraut Relish	Lemon Sherbert
Salt Sticks	Apple Rings	Tossed Green	Strawberry Sundae
Pumpernickel	Spiced Crab Apple	Tomato	Butterscotch Pudding

Menu Suggestions

ENTRÉE	APPETIZER	STARCHY FOOD	OTHER VEGETA
Roast Turkey	Vegetable Juice	Bread Stuffing	Creamed Onic
Cornish Hen	Tomato Soup	Wild Rice Stuffing	Asparagus
Mexican Braised Duck	Jellied Consommé	Sweet Potato Balls	Broccoli
Chicken Mornay	Tomato Juice	Golden Potato Wedges	Spanish Green Peas
Salmon Casserole	Beef Broth	Lima Beans	Buttered Bee
Belgium Baked Codfish	Noodle Soup	Baked Potato	Stewed Tomat
Halibut Supreme	Chicken Soup	French Fried Potatoes	Peas and Carr
Heart	Asparagus Soup	Dublin Cheese and Potato Pie	Stewed Tomat
Kidneys	Orange Sections	Boiled Potatoes	Spinach
Liver	Tomato Bouillon	Creamed Potatoes	Fried Eggplar

BREAD	ACCOMPANIMENT	SALAD	DESSERT
Soft Rolls	Turkey Gravy	Cranberry Orange	Mince Meat Pie
Hard Rolls	Cranberry Sauce	Frozen Fruit	Paradise Pizza
Corn Sticks	Stewed Fruit	Celery Hearts	Cheese Cake
Biscuits	Pickles-Olives	Peach Melba	Rum Balls
Melba Toast	Lemon Cucumber Sauce	Tossed Green	Spice Cake
Hard Rolls	Corn Relish	Head Lettuce	Apple Strudel
Garlic Sticks	Tomato Wedges	Tossed Green	Cardamom Loaf
Soft Rolls	Celery Sticks	Orange Cucumber	Cottage Cheese Cookie Sticks
Toasted Rolls	Spanish Sauce	Confetti Relish Mold	Apple Pie
Corn Muffins	Bacon	Pineapple and Cottage Cheese	Chocolate Cake

Meat Is Important

Down through the centuries meat has always been one of the most universally liked foods. It is the heart of the meal—the center around which the menu is planned.

There is pleasure associated with the eating of foods which have appeal to the eye and to the senses of taste and smell. Meat presents a mouth watering picture, and its aroma and flavor tempt even the most jaded appetite.

Aside from its great palatability, meat is necessary to the daily diet because it is such a rich source of the highest quality protein. It also furnishes valuable amounts of health guarding vitamins and minerals such as iron, copper and phosphorus, which go into the making of good blood and bones.

Meat can always be fitted into the budget because the less tender cuts, which are the least expensive, are just as nutritious as the more expensive tender cuts.

NEED FOR VARIETY

While it is true menus should be planned to give the necessary daily food requirements, it is of equal importance that there is variety.

No article of diet lends itself more readily to variety in menu making than does meat. In addition to the many kinds and cuts of meats, there are hundreds of different methods of preparing and cooking each. Try different cuts, prepare them in different ways and serve a different kind of meat each day.

7 Methods of Cooking Meat and Poultry

There are seven specific methods of cooking meat and poultry. They may be cooked by roasting, broiling, panbroiling, panfrying, deep fat frying, braising and cooking in liquid. The cut of the meat or the age of the poultry usually determines the cooking method.

HOW TO ROAST

Tender cuts of beef, veal, pork or lamb and young birds may be roasted as follows:

1. Season as desired. It makes little difference whether a roast or bird is salted before or after cooking because when done, the salt has penetrated only to a depth of about one half inch.

2. Line shallow roast pan with Alcoa Wrap; place meat, fat side up, poultry breast side up on rack in pan.

3. Add no water; do not cover pan. Roasting is a dry heat method of cooking. If the pan is covered or water added, the meat or poultry will be steamed.

4. Roast at 300°–325° F. to desired degree of doneness.

5. If meat thermometer is used, insert into center of thickest meaty part of meat or bird, being certain end does not touch bone, fat or gristle.

HOW TO BROIL

Tender beef steaks, lamb or mutton chops, sliced ham or bacon, ground beef or lamb, and chicken parts, broiler-fryers or ducklings are suitable for broiling. Fresh pork chops and patties should be broiled slowly to insure complete cooking in center without drying on surface. Veal is seldom broiled.

Steaks and chops should be cut at least one half inch thick. Broiler-fryers and ducklings should be halved or quartered and brushed with butter. To broil:

1. Turn oven regulator to "broil." Preheat as directed by range manufacturer.

2. Line broiler pan with Alcoa Wrap; place rack in pan.

3. Place meat or poultry on rack 2–5 inches from the heat; the thicker the meat the greater the distance from the heat.

4. Broil until top side is thoroughly browned; season with salt, pepper.

5. Turn; brown second side; season; serve at once.

HOW TO PANBROIL

The same tender cuts of meat suitable for broiling may also be pan-broiled.

1. Place FRY PAN or GRIDDLE over medium-high heat.

2. Preheat until a drop of water dances on the surface; add meat; reduce heat to medium. When the cold meat hits the hot pan it will stick but as it cooks and browns it will loosen itself. If juices start to cook out of the meat, increase heat slightly.

3. When meat is brown on one side, turn; brown second side. Do not cover and do not add water.

4. When meat is cooked to desired degree of doneness, season and serve at once.

HOW TO PANFRY

Comparatively thin pieces of tender meat, meat that has been made tender by pounding, cubing, scoring or grinding, or meat that is bread-ed, and broiler-fryers or chicken parts are best suited to panfrying which is the cooking of meat in a small amount of fat. To panfry:

1. Place FRY PAN over medium high heat; add small amount of fat—usually two tablespoons will be sufficient.

2. When fat starts to bubble or sputter, add meat or poultry; cook as in panbroiling.

HOW TO DEEP FAT FRY

This method of cooking is almost always used for breaded meats and poultry or for croquettes made from leftovers. To deep fat fry:

1. Use enough fat or salad oil to cover meat or poultry completely. Allow at least 3 inches between surface of fat and top of kettle so fat will not bubble over during frying.

2. Gradually heat fat to correct temperature using thermometer, or follow manufacturer's instructions when using electric fryer. Temperatures for deep fat frying of meat and poultry range from 300° to 375° F., depending upon the size of the pieces and whether it is cooked or uncooked.

3. Place a few pieces of meat in fry basket; lower slowly into hot fat; cook until brown and thoroughly done.

4. Raise basket; let meat drain; repeat above procedure until all servings are cooked.

5. Fat may be used again if it is strained and stored in refrigerator.

HOW TO BRAISE

Braising, also known as pot roasting, is the method most frequently used for cooking the less tender cuts of meat or older birds. Some tender cuts are also better if braised. These include pork chops, pork steaks, pork cutlets, veal chops, veal steaks, veal cutlets, chicken legs and thighs. To braise:

1. Brown meat on all sides as in panfrying.

2. Season with salt and pepper.

3. Add little or no water; cover tightly.

4. Reduce heat to low; cook until tender, turning frequently. (Meats will cook in their own juices.) May also be done in an oven at 300°–325° F. in covered utensil.

HOW TO COOK IN LIQUID

Stewing, or cooking in liquid, is a method for less tender cuts of meat and stewing chickens. Browning of large cuts or whole birds is optional, however, it does develop flavor and improve color. To cook in liquid:

1. Brown meat on all sides in hot fat.

2. Add just enough water, stock or vegetable juice to cover meat or poultry.

3. Season as desired; cover; simmer until tender.

4. Add vegetables just long enough before serving to be cooked.

5. If the meat is to be served cold, let it cool and then refrigerate in the stock in which it was cooked. The meat is more flavorful and juicy and it will shrink less if cooled in its stock.

Buying Guide for Meat, Poultry

Meat	*Amount to Allow Per Serving (Ready to Cook)*
BEEF, VEAL, PORK, LAMB	Roast, boned and rolled—¼ pound Roast, with bone—½ to ¾ pound Ground—¼ pound Boneless, for stewing—¼ pound For meat stock—3 pounds raw meat to 1 gallon stock
BEEF	Steaks, without bone—⅓ to ½ pound Steaks, with bone—½ to ¾ pound Canned, cooked, boneless meats—3 ounces Short Ribs—½ to 1 pound Chipped dried beef—1½ ounces
VEAL	Chops, thick—⅓ to ½ pound Steak or Cutlet—¼ to ⅓ pound
PORK, FRESH	Chops, thick—½ to ¾ pound Spareribs—¾ to 1 pound Sausage—¼ pound
PORK, SMOKED	Whole ham—½ pound Ham Slice—⅓ pound Bacon—3 to 4 strips (18-20 per pound)
LAMB	Chops, thick—⅓ to ¾ pound Shanks—½ to 1 pound
VARIETY MEATS	Brains—¼ pound Hearts—¼ pound Kidneys—1 veal or lamb kidney, ¼ beef kidney Livers—¼ pound Oxtails—½ to ¾ pound Sweetbreads—¼ Tongue—¼ pound Tripe—¼

POULTRY	Chicken
	  Broiler-Fryer—¼ to ½ bird
	  Roasting, Stewing, Frying—¾ to 1 pound
	Turkey
	  under 12 pounds—¾ to 1 pound
	  over 12 pounds—½ to ¾ pound
	Cornish Hen—1 bird (1 to 1¼ pounds)
	Duckling—¾ to 1 pound
	Goose—1 to 1½ pounds

Beef Chart

Retail Cuts of Beef—Where they come from and how to cook them.

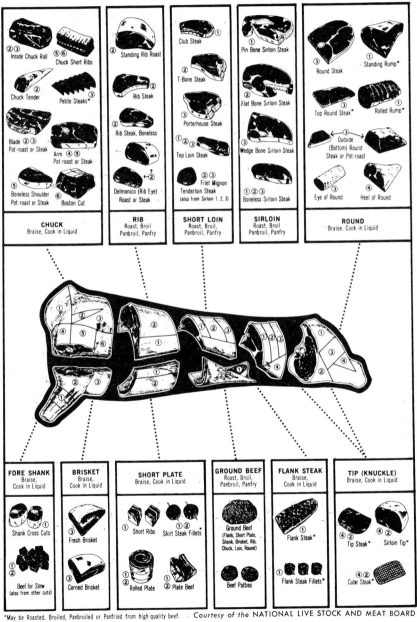

②③ Inside Chuck Roll	⑤⑥ Chuck Short Ribs	② Standing Rib Roast	Club Steak ①	Pin Bone Sirloin Steak ①
Chuck Tender ②	Petite Steaks* ③	Rib Steak ②	T-Bone Steak ②	Flat Bone Sirloin Steak ②
Blade ②③ Pot-roast or Steak	Arm ④⑤ Pot-roast or Steak	Rib Steak, Boneless ②	Porterhouse Steak ③	Wedge Bone Sirloin Steak ③
Boneless Shoulder ⑤ Pot-roast or Steak	Boston Cut ⑥	Delmonico (Rib Eye) Roast or Steak ②→②	Top Loin Steak ①②③	Boneless Sirloin Steak ①②③
			Filet Mignon ②③ Tenderloin Steak (also from Sirloin 1, 2, 3)	

CHUCK
Braise, Cook in Liquid

RIB
Roast, Broil, Panbroil, Panfry

SHORT LOIN
Roast, Broil, Panbroil, Panfry

SIRLOIN
Roast, Broil, Panbroil, Panfry

Round Steak ③ — Standing Rump*

Top Round Steak* ③ — Rolled Rump* ①

Outside (Bottom) Round Steak or Pot-roast

Eye of Round ③ — Heel of Round ④

ROUND
Braise, Cook in Liquid

FORE SHANK
Braise, Cook in Liquid

Shank Cross Cuts ①

Beef for Stew ①② (also from other cuts)

BRISKET
Braise, Cook in Liquid

Fresh Brisket ③

Corned Brisket ③

SHORT PLATE
Braise, Cook in Liquid

Short Ribs ① — Skirt Steak Fillets ①② *

Rolled Plate ①② — Plate Beef ①②

GROUND BEEF
Roast, Broil, Panbroil, Panfry

Ground Beef (Flank, Short Plate, Shank, Brisket, Rib, Chuck, Loin, Round)

Beef Patties

FLANK STEAK
Braise, Cook in Liquid

Flank Steak* ①

Flank Steak Fillets* ①

TIP (KNUCKLE)
Braise, Cook in Liquid

Tip Steak* ④② — Sirloin Tip* ④②

Cube Steak* ④②

*May be Roasted, Broiled, Panbroiled or Panfried from high quality beef. — *Courtesy of the* NATIONAL LIVE STOCK AND MEAT BOARD

Veal Chart

Retail Cuts of Veal—Where they come from and how to cook them.

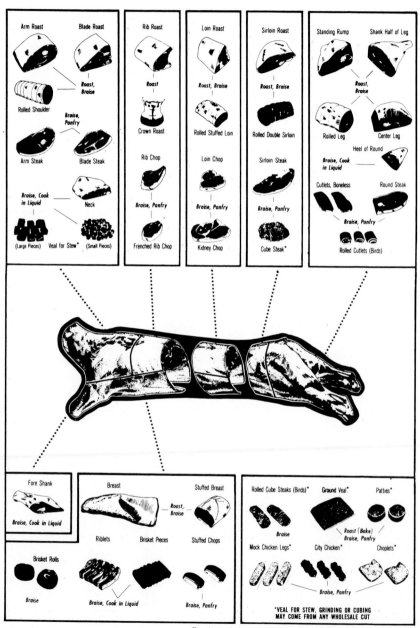

Arm Roast	Blade Roast

Rolled Shoulder

Roast, Braise

Arm Steak · Blade Steak

Braise, Panfry

Braise, Cook in Liquid — Neck

(Large Pieces) Veal for Stew* (Small Pieces)

Rib Roast

Roast

Crown Roast

Rib Chop

Braise, Panfry

Frenched Rib Chop

Loin Roast

Roast, Braise

Rolled Stuffed Loin

Loin Chop

Braise, Panfry

Kidney Chop

Sirloin Roast

Roast, Braise

Rolled Double Sirloin

Sirloin Steak

Braise, Panfry

Cube Steak*

Standing Rump	Shank Half of Leg

Roast, Braise

Rolled Leg · Center Leg

Heel of Round

Braise, Cook in Liquid

Cutlets, Boneless · Round Steak

Braise, Panfry

Rolled Cutlets (Birds)

Fore Shank

Braise, Cook in Liquid

Breast · Stuffed Breast

Roast, Braise

Riblets · Brisket Pieces · Stuffed Chops

Brisket Rolls

Braise

Braise, Cook in Liquid

Braise, Panfry

Rolled Cube Steaks (Birds)* · Ground Veal* · Patties*

Braise

Roast (Bake) Braise, Panfry

Mock Chicken Legs* · City Chicken* · Choplets*

Braise, Panfry

*VEAL FOR STEW, GRINDING OR CUBING MAY COME FROM ANY WHOLESALE CUT

Courtesy of the NATIONAL LIVE STOCK AND MEAT BOARD

Lamb Chart

Retail Cuts of Lamb—Where they come from and how to cook them.

| **SHOULDER** Roast, Broil, Panbroil, Panfry | **NECK** Braise, Cook in Liquid | **RACK** Roast, Broil, Panbroil, Panfry | **LOIN** Roast, Broil, Panbroil, Panfry | **SIRLOIN** Roast, Broil, Panbroil, Panfry | **LEG** Roast, Broil, Panbroil, Panfry |

Square Shoulder — Arm Chop — Rolled Shoulder — Blade Chop — Cushion Shoulder — Saratoga Chops — Cubes for Kabobs* — Neck Slices

Rib Roast — Crown Roast — Rib Chops — Frenched Rib Chops

Loin Roast — Rolled Double Loin — English Chop — Loin Chops

Sirloin Half of Leg — Shank Half of Leg — Leg, Sirloin on — Leg Chop (Steak) — Leg, Sirloin off — Sirloin Roast — Rolled Double Sirloin — Sirloin Chop — Rolled Leg — American Leg — Combination Leg — Center Leg

FORE SHANK Braise, Cook in Liquid

Fore Shank

BREAST Roast, Braise, Broil, Panbroil, Panfry, Cook in Liquid

Breast — Rolled Breast — Stuffed Breast

Riblets — Ribs (for Barbecue, etc.) — Brisket Pieces — Stuffed Chops

HIND SHANK Braise, Cook in Liquid

Hind Shank

GROUND OR CUBED LAMB Roast, Broil, Panbroil, Braise, Cook in Liquid

(Large Pieces) Lamb for Stew* (Small Pieces)

Cube Steak* — Ground Lamb* — Lamburgers*

*LAMB FOR STEW, GRINDING OR CUBING MAY COME FROM ANY WHOLESALE CUT

Courtesy of the NATIONAL LIVE STOCK AND MEAT BOARD

31

Pork Chart

Retail Cuts of Pork—Where they come from and how to cook them.

*These items may come from several areas of the pork side.

Courtesy of the NATIONAL LIVE STOCK AND MEAT BOARD

VARIETY MEATS
AND HOW TO COOK THEM

Brains—Braise, Broil, Panbroil, Panfry, Cook in Liquid

Hearts—Braise, Cook in Liquid

Kidneys
   Beef, Pork—Braise, Cook in Liquid
   Veal, Lamb—Broil, Panbroil, Braise, Cook in Liquid

Livers
   Beef, Pork—Roast, Braise, Panfry
   Veal, Lamb—Broil, Panbroil, Panfry

Oxtails—Braise

Sweetbreads—Braise, Broil, Panbroil, Panfry, Cook in Liquid

Tongues—Cook in Liquid

Tripe—Broil, Panfry

POULTRY SELECTION

Turkey

   Fresh and Frozen
      whole
      halves and quarters
      parts
   Stuffed Frozen Whole
   Frozen Boneless Rolls and
   Roasts
      uncooked
      cooked
   Frozen Breast of Young Turkey

Rock Cornish Game Hen

   Frozen Whole
      unstuffed
      stuffed

Chicken

   Fresh and Frozen
      whole
      halves
      parts
      cut up
   Stuffed Frozen Whole

Capon, Duckling, Goose

   Fresh and Frozen Whole

Care of Meat in the Home

Refrigerator Storage

The meat you buy should be properly cared for to insure its freshness. Keeping it clean and storing it at a low temperature goes a long way in lengthening the storage life of fresh meat and poultry. Remember, as the temperature goes up, storage life goes down.

Of course, you must also exercise some judgment in recognizing spoilage in fresh meat or poultry.

Signs of spoilage:

off-odor   loss of freshness
slippery surface change in color

To insure freshness in meat and poultry, follow these suggestions for storage.

Steaks, Chops, Roasts—Meats wrapped in market paper should be unwrapped, covered loosely with Alcoa Wrap, stored in the coldest part of the refrigerator or in the compartment designed for meat storage. Storage should not exceed three days. Meats prepackaged for self-service may be stored in the refrigerator in the original wrapping if used within one to two days. Loosen ends of wrapping to allow circulation of air.

Ground Meats—They should be handled the same as steaks and chops, however, should be cooked within 24 hours for best eating quality.

Smoked or Cured Meats—Meats such as corned beef, bacon, hams, should be stored in their original wrappers in the refrigerator. For best eating quality, storage time should not exceed one week.

Variety Meats—Since variety meats such as liver, hearts, kidneys, sweetbreads are more perishable than other meats, they should be cooked and served within 24 hours of purchase.

Cooked Meats—They should be cooled, covered or wrapped tightly in Alcoa Wrap, and stored in the coldest part of the refrigerator or in the area designed for meat storage. Cooked meat will keep better if left in larger pieces and not cut until ready to use. Storage time should not exceed 5 days.

Poultry—Fresh poultry should be wrapped loosely to allow some air circulation. It should be stored in the coldest part of the refrigerator or in the compartment designed for meat storage. Storage should not exceed two days. Prompt cooking of the giblets is recommended.

Cooked poultry, stuffing, and any gravy should be cooled promptly, wrapped separately, then stored in coldest part of the refrigerator. Storage should not exceed three days.

Freezer Storage

There are a number of important facts to remember when freezing meats and poultry in the home. Of course, the sooner it is frozen after being purchased, the better.

- Use durable moistureproof wrap such as foil.

- Cover sharp bones with double thickness of foil.

- Wrap tightly and shape foil to surface of meat or poultry to eliminate all air.

- Use drugstore folds.

- Label with name, number of items and/or weight and date.

- Place packages in single layer on coldest part of freezer to freeze as fast as possible.

Steaks, Chops, Roasts—Package steaks and chops according to the number of servings needed. Wrap meats tightly in heavy duty Alcoa Wrap, separating individual servings by a square of foil, and using tight double folds to seal each package. Label packages noting date, cut and weight or number of servings.

Meats, prepackaged as fresh meat for self-service, may be frozen in the original package for short storage, one to two weeks. For long freezer storage, the original package should be overwrapped or rewrapped with Alcoa Wrap.

Recommended Maximum Storage Periods

Fresh Beef —6 to 12 months
Fresh Veal —6 to 9 months
Fresh Lamb—6 to 9 months
Fresh Pork —3 to 6 months

Ground Meats—Shape ground meat into patties or package in portions for loaves or other dishes. Season ground beef after thawing since the flavor of most seasonings is intensified upon freezer storage. Follow wrapping instructions for steaks, chops, roasts.

Recommended Maximum Storage Periods

Ground Beef —3 to 4 months
Ground Veal —3 to 4 months
Ground Lamb—3 to 4 months
Ground Pork —1 to 3 months

Smoked or Cured Meats—Recommended Maximum Storage Periods
Hams, ham slices, sausage . . . . .2 months
Frankfurters, bacon . . . . .1 month
Corned beef . . . . .2 weeks
Luncheon meats, canned hams . . . . .not recommended

Variety Meats—Brains, hearts, kidneys and beef or lamb livers may be frozen uncooked for 3 to 4 months; pork liver for 1 to 2 months.

Sweetbreads should be cooked, cooled, divided into portions before freezing. Storage should not exceed 4 months.

Preferred method for beef and veal tongue is to have them corned or smoked before freezing. Storage should not exceed 4 months.

Cooked Meats—They should be cooked, wrapped tightly in Alcoa Wrap, then frozen for not more than 2 to 3 months.

Poultry—Never freeze an uncooked stuffed bird or a roasted stuffed bird.

Fresh poultry may be frozen and held from 6 to 12 months. Cooked poultry slices or pieces covered with broth or gravy may be held frozen up to 6 months; when not covered with liquid use within 30 days.

Thawing Methods

Meats—Recommended methods:
1. in the refrigerator—in freezer wrapping.
2. at room temperature—in freezer wrapping.
3. during cooking.

Cook frozen roasts at 300° to 325° F., allowing ⅓ to ½ again as long as for cooking thawed roasts.

Poultry—Thawing whole birds at room temperature, unwrapped, is not recommended because of the possibility of contamination.

Recommended methods:
1. in the refrigerator, unwrapped, on a tray—requires 1 to 3 days.
2. with bird still in original water-tight wrap, thaw under cold running water, or immersed in cold water, changing the water frequently—requires 3 to 7 hours, depending on size of bird.

Time-Temperature Charts

ROAST BEEF

300°–325° F. Oven Temperature

Cut	Approx. Weight	Meat Thermometer Reading	Approximate Cooking Time
	Pounds	*Degrees F.*	*Min. per lb.*
Standing Rib	6–8	140 (rare) 160 (med.) 170 (well)	23–25 27–30 32–35
Standing Rib	4–6	140 (rare) 160 (med.) 170 (well)	26–32 34–38 40–42
Rolled Rib	5–7	140 (rare) 160 (med.) 170 (well)	32 38 48
Rib Eye (Delmonico)	4–6	140 (rare) 160 (med.) 170 (well)	18–20 20–22 22–24
Rolled Rump (High Quality)	4–6	150–170	25–30
Sirloin Tip (High Quality)..	3½–4	150–170	35–40

ROAST VEAL

300°–325° F. Oven Temperature

Cut	Approx. Weight	Meat Thermometer Reading	Approximate Cooking Time
	Pounds	*Degrees F.*	*Min. per lb.*
Leg	5–8	170	20–35
Loin	4–6	170	30–35
Rib (Rack)	3–5	170	35–50
Rolled Boned Shoulder	4–6	170	40–45

Time-Temperature Charts

ROAST LAMB
300°–325° F. Oven Temperature

Cut	Approx. Weight	Meat Thermometer Reading	Approximate Cooking Time
	Pounds	*Degrees F.*	*Min. per lb.*
Leg	5–8	175	30–35
Boneless Leg	3–5	175	35–40
Crown Roast	4–6	175	40–45
Rib (Rack)	4–5	175	40–45
Shoulder			
Bone in	4–6	175	30–35
Cushion Style	3–5	175	30–35
Rolled	3–5	175	40–45

FRESH PORK

325°–350° F. Oven Temperature

Cut	Approx. Weight	Meat Thermometer Reading	Approximate Cooking Time
	Pounds	*Degrees F.*	*Min. per lb.*
Loin			
Center	3–5	170	30–35
Half	5–7	170	35–40
End	3–4	170	40–45
Roll	3–5	170	35–45
Boneless Tip	2–4	170	30–35
Crown	4–6	170	35–40
Picnic Shoulder			
Bone in	5–8	185	30–35
Rolled	3–5	170	35–40
Boston Shoulder	4–6	185	45–50
Leg (fresh ham)			
Whole, bone in	10–14	185	30–35
Whole, boneless	7–10	170	30–35
Half, bone in	5–7	170	35–40
Tenderloin	½–1		45–60
Spareribs		Well done	1½–2½ hrs.

Time-Temperature Chart

BAKED HAM
300°–325° F. Oven Temperature

Cut	Approx. Weight	Meat Thermometer Reading	Approximate Cooking Time
	Pounds	*Degrees F.*	*Min. per lb.*
Ham (Cook before eating)			
Whole	10–14	160	18–20
Half	5–7	160	22–25
Shank portion	3–4	160	35–40
Butt portion	3–4	160	35–40
Ham (Fully cooked)			
Whole	10–14	130	10–15
Half	5–7	130	18–24
Loin	3–5	160	25–30
Picnic Shoulder (Cook before eating) ...	5–8	170	35
Picnic Shoulder (Fully cooked)	5–8	130	25–30
Shoulder Roll (Butt)	2–4	170	35
Canadian-Style Bacon	2–4	160	35–40

Time-Temperature Chart

POULTRY
The Tent Method—325° F. Oven Temperature

Type	Purchased Weight	Approx. Total Time—Stuffed*
	Pounds	*Hours*
Chicken	3	2½
	6	4
Capon	6	4
	8	4½
Turkey	8–10	3½–4¼
	10–12	4¼–4¾
	12–14	4¾–5½
	14–16	5½–6
	16–18	6 –6¾
	18–20	6¾–7½
	20–24	7½–8¾
Duck	3	2¼
	6	3¾
Goose	8	4
	11	4½

*NOTE—Times are for stuffed poultry. For unstuffed, deduct 3–5 minutes per pound.

Good to Know: When consulting the Time-Temperature Chart, keep in mind that meat and bone structure of poultry does vary. For this reason, times given are approximate and should serve only as a guide.

Start to test for doneness about one-half hour before bird is supposed to be done. Fowl is done when legs will move up and down freely. Another test is to press the thickest part of the drumstick between the fingers—meat should be soft. Protect fingers with piece of paper towel.

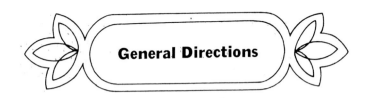

General Directions

ROASTS
Use Tender Cuts of Meat

1. Wipe meat with damp cloth to remove any small loose pieces of bone.
2. If desired, rub meat on all sides with the cut side of a clove of garlic.
3. Sprinkle with salt, pepper.
4. Line shallow roast pan with Alcoa Wrap; place meat fat side up on rack in pan.
5. If using a meat thermometer, insert into thickest part of meat being sure it does not touch bone, gristle or fat.
6. Add no water; do not cover pan.
7. Roast to desired degree of doneness. (See charts on pages 37–38.)

CROWN ROASTS—LAMB OR PORK

1. Have butcher shape two or more rib sections into "crown."
2. Cover ends of bones with cubes of bread or salt pork; remove these before serving.
3. Sprinkle with salt, pepper.
4. Line shallow roast pan with Alcoa Wrap; place meat on rack in pan.
5. Add no water; do not cover pan.
6. Roast to desired degree of doneness. (See charts on page 38.)

POT ROAST
Use beef rump or chuck; beef, veal or lamb shoulder.

4 pounds meat

1. Preheat ROUND ROASTER or 10-inch FRY PAN until a drop of water dances on the surface; add meat; brown thoroughly on all sides.
2. Sprinkle with salt, pepper.
3. Cover; cook over low heat 3–3½ hours or until meat is tender.
4. If desired, potatoes, carrots may be added during last hour of cooking.

BAKED HAM

If packer's wrapper or label contains directions for cooking, they should be followed. If you do not have such directions, use these:

1. Remove outside wrapper but do not remove rind.
2. Line shallow roast pan with Alcoa Wrap; place ham fat side up on rack in pan.
3. If using meat thermometer, insert into thickest part of meat being sure it does not touch bone, gristle or fat.
4. Add no water; do not cover.
5. Bake to desired degree of doneness. (See chart on page 39.)

TO GLAZE BAKED HAM

1. About 45 minutes before baking time is completed, remove ham from oven.
2. Remove rind with TRIMMER or KITCHEN SHEARS.
3. Cut or score fat surface into squares or diamonds using TRIMMER.
4. Stick whole cloves in center of each diamond.
5. Spread or baste with one of the following using SPREADER SPATULA or SOLID SPOON:

¾ cup canned crushed pineapple and ¾ cup brown sugar
Pat brown sugar over ham; drizzle on honey or molasses.

1 cup brown sugar mixed with juice and grated rind of 1 orange
1 cup currant jelly or canned whole cranberry sauce, beaten with fork
1 cup orange, or orange grapefruit marmalade, beaten with fork
1 cup brown sugar combined with 1 cup juice from spiced or pickled peaches
1 cup puréed applesauce, apricots or peaches
1 cup brown sugar mixed with 1 teaspoon dry mustard, 2 tablespoons vinegar, fruit juice or cider or 1 teaspoon horseradish
1 cup brown sugar combined with ¼ cup fine soft bread crumbs
Pat brown sugar over ham; place drained pineapple slices on top and maraschino cherry in center of each slice. Fruit may be fastened to ham with toothpicks and removed before serving. Use pineapple juice for basting.

GENERAL DIRECTIONS FOR TENT METHOD OF
ROASTING POULTRY

1. Line shallow roast pan with Alcoa Wrap.
2. Prepare bird according to recipe.
3. Place bird breast side up on rack in pan.
4. Fold piece of Alcoa Wrap, 4–5 inches longer than fowl, in half lengthwise to form Tent.
5. Place Tent over fowl, pressing one end lightly around drumsticks, other around neck opening.
6. Add no water; occasional basting of bird with drippings in pan is desirable, especially in dry areas; it improves flavor.
7. Roast according to chart on page 40.

ROAST CHICKEN, CAPON OR TURKEY

1. Clean, wash, dry bird.
2. Rub inside with salt, about ⅛ teaspoon per pound.
3. Fill cavity, neck opening with desired stuffing; pack lightly as stuffing swells during cooking.
4. Close cavity with skewers or poultry pins; lace with cord; pull neck skin back over stuffing; fasten with skewers or poultry pins to back of bird.
5. Tie a cord securely around the tail; then tie the ends of the legs to the same cord.
6. Bend tip ends of wings backward so they are held against back of bird.
7. Grease bird thoroughly with soft butter or margarine; sprinkle with salt, pepper.
8. Follow directions for Tent Method Roasting, above.
9. When bird is two-thirds done, cut cord around legs with KITCHEN SHEARS for complete cooking of the thick meated joints.
10. If bird is allowed to set 5–10 minutes after removal from oven it will be easier to carve.

ROAST DUCK

1. Clean, wash, dry duck.
2. Rub inside with salt, allowing ⅛ teaspoon salt per pound.
3. Stuff with desired stuffing or place 1 quartered apple, 1 quartered onion, 2 stalks celery in cavity; remove after roasting.
4. Follow directions for Tent Method Roasting, above.
5. Prick skin using TURNING FORK to allow fat to drain properly; remove excess fat from pan during roasting.

ROAST GOOSE

1. Clean, wash, dry goose.
2. Rub cavity with salt, allowing ⅛ teaspoon salt per pound.
3. To reduce fat: Place goose on rack in shallow open roasting pan lined with Alcoa Wrap; heat 15–20 minutes at 375° F. or until fat runs; dip out fat; repeat until fat ceases to drip.
4. Stuff cavity, neck opening with desired stuffing.
5. Prick fat on back, around tail and skin around wings, legs with TURNING FORK.
6. Follow directions for Tent Method Roasting, page 43.
7. If goose is very fat, remove excess fat from pan during roasting.

CORNISH HEN IN FOIL

| 1 Cornish hen (about 1 pound) | Melted butter or margarine |
| Wild Rice Stuffing | Salt |

1. Clean, wash, dry bird.
2. Stuff bird with Wild Rice Stuffing; tie legs to tail.
3. Brush with melted butter; sprinkle with salt.
4. Place in center of a sheet of Alcoa Wrap; wrap tightly using double folds over top and at each end.
5. Place on rack in shallow pan.
6. Roast 1¼ hours at 425° F.; open foil for last 15 minutes.
7. One–two servings.

ROASTING HALF AND QUARTER TURKEYS

1. Rinse turkey with cold water; pat dry.
2. Skewer skin to meat along cut edges to prevent shrinking from meat during roasting.
3. Tie leg to tail; tie string around breast end to hold wing down.
4. Place turkey on rack in shallow roasting pan, skin side up; brush with butter.
5. Roast at 325° F. as follows:

Pounds	Hours
5–8	2½–3
8–10	3–3½
10–12	3½–4

Broiling Time Tables

BEEF
Turn meat after broiling ½ the time*

Cut	Thickness	Total Approximate Time (Minutes)*		
		Rare	Medium	Well Done
Club Steak	1 inch	8–10	11–13	13–15
	1½ inches	16–18	19–21	21–25
Fillet Mignon	1 inch	5–6	7–8	8–10
(or tenderloin)	1½ inches	8–10	11–13	13–15
	2 inches	11–13	15–17	17–19
Hamburgers	1 inch		8–10	10–12
Porterhouse Steak	1 inch	8–10	11–13	13–15
	1½ inches	16–18	19–21	21–23
	2 inches	27–30	34–36	36–40
Rib Steak	1 inch	8–10	11–13	13–15
Sirloin Steak	1 inch	10–12	12–14	14–16
	1½ inches	18–20	20–24	24–26
	2 inches	34–36	36–40	40–42
T-Bone Steak	1 inch	8–10	11–13	13–15
	1½ inches	16–18	19–21	21–23
	2 inches	27–30	34–36	36–38

LAMB
Turn meat after broiling ½ the time*

Cut	Thickness	TOTAL Approx. Time (Minutes)*
Patties from Ground Lamb	¾ inch	14–15
Rib or Loin Chops	¾–1 inch	12–14
Double Chops	1½ inches	20–25
	2 inches	36–40
English Chops	1½ inches	20–25
	2 inches	36–40
Shoulder Chops	¾–1 inch	14–16
	1½ inches	20–25

Broiling Time Table

PORK

Turn meat after broiling ½ the time*

Cut	Thickness	TOTAL Approx. Time (Minutes)*
SMOKED		
Ham Slice	½ inch	10–12
Ham Slice	1 inch	16–20
Loin Chops	½–¾ inch	15–20
Canadian-Style Bacon		
Sliced	¼ inch	6–8
Sliced	½ inch	8–10
Bacon		4–5
Ham Patties	1 inch	16–20
FRESH**		
Rib or Loin Chops	¾–1 inch	20–25
Shoulder Steaks	½–¾ inch	20–22
Patties	1 inch	20–25

**Fresh pork should be cooked slowly so that it is well done in the center but not dry on the surface.

GENERAL DIRECTIONS

Broiling Steaks, Chops, Ham Slices

1. Preheat broiler as directed by manufacturer.
2. Trim surplus fat from meat using TRIMMER.
3. Slash fat edge of meat at 2-inch intervals to prevent curling.
4. Line broiler pan with Alcoa Wrap; place broiler rack on pan; add meat.
5. Place broiler pan at least 1½ inches below heat—the thicker the meat, the greater the distance.
6. Broil to desired degree of doneness (See Charts on pages 45–46); season as desired.

BROILING MEAT PATTIES

1. Preheat broiler as directed by manufacturer.
2. Line broiler pan with Alcoa Wrap; place broiler rack on pan; add meat.
3. Place broiler pan at least 1½ inches below heat—the thicker the patties, the greater the distance.
4. Broil according to directions in charts on page 45; season as desired.

BROILING BACON

1. Preheat broiler as directed by manufacturer.
2. Line broiler pan with Alcoa Wrap; place broiler rack on pan; add bacon strips or slices.
3. Place broiler pan 3–3½ inches below heat; broil according to directions in chart on page 46.

BROILING CHICKEN PIECES

1. Preheat broiler as directed by manufacturer.
2. Line broiler pan with Alcoa Wrap; place broiler rack on pan; add chicken pieces, skin side down.
3. Brush well with melted butter or margarine.
4. Place broiler rack 3–3½ inches from heat; broil slowly so chicken just begins to brown at end of 10–12 minutes.
5. Turn; brush with melted butter every 10 minutes as browning increases.
6. Broil until tender and evenly browned—about 30 to 45 minutes depending upon size.

PANBROILING MEATS

1. Prepare steaks, chops, ham slices as directed for broiling; shape meat patties as desired.
2. Preheat FRY PAN or GRIDDLE over medium-high heat until a drop of water dances on the surface.
3. Drop meat into FRY PAN or GRIDDLE; brown thoroughly on one side.
4. Turn meat with TURNING FORK or TURNER SPATULA; brown second side; season as desired.

Note: When cold meat hits the hot pan or griddle, it will stick but as it browns it will loosen itself. Heat may be reduced to medium after meat has been added, however, if juices start to cook out of meat, increase heat slightly.

BRAISING PORK CHOPS

1. Prepare chops as directed for broiling.
2. Preheat FRY PAN over medium-high heat until a drop of water dances on the surface.
3. Add chops; reduce heat to medium; brown slowly on both sides.
4. Cover; cook over low heat 35–40 minutes or until tender.

PANBROILING BACON

1. Place bacon strips in cold FRY PAN or GRIDDLE.
2. Place over medium low heat; cook slowly, turning once with TURNING FORK.
3. For crisp bacon, drain off fat as it accumulates.

FRESH PORK SAUSAGES

1. Place links or patties in cold FRY PAN; add small amount of water; cover; bring to boil.
2. Simmer 5–10 minutes depending upon thickness; drain.
3. Cook uncovered over medium heat until golden brown and all pink has disappeared.
4. Drain off fat as it accumulates.

FRYING CHICKEN

1. Wash; clean chicken; cut into desired serving pieces using BUTCHER KNIFE and KITCHEN SHEARS.
2. For each pound of chicken use one of the following coatings:
   a. 2 tablespoons cornmeal, 2 tablespoons flour, ½ teaspoon salt, ⅛ teaspoon pepper, 1 teaspoon paprika blended together in paper bag.
   b. ¼ cup flour, ½ teaspoon salt, ⅛ teaspoon pepper, 1 teaspoon paprika blended together in paper bag.
3. Drop chicken pieces into bag; shake until pieces are coated.
4. Brown thoroughly on all sides in melted fat (part butter, part shortening or cooking oil) in 10-inch FRY PAN or ROUND ROASTER.
5. Cover; cook over low heat 35–60 minutes or until tender—time depends on size of chicken pieces.

OVEN FRYING CHICKEN

1. Prepare chicken for cooking as directed in Fried Chicken.
2. Place chicken pieces in shallow bake pan lined with Alcoa Wrap.
3. Melt ¼ pound butter, ½ cup shortening in 1-quart SAUCE PAN.
4. Spoon some butter mixture over chicken using SOLID SPOON; place in 350° F. oven.
5. Bake 1 hour or until tender, basting every 15 minutes with butter mixture.

BEEF HEART

1 5-pound beef heart

1. With PARING KNIFE remove fat, veins, arteries from cleaned heart.
2. Sauté sliced onion rings in ROUND ROASTER until lightly browned.
3. Add heart; brown thoroughly on all sides.
4. Add salt, pepper; cover with water.
5. Cover; simmer 2½–3 hours or until tender.
6. Thicken cooking liquid for gravy if desired.

SIMMERED BRAINS

1. Wash beef, veal, lamb or pork brains in cold water.
2. Soak ½ hour in salted water, allowing 1 tablespoon salt per quart water.
3. Remove membrane using TRIMMER.
4. Place in SAUCE PAN; add water to cover, 1 teaspoon salt, 1 tablespoon lemon juice or vinegar for each quart water.
5. Cover; simmer over low heat 15–20 minutes.
6. Drain; drop into cold water; drain again.
7. Serve with Mushroom, Tomato or Butter Sauce.
8. Allow four servings per pound.

SAUTEED BRAINS

1. Prepare Simmered Brains.
2. Dip into beaten egg, then fine dry crumbs or corn meal.
3. Sauté in butter in FRY PAN until brown.

BROILED BRAINS

1. Prepare Simmered Brains.
2. Brush with melted butter.
3. Broil 10–15 minutes, turning occasionally using TURNER SPATULA.
4. Serve with lemon wedges, broiled bacon, broiled tomatoes or Beet and Horseradish Relish.

LIVER AND ONIONS

1. Roll slices of liver in seasoned flour.
2. Sauté in butter until brown on both sides.
3. Sauté thinly sliced onion rings in another FRY PAN until golden brown.
4. Place liver on platter; turn onion rings into pan in which liver was cooked. Add 2 tablespoons hot water; stir using MIX-STIR to loosen sediment in pan; mix; pour over liver.

FRESH TONGUE

1 3–5 pound tongue

1. Wash tongue; place in ROUND ROASTER; cover with water; add seasonings.
2. Cover; bring to boil; simmer over low heat until tender, allowing about 50 minutes per pound.
3. Let tongue cool in cooking liquid.
4. Remove skin with TRIMMER; cut off thick end where small bones are apparent.
5. To serve cold: chill, slice thin using TRIMMER.
   To serve hot: reheat; serve with horseradish, barbecue or mustard sauces.

BEEF KIDNEY

1. Cut kidney crosswise into ¼-inch slices using TRIMMER.
2. Remove all fat, gristle; cut into small pieces.
3. Soak in cold water ½ hour; drain.
4. Cover with six cups boiling water; simmer uncovered 1 hour.
5. Cover; simmer ½ hour longer or until tender.
6. Thicken cooking liquid; season to taste.
7. Serve on toast.

BROILED KIDNEYS

1. Wash kidneys; cut in half with TRIMMER; remove fat, tubes with KITCHEN SHEARS.
2. Brush with melted butter or French dressing.
3. Sprinkle with salt, pepper.
4. Broil 5–7 minutes on each side.
5. Serve on toast with melted butter to which a little lemon juice has been added.

SWEETBREADS

1. Wash in cold water; let stand in cold water 20 minutes; drain.
2. Plunge into 2 quarts boiling water to which 2 tablespoons vinegar, 2 teaspoons salt have been added.
3. Cover; simmer 30 minutes.
4. Lift out with PERFORATED SPOON; plunge again into cold water.
5. Drain; remove fat, connecting tissues, fine membrane with TRIMMER; dry.
6. Split into halves lengthwise if very thick.
7. Serve Broiled or Creamed.

   To Broil:
   a. Brush with melted butter; sprinkle with salt, pepper.
   b. Broil until golden brown, about 5–7 minutes per side.
   c. Serve on toast.

   To Cream:
   a. Combine with medium white sauce to which 1½ teaspoons white wine, sherry or lemon juice have been added.
   b. Serve in patty shells.

TRIPE

1. Wash tripe; place in ROUND ROASTER; cover with water; add salt.
2. Cover; simmer over low heat 1 hour.
3. Drain; cut into serving pieces using TRIMMER.
4. Dip into beaten egg, then into dry bread crumbs.
5. Sauté in melted butter or margarine until nicely browned on both sides.

SAUTEED CHICKEN LIVERS

1. Wash; cut livers into halves with TRIMMER.
2. Sauté in butter or margarine until lightly browned.
3. Season with salt, pepper; stir in dairy sour cream if desired (1 cup per ½ pound livers).
4. Serve over cooked rice or on toast.

Entertaining

Successful entertaining is a highly creative exercise in pleasing other people. It is an art worth mastering, and it is fun.

Most of us enjoy having the company of others. The possibilities for party-giving are unlimited—brunches, luncheons, dinners, afternoon teas, morning coffees, Sunday night suppers, engagements, showers, anniversaries, teen-age parties, desserts and coffee, cocktail parties, barbecues.

When we think of entertaining and of having a party, we automatically think of food—what to serve? Here again, the possibilities are unlimited. The recipes on the following pages will be of great help to you in making that decision easier.

How to serve also requires some decision making, but can be a relatively simple task. The two main categories for the serving of food are the Sit-Down Meal and the Buffet Service. Both of these events may be as formal or as simple as you wish to make them.

The Sit-Down Meal

For the Sit-Down Meal, the food may be served in one of the following ways:

- *Food may be served at the table by the host or hostess.*

- *Food may be placed in serving dishes on the table and passed from person to person.*

- *Food may be placed on heated dinner plates in the kitchen and placed before each guest at the table.*

This Sit-Down Service is usually reserved for the heartier type meals such as brunches, luncheons, dinners, suppers, barbecues, although it can be effectively used for the dessert and coffee, showers, and so on.

The COMBO-SERVERS are the perfect companion pieces for the Sit-Down Meal. They can be preheated and used to serve each guest the meat and vegetable course attractively and piping hot. They can also be chilled and used to serve the cold meat and salad course. Alone, the ceramic platters make attractive service pieces for relishes and other side dishes.

The Buffet Service

The Buffet is a form of entertaining that is readily adaptable to a variety of occasions, and is flexible as to the number of guests. It can be as simple as a tray of sweet rolls and a pot of coffee placed on the coffee table in the living room for that morning coffee break with the neighbors. Or, a buffet can be developed using several trays of tiny sandwiches and cakes with a tea service arranged on the dining room table for that afternoon tea for the Women's Club.

The cocktail party is a natural for Buffet service. The more substantial hors d'oeuvres may be arranged attractively on the dining room table, while the lighter snacks, in small bowls and trays, may be conveniently placed around the entire entertaining area on smaller tables.

The Buffet may be expanded considerably so that it can be used to serve the more elaborate brunches, lunches, suppers and even a large dinner party. Regardless of the size or type of Buffet, the food should be arranged in appropriate serving order and the table itself be placed so the guests are able to move around it and reach the food easily. The table should be decorated with an attractive cloth and centerpiece, with plates, napkins and flatware conveniently placed prior to the arrival of guests. The dessert and coffee may be arranged on another smaller table in the dining area, or may be held in the kitchen and brought in at the appropriate time.

As with the Sit-Down Meal, the COMBO-SERVERS are a perfect addition to the Buffet. They can be used side by side in a line to make an attractive display for a variety of foods. Or the ceramic platters and cradles can be used separately for relishes, cold cuts, cheese, and for pretzels, crackers, cookies and breads.

When using the FONDUE SET, the COMBO-SERVERS can be used effectively:

- *to display the bread cubes for the cheese fondues.*

- *to display the meat cubes, slices or balls for the meat fondues.*

- *to display the dunkables for the dessert fondues.*

It is also important to plan the seating of the guests. If the living room or recreation room is to be used, traytables can be effectively used to augment available space on coffee or end tables. If you want to use card tables, it is necessary to have them preset with cloth, napkins, silverware and glasses. In good weather, a patio or terrace can be a most attractive setting for the party.

Now the stage is set for an adventure in good eating, whether it be with the family or entertaining guests.

Appetizers

Stuffed Mushrooms (France)

1 pound large fresh mushrooms
6 green onions
¼ cup butter or margarine
1 cup soft bread crumbs
1 cup canned crabmeat, flaked
1 teaspoon salt
⅛ teaspoon pepper
1 tablespoon ketchup
1 tablespoon lemon juice
3 strips of bacon
½ cup cream

1. Wash mushrooms; remove stems using PARING KNIFE; finely chop stems using FRENCH CHEF'S KNIFE.
2. Mince green onions using FRENCH CHEF'S KNIFE.
3. Melt butter in 8-inch FRY PAN over medium heat; add chopped mushroom stems, minced onions; sauté 5 minutes stirring with TURNING FORK.
4. Stir in bread crumbs, crabmeat; cook 2 minutes.
5. Add salt, pepper, ketchup, lemon juice; stir until well blended.
6. Stuff mushroom cups with above mixture; place in lightly greased bake pan.
7. Cut each strip of bacon in quarters using KITCHEN SHEARS; place two quarters criss-cross fashion on top of stuffing; fasten with toothpicks.
8. Pour cream around mushrooms.
9. Bake 25 minutes at 400° F.
10. Serve immediately.

Barbecued Spareribs

3 pounds spareribs
1 large onion
1 14-ounce bottle ketchup (1¼ cups)
¼ cup Worcestershire sauce
1 cup water
1 teaspoon salt
1 teaspoon chili powder

1. Cut spareribs into serving pieces using BUTCHER KNIFE.
2. Peel onion using PARING KNIFE; cut in thin slices using TRIMMER.
3. Lay spareribs in shallow 13 x 9-inch roast pan; lay onion slices on ribs.
4. Roast 30 minutes at 425° F.; discard onion slices.
5. In 2-quart SAUCE PAN, combine ketchup, Worcestershire sauce, water, salt, chili powder; bring to a boil, stirring with MIX-STIR.
6. Pour ¼ of barbecue sauce over ribs; roast 1 hour at 375° F., basting ribs every 15 minutes with remaining sauce using SOLID SPOON.
7. Eight servings.

55

Appetizers

German Ham Patties

1 medium onion
2 cups canned sauerkraut, well
    drained
1 tablespoon vegetable oil
1 pound ground ham
1 tablespoon prepared mustard
2 eggs, well beaten
1 teaspoon Worcestershire sauce
¼ cup flour
3 eggs well beaten
¾ cup packaged corn flake crumbs
4 tablespoons butter or margarine

1. Peel onion using PARING KNIFE; finely chop using FRENCH CHEF'S KNIFE.

2. Chop sauerkraut using FRENCH CHEF'S KNIFE.

3. Heat oil in 10-inch FRY PAN over medium-high heat; sauté onion 5 minutes stirring with TURNING FORK; remove onions with PERFORATED SPOON.

4. In a large bowl, combine onion, sauerkraut, ham, mustard, eggs, Worcestershire sauce, flour; mix well using TURNING FORK.

5. Cook 10 minutes in FRY PAN over medium-high heat, stirring frequently; cool.

6. Form mixture into small patties (1½ inches in diameter, ¼ inch thick); dip in beaten egg; coat with crumbs.

7. Melt butter in 10-inch FRY PAN over medium heat; fry patties, 10-12 at a time, until well browned on both sides; turn and remove with TURNER.

8. Three–four dozen patties.

Broiled Steak Rolls (Japan)

1 pound sirloin steak, ¼-inch thick
4 green onions
⅓ cup sherry wine
¼ cup Japanese soy sauce
2 teaspoons sugar

1. Cut steak in four sections using BUTCHER KNIFE; pound each section with edge of saucer or meat pounder until ⅛ inch thick.

2. Cut each section in half lengthwise using BUTCHER KNIFE.

3. Cut onions in half lengthwise using PARING KNIFE.

4. Lay onion strips on steak; starting with longest side, roll onion in steak; fasten with toothpick.

5. Combine sherry, soy sauce, sugar in bowl to make Teriyaki Sauce.

6. Brush steak rolls generously with Teriyaki Sauce; place on broiler pan.

7. Broil 3 minutes; turn using TURNER SPATULA; brush with sauce; broil 1 minute.

8. Remove toothpicks; cut in 1-inch-long pieces using TRIMMER.

9. Makes about 2½ dozen hors d'oeuvres.

Gazpacho (Spain)

1 cucumber
2 green peppers
3 stalks celery
1 medium onion
3 hard cooked eggs
3 slices toast
6 tomatoes
1 cup canned tomato juice
1 10-ounce can condensed
   beef consommé
3 tablespoons wine vinegar
1 teaspoon salt

1. Pare cucumber using PARING KNIFE; quarter cucumber lengthwise; remove seeds using TRIMMER; cut in small cubes using FRENCH CHEF'S KNIFE.

2. Seed green peppers using TRIMMER; cut in cubes using FRENCH CHEF'S KNIFE.

3. Dice celery using FRENCH CHEF'S KNIFE.

4. Peel onion using PARING KNIFE; coarsely chop using FRENCH CHEF'S KNIFE.

5. Cube hard cooked eggs, toast using TRIMMER.

6. Place cucumber, green pepper, celery, onion, eggs, toast cubes in individual serving dishes; reserve for serving.

7. Purée tomatoes; combine puréed tomatoes, tomato juice, consommé, vinegar, salt, in bowl; blend using MIX-STIR.

8. Cover with aluminum foil; refrigerate several hours.

9. Serve each guest a bowl of soup to which he adds the accompaniments of his choice.

10. Four–six servings.

Creamed Vegetable Soup (Finland)

1 large carrot
1 stalk celery
1 medium potato
6 green onions
1 cup cauliflower buds
1 cup frozen peas, thawed
1 cup frozen green beans, thawed
3 cups water
2 teaspoons salt
2 tablespoons butter or margarine
1½ tablespoons flour
1 cup light cream
¾ cup milk
2 tablespoons chopped parsley
⅛ teaspoon thyme
   Dash white pepper
1 cup cooked, cleaned shrimp

1. Chop carrot, celery using FRENCH CHEF'S KNIFE.

2. Pare potato using PARING KNIFE; cut in small cubes using FRENCH CHEF'S KNIFE.

3. Slice onions using TRIMMER.

4. Combine carrot, celery, potato, onion, cauliflower, peas, beans, water, salt in 3-quart SAUCE PAN; bring to a boil; boil slowly, uncovered, 10 minutes.

5. Drain vegetables, reserving stock; set vegetables aside.

6. Melt butter in 3-quart SAUCE PAN; blend in flour using MIX-STIR; cook 1 minute, stirring constantly.

7. Gradually stir in vegetable stock, cream, milk; cook until thickened, stirring constantly.

8. Add vegetables, parsley, thyme, pepper, shrimp; cook until vegetables, shrimp are hot, stirring frequently; add more milk if soup is too thick.

9. Six–eight servings.

Note: This is a popular summer soup in Finland. It may be served for lunch or for a late supper.

Salads

Confetti Relish Mold

- 2 medium cucumbers
- 1 green pepper
- 6 green onions
- 12 radishes
- 8 beef bouillon cubes
- 4 3-ounce packages lemon flavored gelatin
- 1 quart boiling water
- ½ cup tarragon vinegar
- 2 teaspoons salt
- 1 quart dairy sour cream

1. Mince cucumbers using FRENCH CHEF'S KNIFE; do not pare.
2. Seed green pepper using TRIMMER; mince using FRENCH CHEF'S KNIFE.
3. Mince onions using FRENCH CHEF'S KNIFE.
4. Cut radishes in very thin slices using TRIMMER.
5. Dissolve bouillon cubes, gelatin in boiling water; add vinegar, salt; chill until partially set.
6. Add sour cream; blend thoroughly.
7. Add cucumber, green pepper, onions, radishes; blend.
8. Pour into 3-quart mold; chill until firm.
9. Fourteen–eighteen servings.

Frozen Fruit Salad

- 2 peaches, fresh (or 4 canned peach halves)
- 1 cup fresh strawberries
- 2 ounces shelled walnuts
- 8 maraschino cherries
- 1 pint dairy sour cream
- ¾ cup sugar
- 2 tablespoons lemon juice
- ⅛ teaspoon salt
- 1 9-ounce can crushed pineapple, drained
- ½ cup blackberries

1. Peel peaches using PARING KNIFE; cut in half; remove seed; slice using TRIMMER.
2. Hull strawberries; cut in half using PARING KNIFE.
3. Chop walnuts using FRENCH CHEF'S KNIFE.
4. Cut cherries in half using PARING KNIFE.
5. Combine sour cream, sugar, lemon juice, salt using MIX-STIR; blend well.
6. Fold in peaches, strawberries, walnuts, cherries, crushed pineapple, blackberries.
7. Pour into 9-inch or 8-inch square bake pan; freeze until firm.
8. Nine servings.

Salads

Orange-Cucumber Salad (Mexico)

---

4 oranges
1 cucumber
½ green pepper
½ onion
   Lettuce
   Vinegar and oil dressing

1. Peel oranges using TRIMMER; cut in ¼-inch slices using TRIMMER.
2. Score cucumber with fork (do not peel); cut in thin slices using TRIMMER.
3. Seed green pepper using TRIMMER; chop finely using FRENCH CHEF'S KNIFE.
4. Peel onion using PARING KNIFE; chop finely using FRENCH CHEF'S KNIFE.
5. Arrange orange slices, cucumber slices on bed of lettuce.
6. Sprinkle chopped green pepper, onion over oranges.
7. Serve with salad dressing.
8. Six servings.

Austrian Cucumber Salad

---

1 cucumber
1 medium onion
½ teaspoon salt
2 tablespoons vegetable oil
2 tablespoons white vinegar
⅓ cup sour cream
   Paprika
   Parsley, fresh

1. Peel cucumber, onion using PARING KNIFE; cut in thin slices using TRIMMER.
2. In small bowl combine cucumber, onion slices; sprinkle with salt.
3. Combine oil, vinegar; mix until blended; pour over cucumber, onion slices; cover; marinate 2 hours; drain well.

4. Add sour cream to cucumbers, onions; blend well; cover; chill 2 hours.
5. Serve on lettuce; sprinkle with paprika; garnish with chopped parsley.
6. Six servings.

Exotic Chicken Salad

---

2 whole cooked chicken breasts
3 stalks celery
1 large green pepper
2 cups grapes
2 cups canned pineapple chunks, drained
2 green onions
1 cup slivered almonds, toasted
⅔ cup mayonnaise
¼ cup light cream
1 teaspoon salt
⅛ teaspoon pepper
2 tablespoons vinegar

1. Cut chicken in large chunks using FRENCH CHEF'S KNIFE.
2. Slice celery diagonally using FRENCH CHEF'S KNIFE.
3. Seed green pepper using TRIMMER; mince using FRENCH CHEF'S KNIFE.
4. Cut grapes in half; seed using PARING KNIFE.
5. Cut pineapple chunks in half using PARING KNIFE.
6. Mince green onions using FRENCH CHEF'S KNIFE.
7. Combine chicken, celery, green pepper, grapes, pineapple, almonds in large bowl.
8. Combine onions, mayonnaise, cream, salt, pepper, vinegar; blend thoroughly.
9. Chill both mixtures separately.
10. Just before serving, blend together, tossing lightly; serve in lettuce cups.
11. Eight–ten servings.

Belgian Green Bean Salad

    1 pound fresh green beans
    2 large potatoes
    4 green onions
    2 tablespoons peanut oil
 1¼ cup canned beef broth
    6 slices bacon
    3 tablespoons vinegar
  ¼ teaspoon thyme
  ⅛ teaspoon pepper

1. Clean beans; cut in 2-inch lengths using FRENCH CHEF'S KNIFE.
2. Pare potatoes using PARING KNIFE; cut into 1-inch cubes using FRENCH CHEF'S KNIFE.
3. Mince green onions using FRENCH CHEF'S KNIFE.
4. Heat oil in 10-inch FRY PAN over medium-high heat; add beans; sauté for 2 minutes, stirring constantly using TURNING FORK.
5. Add broth; cover; simmer 15 minutes.
6. Add potatoes; cover; simmer 30 minutes; drain.
7. In 8-inch FRY PAN, fry bacon until crisp; remove with TURNING FORK; drain on paper towels; reserve ⅓ cup bacon fat; crumble bacon.
8. Combine bacon fat, minced onions, vinegar, thyme, pepper; pour over beans, potatoes; toss until well blended.
9. Sprinkle crumbled bacon over each serving.
10. Six–eight servings.

Sauerkraut Relish Salad

    2 stalks celery
    1 canned pimiento
  ½ medium green pepper
    1 medium onion
    1 14-ounce can sauerkraut,
        well drained
  ⅓ cup vinegar
    3 tablespoons salad oil
  ⅔ cup sugar
  ¼ cup water

1. Cut celery in diagonal slices using FRENCH CHEF'S KNIFE.
2. Chop pimiento using FRENCH CHEF'S KNIFE.
3. Seed green pepper using TRIMMER; chop using FRENCH CHEF'S KNIFE.
4. Peel onion using PARING KNIFE; cut in thin slices using TRIMMER; separate into rings.
5. Combine all ingredients in bowl; mix thoroughly using TURNING FORK.
6. Cover with Alcoa Wrap; (do not press foil onto mixture); refrigerate overnight.
7. Serve in lettuce cup.
8. Six–eight servings.

Note: Also excellent as a relish with sandwiches, meats.

Fresh Mushroom Salad (Finland)

    1 pound fresh mushrooms
    6 green onions
    2 cups water
    2 tablespoons lemon juice
  ½ cup dairy sour cream
  ¼ teaspoon sugar
    1 teaspoon salt
      Dash white pepper

1. Wash, slice mushrooms using TRIMMER.
2. Mince onion using FRENCH CHEF'S KNIFE.
3. Combine water, lemon juice in 2-quart SAUCE PAN; bring to a boil.
4. Add mushrooms; cover; simmer 3 minutes; drain on paper towels until cool.
5. In a small bowl, combine onions, sour cream, sugar, salt, pepper; mix well.
6. Add mushrooms to sour cream; blend well.
7. Serve immediately on lettuce.
8. Five–six servings.

Salads

Senate Salad

½ pound cooked shrimp
1 9-ounce package frozen
　artichoke hearts
1 grapefruit
2 medium tomatoes
2 stalks celery
¼ pound Cheddar cheese
10 ripe olives
6 green onions
2 quarts salad greens (romaine,
　leaf lettuce, escarole, cabbage,
　water cress)
1 3-ounce package lemon gelatin
1 teaspoon salt
½ teaspoon garlic salt
⅛ teaspoon pepper
1½ cups hot water
1 tablespoon vinegar
1 cup Italian dressing

1. Cut shrimp in 1-inch pieces using TRIMMER.
2. Cook artichoke hearts as directed on package; drain; cut each heart in half using TRIMMER.
3. Peel grapefruit; section using TRIMMER.
4. Dip tomato into boiling water for about 1 minute using TURNING FORK; peel, core using PARING KNIFE; dice using FRENCH CHEF'S KNIFE.
5. Cut celery in thin diagonal slices using FRENCH CHEF'S KNIFE.
6. Cut cheese in thin strips using TRIMMER.
7. Slice olives using PARING KNIFE.
8. Chop green onions, salad greens using FRENCH CHEF'S KNIFE.
9. Combine gelatin, salt, garlic salt, pepper; add hot water; stir until gelatin dissolves using MIX-STIR; add vinegar.
10. Pour into 9 x 5-inch loaf pan; chill until slightly thickened.
11. Press shrimp pieces, one inch apart, into thickened gelatin; chill until firm.
12. Combine artichoke hearts, Italian dressing; chill.
13. Combine grapefruit, tomatoes, celery, cheese, olives, onions, greens; toss together lightly in salad bowl; chill.
14. Just before serving, toss artichoke hearts, dressing with other ingredients.
15. Serve in lettuce cups; arrange shrimp squares on top.
16. Four large servings.

Swedish Herring Salad

2 salted herring
4 medium red onions
4 medium boiled potatoes
8 tart apples
6 medium cooked beets
3 small gherkin pickles
⅔ cup white vinegar
½ cup sugar
2 tablespoons capers
　Pepper
　Dairy sour cream
　Hard cooked eggs

1. Soak herring overnight in cold water; drain; split; skin; remove bone using TRIMMER; dice using FRENCH CHEF'S KNIFE.
2. Peel onions using PARING KNIFE; dice using FRENCH CHEF'S KNIFE.
3. Pare potatoes using PARING KNIFE; dice using FRENCH CHEF'S KNIFE.
4. Pare apples using PARING KNIFE; quarter; core using TRIMMER; dice using FRENCH CHEF'S KNIFE.
5. Dice cooked beets, gherkins using FRENCH CHEF'S KNIFE.
6. Combine herring, onions, potatoes, apples, beets, gherkins; mix well.
7. Add vinegar, sugar, capers, pepper; mix well.
8. Top with sour cream, garnish with sliced hard cooked eggs.
9. Eight servings.

Peach Melba Salad

2 1-pound cans sliced peaches
¼ cup lemon juice
2 3-ounce packages lemon gelatin
2 cups hot water
4 teaspoons milk
¼ cup mayonnaise
2 3-ounce packages cream cheese, softened
¼ cup finely chopped pecans
2 10-ounce packages frozen red raspberries, thawed
¼ cup lemon juice
2 3-ounce packages raspberry gelatin
2 cups hot water

1. *Peach Layer:* Drain peaches; combine peach syrup, lemon juice, enough cold water to make 2 cups.
2. Dissolve lemon gelatin in hot water; add syrup mixture; refrigerate until partially set.
3. Blend in peaches; pour into 3-quart mold; refrigerate until set.
4. *Cheese Layer:* Combine milk, mayonnaise, cream cheese; blend well using MIX-STIR; stir in pecans.
5. Spread cheese mixture over peach layer in mold using SPREADER SPATULA; refrigerate.
6. *Raspberry Layer:* Drain raspberries; combine raspberry syrup, lemon juice, enough cold water to make 2 cups.
7. Dissolve raspberry gelatin in hot water; add syrup mixture; refrigerate until partially set.
8. Blend in raspberries; pour over cheese layer in mold; refrigerate until set.
9. Unmold on bed of lettuce.
10. Fourteen–sixteen servings.

Nordic Potato Salad

6 medium potatoes
2 medium, tart red apples
1 pickled herring
1 medium dill pickle
⅔ cup mayonnaise
1 teaspoon prepared mustard
2 tablespoons sherry wine
½ tablespoon chopped chives
2 teaspoons sugar
1 teaspoon salt
⅛ teaspoon pepper

1. Boil potatoes with jackets on until tender; spear with TURNING FORK; remove skins using PARING KNIFE; cube while hot using FRENCH CHEF'S KNIFE.
2. Quarter apples; remove cores using TRIMMER; cube using FRENCH CHEF'S KNIFE.
3. Dice herring, dill pickle using FRENCH CHEF'S KNIFE.
4. Combine potatoes, apples in large bowl.
5. Combine remaining ingredients in small bowl; blend thoroughly.
6. Pour dressing over potatoes, apples; toss lightly to mix.
7. Cover; refrigerate several hours.
8. Six servings.

Entrees

Danish Open Sandwiches

The Danish open-faced sandwich is a typical Danish Lunch. It consists of a single slice of bread topped with a cold filling, attractively arranged and garnished. Although there are an endless variety of fillings, the bread is almost always a well-buttered dark sour rye (white bread with a hard crust is often used for fish or seafood fillings). The Danish sandwich is an excellent disguise for left-overs. Try some of the following combinations or create your own:

1. Sliced smoked salmon on a bed of scrambled eggs, garnished with a twisted cucumber slice. (Use TRIMMER.)

2. Thinly sliced cooked pork topped with strip of crisp bacon, twisted orange slice, pitted prune. (Use PETITE CARVER and TRIMMER.)

3. Thinly sliced cooked ham topped with scrambled eggs, chopped chives, sprig of parsley. (Use SLICER.)

4. Sliced cooked sausage patty topped with sliced boiled potato, sliced green onion, chopped pimiento. (Use TRIMMER and FRENCH CHEF'S KNIFE.)

5. Chopped cooked shrimp on bed of lettuce topped with shrimp sauce, twisted slice of lemon. (Use FRENCH CHEF'S KNIFE and TRIMMER.)

6. Ham salad topped with an orange section and twisted cucumber slice. (Use SPREADER SPATULA and TRIMMER.)

7. Sliced braunsweiger topped with piece of lettuce, strip of crisp bacon, slice of pimiento. (Use TRIMMER.)

8. Thinly sliced roast beef topped with tomato wedge, sliced pickle. (Use SLICER and TRIMMER.)

9. Marinated herring topped with onion rings. (Use TRIMMER.)

10. Curried macaroni and herring salad on bed of lettuce topped with twisted cucumber slice. (Use TRIMMER.)

11. Thinly sliced ham topped with sliced Swiss cheese, lettuce, cherry tomato. (Use PETITE CARVER.)

12. Grape jelly topped with sliced apples. (Use SPREADER SPATULA and TRIMMER.)

13. Peanut butter topped with crisp bacon slice, celery strips. (Use SPREADER SPATULA and TRIMMER.)

Entrees

Steak Eszterhazy (Hungary)

2 pounds top round steak, ½-inch thick
Salt, pepper
1 medium onion
1 stalk celery
1 small carrot
3 large sprigs parsley
1 medium carrot
2 gherkin pickles
⅓ cup flour
¼ cup vegetable oil
2 cups canned condensed beef consommé
¼ cup wine vinegar
6 whole allspice
2 bay leaves
⅛ teaspoon thyme
½ cup dairy sour cream

1. Cut steak into six equal portions using PETITE CARVER; sprinkle with salt, pepper.
2. Peel onion using PARING KNIFE; chop using FRENCH CHEF'S KNIFE.
3. Chop celery, carrot using FRENCH CHEF'S KNIFE.
4. Snip parsley using KITCHEN SHEARS.
5. Cut carrot in thin strips about 1½ inches long using FRENCH CHEF'S KNIFE.
6. Cut gherkins in thin strips about 1½ inches long using TRIMMER.
7. Coat steak with flour; pound with edge of saucer.
8. Heat oil in 10-inch FRY PAN over medium heat 4–5 minutes; quickly brown meat on both sides; remove with TURNER.
9. Sauté onion, celery, chopped carrot about 5 minutes stirring with TURNING FORK.
10. Stir in remaining flour (3–4 tablespoons) using MIX-STIR; slowly blend in consommé, vinegar; add allspice, bay leaves, thyme, chopped parsley.
11. Bring to boil; return meat to pan; cover; simmer 60–70 minutes.

12. Blend in sour cream; simmer additional 5 minutes.
13. Serve meat with gravy; garnish with carrot, gherkin strips.
14. Six servings.

Australian Curried Beef

1½ pounds boneless chuck
1 tart apple
1 medium onion
2 medium tomatoes
2 large sprigs parsley
2 tablespoons vegetable oil
1 teaspoon curry powder
1 tablespoon instant-type flour
1 10½-ounce can condensed beef bouillon
⅓ cup seedless raisins
1 tablespoon brown sugar
2 teaspoons salt
⅛ teaspoon pepper

1. Cut meat in thin strips 1½ " x ½ " using PETITE CARVER.
2. Pare, core apple using PARING KNIFE; dice using FRENCH CHEF'S KNIFE.
3. Peel onion using PARING KNIFE; slice using TRIMMER.
4. Dice tomatoes using FRENCH CHEF'S KNIFE.
5. Snip parsley using KITCHEN SHEARS.
6. In 10-inch FRY PAN, brown meat quickly in oil over medium-high heat stirring with TURNING FORK.
7. Add apple, onion; sauté 2–3 minutes; stir in curry powder.
8. Add tomatoes, parsley, flour, bouillon, raisins, brown sugar, salt, pepper; blend well.
9. Cover; simmer 40–45 minutes until meat is tender.
10. Six servings.

Argentine Beef Pie

Pastry
2¼ cups sifted all-purpose flour
½ cup sugar
½ teaspoon salt
½ cup butter or margarine
2 egg yolks, slightly beaten
¼ cup water or Muscatel wine
Filling
2 medium potatoes
1 carrot
1 medium onion
1½ pounds cooked beef roast
½ teaspoon salt
1 10¾-ounce can beef gravy
⅓ cup raisins
½ teaspoon cinnamon
¼ teaspoon ground cloves
½ teaspoon oregano
⅛ teaspoon pepper
1 can (1 lb. 13 oz.) peach halves, drained
2 egg whites
2 tablespoons sugar

Pastry

1. Sift together flour, sugar, salt into bowl.
2. Cut in butter with pastry blender or 2 knives until mixture resembles coarse meal.
3. Add egg yolks; quickly blend in with fork.
4. Add water by tablespoons blending with fork after each addition until mixture clings together.
5. Form dough into ball; wrap in aluminum foil; refrigerate 30 minutes or longer.

Filling

1. Pare potatoes, carrot, onion using PARING KNIFE; coarsely chop using FRENCH CHEF'S KNIFE.
2. Cut meat in ½-inch cubes using PETITE CARVER.
3. In a 3-quart SAUCE PAN, cook potatoes, carrots, onions until tender; add salt.
4. Add meat cubes, gravy, raisins, cinnamon, cloves, oregano, pepper; heat 5 minutes.
5. Roll out pastry on floured board into two 13-inch squares; line bottom and sides of 9-inch square bake pan with pastry.
6. Pour filling into pan; arrange peach halves on top; cover with pastry; crimp edge of pastry.
7. Bake 30 minutes at 375° F.
8. Beat egg whites until soft peaks are formed; beat in sugar until meringue is stiff and glossy.
9. Spread meringue over top of pie; bake 3–5 minutes at 425° F. or until meringue is golden brown.
10. Cut in squares.
11. Eight–nine servings.

Hungarian Beef Strips

2 pounds of beef tenderloin
1 medium onion
4 large mushrooms
1 green pepper
1 red pepper
3 tablespoons vegetable oil
1¼ teaspoons paprika
½ teaspoon salt

1. Cut tenderloin in 3 x 1 x ¼-inch strips using PETITE CARVER.
2. Peel onion using PARING KNIFE; cut in thin slices using TRIMMER.
3. Chop mushrooms using FRENCH CHEF'S KNIFE.
4. Seed peppers; cut into thin strips using TRIMMER.
5. Heat 2 tablespoons oil in 10-inch FRY PAN over medium-high heat; brown beef strips well on both sides; remove from pan using PERFORATED SPOON.
6. Add 1 tablespoon oil; sauté onions 5–8 minutes stirring with TURNING FORK; remove from heat; stir in paprika.
7. Add browned meat, mushrooms, green pepper, red pepper, salt.
8. Heat until sizzling begins; reduce heat to low; cover; simmer 25–30 minutes.
9. Serve with hot buttered rice.
10. Four–five servings.

Entrees

Belgian Beef Casserole

3 pounds round steak
2 medium onions
6 tablespoons butter or margarine
½ cup instant-type flour
1½ cups hot water
1 cup light beer
2 teaspoons salt
⅛ teaspoon garlic powder
1 bay leaf
½ teaspoon sugar
⅛ teaspoon nutmeg
¼ teaspoon oregano
1½ teaspoons vinegar

1. Cut round steak in 1-inch cubes using PETITE CARVER.

2. Peel onions using PARING KNIFE; cut in thin slices using TRIMMER.

3. Melt 2 tablespoons butter in 10-inch FRY PAN over medium-high heat; brown meat cubes, stirring with TURNING FORK; transfer to 2-quart casserole using PERFORATED SPOON.

4. Melt remaining butter over medium heat; brown onions; transfer to casserole.

5. Stir in flour using MIX-STIR; cook 1 minute; gradually add water, beer, stirring constantly.

6. Add salt, garlic powder, bay leaf, sugar, nutmeg, oregano, vinegar; bring to a boil.

7. Pour gravy over meat, onions; cover; bake 2 hours at 325° F.

8. Serve with hot buttered noodles.

9. Five–six servings.

Flank Steak Bourbon

2 cups tomato sauce
¼ cup chopped chives
1 teaspoon seasoned salt
¼ teaspoon pepper
½ teaspoon celery salt
¼ cup bourbon
1 4-ounce can chopped mushrooms
    plus liquid
1 flank steak, 1-1¼ pounds

1. Combine tomato sauce, chives, seasoned salt, bourbon, mushrooms plus liquid; blend well using MIX-STIR.

2. Score flank steak on both sides with criss-cross cuts using PETITE CARVER; cover with Alcoa Wrap. (Do not press foil onto meat.)

3. Refrigerate about 12 hours; spoon marinade over beef several times using SOLID SPOON.

4. Bake uncovered 1½–2 hours at 325° F.; baste occasionally with marinade.

5. Four–five servings.

Beef Burgundy

1 garlic clove
1½ cups red wine
1 tablespoon pickling spice
3 pound bottom round beef,
    1-inch thick
1 medium carrot
1 medium onion
1 stalk celery

1. Mince garlic clove using FRENCH CHEF'S KNIFE; add wine, pickling spices; blend well.

2. Place beef in shallow bake pan; pour marinade over beef; cover with Alcoa Wrap. (Do not press foil onto meat.)

3. Refrigerate about 12 hours; spoon marinade over beef several times using SOLID SPOON.

4. Scrape carrot, peel onion using PARING KNIFE; slice using TRIMMER.

5. Cut celery in ½-inch pieces using FRENCH CHEF'S KNIFE.

6. Strain marinade; pour over beef once again; add carrots, onions, celery.

7. Bake uncovered 2–2½ hours at 325° F.; baste occasionally with marinade.

8. Eight servings.

Beef Teriyaki (Japan)

2 pounds boneless sirloin,
    ¼-inch thick
¼ cup sherry wine
⅓ cup Japanese soy sauce
⅓ cup canned chicken broth
1 tablespoon sugar
2 teaspoons cornstarch
1 tablespoon cold water

1. Trim meat of excess fat using TRIMMER; cut into 12 pieces using BUTCHER KNIFE; pound meat slightly with edge of saucer or meat pounder.
2. To make Teriyaki Sauce: Blend together sherry, soy sauce, broth using MIX-STIR; reserve ¼ cup sauce.
3. Marinate meat in Teriyaki Sauce about 1 hour.
4. To make Teriyaki Glaze: Combine the reserved ¼ cup sauce, sugar in 1-quart SAUCE PAN heat but do not boil.
5. Dissolve cornstarch in water; stir into hot sauce using MIX-STIR; cook over medium heat until thick and clear; pour into bowl; set aside.
6. Broil meat for 1–2 minutes per side (medium or well done).
7. Cut meat into 1-inch wide strips using TRIMMER; arrange on platters of COMBO SERVERS; top with Teriyaki Glaze.
8. Six servings.

Variation: Boned chicken breasts, cut in half, may be substituted for beef; broil 4–5 minutes per side.

Flank Steak Teriyaki

1 clove garlic
4 green onions
½ cup vegetable oil
¼ cup soy sauce
¼ cup honey
2 tablespoons cider vinegar
2 tablespoons sherry wine
2 teaspoons ground ginger
2 pounds flank steak, not scored

1. Mince garlic, green onions using FRENCH CHEF'S KNIFE.
2. Press garlic against side of small bowl with back of wooden spoon.
3. Add onions, oil, soy sauce, honey, vinegar, sherry, ginger; beat until well blended using MIX-STIR.
4. Pour marinade over steak; cover; refrigerate at least six hours.
5. Place steak on broiler rack; broil 5–8 minutes per side.
6. To carve: Cut steak in thin slices with grain using PETITE CARVER; serve on COMBO SERVERS.
7. Six servings.

Delicious Meat Balls

2 pounds round steak, ground
1 pound pork tenderloin, ground
6 eggs, beaten
2 teaspoons salt
¼ teaspoon pepper
¼ cup all purpose flour
¼ cup salad oil or shortening
2 tablespoons all purpose flour
2 10½-ounce cans condensed beef
    consommé, undiluted
1 tablespoon bottled sauce for gravy
1 cup sherry wine

1. Combine beef, pork, eggs, salt, pepper, flour; toss together lightly using TURNING FORK.
2. Shape meat into balls, ¾ to 1-inch in diameter.
3. Heat oil in 10-inch FRY PAN.
4. Brown meat balls a few at a time in hot fat; remove with PERFORATED SPOON when browned.
5. When browning is complete, add the 2 tablespoons flour to fat in FRY PAN; stir until smooth using MIX-STIR.
6. Add consommé, bottled sauce; cook several minutes, stirring constantly using MIX-STIR.
7. Add sherry, meat balls; simmer 10 minutes over low heat.
8. Seven–eight servings as entrée: Serve over buttered noodles. Approximately 70 meat balls as hot hors d'oeuvres.

Entrees

Chuck Wagon Special

1 small baking potato
2 small onions
1 small carrot
1 stalk celery
¼ pound beef sirloin
2 tablespoons chili sauce
1 teaspoon quick-cooking tapioca
¼ teaspoon salt
⅛ teaspoon pepper

1. Peel potato, onions using PAR-ING KNIFE; cut potato in half using TRIMMER.
2. Scrape carrot with PARING KNIFE; cut into quarters using FRENCH CHEF'S KNIFE.
3. Chop celery using FRENCH CHEF'S KNIFE.
4. Cut beef into 1-inch cubes using TRIMMER.
5. Combine chili sauce, tapioca; spread in center of double-thick square of Alcoa Wrap.
6. On sauce, arrange potato, onions, carrot, celery; top with meat cubes; sprinkle with salt, pepper.
7. Bring torn edges of foil over food; fold together tightly with double folds; make double fold on each end.
8. Place on baking sheet; bake 1 hour at 425° F.
9. Serve in opened package; idea fare for the patio supper.
10. One serving.

Spicy Beef Casserole

2½ pounds boneless rump
¼ cup flour
1 tablespoon sugar
1 teaspoon salt
½ teaspoon dry mustard
¼ teaspoon ground allspice
⅛ teaspoon pepper
1 8-ounce can tomato sauce
¼ cup Burgundy wine
½ cup canned beef broth
2 tablespoons vinegar
1½ tablespoons Worcestershire sauce

1. Cut beef in 2-inch cubes using BUTCHER KNIFE.
2. Combine flour, sugar, salt, mustard, allspice, pepper; coat meat.
3. Place meat in 2-quart casserole; sprinkle remaining flour mixture over meat.
4. Blend together tomato sauce, Burgundy, beef broth, vinegar, Worcestershire sauce using MIX-STIR; pour over meat; cover.
5. Bake 2½ hours at 325° F.
6. Serve with hot buttered noodles.
7. Five–six servings.

Swiss Steak

1½ pounds round steak, 1½ inches thick
3 large onions
2 tablespoons flour
1 teaspoon salt
⅛ teaspoon pepper
2 tablespoons shortening
1 cup hot water

1. Trim excess fat from meat; cut into serving size pieces using PE-TITE CARVER.
2. Peel onions using PARING KNIFE; slice using TRIMMER.
3. Combine flour, salt, pepper.
4. Coat meat with flour mixture; pound with edge of saucer.
5. Melt shortening in 10-inch FRY PAN; brown meat on both sides over medium heat.
6. Add water, onions; cover; cook over low heat about 2 hours or until meat is tender; add more water if necessary.
7. Four–six servings.

Variations:

1. Use 1½ cups canned tomatoes instead of water.
2. Substitute tomato sauce or vegetable juice for all or part of water.
3. Add 2 tablespoons ketchup, ½ teaspoon prepared mustard to water.
4. Add 1 green pepper, seeded and cut into rings.

Sukiyaki (Japan)

12 green onions
4 large mushrooms
2 leaves Chinese cabbage
1½ pounds boneless sirloin
1 cup fresh spinach leaves
2 tablespoons peanut oil
1 5-ounce can bamboo shoots, drained
½ cup canned bean sprouts
⅓ cup Japanese soy sauce
2 tablespoons sugar
½ cup canned chicken broth
2 tablespoons sherry wine

1. Slice green onions diagonally in 2-inch lengths using TRIMMER.
2. Cut mushrooms in thin slices using TRIMMER.
3. Slice cabbage diagonally using TRIMMER.
4. Cut sirloin in very thin 1 x 2-inch slices using PETITE CARVER.
5. Chop spinach using FRENCH CHEF'S KNIFE.
6. Heat oil in 10-inch FRY PAN over medium-high heat.
7. Add onions, mushrooms, cabbage, bamboo shoots, bean sprouts; sauté 2 minutes, stirring constantly using TURNING FORK.
8. Combine soy sauce, sugar, broth, sherry; blend well using MIX-STIR; pour over vegetables; simmer 8–10 minutes, stirring occasionally.
9. Add meat; bring liquid to boil; add spinach; simmer 3–5 minutes or until meat loses its red color.
10. Serve with steamed rice.
11. Four servings.

Note: Sukiyaki may be prepared at table in electric FRY PAN or in blazer pan of chafing dish. Arrange vegetables and meat attractively on platters of COMBO SERVERS; pour broth mixture into pitcher. Use chop sticks or two forks when adding vegetables and meat to FRY PAN.

Meat Loaf

3 slices white bread
1 small onion
½ small green pepper
2 eggs
1½ pounds ground beef
½ pound ground pork
2 tablespoons bottled horseradish
1 tablespoon salt
¼ cup milk
¼ cup ketchup
1 teaspoon dry mustard

1. Cut bread into small cubes using SLICER.
2. Peel onion using PARING KNIFE; finely chop using FRENCH CHEF'S KNIFE.
3. Finely chop green pepper using FRENCH CHEF'S KNIFE.
4. Beat eggs using MIX-STIR.
5. Add eggs to ground meats; blend lightly with TURNING FORK.
6. Add remaining ingredients; mix thoroughly but do not stir more than necessary as it tends to toughen loaf.
7. Shape into an oval loaf; place in shallow cake pan.
8. Bake 1 hour at 400° F.
9. Six–eight servings.

Variations:

1. Pack mixture into 9 x 5 x 3-inch loaf pan; bake as above. To remove from pan, drain off liquid; unmold on cake rack; then turn right side up on heated platter.
2. Spread top with ½ cup ketchup before baking.
3. Place ½ of meat mixture in loaf pan; make three depressions using a tablespoon; place a shelled hard cooked egg in each depression; add remaining meat.
4. Pack mixture into ring mold. To serve, fill center with mashed potatoes.

Entrees

Sloppy Joes

1 small onion
½ small green pepper
2 medium tomatoes
1 4-ounce can button mushrooms
2 tablespoons fat
½ pound ground beef
1 cup tomato juice
¼ teaspoon paprika
¼ teaspoon pepper
½ teaspoon salt
4 sandwich buns

1. Peel onion using PARING KNIFE; slice using TRIMMER.

2. Finely chop green pepper using FRENCH CHEF'S KNIFE.

3. Dip tomatoes into boiling water for about 1 minute using TURNING FORK; peel; core using PARING KNIFE; cut into eighths using TRIMMER.

4. Drain mushrooms; finely chop using FRENCH CHEF'S KNIFE.

5. Sauté onion, green pepper in fat in 10-inch FRY PAN until lightly browned, stirring with TURNING FORK.

6. Add tomatoes, mushrooms, beef, tomato juice, paprika, pepper, salt; cover.

7. Cook over low heat 15–20 minutes; thicken juice if desired.

8. Slice buns in half using SLICER; toast under broiler.

9. Serve over toasted buns.

10. Four servings.

Double Decker Hamburger

4 large stuffed olives
1 medium onion
1½ pounds ground round steak
¾ cup cold water
1 teaspoon salt
¼ teaspoon pepper
¼ cup ketchup
3 tablespoons soft butter or margarine

1. Slice olives using TRIMMER.

2. Peel onion using PARING KNIFE; slice using TRIMMER; separate into rings.

3. Combine meat, water, salt, pepper; shape into 8 flat patties.

4. Preheat 10-inch FRY PAN until drop of water dances on the surface; add meat patties; brown quickly on both sides.

5. Line shallow baking pan with Alcoa Wrap; place 4 patties in pan.

6. Spread ketchup over top of patties using SPREADER SPATULA; arrange olive slices over ketchup.

7. Top with remaining 4 patties; spread with butter using SPREADER SPATULA.

8. Insert toothpick through center of each patty; hang onion rings over toothpicks.

9. Bake 25–30 minutes at 375° F.

10. Four servings.

Chili Con Carne

1 small onion
1 tablespoon butter or margarine
1 pound ground beef
1 No. 2 can red kidney beans
1 10½-ounce can condensed tomato soup
1 teaspoon salt
¼ teaspoon chili powder

1. Peel onion using PARING KNIFE; finely chop using FRENCH CHEF'S KNIFE.

2. Melt butter in 10-inch FRY PAN; add onions, meat; cook until brown, stirring frequently with TURNING FORK.

3. Add kidney beans, tomato soup, salt, chili powder; stir; cover.

4. Cook over low heat 20–25 minutes; stir occasionally.

5. Four servings.

Corned Beef

4-5 pounds mild cure brisket of beef
3 medium onions
1 clove garlic
1 stalk celery
1 medium carrot
2 sprigs parsley
3 whole cloves
6 peppercorns
1 bay leaf

1. Wipe meat with damp cloth; place in ROUND ROASTER; cover with cold water.
2. Peel onions using PARING KNIFE; slice using TRIMMER.
3. Peel garlic clove; cut into quarters using PARING KNIFE.
4. Cut celery, carrot in 2-inch pieces using FRENCH CHEF'S KNIFE.
5. Snip parsley using KITCHEN SHEARS.
6. Add onions, garlic, celery, carrot, parsley, cloves, peppercorns, bay leaf to ROUND ROASTER; cover.
7. Bring to boil over medium-high heat; reduce to low; simmer 4–5 hours or until meat is tender; remove any scum that appears with the PERFORATED SPOON.
8. Remove from stock; slice with the SLICER; serve with horseradish sauce.

20th Century Wieners

3 tomatoes
2 medium onions
8 wieners
⅛ teaspoon basil
⅓ cup shredded sharp cheese

1. Core tomatoes using PARING KNIFE; slice using TRIMMER.
2. Peel onions using PARING knife; slice using TRIMMER.
3. Cut wieners in 1-inch pieces using TRIMMER.
4. Alternate tomatoes, onions, wieners in 10-inch FRY PAN; sprinkle basil on top.
5. Cover; cook over low heat 20–25 minutes.

6. Sprinkle cheese over top just before serving.
7. Four servings.

Corned Beef and Cabbage

1. Follow directions for Corned Beef.
2. Wash; quarter medium head cabbage using BUTCHER KNIFE; remove core.
3. About 20 minutes before corned beef is done, place cabbage wedges on top of meat.
4. Cover; boil until cabbage is just tender.

Calves Liver, German Style

4 medium red cooking apples
3 medium onions
1 pound calves liver
3 large sprigs parsley
3 tablespoons butter or margarine
Salt, pepper
3 tablespoons flour
1 tablespoon butter or margarine

1. Core apples using PARING KNIFE; cut in ¼-inch rings using TRIMMER.
2. Peel onions using PARING KNIFE; slice using TRIMMER; separate into rings.
3. Cut liver into ¼-inch slices using PETITE CARVER.
4. Snip parsley using KITCHEN SHEARS.
5. Melt butter in 10-inch FRY PAN; sauté apple rings until just tender; remove from pan using TURNER; keep warm in oven.
6. Sauté onion rings until transparent; remove from pan using TURNER; keep warm in oven.
7. Season liver with salt, pepper; coat with flour.
8. Melt remaining 1 tablespoon butter in FRY PAN; sauté liver until nicely browned, about 3–5 minutes per side.
9. Serve liver topped with apple rings, onion rings, snipped parsley.
10. Four servings.

Entrees

Exotic Greek Stew

- 3 pounds lean beef
- 2½ pounds small onions
- 1 tablespoon salt
- ⅓ cup butter or margarine, melted
- 1 6-ounce can tomato paste
- ⅓ cup red wine
- 2 tablespoons wine vinegar
- 1 tablespoon brown sugar
- ⅛ teaspoon garlic salt
- 1 bay leaf
- 1 small cinnamon stick
- ½ teaspoon whole cloves

1. Cut meat into 1½-inch cubes using PETITE CARVER.
2. Peel onions using PARING KNIFE.
3. Place meat, onions in ROUND ROASTER; sprinkle with salt; add melted butter. *(Do not brown meat.)*
4. Combine remaining ingredients; pour over meat; *do not stir.*
5. Cover; bake 5 hours at 250° F.; stir gently to blend meat and sauce before serving.
6. Six–eight servings.

5-Hour Stew

- 2 pounds lean chuck, lamb or veal
- 1 5¼-ounce can water chestnuts, drained
- 1 1-pound can tomatoes
- 1½ pound package frozen stew vegetables
- 1 tablespoon sugar
- 3 tablespoons quick cooking tapioca
- 1 tablespoon salt
- ¼ teaspoon pepper
- ¼ cup red wine

1. Cut meat into 1½-inch cubes using PETITE CARVER.
2. Slice water chestnuts with TRIMMER.

3. Combine all ingredients in a 3-quart casserole or ROUND ROASTER. *(Do not brown meat);* stir gently to blend.
4. Cover; bake 5 hours at 250° F.; stir gently before serving.
5. Five–six servings.

Braised Veal Chops (France)

- 4 loin veal chops, 1-inch thick
- 1 medium onion
- 1 carrot
- 1 stalk celery
- 3 large sprigs parsley
- Salt, pepper
- ½ teaspoon basil
- 3 tablespoons vegetable oil
- 1 cup dry white wine
- ½ cup canned chicken broth
- 2 tablespoons butter or margarine
- ¾ cup fresh bread crumbs

1. Trim chops of excess fat using TRIMMER.
2. Peel onion using PARING KNIFE; chop onion, carrot, celery using FRENCH CHEF'S KNIFE.
3. Snip parsley using KITCHEN SHEARS.
4. Season chops with salt, pepper, basil.
5. Heat oil in 10-inch FRY PAN over medium-high heat; brown chops on both sides; remove using TURNING FORK.
6. Sauté onion, carrot, celery in oil 5 minutes; stir with TURNING FORK.
7. Add wine; boil several minutes or until liquid is reduced to ½ cup; add chicken broth.
8. In 8-inch FRY PAN, melt butter; stir in bread crumbs, parsley until thoroughly coated with butter.
9. Return chops to large FRY PAN; top with bread crumbs; cover; simmer 45 minutes.
10. Four servings.

Sesame Veal

1 pound veal steak
2 tablespoons flour
½ teaspoon salt
½ teaspoon poultry seasoning
½ teaspoon paprika
⅛ teaspoon pepper
2 tablespoons fat
½ cup soft bread crumbs
1 tablespoon butter or margarine, melted
¼ cup grated Parmesan cheese
2 tablespoons sesame seeds, toasted
½ cup hot water

1. Cut veal into serving pieces using PETITE CARVER.
2. Combine flour, salt, poultry seasoning, paprika, pepper; coat veal in flour mixture.
3. Melt fat in 10-inch FRY PAN; add veal; brown on all sides.
4. Place meat in shallow baking pan.
5. Combine bread crumbs, melted butter, Parmesan cheese, sesame seed; spoon over veal.
6. Pour water around veal.
7. Bake 45–50 minutes at 350° F.
8. Serve sauce from pan over veal.
9. Three–four servings.

Veal Cacciatora

1½ pounds veal round steak
1 medium onion
1 medium green pepper
2 large sprigs parsley
¼ cup olive oil
1 15-ounce can tomato sauce
⅓ cup white wine
1 teaspoon salt
¼ teaspoon pepper
¼ teaspoon instant minced garlic
1 teaspoon oregano
1 bay leaf

1. Cut veal steak into 2 x ½-inch strips using TRIMMER.
2. Peel onion using PARING KNIFE; slice using TRIMMER.
3. Seed green pepper; cut into thin strips using TRIMMER.
4. Snip parsley using KITCHEN SHEARS.
5. Heat oil in 10-inch FRY PAN; brown veal on both sides.
6. Add onion, green pepper; sauté 3 minutes.
7. Blend in remaining ingredients; cover; simmer 55–60 minutes.
8. Serve with hot buttered spaghetti or noodles.
9. Six servings.

Variation: Six serving pieces of chicken may be substituted for veal.

Wiener Schnitzel

1 pound veal cutlet, ½-inch thick
½ cup flour
1 teaspoon salt
2 eggs, beaten
1 cup crushed cornflakes
2 tablespoons butter or margarine
½ cup blanched, toasted almonds

1. Cut veal into serving pieces using PETITE CARVER.
2. Combine flour, salt; sprinkle half of flour mixture over veal; pound into meat using rim of saucer.
3. Turn meat; pound remaining flour into second side.
4. Dip meat into beaten egg, then into crushed cornflakes.
5. Melt butter in 10-inch FRY PAN; brown veal on both sides; cover; simmer until tender, about 30 minutes.
6. Sprinkle toasted almonds over each serving.
7. Three–four servings.

Fry Pan Kebabs

- 1 pound leg of lamb
- 2 green peppers
- 2 tomatoes
- 6 tablespoons wine vinegar
- 6 tablespoons water
- ¼ cup butter or margarine
- ½ teaspoon salt
- ¼ teaspoon pepper

1. Cut lamb in 1-inch cubes using TRIMMER.
2. Seed green peppers using TRIMMER; pour boiling water over peppers; let stand 5 minutes; drain; cut into 24 one-inch squares using FRENCH CHEF'S KNIFE.
3. Cut each tomato in eight wedges using TRIMMER.
4. Combine vinegar, water; pour over lamb; cover with aluminum foil; refrigerate 1 hour; turn meat once or twice.
5. Melt butter in 10-inch FRY PAN over medium heat; brown marinated lamb thoroughly on all sides about 15 minutes; stir with TURNING FORK; remove from pan using PERFORATED SPOON; cool slightly.
6. Arrange lamb, green pepper, tomato alternately on 8 short skewers; sprinkle with salt, pepper.
7. Place kebabs in FRY PAN; cover.
8. Cook 15 minutes, turning occasionally using TURNING FORK.
9. Eight servings.

Grecian Lamb Balls

- 1 small onion
- 1 medium eggplant
- 2 large sprigs parsley
- 1½ pounds ground lamb
- 1 teaspoon salt
- ⅛ teaspoon pepper
- 3 tablespoons vegetable oil
- 1 8-ounce can tomato sauce
- 2 tablespoons instant onion flakes
- 2 tablespoons vinegar
- 1 tablespoon brown sugar
- ¼ teaspoon salt
- ⅛ teaspoon pepper
- ⅛ teaspoon mustard
- ½ teaspoon cinnamon
- ¼ teaspoon ground cloves

1. Peel onion using PARING KNIFE; finely chop using FRENCH CHEF'S KNIFE.
2. Slice eggplant using PETITE CARVER; peel using PARING KNIFE; finely chop enough to make 2½ cups using FRENCH CHEF'S KNIFE.
3. Snip parsley using KITCHEN SHEARS.
4. Lightly toss together onion, eggplant, parsley, lamb, salt, pepper using TURNING FORK.
5. Shape into 20 balls using about ¼ cup mixture for each.
6. Heat oil in 10-inch FRY PAN over medium heat; brown meatballs on all sides; drain off excess fat.
7. Combine remaining ingredients; pour over meatballs.
8. Cover; simmer 45 minutes.
9. Four–five servings.

County Kerry Pork Chops

4 pork chops, ½-inch thick
1 small onion
3 medium potatoes
1 pound cabbage
2 tablespoons vegetable oil
1 10½-ounce can condensed cream
    of celery soup
½ cup milk
¼ cup flour
1½ teaspoons salt
⅛ teaspoon pepper

1. Trim excess fat from chops using TRIMMER.
2. Peel onion using PARING KNIFE; dice using FRENCH CHEF'S KNIFE.
3. Pare potatoes using PARING KNIFE; cut in thin slices using FRENCH CHEF'S KNIFE.
4. Cut cabbage in wedges using BUTCHER KNIFE; shred using SLICER.
5. Heat oil in 10-inch FRY PAN over medium-high heat; quickly brown chops; remove using TURNING FORK.
6. Add onion, soup, milk to FRY PAN; blend; set aside.
7. Starting with potatoes, put alternate layers of potatoes, cabbage into a 2-quart casserole; sprinkle each layer with mixture of flour, salt, pepper; pour soup mixture over each layer.
8. Place chops on top; cover; bake 1¼ hours at 350° F.
9. Four servings.

Pork Chops Pierre

1 small onion
2 stalks celery
1 large onion
1 large green pepper
1 tablespoon butter or margarine
¼ cup water
½ cup ketchup
2 tablespoons vinegar
1 tablespoon lemon juice
1 tablespoon Worcestershire sauce
1 tablespoon brown sugar
½ teaspoon salt
⅛ teaspoon pepper
8 loin pork chops, ½-inch thick

1. Peel small onion using PARING KNIFE; finely chop onion, celery using FRENCH CHEF'S KNIFE.
2. Peel large onion using PARING KNIFE; thinly slice using PETITE CARVER.
3. Seed green pepper; cut into rings using TRIMMER.
4. Combine butter, onion, celery in 2-quart SAUCE PAN; sauté until tender.
5. Add water, ketchup, vinegar, lemon juice, Worcestershire sauce, sugar, salt, pepper; cover; simmer 20 minutes.
6. Brown chops on both sides in preheated 10-inch FRY PAN.
7. Place chops in 9 x 13-inch bake pan; pour sauce over chops; top with onion slices; pepper rings.
8. Cover pan with Alcoa Wrap; bake 45–50 minutes at 400° F.
9. Eight servings.

Maggie's Lamb Chops

4 loin lamb chops, 1-inch thick
    Salt, pepper
4 slices American cheese
4 slices Bermuda onion
8 tablespoons dairy sour cream

1. Trim chops of excess fat using TRIMMER; secure tails to thickest part of chops with toothpicks.
2. Sprinkle with salt, pepper.
3. Place chops in shallow baking pan.
4. Place 1 slice cheese, 1 slice onion on each chop.
5. Put 2 tablespoons sour cream on each chop.
6. Add no water; do not cover.
7. Bake 1 hour at 375° F.
8. Four servings.

Entrees

Glazed Ham Balls

- 1 small onion
- 1 pound ground ham
- 1 pound ground pork
- ⅔ cup cracker crumbs
- 2 eggs, beaten
- 1¼ cups evaporated milk
- ¼ teaspoon salt
- ¼ teaspoon thyme
- 1 cup brown sugar, firmly packed
- 1 teaspoon dry mustard
- 3 tablespoons vinegar

1. Peel onion using PARING KNIFE; finely chop using FRENCH CHEF'S KNIFE.
2. Combine ham, pork, cracker crumbs, eggs, evaporated milk, salt, thyme, onion; toss together lightly using TURNING FORK.
3. Make 16 balls (using #16 ice cream scoop); place balls in 9 x 13-inch bake pan.
4. Combine brown sugar, mustard, vinegar in 1-quart SAUCE PAN; bring to boil over medium heat; pour over ham balls.
5. Bake uncovered 1 hour at 350° F.
6. Eight servings.

Pork Chops Alexander

- 1 cup dried apricots
- 2 cups warm water
- ½ cup flour
- ½ teaspoon salt
- ¼ teaspoon pepper
- ¼ teaspoon thyme
- 6 loin pork chops, ¾-inch thick
- 2 tablespoons oil
- ¼ cup maple syrup

1. Combine apricots, water in 1-quart SAUCE PAN; cook until tender; drain.

2. Combine flour, salt, pepper, thyme; dust over both sides of chops.
3. Heat oil in 10-inch FRY PAN; brown chops on both sides.
4. Combine apricots, syrup; pour over chops.
5. Cover; cook 1 hour over low heat until chops are tender.
6. Six servings.

Hawaiian Ribs

- 4 pounds spareribs
- 2 green peppers
- ¾ cup cornstarch
- ¼ cup molasses
- ¼ cup soy sauce
- ½ cup sugar
- ¾ cup vinegar
- ¾ cup water
- ¾ cup pineapple juice
- 1 cup pineapple chunks

1. Cut spareribs into 1½-inch strips using BUTCHER KNIFE.
2. Seed green peppers; cut into 1-inch cubes using TRIMMER.
3. Brown ribs in ROUND ROASTER; remove from pan.
4. Combine cornstarch, molasses, soy sauce to make paste.
5. Spread paste on both sides of ribs using SPREADER SPATULA.
6. Rebrown quickly in ROUND ROASTER.
7. Combine sugar, vinegar, water, pineapple juice in 1-quart SAUCE PAN; heat until sugar dissolves; pour over ribs.
8. Cover; simmer 25–30 minutes.
9. Add pineapple chunks, green pepper cubes; simmer additional 5 minutes.
10. Four–five servings.

Spaghetti Carbonara (Italy)

1 clove garlic
8 large sprigs parsley
8 ounces uncooked spaghetti
2 tablespoons butter or margarine
2 cups diced cooked ham
3 eggs
½ cup grated Parmesan cheese

1. Mince garlic using FRENCH CHEF'S KNIFE.
2. Snip parsley using KITCHEN SHEARS.
3. Cook spaghetti in 4-quart SAUCE PAN following package directions; drain; return to pan.
4. Melt butter in 8-inch FRY PAN; sauté garlic, ham 3–4 minutes over medium heat, stirring with TURNING FORK.
5. Beat eggs using MIX-STIR; add cheese, parsley; pour over hot drained spaghetti; add ham; toss quickly with two forks until all strands are coated.
6. Four–six servings.

Lasagne (Italy)

1 small onion
2 small sprigs parsley
1 pound ground beef
2 cups canned tomatoes
1 15-ounce can tomatoe sauce
⅛ teaspoon instant minced garlic
1 teaspoon oregano
1 teaspoon salt
½ pound lasagne noodles
¾ pound Mozzarella cheese, grated
6 ounces Cheddar cheese, grated
4 ounces Parmesan cheese, grated

1. Peel onion using PARING KNIFE; chop using FRENCH CHEF'S KNIFE.
2. Snip parsley using KITCHEN SHEARS.
3. Preheat 10-inch FRY PAN until drop of water dances on the surface; add beef; brown thoroughly using TURNING FORK to stir.

4. Add onion, parsley, tomatoes, tomato sauce, garlic, oregano, salt; cover; simmer 1 hour.
5. Cook noodles in 4-quart SAUCE PAN according to package directions; drain.
6. Cover bottom of 9 x 13-inch bake pan with sauce; add a layer of noodles.
7. Sprinkle with ½ the Mozzarella cheese, then more sauce; repeat layers.
8. Top with Cheddar, Parmesan cheese.
9. Bake 30 minutes at 350° F.
10. Let stand 5 minutes for easier cutting; remove serving pieces with TURNER.
11. Twelve servings.

Egg Foo Yung (China)

¼ pound cooked chicken
¼ pound cooked shrimp
4 mushrooms
8 green onions
1 stalk celery
5 eggs
½ teaspoon salt
½ cup bean sprouts
3-4 tablespoons peanut oil

1. Coarsely chop chicken, shrimp, mushrooms using FRENCH CHEF'S KNIFE.
2. Mince green onions, celery using FRENCH CHEF'S KNIFE.
3. Beat eggs using MIX-STIR; blend in salt.
4. Stir in chicken, shrimp, mushrooms, onions, celery, bean sprouts.
5. Heat ½ tablespoon oil in 8-inch FRY PAN over medium-high heat; reduce heat to medium.
6. Pour ¼ cup egg mixture into FRY PAN; cook 1 minute on each side (should be lightly browned); keep warm in 200° F. oven; repeat until all batter is used; add more oil as needed.
7. Serve with Foo Yung Sauce.
8. Four servings.

Entrees

Onion Quiche (Switzerland)

2 medium onions
2 hard cooked eggs
Pastry for one crust
2 tablespoons butter or margarine
¼ pound Swiss cheese, grated
4 eggs
1 cup whipping cream
½ cup milk
¾ teaspoon salt
⅛ teaspoon nutmeg
⅛ teaspoon pepper

1. Peel onion using PARING KNIFE; slice in thin rings using TRIMMER.
2. Slice hard cooked eggs using TRIMMER.
3. Line Quiche Lorraine pan or 9-inch pie pan with pastry; trim and flute at top edge.
4. Prick well with TURNING FORK; bake 10–15 minutes at 425° F. until pastry just begins to brown; cool.
5. Melt butter in 10-inch FRY PAN over medium-high heat; sauté onions until tender but not brown, stirring with TURNING FORK.
6. Sprinkle ½ the grated cheese over bottom of pastry shell; arrange onions over cheese; sprinkle with remaining cheese.
7. Beat eggs thoroughly using MIX-STIR in medium sized bowl; blend in cream, milk, salt, nutmeg, pepper; pour over cheese, onion.
8. Arrange sliced eggs on top; push to submerge slices slightly.
9. Bake 15 minutes at 425° F., then reduce temperature to 300° F. for 30 minutes or until golden brown, custard set.
10. Seven–eight servings.

Maggie's Chicken Mornay

3 whole chicken breasts
½ cup flour
1 teaspoon salt
⅛ teaspoon pepper
⅛ teaspoon ginger
½ cup butter or margarine
1 cup water
Sauce
¼ cup butter or margarine
¼ cup flour
1 teaspoon salt
½ cup light cream
½ cup milk
1 cup grated American cheese
1 4-ounce can diced mushrooms, drained

1. Split chicken breasts in half using BUTCHER KNIFE and KITCHEN SHEARS.
2. Coat chicken breasts with combined flour, salt, pepper, ginger mixture.
3. Melt butter in 10-inch FRY PAN; brown chicken breasts on both sides; cover; cook over low heat 30–45 minutes or until tender.
4. Transfer chicken breasts to 9 x 13-inch bake pan.
5. Add water to drippings in FRY PAN; stir with MIX-STIR to loosen any sediment; set aside.
6. Melt butter in 2-quart SAUCE PAN; blend in flour, salt with MIX-STIR.
7. Gradually add cream, milk, reserved liquid from FRY PAN; cook over low heat until thickened, stirring constantly with MIX-STIR.
8. Add ½ cup cheese, mushrooms; blend well.
9. Pour sauce over chicken; sprinkle with remaining cheese; bake 25–30 minutes at 350° F. until just lightly browned.
10. Six servings.

Chicken Fricassee (France)

1 medium onion
1 stalk celery
1 carrot
6 medium mushrooms
3 pound frying chicken, cut up
¼ cup flour
½ teaspoon salt
⅛ teaspoon white pepper
¼ cup butter or margarine
1 14-ounce can chicken broth
1 cup dry white wine
½ cup whipping cream
Salt, pepper

1. Peel onion using PARING KNIFE; cut in thin slices using TRIMMER.
2. Slice celery diagonally using TRIMMER.
3. Slice carrot thinly using FRENCH CHEF'S KNIFE.
4. Slice mushrooms using TRIMMER.
5. Coat chicken with mixture of flour, salt, pepper; reserving any remaining flour.
6. Melt 3 tablespoons butter in 10-inch FRY PAN over medium heat; quickly fry chicken on all sides, turning frequently with TURNING FORK; do *not* brown; remove.
7. Add 1 tablespoon butter to FRY PAN; sauté onion, celery, carrot, mushrooms 5 minutes, stirring with TURNING FORK.
8. Blend in any remaining flour mixture; slowly stir in broth, wine using MIX-STIR.
9. Add chicken; bring to a boil; cover; simmer 25–30 minutes or until chicken is tender.
10. Remove chicken; boil liquid until reduced to 2 cups.
11. Gradually stir in cream using MIX-STIR; season with salt, pepper to taste.
12. Return chicken to sauce; heat.
13. Six servings.

Belgium Baked Codfish

2 pounds codfish fillets
Salt, pepper
2 medium onions
½ cup dry white wine
2 tablespoons dry bread crumbs
3 tablespoons grated Cheddar cheese
1 teaspoon paprika
¼ cup butter or margarine
2 parsley sprigs

1. Place fillets in 9 x 13-inch bake pan; season with salt, pepper.
2. Peel onions using PARING KNIFE; cut in thin slices using TRIMMER.
3. Lay onion slices over fillets; pour wine around fillets.
4. Combine bread crumbs, cheese, paprika; sprinkle over fillets; dot with butter.
5. Snip parsley using KITCHEN SHEARS; sprinkle over top.
6. Bake 25 minutes at 350° F.
7. Six servings.

Baked Salmon with Herb Butter

1 small onion
1 clove garlic
2 sprigs parsley
2 pounds salmon fillets
¼ cup butter or margarine, softened
3 tablespoons lemon juice
½ teaspoon basil
1 teaspoon salt
½ teaspoon pepper

1. Peel onion using PARING KNIFE; finely chop using FRENCH CHEF'S KNIFE.
2. Mince garlic, parsley using FRENCH CHEF'S KNIFE.
3. Place salmon fillets in 9 x 13-inch bake pan.
4. Combine onion, garlic, parsley, butter, lemon juice, basil, salt, pepper; blend well using TURNING FORK.
5. Spread over salmon using SPREADER SPATULA.
6. Bake 25–30 minutes at 300° F. or until fish flakes.
7. Six–eight servings.

Entrees

Mexican Braised Duck

4-5 pound duck
¼ cup lemon juice
½ teaspoon salt
⅛ teaspoon pepper
 2 tablespoons olive oil
 2 12-ounce cans light beer
 1 cup raw rice
 1 cup frozen green peas, thawed
½ teaspoon salt
　Pepper
½ teaspoon ground coriander
 2 sprigs parsley

1. Cut duck into serving pieces using BUTCHER KNIFE, KITCHEN SHEARS; trim off all fat using TRIMMER.
2. Brush duck with lemon juice; season with salt, pepper; cover; let stand 3 hours.
3. Heat olive oil in 10-inch FRY PAN over medium-high heat; brown duck well on both sides; pour off fat.
4. Add beer to FRY PAN; cover; simmer 45 minutes.
5. Remove duck; keep warm in 200° F. oven.
6. Skim fat from broth; measure 2 cups broth (add water, if necessary).
7. Combine broth, rice in FRY PAN; bring to a boil.
8. Add peas, salt, pepper, coriander; cover; simmer about 15 minutes or until all liquid has been absorbed.
9. Snip parsley with KITCHEN SHEARS; stir into rice; place in serving dish; top with duck.
10. Four–five servings.

Phillipine Red Snapper

 1 large onion
½ green pepper
 3 stalks celery
 1 carrot
 2 pounds red snapper fillets
 2 tablespoons lemon juice
½ teaspoon salt
 2 tablespoons olive oil
 1 1-pound can tomatoes
 2 tablespoons ketchup
½ teaspoon salt
⅛ teaspoon pepper

1. Peel onion using PARING KNIFE; finely chop using FRENCH CHEF'S KNIFE.
2. Seed green pepper using TRIMMER; chop using FRENCH CHEF'S KNIFE.
3. Chop celery, carrot using FRENCH CHEF'S KNIFE.
4. Place fish fillets on large plate; sprinkle with lemon juice, salt; let stand 30 minutes; place fillets in 9 x 13-inch bake pan, discarding excess lemon juice.
5. Heat olive oil in 10-inch FRY PAN over medium-high heat; sauté onion, green pepper, celery, carrot 5 minutes, stirring with TURNING FORK.
6. Add tomatoes, ketchup, salt, pepper; cover; simmer 30 minutes.
7. Pour vegetable mixture over fillets; bake 35 minutes at 400° F.
8. Six servings.

Mexican Style Perch

1 small onion
¼ green pepper
1 canned pimiento
¼ cup soft butter or margarine
1 teaspoon salt
¾ teaspoon chili powder
⅛ teaspoon thyme
⅛ teaspoon pepper
3 tablespoons dry bread crumbs
1½ pounds perch fillets

1. Peel onion using PARING KNIFE; mince using FRENCH CHEF'S KNIFE.
2. Seed green pepper using TRIMMER; mince using FRENCH CHEF'S KNIFE.
3. Mince pimiento using FRENCH CHEF'S KNIFE.
4. Combine onion, green pepper, pimiento, butter, salt, chili powder, thyme, pepper, bread crumbs; blend well using TURNING FORK.
5. Place fillets side by side in 9 x 13-inch bake pan; spread butter mixture over fillets using SPREADER SPATULA.
6. Bake 25–30 minutes at 425° F.
7. Six servings.

Salmon Casserole

2 tablespoons instant minced onion
¼ cup cold water
3 cups cooked rice
1 pound can salmon, drained, flaked
2 teaspoons salt
¼ teaspoon pepper
1 whole egg
2 egg whites
2 tablespoons butter or margarine, melted

1. Combine onion, water; let stand 5 minutes.
2. Combine onion, rice, salmon, salt, pepper; toss together lightly with TURNING FORK.
3. Beat egg, egg whites with MIX-STIR; add to salmon mixture; blend together.
4. Press into greased 1½-quart casserole; brush top with melted butter.
5. Bake 30 minutes at 375° F.
6. Garnish with lemon wedges, parsley; serve with Lemon Cucumber Sauce.
7. Four–five servings.

Halibut Supreme

1½ pounds halibut fillets
1 cup water
¼ cup dry white wine
¼ cup lemon juice
2 tablespoons butter or margarine
2 tablespoons flour
1 cup milk
¼ teaspoon salt
⅛ teaspoon pepper
¼ teaspoon onion salt
2 cups chopped, cooked spinach
¾ cup grated sharp cheese
2 eggs
1 tablespoon butter or margarine

1. Place fish in 10-inch FRY PAN; add water, wine, lemon juice; cover; simmer 5 minutes.
2. Remove fish using TURNER; place in 2-quart casserole.
3. Boil liquid until ¾ cup broth remains.
4. Melt butter in 2-quart SAUCE PAN; stir in flour using MIX-STIR; gradually add milk; cook, stirring constantly until thickened.
5. Add salt, pepper, onion salt, spinach, ¼ cup cheese; cook 5 minutes.
6. Beat eggs with MIX-STIR; stir into sauce.
7. Pour sauce over fish; sprinkle top with remaining cheese; dot with butter.
8. Bake 10–12 minutes at 400° F. until bubbly, cheese melts.
9. Six servings.

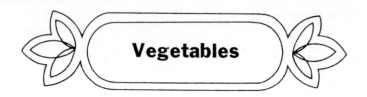

Vegetables

Stuffed Zucchini Boats

2 medium zucchini
2 hard cooked eggs
1 small stalk celery
2 green onions
1 tablespoon butter or margarine
1 tablespoon flour
½ cup milk
1 4½-ounce can deviled ham
1 teaspoon chopped parsley
1 teaspoon chopped chives
1 teaspoon salt
¼ teaspoon pepper
¼ teaspoon nutmeg
¾ cup whole wheat cracker crumbs

1. Slice zucchini in half lengthwise using BUTCHER KNIFE; scoop out centers, reserving pulp.
2. Chop eggs, celery using FRENCH CHEF'S KNIFE.
3. Mince green onions using FRENCH CHEF'S KNIFE.
4. Place zucchini pulp in 1-quart SAUCE PAN; cover with cold water; bring to a boil; simmer 5 minutes; drain.
5. Melt butter in 2-quart SAUCE PAN; stir in flour using MIX-STIR; add milk; cook until thick, smooth, stirring constantly.
6. Add zucchini pulp, eggs, celery, onions, deviled ham, parsley, chives, salt, pepper, nutmeg, ½ cup crumbs; blend thoroughly using TURNING FORK.
7. Fill each zucchini shell with stuffing; sprinkle with remaining crumbs; place in 9 x 13-inch bake pan.
8. Bake 30 minutes at 375° F.
9. Four servings.

Summer Vegetable Medley

2 cloves garlic
3 medium potatoes
4 carrots
2 onions
2 green peppers
1 small eggplant
2 zucchini
2 summer squash
¼ cup butter or margarine
1 8-ounce can tomato sauce
1 cup water
  Dash Tabasco sauce
  Salt, pepper

1. Cut garlic cloves in half using PARING KNIFE.
2. Pare potatoes using PARING KNIFE; cut in cubes using FRENCH CHEF'S KNIFE.
3. Scrape carrots using PARING KNIFE; cut in thin crosswise slices using FRENCH CHEF'S KNIFE.
4. Peel onions using PARING KNIFE; cut in thin slices using TRIMMER.
5. Seed green peppers; cut in eighths using TRIMMER.
6. Cut eggplant in cubes (do *not* pare) using FRENCH CHEF'S KNIFE.
7. Cut zucchini, summer squash, in thin slices using FRENCH CHEF'S KNIFE.
8. Sauté garlic in butter in 10-inch FRY PAN stirring with TURNING FORK; remove pieces.
9. Add vegetables, tomato sauce, water, Tabasco; cover; simmer 20–25 minutes, or until vegetables are tender.
10. Season with salt, pepper.
11. Eight servings.

Vegetables

Eggplant-Tomato Casserole

- 2 medium eggplants
- 1 teaspoon salt
- 2 tablespoons flour
- 2 1-pound cans stewed tomatoes
- 1 tablespoon instant chopped onion
- 2 teaspoons sugar
- ½ teaspoon paprika
- ¼ teaspoon oregano
- ⅛ teaspoon pepper
- ½ cup olive oil
- ½ cup grated Parmesan cheese

1. Slice eggplants in ¼-inch slices using PETITE CARVER; pare using PARING KNIFE; sprinkle with salt.
2. Blend flour, liquid from tomatoes together in 2-quart SAUCE PAN using MIX-STIR.
3. Add tomatoes, onion, sugar, paprika, oregano, pepper; bring to boil; simmer 5 minutes.
4. Heat 2 tablespoons olive oil in 10-inch FRY PAN over medium heat; fry eggplant slices until lightly browned, tender; drain on paper toweling; continue until all slices have been browned, adding more oil as necessary.
5. Line bottom of 9 x 13-inch bake pan with eggplant slices; top with half the tomato sauce; repeat layers; sprinkle cheese over top.
6. Bake 30 minutes at 350° F.
7. Six–eight servings.

Corn Curry (New Zealand)

- 3 tablespoons butter or margarine
- 2 tablespoons chopped green pepper
- 1 tablespoon instant minced onion
- 1 10-ounce package frozen corn
- ½ teaspoon salt
- ½ teaspoon curry powder
  Dash pepper
- ½ cup dairy sour cream

1. Melt butter in 8-inch FRY PAN; sauté green pepper, onion about 1 minute over medium heat, stirring with TURNING FORK.
2. Add corn, salt, curry powder, pepper; cover; simmer 8–10 minutes or until corn is tender.
3. Stir in sour cream; heat, stirring constantly.
4. Four servings.

Cucumber Au Gratin (Ireland)

- 2 cucumbers
- 2 tomatoes
  Salt, pepper
- 3 tablespoons butter or margarine
- 3 tablespoons flour
- ¼ teaspoon salt
- 1 cup milk
- ½ cup grated Cheddar cheese
- 2 tablespoons grated Cheddar cheese

1. Pare cucumbers using PARING KNIFE; cut in thin slices using TRIMMER.
2. Cut tomatoes in ¼-inch slices using TRIMMER.
3. Cook cucumber slices in boiling, salted water about 10 minutes; drain.
4. Arrange in shallow baking dish; sprinkle lightly with salt, pepper.
5. In a 1-quart SAUCE PAN, melt butter over low heat; stir in flour, salt using MIX-STIR, gradually stir in milk.
6. Cook over low heat, stirring constantly until thickened; add ½ cup grated cheese; stir until cheese melts.
7. Pour sauce over cucumbers; top with tomato slices, grated cheese.
8. Bake 10–15 minutes at 400° F. or until lightly browned.
9. Five–six servings.

Chinese Green Beans

1 pound fresh green beans
3 tablespoons peanut oil
1 4-ounce can sliced mushrooms, drained
1 teaspoon salt
1 teaspoon sugar
⅓ cup canned chicken broth
1 teaspoon cornstarch
1 tablespoon chicken broth

1. Remove ends from beans using PARING KNIFE; cut diagonally in 2-inch pieces using FRENCH CHEF'S KNIFE.
2. Heat oil in 10-inch FRY PAN over medium-high heat; add beans; fry 3–4 minutes, stirring constantly using TURNING FORK.
3. Add mushrooms, salt, sugar, chicken broth; blend together.
4. Cover; cook over medium heat 5 minutes until beans are tender but crisp.
5. Dissolve cornstarch in chicken broth; stir into beans; cook until thickened, stirring constantly.
6. Four–five servings.

Spanish Green Peas

2 whole canned pimientos
¼ cup ripe olives
2 tablespoons butter or margarine
½ teaspoon onion salt
¼ teaspoon crushed oregano
¼ teaspoon pepper
1 1-pound can green peas, drained

1. Chop pimientos using FRENCH CHEF'S KNIFE.
2. Slice olives using TRIMMER.
3. Melt butter in 1-quart SAUCE PAN; add onion salt, oregano, pepper; simmer 3 minutes.
4. Add peas, pimientos, olives; toss lightly to mix using TURNING FORK; cover; simmer 10 minutes or until peas are hot; shake pan occasionally.
5. Four servings.

French Green Peas

3 slices bacon
2 small onions
2 sprigs parsley
½ canned pimiento
3 tablespoons flour
1½ cups canned chicken broth
½ teaspoon salt
Dash pepper
1 10-ounce package frozen peas

1. Dice bacon using TRIMMER.
2. Peel onions using PARING KNIFE; slice using TRIMMER.
3. Snip parsley using KITCHEN SHEARS.
4. Cut pimiento into strips using TRIMMER.
5. Fry bacon until crisp in 8-inch FRY PAN over medium heat; remove using PERFORATED SPOON; drain on paper toweling.
6. Add flour to bacon fat in pan; blend until smooth using MIX-STIR; cook over low heat 1–2 minutes.
7. Add chicken broth, salt, pepper; cook over medium heat, stirring constantly, until smooth, thickened.
8. Add peas, onions, parsley; cover; cook over low heat until peas are tender, about 20 minutes.
9. Garnish with crisp bacon, pimiento strips.
10. Four servings.

Vegetables

Mushrooms Baked in Foil

1 pint fresh mushrooms
Salt, pepper

1. Trim stems of mushrooms, remove blemishes using PARING KNIFE; wash; drain; dry.
2. Place mushrooms on double thick sheet of Alcoa Wrap; add salt, pepper.
3. Place sheet of Alcoa Wrap over mushrooms; fold each side over in double fold; seal tightly.
4. Place foil package on baking sheet; bake 30 minutes at 350° F.
5. Three–four servings.

Baked Stuffed Onions

6 large onions
¾ cup seasoned bread stuffing
¾ cup chopped cooked chicken
¾ cup thin white sauce
1 egg yolk
Salt, pepper
½ cup buttered cracker crumbs

1. Peel onions using PARING KNIFE; boil 10 minutes in salted water; drain; turn upside down to cool.
2. Remove centers of onions, leaving shell thick enough to retain shape.
3. Chop onion centers using FRENCH CHEF'S KNIFE; combine with stuffing, chicken, white sauce, egg yolk, salt, pepper using TURNING FORK.
4. Place each onion in center of square of Alcoa Wrap; bring sides of foil up around onion to form cup.
5. Fill onions with stuffing mixture; sprinkle cracker crumbs on top; place foil cups on baking sheet.
6. Bake 40 minutes at 350° F.
7. Serve in foil cups.
8. Six servings.

Souffléed Cauliflower

2 10-ounce packages frozen cauliflower
2 eggs, separated
1 10½-ounce can condensed mushroom soup, undiluted
2 tablespoons sherry wine
1 tablespoon light cream
¼ teaspoon salt
⅛ teaspoon pepper
½ cup grated Cheddar cheese
Paprika

1. Cook cauliflower as directed on package; drain; arrange in 1½-quart casserole.
2. Beat egg yolks slightly using MIX-STIR; add mushroom soup, sherry, cream, salt, pepper; beat thoroughly; add cheese.
3. Beat egg whites until stiff; fold into egg yolk mixture.
4. Pour over cauliflower; sprinkle with paprika.
5. Bake 20 minutes at 425° F.
6. Five–six servings.

Stuffed Artichokes with Mornay Sauce

4 artichokes
1 10-ounce package frozen cut asparagus
3 tablespoons butter or margarine
3 tablespoons flour
½ teaspoon salt
½ cup light cream
½ cup grated American cheese

1. Wash artichokes; drain; remove loose discolored leaves around base using PARING KNIFE.

2. Drop artichokes into boiling unsalted water to cover; simmer 15–20 minutes or until just tender. (Retain 1 cup liquid for sauce.)

3. Cut away fuzzy centers or "chokes" of artichokes using PARING KNIFE; discard; set artichokes aside.

4. Cook asparagus according to directions on package.

5. To make Mornay Sauce: Melt butter in 1-quart SAUCE PAN; add flour, salt, stirring with MIX-STIR.

6. Gradually add cream, the 1 cup artichoke liquid; cook over low heat, stirring constantly with MIX-STIR until thickened.

7. Add cheese; stir until melted.

8. Place each artichoke in center of sheet of Alcoa Wrap; crush foil around artichokes to form cups.

9. Fill centers of artichokes with asparagus; pour Mornay Sauce over top.

10. Place foil cups on baking sheet; bake 25–30 minutes at 350° F. or until sauce is bubbly, lightly browned.

11. Serve in foil cups.

12. Four servings.

Deviled Mushrooms

1 pint fresh mushrooms
Salt, pepper
2 teaspoons lemon juice
1 hard cooked egg yolk
1 raw egg yolk
½ cup dry bread crumbs
1 tablespoon butter or margarine, softened
Dash Tabasco sauce

1. Wash mushrooms; remove stems using PARING KNIFE.

2. Place mushroom caps and stems in 1-quart casserole; season with salt, pepper, lemon juice.

3. Mash hard cooked egg yolk using TURNING FORK; add raw yolk, bread crumbs, butter, Tabasco; blend thoroughly.

4. Sprinkle egg-bread crumb mixture over top of mushrooms.

5. Bake 20–25 minutes at 350° F.

6. Four servings.

Carrots in Sauce

1 pound carrots
4 whole cloves
1 bay leaf
2 tablespoons butter or margarine
2 tablespoons flour
1 cup milk
1 teaspoon chopped parsley
½ teaspoon salt
Dash cayenne pepper

1. Wash carrots; scrape using PARING KNIFE; dice using FRENCH CHEF'S KNIFE.

2. Put in 2-quart SAUCE PAN along with cloves, bay leaf; cover with boiling water; cover pan; simmer until tender.

3. Drain, reserving 1 cup water; set carrots aside.

4. Melt butter in SAUCE PAN; add flour, blending with MIX-STIR.

5. Add milk, reserved liquid; cook until thickened.

6. Add parsley, salt, cayenne, carrots; heat about 5 minutes.

7. Garnish with lemon slices if desired.

8. Six servings.

Vegetables

Baked Asparagus with Basil Sour Cream

¾ pound fresh asparagus spears
½ cup dairy sour cream
½ cup butter or margarine, melted
2 cups soft bread crumbs
1 teaspoon sweet basil
½ teaspoon salt

1. Wash asparagus; trim ends using FRENCH CHEF'S KNIFE.
2. Cook asparagus spears until just tender; place spears in 9-inch square bake pan; spread sour cream over spears using SPREADER SPATULA.
3. Combine melted butter, bread crumbs, basil, salt; toss together using TURNING FORK; sprinkle over sour cream.
4. Bake 15–20 minutes at 375° F. or until crumb topping is browned.
5. Three–four servings.

Golden Potato Wedges

2 medium baking potatoes
¼ cup butter or margarine, melted
½ cup fine dry bread crumbs
Salt, pepper
2 tablespoons butter or margarine

1. Pare potatoes using PARING KNIFE; cut potatoes in half crosswise using FRENCH CHEF'S KNIFE; cut each half in four long wedges.
2. Dip wedges in melted butter, then into bread crumbs; place in greased shallow baking dish; sprinkle with salt, pepper; dot with butter.
3. Bake 35–40 minutes at 400° F. or until tender, golden brown.
4. Two–three servings.

Corn Pudding

1 large green pepper
1 medium onion
4 slices white bread
¼ cup butter or margarine
¼ cup flour
2 teaspoons salt
1 teaspoon paprika
1 teaspoon dry mustard
⅛ teaspoon cayenne pepper
1 cup milk
2 eggs
2 No. 303 cans cream-style corn
3 tablespoons butter or margarine

1. Seed green pepper using PARING KNIFE; finely chop using FRENCH CHEF'S KNIFE.
2. Peel onion using PARING KNIFE; finely chop using FRENCH CHEF'S KNIFE.
3. Cut bread slices into cubes using FRENCH CHEF'S KNIFE.
4. Melt butter in 10-inch FRY PAN; sauté green pepper, onion 5 minutes using TURNING FORK to stir.
5. Add flour, salt, paprika, dry mustard, cayenne; blend using MIX-STIR.
6. Add milk; cook stirring constantly until thickened.
7. Beat eggs using MIX-STIR; add to sauce along with corn; blend well.
8. Melt butter in 8-inch FRY PAN; sauté bread cubes until brown, stirring with TURNING FORK; blend into corn pudding.
9. Pour pudding into greased 2-quart casserole; bake 1 hour at 350° F.
10. Eight servings.

Cottage Potatoes

2 medium potatoes
3 large sprigs parsley
Salt, pepper
1 tablespoon butter or margarine
¼ cup light cream
Grated Parmesan cheese

1. Pare potatoes using PARING KNIFE; cut into ⅜-inch strips using FRENCH CHEF'S KNIFE.
2. Snip parsley using KITCHEN SHEARS.
3. Place potato strips in center of double thick square of Alcoa Wrap; sprinkle with parsley, salt, pepper; dot with butter; pour on cream; sprinkle top with Parmesan cheese.
4. Bring torn edges of foil together; fold in tight double folds over top and at each end.
5. Place foil package on baking sheet; bake 40–45 minutes at 425° F.
6. Two–three servings.

Cottage Cheese Herbed Onions

2 pounds whole small onions
¼ cup butter or margarine
¼ cup flour
½ cup milk
½ teaspoon salt
Dash pepper
1 teaspoon marjoram
1½ cups cottage cheese, cream style
1½ cups buttered fresh bread crumbs

1. Peel onions using PARING KNIFE; cook in boiling salted water 20 minutes or until tender; drain.
2. Place onions in greased 2-quart casserole.
3. Melt butter in 1-quart SAUCE PAN; blend in flour using MIX-STIR; add milk; cook until thick, stirring constantly.
4. Quickly blend in salt, pepper, marjoram, cottage cheese; spread over onions using SPREADER SPATULA; top with buttered crumbs.
5. Bake 25 minutes at 375° F.
6. Six servings.

Asparagus à la King

1 pound fresh asparagus
4 hard cooked eggs
¼ cup butter or margarine
¼ cup flour
2 cups milk
½ teaspoon salt
Dash pepper
1 teaspoon leaf oregano
2 cups grated Cheddar cheese

1. Wash asparagus; cut into 1-inch pieces using FRENCH CHEF'S KNIFE.
2. Cook asparagus until just tender; set aside.
3. Dice eggs using FRENCH CHEF'S KNIFE.
4. Melt butter in 3-quart SAUCE PAN; add flour, blending with MIX-STIR.
5. Add milk; cook over low heat stirring constantly until thickened.
6. Add salt, pepper, oregano, cheese; stir until cheese melts.
7. Add asparagus, eggs; blend well; heat 5 minutes.
8. Serve in patty shells or over chow mein noodles.
9. Five–six servings.

Vegetables

Chow String Beans with Sour Cream

2 10-ounce packages frozen cut green beans
¼ cup vegetable oil
3 tablespoons chopped onion
1 teaspoon flour
1 tablespoon water
½ teaspoon salt
⅛ teaspoon pepper
¼ teaspoon grated lemon peel
1½ tablespoons chopped parsley
½ cup dairy sour cream
2 tablespoons cornflake crumbs
¼ cup grated Cheddar cheese

1. Thaw green beans.
2. Heat oil in 10-inch FRY PAN over medium-high heat; add green beans, onions; cook stirring constantly 1 minute using TURNING FORK; cover; cook additional 1 minute. (Note: Beans should be bright green with crisp, crunchy texture.)
3. Stir in flour; add water, salt, pepper, lemon peel, parsley, sour cream; blend thoroughly.
4. Pour into 1-quart casserole; sprinkle with cornflake crumbs; top with grated cheese.
5. Bake 20 minutes at 350° F.
6. Six servings.

Sweet Potato Balls

2 cups mashed sweet potatoes
2 tablespoons flour
2 tablespoons sugar
1 egg, beaten
1 quart oil for frying
Confectioners' Sugar

1. Combine potatoes, flour, sugar, egg; blend together using TURNING FORK.
2. Form mixture in balls, 1-inch in diameter.
3. Pour oil into 10-inch FRY PAN; heat to 375° F.
4. Drop potato balls into hot oil; fry to golden brown, turning with TURNING FORK; remove using PERFORATED SPOON; drain on paper toweling.
5. Sprinkle with confectioners' sugar; serve hot.
6. Four servings.

Italian Rice with Peas

1 small onion
3 tablespoons butter or margarine
¾ cup raw rice
½ 10-ounce package frozen peas
1 cup diced cooked ham
2½ cups canned chicken broth
1 tablespoon butter or margarine
¼ cup grated Parmesan cheese

1. Peel onion using PARING KNIFE; chop using FRENCH CHEF'S KNIFE.
2. Melt butter in 2-quart SAUCE PAN; sauté onions over medium heat 2-3 minutes, stirring with TURNING FORK.
3. Stir in rice, peas, ham, chicken broth; bring to boil.
4. Cover; simmer 15–20 minutes or until all broth is absorbed.
5. Stir in butter, cheese.
6. Six servings.

Dublin Cheese and Potato Pie

4 medium potatoes
2 medium onions
1 cup milk
1 cup grated Cheddar cheese
1 teaspoon Worcestershire sauce
1 teaspoon salt
¼ teaspoon pepper
1 tablespoon flour
3 tablespoons butter or margarine
2 tablespoons dry bread crumbs

1. Pare potatoes using PARING KNIFE; cut into ⅛-inch slices using FRENCH CHEF'S KNIFE.
2. Peel onions using PARING KNIFE; cut into thin slices using TRIMMER.
3. Combine milk, cheese in 1-quart SAUCE PAN; heat over low heat until cheese melts; stir constantly with MIX-STIR; add Worcestershire sauce.
4. Combine salt, pepper, flour.
5. Place layer of sliced potatoes in bottom of greased 1½-quart casserole; sprinkle one half of flour mixture over top; add layer of onions; dot with half of butter; repeat layers using remaining ingredients.
6. Pour cheese sauce over all; top with bread crumbs.
7. Bake 1 hour at 350° F.
8. Four–five servings.

Rarebit Stuffed Peppers

3 large green peppers
½ pound Cheddar cheese
2 tablespoons butter or margarine
2 tablespoons minced onion
1 No. 2 can kidney beans, drained
2 tablespoons ketchup
½ teaspoon Worcestershire sauce
½ teaspoon salt
Dash pepper

1. Cut green peppers in half lengthwise using TRIMMER; remove seeds; panbroil 5 minutes; drain.
2. Cut cheese into small cubes using FRENCH CHEF'S KNIFE.
3. Melt butter in 10-inch FRY PAN; sauté onion until tender, stirring with TURNING FORK; remove from heat.
4. Add cheese, kidney beans, ketchup, Worcestershire sauce, salt, pepper; blend.
5. Fill peppers with cheese mixture; place filled peppers in 9 x 13-inch bake pan.
6. Bake 30 minutes at 350° F.
7. Six servings.

Sauces

Foo Yung Sauce (China)

1 cup canned chicken broth
⅓ cup frozen peas, thawed
1 tablespoon cornstarch
2 tablespoons canned chicken broth
1 tablespoon soy sauce

1. Combine chicken broth, peas in 1-quart SAUCE PAN; bring to boil; simmer 3 minutes.
2. Dissolve cornstarch in 2 tablespoons chicken broth; blend into hot broth using MIX-STIR.
3. Add soy sauce; cook 2 minutes, stirring constantly.
4. Serve over Egg Foo Yung.
5. About 1 cup sauce.

Lemon Cucumber Sauce

2 egg yolks
¼ cup lemon juice
½ cup butter or margarine
½ cup well-drained, grated cucumber

1. Beat egg yolks slightly in 1-quart SAUCE PAN using MIX-STIR.
2. Add lemon juice, ¼ cup butter; stir over low heat until blended.
3. Add remaining ¼ cup butter; continue cooking, stirring constantly, until thickened, smooth.
4. Stir in grated cucumber.
5. Serve over Salmon Casserole.
6. About 1 cup sauce.

Chateau Sauce (France)

1 small onion
2 tablespoons pickled onions
¼ cup butter or margarine
¼ cup flour
6 beef bouillon cubes
3 cups boiling water
⅓ cup tomato purée
2 tablespoons bottled meat sauce
¼ cup chopped canned mushrooms
¼ cup white wine
½ cup butter or margarine

1. Peel onion using PARING KNIFE; chop onion, pickled onions using FRENCH CHEF'S KNIFE.
2. Melt butter in 10-inch FRY PAN; sauté onions until lightly browned, stirring with TURNING FORK.
3. Blend in flour using MIX-STIR; cook over medium heat 8–9 minutes or until browned, stirring constantly.
4. Dissolve bouillon cubes in boiling water; stir in tomato purée, meat sauce; add to sautéed onions; blend well.
5. Cook over medium heat about 10 minutes or until thickened, stirring constantly.
6. Combine mushrooms, wine in 1-quart SAUCE PAN; cook uncovered over medium heat until liquid has evaporated; add to sauce.
7. Add butter; blend thoroughly.
8. Serve with meat.
9. About 4 cups sauce.

Sauces

Sweet-Sour Sauce (Polynesia)

1 tablespoon butter or margarine
1 cup water
½ cup cider vinegar
3 tablespoons soy sauce
¼ cup sugar
1 tablespoon cornstarch
3 tablespoons sherry wine

1. Melt butter in 2-quart SAUCE PAN; add water, vinegar, soy sauce, sugar; blend thoroughly using MIX-STIR; bring to boil; simmer 5 minutes.
2. Dissolve cornstarch in sherry; slowly stir into simmering liquid.
3. Simmer, stirring constantly until thickened.
4. Serve with pork, spareribs.
5. About 2 cups sauce.

Parsley Sauce (Denmark)

2 tablespoons butter or margarine
2 tablespoons flour
1 cup canned chicken broth
¼ teaspoon salt
1 teaspoon lemon juice
1 teaspoon grated lemon peel
2 tablespoons chopped parsley

1. Melt butter in 1-quart SAUCE PAN; stir in flour using MIX-STIR; cook over low heat 2 minutes.
2. Gradually stir in broth, salt; cook over low heat until thickened, stirring constantly.
3. Add lemon juice, lemon peel, parsley; blend well.
4. Serve with fish.
5. About 1 cup sauce.

Mexican Chili Sauce

2 8-ounce cans tomato purée
¼ cup tomato paste
¾ cup canned chicken broth
¼ cup instant chopped onion
1 teaspoon chili powder
½ teaspoon cinnamon
½ teaspoon ground cloves
½ teaspoon ground coriander
⅛ teaspoon instant minced garlic
1 tablespoon sugar
1 teaspoon salt
¼ teaspoon pepper
1 1-ounce square unsweetened chocolate

1. Combine all ingredients except chocolate in 2-quart SAUCE PAN; blend thoroughly using MIX-STIR.
2. Bring to boil over medium heat; add chocolate; simmer over low heat until chocolate melts; stir frequently.
3. Serve with roast turkey, chicken or pork.
4. About 4 cups sauce.

Sauce Béarnaise (France)

1 teaspoon tarragon
1 teaspoon chervil
2 tablespoons finely chopped
    scallions
4 whole black peppercorns, ground
¼ cup tarragon vinegar
¼ cup white wine
3 egg yolks
1 tablespoon water
½ pound butter or margarine
1 teaspoon salt
¼ teaspoon cayenne

1. Combine tarragon, chervil, scallions, ground pepper, vinegar, wine in 1-quart SAUCE PAN; blend well using MIX-STIR.
2. Cook over medium heat until reduced to a thick paste, stirring constantly; remove from heat; cool slightly.
3. Combine egg yolks, water; blend well using MIX-STIR; add to seasoned paste, beating until light, fluffy.
4. Place over low heat; add butter in thirds, beating well after each addition.
5. Add salt, cayenne; blend well.
6. Serve with broiled fish.
7. About 1 cup sauce.

Raisin Sauce

½ cup brown sugar, firmly packed
1½ teaspoons dry mustard
1½ tablespoons flour
½ cup seedless raisins
¼ cup vinegar
1¾ cups water

1. Combine all ingredients in 1-quart SAUCE PAN; blend thoroughly using MIX-STIR.
2. Bring to boil over medium heat; simmer 15 minutes over low heat; stir occasionally.
3. Serve with ham or fresh pork.
4. About 2 cups sauce.

Steak Sauce

6 tablespoons butter or margarine
6 tablespoons lemon juice
1 teaspoon dry mustard
2 tablespoons Worcestershire sauce
Salt, pepper

1. Melt butter in 1-quart SAUCE PAN; blend in remaining ingredients using MIX-STIR; simmer 5 minutes.
2. Serve with broiled steaks.
3. About ½ cup sauce.

Mint Sauce

Fresh mint
½ cup vinegar
1 cup water
¼ cup lemon juice
½ cup water
2 tablespoons sugar
¼ teaspoon salt

1. Snip enough fresh mint to make ½ cup using KITCHEN SHEARS.
2. Add ¼ cup mint to 1-quart SAUCE PAN along with vinegar, 1 cup water; simmer until liquid is reduced one half; strain.
3. Add lemon juice, the ½ cup water, sugar, salt; blend using MIX-STIR; chill.
4. Just before serving add remaining ¼ cup mint.
5. Serve with cold roast lamb.
6. About 1 cup sauce.

Sauces

Allemande Sauce (France)

3 tablespoons butter or margarine
2 tablespoons flour
1 cup canned chicken broth
¼ teaspoon salt
¼ teaspoon paprika
1 egg yolk
1 teaspoon lemon juice

1. Melt butter in 1-quart SAUCE PAN over medium heat; stir in flour using MIX-STIR; gradually add broth; blend well.
2. Cook over low heat until thickened, stirring constantly.
3. Add salt, paprika, egg yolk; beat thoroughly; continue cooking 1–2 minutes, stirring constantly.
4. Stir in lemon juice.
5. Serve with asparagus or green beans.
6. About 1 cup sauce.

Egg-Lemon Sauce (Greece)

4 eggs
2 tablespoons lemon juice
1 cup hot canned chicken broth
½ teaspoon salt
Dash white pepper

1. Beat eggs in 1-quart SAUCE PAN using MIX-STIR; gradually blend in lemon juice.
2. Slowly add hot chicken broth, beating constantly; add salt, pepper.
3. Cook over low heat 5–8 minutes or until thickened; stir constantly; do not boil.
4. Serve with broccoli, asparagus, green beans, artichoke hearts.
5. About 1½ cups sauce.

White Clam Sauce (Italy)

3 cloves garlic
2 large sprigs parsley
2 tablespoons olive oil
1 cup canned clam juice
¼ teaspoon salt
Dash pepper
2 7½-ounce cans minced clams, drained

1. Mince garlic cloves using FRENCH CHEF'S KNIFE.
2. Snip parsley using KITCHEN SHEARS.
3. Heat oil in 1-quart SAUCE PAN; sauté garlic 3 minutes over medium heat, stirring with TURNING FORK.
4. Add parsley, clam juice, salt, pepper; simmer 10 minutes.
5. Add clams; simmer 2 minutes.
6. Serve with spaghetti.
7. About 2 cups sauce.

Variation: For Red Clam Sauce, add ¼ cup tomato paste.

Old-Fashioned Lemon Sauce

½ cup butter or margarine
1 cup sugar
¼ cup water
1 egg
3 tablespoons lemon juice
Grated peel of 1 lemon

1. Combine all ingredients in 1-quart SAUCE PAN; blend thoroughly using MIX-STIR.
2. Cook over medium heat, stirring constantly, just until mixture comes to a boil.
3. Serve warm over Blueberry Buckle, gingerbread.
4. About 1⅓ cups sauce.

Ginger Sauce (Lebanon)

½ cup sugar
2 tablespoons cornstarch
⅛ teaspoon nutmeg
½ teaspoon ginger
Grated peel of 1 lemon
1¼ cups pineapple juice
1 12-ounce can apricot nectar
2 tablespoons lemon juice

1. Combine sugar, cornstarch, nutmeg, ginger, lemon peel in 2-quart SAUCE PAN; blend together with MIX-STIR.
2. Add pineapple juice, apricot nectar, lemon juice; stir until smooth.
3. Bring to a boil; cook over low heat, stirring constantly, about 10 minutes or until smooth, thickened.
4. Cool, stirring occasionally to prevent film from forming.
5. Store in covered container in refrigerator.
6. Serve cold with fresh, canned, or frozen fruits.
7. About 3 cups sauce.

Almond Apricot Sauce

2 cups dried apricots
2 cups water
½ cup sugar
1 teaspoon lemon juice
½ cup slivered blanched almonds

1. Cut apricots into eighths using KITCHEN SHEARS.
2. Place in 2-quart SAUCE PAN along with water; simmer about 20 minutes or until apricots are tender.
3. Add sugar, lemon juice, almonds; stir.
4. Serve warm over plain sponge cake or pound cake.
5. About 2½ cups sauce.

Nutmeg Sauce

¼ cup butter or margarine
1½ tablespoons flour
½ cup sugar
1 egg yolk
1 teaspoon vanilla
1¼ cups boiling water
¼ teaspoon nutmeg

1. Melt butter in 1-quart SAUCE PAN; remove from heat; blend in flour, sugar using MIX-STIR.
2. Blend in egg yolk, vanilla; gradually add boiling water, blending thoroughly.
3. Cook over low heat, stirring constantly, until thickened.
4. Stir in nutmeg.
5. Serve warm over gingerbread, spice cake.
6. About 2 cups sauce.

Rum Sauce

2 eggs
1 cup sugar
1 cup heavy cream, whipped
Rum or rum extract

1. Beat eggs until light using MIX-STIR.
2. Add sugar gradually, continuing to beat until mixture loses its grainy texture.
3. Fold into whipped cream; flavor to taste with rum or rum extract
4. Serve over plum pudding, apple crisp.
5. About 1½ cups sauce.

Desserts

Danish Apple Cake

2 pounds cooking apples
¼ cup sugar
½ cup water
1 teaspoon vanilla
2 cups dry bread crumbs
1 cup oatmeal, uncooked
¼ cup brown sugar, firmly packed
1 teaspoon cinnamon
1 cup butter or margarine, melted
¾ cup strawberry preserves

1. Pare, quarter, core apples using PARING KNIFE; slice using TRIMMER.
2. Combine apple slices, sugar, water, vanilla in 2-quart SAUCE PAN; bring to boil; simmer 5–10 minutes or until apples are just tender; cool slightly.
3. In bowl combine bread crumbs, oatmeal, brown sugar, cinnamon.
4. Spread ½ the crumb mixture in bottom of greased 9-inch square bake pan; top with apples; pour ½ cup melted butter over apples.
5. Spread preserves over apples using SPREADER SPATULA; top with remaining crumb mixture, melted butter.
6. Bake 30 minutes at 400° F.
7. Serve warm.
8. Eight–nine servings.

Norwegian Fruit Dessert

2 oranges
1 small banana
¾ cup seedless white grapes
2 ounces shelled walnuts
1 small red apple
1 teaspoon lemon juice
1 teaspoon water
3 eggs
3 tablespoons sugar
½ tablespoon brandy or rum

1. Peel oranges using TRIMMER; separate into sections.
2. Peel banana; coarsely chop using FRENCH CHEF'S KNIFE.
3. Cut grapes in half using PARING KNIFE.
4. Chop walnuts using FRENCH CHEF'S KNIFE.
5. Cut apple in quarters using TRIMMER; core using PARING KNIFE; coarsely chop using FRENCH CHEF'S KNIFE; sprinkle with diluted lemon juice.
6. Combine fruits, walnuts; refrigerate.
7. When ready to serve, beat eggs until soft peaks form; gradually beat in sugar, brandy.
8. Serve sauce over chilled fruit mixture.
9. Six servings.

Desserts

Deep Dish Apple-Cheese Pie

  Pastry for 1 crust 8-inch square pan
4 medium apples
¼ cup sugar
¼ teaspoon cinnamon
¼ teaspoon nutmeg
2 eggs
½ cup sugar
⅛ teaspoon salt
1 cup milk, scalded
1 teaspoon vanilla
1 cup creamed cottage cheese

1. Line 8-inch square bake pan with pastry; flute edges.
2. Pare, quarter, core apples using PARING KNIFE; slice thinly using TRIMMER; arrange slices in pastry shell.
3. Combine sugar, cinnamon, nutmeg; sprinkle over apples.
4. Bake 15 minutes at 425° F.; remove from oven; reduce temperature to 325° F.
5. Beat eggs using MIX-STIR; add sugar, salt, milk, vanilla, cottage cheese; blend thoroughly.
6. Pour cheese mixture over apples; spread evenly using SPREADER SPATULA.
7. Bake 40–50 minutes at 325° F.
8. Cool before serving.
9. Six servings.

Rhubarb Custard Pie

  Pastry for 1 crust 9-inch pie
  Pastry for lattice strips
1¼ pounds fresh rhubarb
3 eggs
3 tablespoons milk
2 cups sugar
¼ cup flour
¾ teaspoon nutmeg
1 tablespoon butter or margarine

1. Line 9-inch pie pan with pastry; flute edge.
2. Trim root, leaf ends of rhubarb using TRIMMER; cut stocks into 1-inch pieces (to make 4 cups) using FRENCH CHEF'S KNIFE; arrange in pie shell.
3. Beat eggs, milk using MIX-STIR; add sugar, flour, nutmeg; blend thoroughly.
4. Pour egg mixture over rhubarb; dot with butter; arrange lattice strips over top.
5. Bake 50–60 minutes at 400° F. or until nicely browned.
6. Serve warm.
7. Six–seven servings.

Southern Pecan Pie

  Pastry for 1 crust 9-inch pie
½ cup butter or margarine
½ cup sugar
3 eggs
¾ cup white corn syrup
2 tablespoons honey
1 teaspoon vanilla
2 cups pecan halves

1. Line 9-inch pie pan with pastry; flute edge.
2. Cream butter until soft; add sugar gradually, continuing to beat until light, fluffy.
3. Beat eggs using MIX-STIR; add syrup, honey, vanilla; blend thoroughly.
4. Slowly beat egg mixture into butter-sugar mixture; add 1 cup pecans.
5. Pour into pie shell; arrange remaining 1 cup pecans on top.
6. Bake 50–55 minutes at 350° F.; cool.
7. Top with whipped cream if desired.
8. Six–seven servings.

Black Bottom Pie

Vanilla Wafer Crust:
1⅓ cups fine vanilla wafer crumbs
    (about 24)
¼ cup soft butter or margarine
¼ cup sugar

Filling:
4 egg yolks
1 cup milk
1 cup light cream
½ cup sugar
4 teaspoons cornstarch
1½ squares unsweetened chocolate,
    melted
½ teaspoon vanilla
1 tablespoon unflavored gelatin
¼ cup cold water
1 tablespoon rum
3 egg whites
¼ teaspoon salt
¼ teaspoon cream of tartar
¼ cup sugar

1. Combine wafer crumbs, butter, sugar; blend together with TURNING FORK until crumbly.

2. Pour into 9-inch pie pan; press crumbs evenly, firmly to bottom, sides of pan.

3. Bake 8 minutes at 375° F.; cool.

4. Combine egg yolks, milk, cream in 1-quart SAUCE PAN; beat thoroughly using MIX-STIR.

5. Combine sugar, cornstarch; blend into milk mixture; cook over low heat about 20 minutes or until mixture coats spoon heavily; stir occasionally.

6. Remove 1 cup custard; add melted chocolate, vanilla to it; beat until cool; pour into prepared shell; spread evenly using SPREADER SPATULA.

7. Stir gelatin into water; add to remaining custard; stir until dissolved; cool slightly; stir in rum.

8. Beat egg whites, salt until frothy; add cream of tartar; beat until stiff; beat in sugar, 1 tablespoon at a time.

9. Fold gelatin-custard mixture into egg whites; pour on top of chocolate custard; spread evenly using SPREADER SPATULA; chill until firm.

10. Top with sweetened whipped cream if desired.

11. Six–seven servings.

Fresh Pear Pie (Canada)

Pastry for 2 crust 9-inch pie
5-6 fresh pears
½ cup sugar
2 tablespoons quick cooking tapioca
⅛ teaspoon salt
¼ teaspoon cinnamon
¼ teaspoon nutmeg
¼ teaspoon ginger
1 tablespoon lemon juice

1. Line 9-inch pie pan with pastry.

2. Pare, quarter, core pears using TRIMMER; arrange slices in pie shell.

3. In small bowl combine sugar, tapioca, salt, cinnamon, nutmeg; ginger; pour over slices; sprinkle with lemon juice.

4. Cover with top crust; seal edges; flute; bake 40 minutes at 425° F.

5. Six–seven servings.

Desserts

Paradise Pie

Meringue Shell:
- 6 egg whites, room temperature
- 2 cups sugar
- 2 teaspoons vinegar
- 1½ teaspoons vanilla
- ⅛ teaspoon salt

Filling:
- 2 squares unsweetened chocolate
- ½ cup sugar
- ¼ cup cold water
- 4 egg yolks
- 1 cup butter or margarine
- 1 cup confectioners' sugar
- 4 egg whites
- 1 cup whipping cream
- 1 teaspoon vanilla

1. Beat egg whites, using electric mixer at high speed, until stiff but not dry.
2. Add one half the sugar, 2 tablespoons at a time, beating well after each addition.
3. Add vinegar, vanilla, salt; blend; add remaining sugar, beating thoroughly.
4. Pour mixture into 12-inch pizza pan; spread over bottom using SPATULA SPREADER; shape so there is a 1-inch high rim around edge.
5. Bake 1 hour at 250° F.; cool.
6. Combine chocolate, sugar, water in 3-quart SAUCE PAN; heat until melted.
7. Beat egg yolks until lemon-colored using MIX-STIR; add to chocolate mixture; cook until thick, stirring constantly; cool.
8. Cream butter, sugar together until light, fluffy; add to chocolate mixture; blend well using MIX-STIR.
9. Beat egg whites until stiff; fold into chocolate mixture; refrigerate until serving time.
10. To Serve: Fill meringue shell with chocolate mixture; whip cream; add vanilla; spread over top of chocolate filling using SPREADER SPATULA.
11. Twelve servings.

Cheese Cake

- 2 eggs
- ½ cup sugar
- 12 ounces cream cheese, softened
- ½ teaspoon vanilla
- 1 teaspoon lemon juice
- 1½ cups graham cracker crumbs
- 2 tablespoons sugar
- ¼ cup butter or margarine
- 1 cup dairy sour cream
- 2 tablespoons sugar
- ½ teaspoon vanilla
- Nutmeg

1. Beat eggs until light using MIX-STIR; add sugar gradually, beating after each addition.
2. Add cream cheese, vanilla, lemon juice; beat thoroughly.
3. Combine cracker crumbs, sugar, butter using TURNING FORK; press onto bottom, up sides of 9-inch pie pan.
4. Pour in cheese mixture; spread evenly with SPREADER SPATULA.
5. Bake 20 minutes at 375° F.; cool 1 hour.
6. Combine sour cream, sugar, vanilla; spread evenly over cooled cake using SPREADER SPATULA.
7. Bake 10 minutes at 400° F.; sprinkle top with nutmeg; cool; chill.
8. Six–seven servings.

Pêches Cardinal (France)

6 fresh peaches
5 cups water
1½ cups sugar
2½ tablespoons vanilla
1 10-ounce package frozen red raspberries, thawed, drained
1½ tablespoons confectioners' sugar
1 tablespoon brandy or kirsch
Sweetened whipped cream

1. Pare peaches using PARING KNIFE; cut in half using TRIMMER; remove pits.
2. Combine water, sugar in 3-quart SAUCE PAN; bring to a boil; boil 4 minutes, stirring until sugar dissolves.
3. Add vanilla, peach halves; simmer slowly for 10–15 minutes until peaches are just tender.
4. Cool; cover; refrigerate until cold.
5. Purée raspberries in electric blender; put liquid through sieve to remove seeds.
6. Add sugar, brandy to purée; blend well; cover; refrigerate.
7. To serve: Remove peach halves from syrup using PERFORATED SPOON; place in individual dessert dishes; cover with raspberry sauce; garnish with whipped cream.
8. Twelve servings.

Cardamom Loaf (Iceland)

1 cup butter or margarine
1 cup sugar
2 eggs
3 cups sifted all purpose flour
3 teaspoons baking powder
½ teaspoon salt
1 teaspoon ground cardamom
¾ cup milk
1 cup seedless raisins

1. Cream butter; add sugar gradually, continuing to cream until light, fluffy.
2. Add eggs; beat well.
3. Sift together flour, baking powder, salt, cardamom; add to butter mixture; mix well.
4. Blend in milk; fold in raisins.
5. Pour into greased, floured 9 x 5 x 3-inch loaf pan.
6. Bake 70 minutes at 375° F.
7. Slice thin to serve using SLICER.
8. Serve with fresh fruit if desired.
9. One medium loaf.

Belgian Apple Fritters

1 egg
1 cup flour
1 tablespoon sugar
¾ cup flat beer
½ tablespoon brandy
6 firm cooking apples
Vegetable oil
½ cup sugar
1 teaspoon cinnamon

1. Beat egg using MIX-STIR; blend in ¼ cup flour, sugar.
2. Add beer alternately with remaining flour, beating well after each addition; blend in brandy.
3. Let batter stand at room temperature at least one hour.
4. To prepare Fritters: Pare apples using PARING KNIFE; core; cut in ¼-inch rings using TRIMMER.
5. Pour 1 inch of oil into 10-inch FRY PAN; heat oil to 375° F.
6. Coat apple rings with batter; fry in hot oil until lightly browned on both sides; remove with PERFORATED SPOON; drain on paper toweling.
7. Combine sugar, cinnamon; sprinkle over fritters.
8. Keep warm, crisp in 250° F. oven until all fritters are cooked; serve immediately.
9. Eight–ten servings.

Desserts

Canadian Apple Kuchen

2 cups sifted all purpose flour
½ teaspoon salt
¼ teaspoon baking powder
2 tablespoons sugar
6 tablespoons butter or margarine
4–5 apples
⅓ cup golden raisins
¾ cup sugar
1 teaspoon cinnamon
¼ teaspoon nutmeg
2 egg yolks
1 cup dairy sour cream

1. Sift together flour, salt, baking powder, sugar.
2. Cut in butter with 2 knives or pastry blender until mixture looks like corn meal.
3. Pile into ungreased 8-inch square cake pan; pat an even layer over bottom, halfway up sides of pan.
4. Pare apples, core using PARING KNIFE; cut in thin slices using TRIMMER; arrange in pastry shell.
5. Sprinkle raisins over apples.
6. Combine sugar, cinnamon, nutmeg; sprinkle over top.
7. Bake 15 minutes at 400° F.
8. Beat egg yolks slightly using MIX-STIR; blend in sour cream; pour over kuchen, spreading evenly with SPREADER SPATULA.
9. Bake 30 minutes longer.
10. Serve warm.
11. Six–eight servings.

Variation: For Peach Kuchen, use 12 peach halves and eliminate raisins.

Banana Flambé (Brazil)

4 ripe bananas
3 tablespoons butter or margarine
1 tablespoon grated orange peel
1 tablespoon brown sugar
1 10-ounce package frozen red raspberries, thawed
2 tablespoons brandy
Brandy

1. Peel bananas; cut in half lengthwise using TRIMMER.
2. Melt butter in 10-inch FRY PAN; stir in orange peel, brown sugar using MIX-STIR; bring to boil.
3. Sauté banana halves on both sides about 3 minutes total, turning with TURNING FORK.
4. Purée raspberries in electric blender; add brandy; pour over bananas; heat.
5. To serve: Pour 2 tablespoons warmed brandy into LADLE; ignite; pour over bananas; when flame dies out, serve.
6. Four servings.

Blueberry Buckle

¾ cup sugar
¼ cup shortening
1 egg
½ cup milk
2 cups sifted all purpose flour
2 teaspoons baking powder
½ teaspoon salt
1 cup blueberries, well-drained
½ cup sugar
⅓ cup sifted all purpose flour
½ teaspoon cinnamon
¼ cup soft butter or margarine

1. Beat together sugar, shortening, egg; stir in milk.
2. Sift together flour, baking powder, salt; stir into sugar mixture.
3. Carefully blend in blueberries.
4. Pour batter into greased, floured 9-inch square bake pan; spread evenly using SPREADER SPATULA.
5. Combine sugar, flour, cinnamon, butter using TURNING FORK; sprinkle over batter.
6. Bake 45–50 minutes at 375° F.
7. Serve warm with Old-Fashioned Lemon Sauce.
8. Nine servings.

Swiss Fir Cone
(Cake for Christmas Season)

Sponge Cake:
¾ cup sugar
4 eggs
Grated peel of one lemon
¼ cup sifted all purpose flour
¼ cup cornstarch
½ teaspoon baking powder

1. Combine sugar, eggs in large mixing bowl; set in deep pan or bowl of warm water.
2. Beat 15 minutes with electric mixer; remove from warm water; beat another 5 minutes; add grated lemon peel.
3. Sift flour, cornstarch, baking powder together; fold into egg mixture.
4. Line bottom, sides of 15 x 10 x 1-inch bake pan with waxed paper; pour in batter; spread evenly using SPREADER SPATULA.
5. Bake 30–35 minutes at 350° F.
6. When cake is removed from oven, loosen around edges with SPREADER SPATULA; turn upside down on cooling racks; remove pan; quickly peel off paper.

Coffee Butter Cream Frosting:
1¼ cups butter or margarine
2 cups sifted confectioners' sugar
½ cup strong coffee
2 cups blanched almonds, split, toasted

1. Cream butter until fluffy; add sugar gradually, blending well.
2. Add coffee; beat until creamy.

Assembling Fir Cone:
1. Cut three patterns from double thickness of Alcoa Wrap using bottom of an ordinary iron to obtain shape. Dimensions should be:

   #1, 9½ inches in length, 6 inches at broad end.
   #2, 9 inches by 5½ inches.
   #3, 8 inches by 4 inches.

2. Arrange patterns on cake; cut around patterns using TRIMMER to make fir cone shapes.
3. Assemble fir cone using largest cone shape for base; frost between each layer, around sides and over top with Coffee Butter Cream Frosting using SPREADER SPATULA.
4. Beginning at point of cake, place toasted split almonds into frosting in overlapping pattern to resemble fir cone scales.
5. Sprinkle confectioners' sugar lightly over entire surface to resemble snow.
6. At blunt end, fasten small twig of fir branch, red ribbon bow.
7. Eight–ten servings.

Rum Balls

2 tablespoons cocoa
1 cup confectioners' sugar
¼ cup light rum
2 tablespoons light corn syrup
2½ cups vanilla wafer crumbs
1 cup chopped pecans

1. Sift cocoa, confectioners' sugar together; blend in rum, corn syrup.
2. Add wafer crumbs, pecans; mix thoroughly using TURNING FORK.
3. Form mixture into 1-inch balls; roll in confectioners' sugar.
4. About 2½–3 dozen balls.

Variation: For Bourbon Balls, substitute bourbon for rum.

Desserts

Cottage Cheese Cookie Sticks

- 1 cup creamed cottage cheese
- 1 cup butter or margarine
- 2 cups sifted all purpose flour
- ¼ cup melted butter or margarine
- ¾ cup finely chopped walnuts
- ¾ cup brown sugar, firmly packed

1. Blend cottage cheese, butter together with pastry cutter.
2. Blend flour into mixture until dough holds together.
3. Roll out on lightly floured board to ⅛-inch thickness.
4. Brush melted butter over dough; sprinkle walnuts, brown sugar over entire surface.
5. Cut into equal strips, about 3 inches wide using SPATULA SPREADER; cut each strip into triangles, each about 3 inches wide at base.
6. Lift triangles from board using SPATULA SPREADER; beginning at base of triangle, roll dough into sticks.
7. Place sticks on ungreased cookie sheet, point side down.
8. Bake 20 minutes at 400° F. or until golden brown.
9. About 4–4½ dozen cookies.

Nut Pie

- 4 egg whites
- ½ cup granulated sugar
- ½ cup light brown sugar, firmly packed
- ½ teaspoon salt
- 1 teaspoon vanilla
- ¾ cup crushed round crackers (about 21)
- ¾ cup chopped nuts
- 1 teaspoon baking powder

1. Beat egg whites until stiff but not dry.
2. Gradually add sugars, continuing to beat until thoroughly blended, stiff.
3. Add salt, vanilla; blend.

4. Combine cracker crumbs, nuts, baking powder; fold into egg white mixture.
5. Pour into ungreased 9-inch pie pan; spread evenly using SPREADER SPATULA.
6. Bake 30 minutes at 325° F.
7. To serve: Fill with ice cream; top with whipped cream.
8. Six servings.

Pineapple Fritters

- ¼ cup flour
- 2 eggs
- ½ teaspoon salt
- 6 pineapple slices
  Vegetable shortening
  Confectioners' sugar

1. Blend flour, eggs, salt together to make batter using MIX-STIR.
2. Cut pineapple slices in half using TRIMMER; drain on paper toweling.
3. Pour 1 inch of oil in 10-inch FRY PAN; heat oil to 375° F.
4. Coat pineapple slices with batter; fry in hot oil until lightly browned on both sides; remove with PERFORATED SPOON; drain on paper toweling.
5. Sprinkle with confectioners' sugar; serve hot.
6. Six servings.

Fruit Medley

cups crisp macaroon crumbs
    (about 40)
No. 303 can sliced peaches, drained
1-pound can pitted purple plums,
    drained
No. 2 can pineapple chunks,
    drained
1-pound can pitted Bing Cherries,
    drained
cup sherry wine

Lightly grease 9-inch square bake
pan; sprinkle ½ cup macaroon
crumbs in bottom.

Combine peaches, plums, pineapple, cherries; toss together using
TURNING FORK.

Spoon layer of fruit into pan using
SOLID SPOON; sprinkle with
crumbs.

Continue layering fruit, crumbs,
ending with layer of crumbs.

Pour sherry over top of crumbs.

Bake 40–45 minutes at 350° F.

Serve warm topped with sweetened whipped cream or dairy sour
cream, if desired.

Six–eight servings.

tch Shortbread

cup butter or margarine
cup + 2 tablespoons sugar
egg yolk
cups sifted all purpose flour

Cream butter until soft; add sugar
gradually; beat until light, fluffy;
blend in egg yolk.

Add flour in three additions, beating well after each addition.

Divide mixture in half; roll out
each half on lightly floured board
to ½-inch thickness (about 7
inches in diameter); place in bottom of two 9-inch pie pans.

Score each round into 8 pie-shaped
wedges using TRIMMER; pierce
with TURNING FORK in several
places over top.

Bake 25 minutes at 325° F.; separate into wedges using TRIM-
MER; cool on rack.

Sixteen servings.

Fruit Curry

⅓ cup butter or margarine
¾ cup light brown sugar, firmly
    packed
1 tablespoon curry powder
1 No. 2 can peach halves, drained
1 No. 2 can pear halves, drained
1 No. 2 can pineapple chunks, drained
12 maraschino cherries, drained

1. Melt butter in 1-quart SAUCE
   PAN; add brown sugar, curry;
   blend well using MIX-STIR.
2. Arrange peaches, pears, pineapple
   in 9-inch square bake pan; place
   cherries in peach and pear centers; spoon syrup over fruit using
   SOLID SPOON.
3. Bake 45 minutes at 350° F.
4. Serve warm.
5. Six–eight servings.

Raspberry Cream Parfait

3 tablespoons quick cooking tapioca
¼ cup sugar
¼ teaspoon salt
1⅓ cups milk
½ cup heavy cream
2 cups fresh red raspberries
2 tablespoons sugar

1. Mix tapioca, sugar, salt in 1-quart
   SAUCE PAN using MIX-STIR.
2. Add milk gradually; cook, stirring constantly until mixture
   boils.
3. Remove from heat; cool.
4. Whip cream; fold into tapioca
   mixture; chill.
5. Crush raspberries slightly using
   MIX-STIR; add sugar.
6. Spoon raspberries, tapioca mixture into parfait glasses in alternate layers.
7. Serve plain or topped with
   whipped cream.
8. Four servings.

Variation: Fresh strawberries, black
raspberries, etc., may be substituted
for red raspberries.

Fondues

Fondue Bourguigonne
(Beef Fondue)

- **2 pounds beef tenderloin, ¾-inch thick**
- **2 cups vegetable oil**
- **Variety of sauces and side dishes**

1. Cut beef in ¾-inch cubes using PETITE CARVER; arrange on platter lined with lettuce; garnish with parsley.
2. Pour oil into FONDUE PAN; heat on range to 400° F.
3. Place FONDUE PAN on stand; place adapter in pan; light alcohol burner; adjust burner to have 3 small holes closed.
4. Eight–ten servings for appetizers. Four–five servings as entrée.

To Serve:

Provide each guest with a salad plate, FONDUE FORK and regular fork. Place platter of beef cubes, salt shaker, pepper mill, sauces and accompaniments on the table near the FONDUE PAN.

To Cook and Eat:

Each guest helps himself to sauces and other accompaniments which he puts on his salad plate. He then spears a cube of beef with the FONDUE FORK and dips it into the hot oil, cooking it to his liking. (Only four fondue forks should be in the FONDUE PAN at one time.) Since the FONDUE FORK will become very hot, the guest transfers his meat to the regular fork and dips it into the sauce of his choice.

Flame beneath the pan should be kept regulated so that the oil remains hot.

Suggested Accompaniments:

Hot and mild mustards
Mixed pickles
Chutney
Pickled onions
Olives

Variations:

1. Chicken Fondue: Substitute 3 whole chicken breasts (boned and skinned) cut into ½-inch cubes.
2. Shrimp Fondue: Substitute 2 pounds medium shrimp (shelled and deveined).

Use your favorite sauce recipes or try several of the following. Combine all ingredients using MIX-STIR; chill.

Tangy Blue Cheese Sauce 1¼ cups

- **1 cup mayonnaise**
- **¼ cup crumbled blue cheese**
- **1 teaspoon lemon juice**
- **2 tablespoons chopped parsley**

Tartar Sauce 1 cup

- **½ cup mayonnaise**
- **½ cup dairy sour cream**
- **2 tablespoons sweet relish**
- **1 tablespoon chopped chives**
- **1 teaspoon lemon juice**

Fondues

Combine all ingredients using MIX-STIR; chill.

Horseradish Sauce   1¼ cups

1 cup dairy sour cream
¼ cup chopped pimiento
2 tablespoons horseradish
2 tablespoons lemon juice
1 teaspoon sugar
4 drops Tabasco sauce

Curry Sauce   1 cup

1 cup dairy sour cream
½ cup mayonnaise
1 tablespoon chopped parsley
2 teaspoons curry powder
1 teaspoon lemon juice
½ teaspoon Worcestershire sauce
¼ teaspoon salt

Fondue Orientale

2 pounds lean, boneless pork, veal,
   or beef, ¾-inch thick
6 chicken or beef bouillon cubes
3 cups water
   Variety of sauces and side dishes

1. Cut meat in wafer-thin strips, ¾ inch x 2 inch using PETITE CARVER; roll strips; arrange on platter lined with lettuce; garnish with parsley.
2. Place bouillon cubes, water in FONDUE PAN; heat on range until cubes dissolve, bouillon boils.
3. Place FONDUE PAN on stand; place adapter in pan; light alcohol burner; adjust burner to have 3 small holes closed.
4. Eight–ten servings for appetizers. Four–five servings as entrée.

Follow the Fondue Bourguignonne cooking and eating procedures, and serve with the same sauces and accompaniments.

Flame beneath the pan should be kept regulated so that the bouillon continues to boil.

Fondue Neuchâtel (Swiss Fondue)

½ pound natural Swiss cheese, grated
2 tablespoons flour
1 clove fresh garlic
1 cup Neuchâtel wine or other light,
   dry wine
½ tablespoon lemon juice
2 tablespoons kirsch or brandy
   Nutmeg, pepper to taste
1 small loaf French or Italian bread,
   cut in cubes, with some crust
   on each cube

1. Coat cheese with flour.
2. Rub cut garlic clove over inside of FONDUE PAN.
3. Pour wine into pan; place on range over low heat; when air bubbles rise to surface, add lemon juice.
4. Add cheese by handfuls, stirring constantly using MIX-STIR until cheese melts.
5. Add kirsch, nutmeg, pepper; blend thoroughly.
6. Place FONDUE PAN on stand; light alcohol burner; adjust burner to have all 6 small holes closed.
7. Six–eight servings for appetizers. Three–four servings as entrée.

To Serve:

Provide each guest with a salad plate, FONDUE FORK and regular fork. Place platter of bread cubes on table near FONDUE PAN.

To Eat:

In eating the Swiss Fondue each guest spears a cube of bread on the FONDUE FORK, going through the soft side into the crust. He then dunks the bread in the fondue in a stirring motion until coated, then transfers the bread to a regular fork. Each person takes his leisurely turn in rotation. The stirring will help maintain the proper consistency of the fondue and will assure that each piece of bread is thoroughly coated with melted cheese.

Flame beneath the pan should be kept regulated so that the fondue bubbles lightly. If fondue becomes too thick, stir in a little preheated wine.

Fontina

2 tablespoons butter or margarine
3 tablespoons flour
1 cup milk
½ pound natural Swiss cheese, grated
Dash salt, nutmeg

1. Melt butter in FONDUE PAN on range; add flour; stirring until blended using MIX-STIR.
2. Gradually add milk, stirring constantly; cook several minutes over low heat.
3. Add cheese by handfuls, stirring constantly until cheese melts; add salt, nutmeg.
4. Place FONDUE PAN on stand; light alcohol burner; adjust burner to have all 6 small holes closed.
5. Six–eight servings for appetizers. Three–four servings as entrée.

The Fontina, a milder version of the typical Swiss Fondue Neuchâtel, can be enjoyed by young and old alike. Follow the same serving and eating procedures. If the Fontina becomes too thick, stir in a little pre-heated milk.

Pizza Fondue

1 envelope onion soup mix
1 15-ounce can tomato sauce
1 tablespoon Worcestershire sauce
1 teaspoon oregano
1½ cups (6 ounces) grated Cheddar cheese

1. Combine onion soup mix, tomato sauce, Worcestershire sauce, oregano in FONDUE PAN using MIX-STIR.
2. Heat on range over medium heat 5–10 minutes.
3. Add cheese by handfuls, stirring constantly until cheese melts.
4. Place FONDUE PAN on stand; light alcohol burner; adjust burner to have all 6 small holes closed.
5. Six–eight servings as hors d'oeuvre. Three–four servings as entrée.

Follow the same serving and eating procedure as for Swiss Fondue.

German Fondue

1¼ cups sifted flour
2½ teaspoons baking powder
3 tablespoons sugar
¾ teaspoon salt
1 egg
¾ cup milk
1 1-pound package frankfurters
3 cups (1½ pints) vegetable oil
Variety of sauces and side dishes

1. Sift together flour, baking powder, sugar, salt.
2. Beat egg using MIX-STIR; blend in milk.
3. Stir egg mixture into dry ingredients until well blended; pour into attractive bowl.
4. Cut each frankfurter into eight slices using TRIMMER; arrange on platter lined with lettuce; garnish with parsley.
5. Heat oil to 400° F. in FONDUE PAN on range.
6. Place FONDUE PAN on stand; place adapter in pan; light alcohol burner; adjust burner to have 3 small holes closed.
7. Eight–ten servings as hors d'oeuvre.
   Four–five servings as entrée.

To Serve:
Provide each guest with salad plate, FONDUE FORK, regular fork. Place bowl of batter, platter of frankfurters, sauces and side dishes on table near FONDUE PAN. Each guest helps himself to the sauces which he puts on his salad plate; then spears a slice of frankfurter with the FONDUE FORK, coats it with batter and cooks it in the hot oil. He transfers the cooked "fritter" to a regular fork and dips it in the sauces of his choice.

Suggested Sauces and Side Dishes:
Hot and mild mustards
Mustard-Dill Sauce
Tomato Sauce
Ketchup
Pancake Syrup

Fondues

Italian Bagna Cauda

This hot garlic-anchovy dip is a popular Italian specialty. It can be served as an hors d'oeuvre or an entrée.

8 cloves garlic, minced
¼ cup butter or margarine
1 2-ounce flat can anchovy fillets, finely chopped
1 cup olive oil
Assorted fresh vegetables
1 loaf Italian bread, cut in 1-inch slices

1. Press minced garlic against side of FONDUE PAN with back of spoon to extract oil.
2. Add butter; bring to a simmer on range over medium heat.
3. Add anchovies; simmer slowly over low heat until anchovies lose their shape.
4. Slowly stir in olive oil; bring to a simmer.
5. Place FONDUE PAN on stand; light alcohol burner; adjust burner to have 3 small holes closed. (Sauce should simmer slowly.)
6. Eight servings as hors d'oeuvre. Four servings as entrée.

To Serve:

Provide each guest with salad plate, FONDUE FORK, regular fork. Arrange vegetables attractively on a platter; place platter, bread on table near FONDUE PAN. Each guest spears a vegetable on a FONDUE FORK and swirls it in the hot sauce. He then transfers it to a regular fork or to a slice of bread.

Suggested Fresh Vegetables:

Lettuce, small whole leaves
Cabbage, small whole leaves
Celery, cut in 2 x ½-inch strips
Green pepper, cut in 2 x ½-inch strips
Carrots, cut in 2 x ½-inch strips
Cucumber, seeded, cut in 2 x ½-inch strips
Green onions, in 2-inch lengths
Mushrooms, small whole
Cherry tomatoes

Meat Ball Fondue

2 pounds ground round
½ teaspoon salt
⅛ teaspoon onion salt
⅛ teaspoon pepper
¼ pound Cheddar or Swiss cheese
2 cups (1 pint) vegetable oil
Variety of sauces and side dishes

1. Combine meat, salt, onion salt, pepper; form in balls about ¾ inch in diameter.
2. Cut cheese into small cubes about ¼ inch using TRIMMER; insert cheese cube in center of each meatball; arrange on platter with lettuce; garnish with parsley.
3. Heat oil to 400° F. in FONDUE PAN on range over medium-high heat.
4. Place FONDUE PAN on stand; place adapter in pan; light alcohol burner; adjust burner to have 3 small holes closed.
5. Eight–ten servings as hors d'oeuvre.
   Four–five servings as entrée.

To Serve:

Provide each guest with salad plate, FONDUE FORK, regular fork. Arrange meatballs attractively on a platter; place platter, sauces and accompaniments on table near FONDUE PAN. Each guest spears a meatball on a FONDUE FORK and cooks it in the hot oil. He then transfers his meatball to a regular fork and dips it into the sauce of his choice.

Sauces:

Tomato Sauce
Curry Sauce
Tartar Sauce

Accompaniments:

Hot and mild mustards
Ketchup
Mixed pickles

Variations:

Cubes of onion, green pepper, mushroom, water chestnut may be substituted for cheese.

Fondue Chocolat

2 9-ounce milk chocolate candy bars
2 1-ounce squares unsweetened
baking chocolate
1 cup light cream
3 tablespoons kirsch, cognac or
Cointreau

1. Break chocolate candy bars and baking chocolate into pieces; place in FONDUE PAN.
2. Add cream, kirsch.
3. Place on range over low heat until chocolate is melted, mixture is smooth; stir constantly using MIX-STIR.
4. Place FONDUE PAN on stand; light alcohol burner; adjust burner to have all 6 small holes closed.
5. Eight–ten servings for snack.
   Four–five servings for dessert.

To Serve:
Provide each guest with a salad plate, FONDUE FORK and regular fork. Place dishes of dunkables on table near FONDUE PAN.

To Eat:
Each guest spears a dunkable on the FONDUE FORK, then swirls it through the chocolate, transferring the coated dunkable to regular fork.

Flame beneath the pan should be kept regulated so that the fondue bubbles lightly.

Suggested Dunkables:
Fresh Fruits
tangerine or orange sections
pineapple, pear, peach, banana chunks
grapes, strawberries, cherries
Canned fruits, well drained
Angel food cake, cut in chunks
Doughnuts, cut in chunks
Marshmallows, popcorn

Fondue Chocolateen

Prepared the same as the Fondue Chocolat except that ½ teaspoon ground cinnamon and ½ teaspoon ground cloves should be substituted for the kirsch. Follow the same serving, eating and dunkable suggestions.

Butterscotch Fondue

2 12-ounce jars butterscotch ice
cream topping
2 tablespoons butter or margarine
Assorted dunkables

1. Heat butterscotch topping, butter in FONDUE PAN on range until butter melts.
2. Place FONDUE PAN on stand; light alcohol burner; adjust burner to have all 6 small holes closed.
3. Eight servings as snack.
   Four servings as dessert.

Follow the Fondue Chocolat serving, eating and dunkable suggestions.

Apple Cheddar Fondue

2 tablespoons butter or margarine
3 tablespoons flour
1 cup milk
½ pound Cheddar cheese, grated
Dash salt
Sliced green apples

1. Melt butter in FONDUE PAN on range over medium heat; add flour, stirring until well blended using MIX-STIR.
2. Gradually add milk, stirring constantly; cook several minutes over low heat.
3. Add cheese by handfuls, stirring constantly until cheese melts; add salt.
4. Place FONDUE PAN on stand; light alcohol burner; adjust burner to have all 6 small holes closed.
5. Eight–ten servings as snack.
   Four–five servings as dessert.

To Serve:
Provide each guest with a salad plate, FONDUE FORK, regular fork. Place tray of sliced apples on table near FONDUE PAN. Each guest spears a slice of apple on the FONDUE FORK. He dunks the apple in the fondue in a stirring motion to coat, then transfers it to a regular fork.

Outdoor Cooking

BUILDING THE FIRE

The easiest way is to spray the charcoal with any one of several good fire starters to be found on the market, following the instructions on the container. Only a sheet of newspaper is needed for igniting and the coals are ready in ten to fifteen minutes. As a rule, less charcoal is needed because a single layer is sufficient for most charcoal broiling.

When the coals have all turned white on top and you can see a steady red glow underneath, the fire is ready. For best results, don't rush this preparation time. Flames, even little ones, do nothing but scorch the meat, spoiling the true charcoal flavor. It's better to be hungry a little longer than to serve meat resembling a piece of charred wood.

ALCOA WRAP A MUST

Heavy Duty Alcoa Wrap is practically indispensable in Outdoor Cookery.

A sheet of foil accordion pleated into one-inch pleats, placed under the charcoal, reflects the heat. The charcoal can be placed about an inch apart—thus less charcoal is needed.

When doing meat on the rotisserie, make the drip pan from Heavy Duty Alcoa Wrap. It catches all the fat and can be tossed away later.

For greater heat reflectivity, line sides and top of Barbecue with Heavy Duty Alcoa Wrap; also makes cleaning easier.

Shape double thick squares of Heavy Duty Alcoa Wrap into little bowls for holding sauces or garlic butter brushed onto meat during cooking. No pans to wash later.

Corn on the cob and potatoes, snugly wrapped in foil, may be cooked right in the coals; turn several times. Fresh or frozen vegetables, wrapped in Heavy Duty Alcoa Wrap can be done on the grill; turn packages several times to insure even cooking.

When cooking for a crowd and the grill is not large enough to cook all the meat at one time, keep the cooked batches hot by wrapping them in foil.

Use Heavy Duty Alcoa Wrap to keep corn on the cob and rolls hot during serving. Covering serving platters with foil eliminates dishwashing later.

OUTDOOR SMOKE OVEN COOKERY

This is the simplest and easiest method of Outdoor Cooking. While the food cooks you are free to enjoy your guests. The result, the most delicious meat, fish or fowl you ever tasted, all delicately seasoned with a true smoky flavor.

Any outdoor Barbecue or Grill can be converted into a Smoke Oven by making a Hood from Alcoa Wrap.

Here's how:

1. Before starting the fire, completely line the bowl or fire box with double-thick sheets of Heavy Duty Alcoa Wrap, allowing each strip to extend about three inches over the rim. Depending on size, you will have one to three double-thick sheets running from north to south and one to three double-thick sheets running from east to west.

2. Press overhang tightly to form a firm rim. The Hood now looks like an umbrella. Remove from bowl or fire box.

3. Cut a hole about 2 inches in diameter in the center of the top. This makes the vent necessary for good browning.

4. The Hood is now ready to use. It can be used over and over again —any time you want to do Smoke Oven Cookery.

To Do Smoke Oven Cookery:

1. Line fire box or bowl with Alcoa Wrap.

2. Build fire in usual way; put grill in place.

3. When coals start to turn gray, set a portable oven thermometer on the grill; cover with the Alcoa Wrap Hood; let Smoke Oven pre-heat to desired temperature.

4. Prepare food according to recipe; place on grill; add Hood; bake as directed in recipe.

GOOD TO KNOW: Alcoa Wrap Hood may be removed by inserting the tines of a barbecue fork into the vent. If Smoke Oven gets too hot, prop Hood up slightly.

BARBECUE SET

The long handled TONGS, TURNER and FORK are essential for the many turning and lifting jobs around the outdoor grill.

ACCESSORIES

While you will find the Barbecue Shop in any store well stocked with all kinds of tricky gadgets, there are only a few that are really necessary. Start with these and then let your continued interest in outdoor cookery be your guide on future purchases.

Gloves—A pair of heavy canvas work gloves are indispensable for handling the charcoal when starting the fire. Asbestos gloves are good to have for adjusting the spit, moving hot coals when additional charcoal needs to be added or for other hot jobs.

Sprinkling Bottle—A large bottle with a sprinkler such as is used for sprinkling clothes is needed to extinguish flames that flare up during broiling.

Sauce Brush—A regular pastry brush with a fairly long handle is necessary for brushing meats either when broiling or doing meat on the spit.

Thermometers—A regular meat thermometer goes a long way toward doing a perfect roast over the grill. Knowing the right internal temperature is the only sure way of knowing the roast is done to your liking. An oven thermometer is necessary when using a Smoke Oven in order that it can be preheated to the proper temperature.

Hinged Broilers—Several of these with medium to fine grids are convenient for broiling bacon, chicken livers, oysters, tidbits, shrimp, etc.

Skewers—These should be 12–18 inches long and preferably of a nonrusting metal. They are desirable for all kinds of skewered foods.

Wire Brush—A stiff wire brush, resembling a regular scrubbing brush in size and shape, makes the cleaning of the grill an easy task.

CHARCOAL ROTISSERIE TIME CHARTS

	Thermometer Reading	Approximate Time
Beef		
Standing Rib		
Rare	140° F.	2–2½ hours
Medium	140°–150° F.	2½–3 hours
Well Done	160°–170° F.	3–4 hours

Rolled Rib: Allow about 25–35 minutes longer. Thermometer reading will be the same.

	Thermometer Reading	Approximate Time
Lamb		
Leg		
Medium	150°–160° F.	1½–2 hours
Well Done	175°–180° F.	2–2½ hours

Boned Shoulder: Same as for leg of lamb.

	Thermometer Reading	Approximate Time
Pork		
Fresh Loin	170°–175° F.	2–2½ hours
Fresh Ham—12 pounds	170°–175° F.	4 hours
Veal		
Rolled Roast—3 pounds	165°–170° F.	45–60 minutes

	Weight	Approximate Time
Poultry		
Chicken	3–4 lbs.	1–1½ hours
Turkey	15 lbs.	3–4 hours
Duck	4–6 lbs.	1–1½ hours
Goose	4–7 lbs.	1¾–2½ hours
Rabbit	3–5 lbs.	40 min.–2 hours
Wild Duck	1–2½ lbs.	20–30 minutes
Cornish Hens	1–2 lbs.	1–1½ hours

ROTISSERIE ROASTED MEATS

1. Start charcoal fire early to have coals burning evenly for a low, steady heat.
2. Wipe meat with damp cloth; rub with cut side of clove of garlic; sprinkle with salt, pepper.
3. Insert spit rod completely through center of meat; insert spit fork into each end; tighten screws.
4. Check meat for balance by rotating spit between palms of hands.
5. If using a meat thermometer, insert it into thickest part, being sure bulb does not rest on bone, fat or gristle.

6. Arrange charcoal briquettes at back of fire box; knock off the gray ash.
7. Place a drip pan fashioned from heavy duty Alcoa Wrap in front of the coals.
8. Attach spit; start motor, having fire box at highest position until meat is seared.
9. Lower fire box 6–7 inches; continue roasting.
10. Roast according to Rotisserie Chart.

CHARCOAL BROILING TIME CHART

	Thickness	Rare	Medium	Well Done
Beef				
Steaks	1 inch	8–12 min.	12–15 min.	15–20 min.
	1½ inches	10–15 min.	14–18 min.	18–25 min.
	2 inches	18–30 min.	25–30 min.	45–60 min.
	2½ inches	30–35 min.	35–45 min.	60–75 min.
Hamburgers			14–15 min.	18–20 min.
Lamb				
Chops, steaks	1 inch		6–14 min.	18–25 min.
	1½ inches		8–16 min.	20–30 min.
	2 inches		12–20 min.	25–30 min.

	Thickness	Time
Pork		
Chops, steaks	1 inch	25–35 minutes
	1½ inches	30–45 minutes
Ham Steaks	¾ inch	25–30 minutes
	1 inch	30–35 minutes
	1½ inches	35–45 minutes
	2 inches	45–60 minutes
Poultry		
Chicken	Split	25–45 minutes
Duck	Split	30–50 minutes
Squab	Split	25–35 minutes
Fish		
Fish Steaks	1 inch	6–9 minutes
	1½ inches	8–12 minutes
	2 inches	10–18 minutes
Fish Fillets		6–18 minutes
Split Fish	Small	8–12 minutes
Whole Fish	Small	12–18 minutes
Whole Fish	Large	30–60 minutes

Outdoor Cooking

Chuck Steak Aruba

Juice of 2 large lemons
¼ cup olive oil
2 tablespoons grated onion
1 tablespoon chili powder
2 teaspoons ginger
1 clove garlic, mashed to a pulp
1 tablespoon salt
1 chuck steak, 1-inch thick

1. Combine lemon juice, oil, onion, chili powder, ginger, garlic, salt; blend thoroughly using MIX-STIR.
2. Place steak in shallow pan; pour marinade over meat; turn so both sides are coated; cover pan with Alcoa Wrap; refrigerate overnight or at least 10 hours; spoon marinade over steak several times using SOLID SPOON.
3. Place on grill over very hot coals, approximately 5–7 minutes per side; have coals as close to meat as possible.
4. Heat remaining marinade; use as sauce with meat.
5. Carve steak using PETITE CARVER.
6. Four servings.

Variation: Use ¾ cup bottled Italian Salad Dressing as marinade.

Fish Barbecue

2 1-pound packages frozen fish fillets
Prepared barbecue sauce

1. Allow fish to defrost enough to separate fillets.
2. Divide fillets into six servings.
3. Place each serving in center of double thick square of Alcoa Wrap.
4. Brush each fillet generously with a favorite barbecue sauce.
5. Bring up sides of Alcoa Wrap; fold down onto fish in tight double fold; fold ends up in tight double folds.
6. Place packages on grill over medium coals; grill 20–25 minutes.
7. Serve in opened foil packages.
8. Six servings.

Marinated Lobster Tails

6 tablespoons lemon juice
1½ tablespoons soy sauce
½ teaspoon ginger
½ teaspoon salt
½ teaspoon tarragon
½ teaspoon Tabasco sauce
1 cup sherry wine
1 clove garlic
8 frozen lobster tails, thawed

1. Combine lemon juice, soy sauce, ginger, salt, tarragon, Tabasco, sherry; blend well using MIX-STIR.
2. Finely mince garlic clove using FRENCH CHEF'S KNIFE; add to marinade.
3. Cut under-shell around edge of lobster tails with KITCHEN SHEARS; remove membrane.
4. Place lobster tails in shallow bake pan; pour marinade over lobster; cover pan with Alcoa Wrap; refrigerate several hours or overnight; spoon marinade over lobster several times using SOLID SPOON.
5. Preheat charcoal grill with Alcoa Wrap Smoke Oven Hood to 350° F.
6. Remove lobster tails from marinade; place directly on grill above charcoal with shell side down on grill; add Hood; grill 6–9 minutes, basting occasionally with marinade.
7. Four servings.

Herb Lamb Chops

1 medium onion
6 large sprigs parsley
1 cup olive oil
½ cup lemon juice
1½ teaspoons salt
1½ teaspoons marjoram
1½ teaspoons thyme
¾ teaspoon pepper
¼ teaspoon garlic salt
6 shoulder lamb chops, ½-inch thick

1. Peel onion using PARING KNIFE; chop using FRENCH CHEF'S KNIFE.

2. Snip parsley using KITCHEN SHEARS.

3. Combine onion, parsley, olive oil, lemon juice, salt, marjoram, thyme, pepper, garlic salt; blend well using MIX-STIR.

4. Place lamb chops in shallow bake pan; pour marinade over chops; cover pan with Alcoa Wrap; refrigerate several hours or overnight; spoon marinade over chops several times using SOLID SPOON.

5. Preheat charcoal grill with Alcoa Wrap Smoke Oven Hood to 350° F.

6. Remove chops from marinade; place directly on grill above charcoal; add Hood; grill 8 minutes per side.

7. Heat marinade; serve with grilled chops.

8. Six servings.

Grilled Lamb Steaks

4 lamb steaks from leg, 1-inch thick
¾ cup olive oil
¼ cup vinegar
1 clove garlic, mashed to a pulp
1 teaspoon salt
¼ teaspoon pepper
½ teaspoon crushed dried mint

1. Place steaks in shallow baking pan.

2. Combine oil, vinegar, garlic, salt, pepper, mint; blend well using MIX-STIR; pour over steaks.

3. Cover pan with Alcoa Wrap; refrigerate 3–4 hours, turning once.

4. Preheat charcoal grill with Alcoa Wrap Smoke Oven Hood to 350° F.

5. Remove steaks from marinade; place directly on grill above charcoal; add Hood; grill 10–12 minutes per side; baste frequently with marinade.

6. Four servings.

Smothered Onions

1 medium onion
1 tablespoon butter or margarine
Salt, pepper

1. Peel onion using PARING KNIFE; slice using TRIMMER.

2. Place sliced onion in center of double thick square of Alcoa Wrap.

3. Place butter on top; sprinkle with salt, pepper.

4. Bring up sides of Alcoa Wrap; fold down onto onions in tight double fold; fold ends up in tight double folds.

5. Place package on grill over medium coals; grill 25–30 minutes; turn package several times.

6. Serve in open package.

7. One serving.

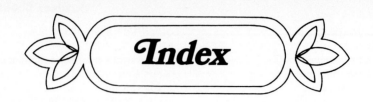

Index

Index

Index

Equivalents and Substitutions

Baking Powder		
Rising Equivalent	1 teaspoon	⅓ teaspoon baking soda plus ½ teaspoon cream of tartar
	1 teaspoon	¼ teaspoon baking soda plus ½ cup buttermilk
Bread Crumbs		
Dry	⅓ cup	1 slice
Soft	¾ cup	1 slice
Butter or Margarine		
1 stick	8 tablespoons	½ cup (¼ lb.)
4 sticks	2 cups	1 pound
Cheese, Cheddar	1 cup grated	¼ pound
Cheese, Cream	6 tablespoons	3-oz. package
Cheese, Cottage	1 cup	½ pound
Chocolate	1 square	1 ounce
Chocolate	1 square	4 tablespoons, grated
Chocolate	1 oz. plus 4 teaspoons sugar	1⅔ oz. semi-sweet chocolate
Cocoa	3 tablespoons cocoa plus 1 tablespoon fat	1 oz. chocolate
Coconut, fine grated	1 cup	3½ ounces
Coconut, flaked	1⅓ cups	3½ ounces
Cornstarch		
For thickening	1 tablespoon	2 tablespoons flour
Dates, pitted	1¼ cups cut-up	8-oz. package
Eggs, whole		
Large	5	about 1 cup
Medium	6	about 1 cup
Small	7	about 1 cup
Eggs, whites		
Large	8	about 1 cup
Medium	10-11	about 1 cup
Small	11-12	about 1 cup
Eggs, yolks		
Large	12	about 1 cup
Medium	13-14	about 1 cup
Small	15-16	about 1 cup
Flour		
All-purpose	1 cup sifted	1 cup plus 2 tablespoons cake flour
Cake	1 cup sifted	1 cup minus 2 tablespoons all-purpose flour